Also by Robert Goddard

In order of publication

PAST CARING

A young graduate starts to investigate the fall from grace of an Edwardian cabinet minister and sets in train a bizarre and violent chain of events.

'A hornet's nest of jealousy, blackmail and violence. Engrossing'
DAILY MAIL

IN PALE BATTALIONS

An extraordinary story unfolds as Leonora Galloway strives to solve the mystery of her father's death, her mother's unhappy childhood and a First World War murder.

'A novel of numerous twists and turns and surprises'
SUNDAY TELEGRAPH

PAINTING THE DARKNESS

On a mild autumn afternoon in 1882, William Trenchard's life changes for ever with the arrival of an unexpected stranger.

'Explodes into action'
SUNDAY INDEPENDENT

INTO THE BLUE

When a young woman disappears and Harry Barnett is accused of her murder he has no option but to try and discover what led her to vanish into the blue.

'A cracker, twisting, turning and exploding with real skill'
DAILY MIRROR

TAKE NO FAREWELL

September 1923, and architect Geoffrey Staddon must return to the house called Clouds Frome, his first important commission, to confront the dark secret that it holds.

'A master storyteller'
INDEPENDENT ON SUNDAY

HAND IN GLOVE

The death of a young English poet in the Spanish Civil
War casts a shadow forward over half a century.

'Cliff-hanging entertainment'
GUARDIAN

CLOSED CIRCLE

1931, and two English fraudsters on a transatlantic liner stumble
into deep trouble when they target a young heiress.

*'Full of thuggery and skulduggery, cross and
doublecross, plot and counter-plot'*
INDEPENDENT

BORROWED TIME

A brief encounter with a stranger who is murdered soon afterwards draws
Robin Timariot into the complex relationships and motives of the dead
woman's family and friends.

*'An atmosphere of taut menace...
heightened by shadows of betrayal and revenge'*
DAILY TELEGRAPH

OUT OF THE SUN

Harry Barnett becomes entangled in a sinister
conspiracy when he learns that the son he never
knew he had is languishing in hospital in a coma.

*'Brilliantly plotted, full of good,
traditional storytelling values'*
MAIL ON SUNDAY

BEYOND RECALL

The scion of a wealthy Cornish dynasty reinvestigates a 1947 murder
and begins to doubt the official version of events.

*'Satisfyingly complex...
finishes in a rollercoaster of twists'*
DAILY TELEGRAPH

PLAY TO THE END

Actor Toby Flood finds himself a player in a much bigger
game when he investigates a man who appears to be a stalker.

'An absorbing display of craftsmanship'
SUNDAY TIMES

SIGHT UNSEEN

An innocent bystander is pulled into a mystery which takes over
twenty years to unravel when he witnesses the abduction of a child.

*'A typically taut tale of wrecked lives, family tragedy,
historical quirks and moral consequences'*
THE TIMES

NEVER GO BACK

The convivial atmosphere of a reunion weekend is
shattered by an apparent suicide.

*'Meticulous planning, well-drawn characters and an immaculate
sense of place... A satisfying number of twists and shocks'*
THE TIMES

NAME TO A FACE

A centuries old mystery is about to unravel...

*'Mysterious, dramatic, intricate,
fascinating and unputdownable'*
DAILY MIRROR

LONG TIME COMING

For thirty-six years they thought he was dead...
They were wrong...

*'When it comes to duplicity and intrigue,
Goddard is second to none'*
DAILY MAIL

PLAY TO THE END

Actor Toby Flood finds himself a player in a much bigger game when he investigates a man who appears to be a stalker.

'An absorbing display of craftsmanship'
SUNDAY TIMES

SIGHT UNSEEN

An innocent bystander is pulled into a mystery which takes over twenty years to unravel when he witnesses the abduction of a child.

'A typically taut tale of wrecked lives, family tragedy, historical quirks and moral consequences'
THE TIMES

NEVER GO BACK

The convivial atmosphere of a reunion weekend is shattered by an apparent suicide.

'Meticulous planning, well-drawn characters and an immaculate sense of place... A satisfying number of twists and shocks'
THE TIMES

NAME TO A FACE

A centuries-old mystery is about to unravel...

'Mysterious, dramatic, intricate, fascinating and unputdownable'
DAILY MIRROR

FOUND WANTING

Catapulted into a breathless race against time, Richard's life will be changed for ever in ways he could never have imagined...

'The master of the clever twist'
SUNDAY TELEGRAPH

LONG TIME COMING

For thirty-six years they thought he was dead...
They were wrong.

'When it comes to duplicity and intrigue,
Goddard is second to none'
DAILY MAIL

BLOOD COUNT

There's no such thing as easy money.
As surgeon Edward Hammond is about to find out.

'Mysterious, dramatic, intricate,
fascinating and unputdownable...
The crime writers' crime writer'
DAILY MIRROR

IN PALE BATTALIONS

ROBERT GODDARD

CORGI BOOKS

TRANSWORLD PUBLISHERS
61–63 Uxbridge Road, London W5 5SA
A Random House Group Company
www.rbooks.co.uk

IN PALE BATTALIONS
A CORGI BOOK: 9780552162968

First published in Great Britain
in 1988 by Bantam Press
an imprint of Transworld Publishers
Corgi edition published 1989
Corgi edition reissued 2010

Addresses for Random House Group Ltd companies outside the UK
can be found at: www.randomhouse.co.uk
The Random House Group Ltd Reg. No. 954009

The Random House Group Limited supports The Forest Stewardship
Council (FSC), the leading international forest certification organisation.
All our titles that are printed on Greenpeace approved FSC certified paper
carry the FSC logo. Our paper procurement policy can be found at
www.rbooks.co.uk/environment

Typeset in 11/13pt Giovanni Book by
Falcon Oast Graphic Art Ltd.
Printed in the UK by CPI Cox & Wyman, Reading, RG1 8EX.

3 5 7 9 10 8 6 4 2

IN MEMORIAM

Frederick John Goddard, First Battalion, the Hampshire
Regiment
Born Kimpton, Hampshire, 18th August 1885
Missing, presumed killed in action, Ypres, Belgium,
27th April 1915

HIS NAME LIVETH FOR EVERMORE

ACKNOWLEDGEMENTS

The lines quoted at the beginning and end of the book are the opening and closing lines of a sonnet by Charles Hamilton Sorley (1895–1915).

The lines from the poem 'Not Waving but Drowning' by Stevie Smith (1902–71), quoted on page 405, are reproduced by kind permission of James MacGibbon.

When you see millions of the mouthless dead
Across your dreams in pale battalions go,
Say not soft things as other men have said,
That you'll remember. For you need not so.

IN PALE
BATTALIONS

PROLOGUE

This is the day and this the place where a dream turns a corner and a secret is told. This is Thiepval, where only the clamping mist of an autumn morning can hide the massive, brick-arched statement of our collective conscience that is the Memorial to the Missing of the Somme. And this is where Leonora Galloway has brought her devoted daughter to begin her explanation of what has taken her most of a long life to understand.

To Monsieur Lefebvre, taxi-driver of Amiens, it is merely another fare, though more remunerative than most. A mother and daughter, elegantly dressed, breaking the rail journey from Calais to Paris, and requesting, in hesitant English-accented French, that he drive them the twenty-eight kilometres north-east along the flat, straight road to Albert, then up into the rolling hills above the Ancre valley to 'le Mémorial Britannique de Thiepval'. He was scarcely likely to refuse, though to him such reminders of a long-ago conflict hold no appeal. Monsieur Lefebvre is himself possessed of a total and unaffected oblivion to the past and is comfortable in that condition. He has driven obediently to the place –

the mist not at all restraining his speed – and sits now in his taxi, smoking a cigarette and watching the waiting-time tick up on his meter, flicking ashy towards the sycamore trees fringing the car park and wondering idly how long his customers will decide to spend in this literally God-forsaken spot.

They left him some time ago and walked up the gravelled approach to the memorial, still hidden at that stage by mist and screening fir trees. At length, it loomed through its seldom-worn shroud: huge, dis-proportionate, vaguely alien in the silent, cold-dewed modesty of the surrounding countryside. The two visitors spread anoraks on the long, curved stone bench that faces the Memorial and sit now, watching it slowly emerge into view as the mist begins to give way to the sun that burns above.

Leonora Galloway is a lady of seventy, tall, finely boned and well bred, grey-haired and slightly gaunt in a way that suggests youthful good looks: her faceful bearing owes more to taste and training than to delicacy of manner. Her daughter, Penelope, some thirty-five years her junior, appears, as they sit together, quite obviously her child: the same height, the same open, high-cheeked face, flaxen hair that flows to her shoulders but will one day be as grey and trimmed as her mother's. Not as determined, perhaps, not as vigorous, but, if anything, more patient, more gentle, perhaps even more reliable. Part of Penelope's charm lies in her early assumption of elderly virtues, part of Leonora's in her resistance of them.

Earlier in the year, Leonora's husband died suddenly at their cottage home in Somerset. She bore the blow with the fortitude expected of her. Now, six months later, she has set off for a holiday in Paris designed to

16

aid her adjustment to the solitary life. Of her two children, Penelope was the obvious choice to accompany her, being long accustomed to such a life and possessing, unlike her married, more prosperous brother, one quality immediately endearing to Leonora: the capacity to think.

From Penelope's point of view, there was also much to be said for the venture. Through thirty years of reliable memories, her mother has somehow contrived to evade her definition, her manner always brittly restrained, her accounts of herself cautiously vague. Penelope has been left with an abiding curiosity about the strangely distant, private woman who is her mother – a curiosity which, her daughter's instincts have told her, this trip may at last satisfy. Already, her expectancy has been encouraged. The break of journey in Amiens was unscheduled, the taxi drive to Thiepval unexpected. Here, she feels certain, the explanations will begin.

'I expect you're wondering why we've come here,' Leonora remarks, her words breaking in on her daughter's thoughts.

'Of course I am. But I'm sure you'll tell me when you're ready.' It is something she remembers her father telling her long ago, a piece of good advice from a patient, self-effacing man: 'Your mother will confide in you when she wants to, not when you want her to.'

The mist is thinner now, the brick-wrought, statement of official mourning clearer as its backdrop shifts imperceptibly from muffled grey to verdant green and hazy blue. The two onlookers are dwarfed by the emergent edifice, a little shocked by its massive, graceless presence, huge and finely sculpted as it is.

'The sun will be out soon,' Leonora says. 'Shall we go and look for his name?'

17

'Whose name?'

'My father's. That's why we've come here, you see.'

She rises from the bench, crosses the gravel drive and sets off across the wide lawn fronting the Memorial, her feet leaving dark prints behind her in the saturated grass. Penelope follows, patient as ever. To her the Somme means one battle, larger than most, amongst the mindless many of the First World War. She knows – because she has read of it – that thousands died there, her grandfather among them. Now, as she approaches the Memorial, she sees the huge brick pillars supporting its central archway are faced in stone and that the stone is minutely etched with names. At last its vastness is in part explained, for the names are the thousands of the missing of the Somme. Penelope stares up at them, still ranked and filed for war, lists reaching higher than her eye can follow. She is taken aback. She has read of it, of course, but nobody has told her, nobody has prepared her for 73,412 men without a grave.

Leonora has gone ahead of her across the flagstoned plinth beneath the pillars, scanning the walls quickly, looking for the one she seeks. At the foot of one stone-wreathed column of names, she halts. There Penelope catches her up and follows with her eyes the direction of her gaze. Near the top of the pillar, the names of the Hampshire Light Infantry are assembled in order of rank. At the head, Captains Arnell, Bailey, Bland, Cade, Carrington, Cromie . . . and Hallows, Leonora's maiden name. So there he is. Suddenly, to Penelope, it seems a long way to have come just for this.

'Why didn't you come before, Mother? There must have been visits arranged for relatives. We could all have come together.'

'I hardly think so.'

18

'Why on earth not?'

'Because of what we'd have found here.'

'What do you mean?'

'Come and see.'

The two women move back towards the steps by which they ascended to the Memorial. At the base of each of the two gigantic pillars flanking the steps is a metal door let into the wall. Leonora opens the one to the left. Within are stacked several dog-eared but faithfully preserved volumes constituting the Memorial register. She leafs through one until she finds the place she wants, then holds it up for Penelope to see.

'HALLOWS. Captain the Hon. John, son of Edward, Lord Powerstock, of Meongate, Droxford, Hampshire. Missing, presumed killed in action, Mametz, 30th April 1916, aged 29 years.'

The family's sundered connection with the aristocracy is not new to Penelope. The Powerstock title ended, she knows, with this death on the Somme. Leonora's mother died when she was only a few days old, leaving her to be brought up by her grandparents. After their death, the Meongate estate was dismantled. Neither money nor title ever found its way to Leonora, nor reminiscence of an aristocratic childhood, through her, to Penelope.

'What's wrong with this?' she says, after staring blankly at the entry.

'Come on, Penny. My father was killed on 30th April 1916, but I wasn't born until 14th March 1917. Don't you see now?'

'Ah.' Penelope smiles. 'So that's it. Well, this sort of thing was common enough in wartime, wasn't it?'

'Oh yes. Common enough, I dare say.' Leonora replaces the book and pushes the door shut. 'But not quite the point. I've always known my father wasn't . . . well, wasn't my father. Lady Powerstock made sure I knew and she made sure Tony knew as well.'

'Then . . . where's the harm?'

'There wouldn't be any, if it were as simply as that.'

Leonora turns and walks back through the archway, past the pillar bearing her father's name and on to the steps at the rear of the Memorial. These lead down to a cemetery of unknown soldiers. To the left, French, marked with crosses, to the right, British, marked with plain stones. The stone appears white and painfully bright in the ever strengthening sunlight. Beyond the fir trees that bound the cemetery on three sides, the valleys of the Ancre and the Somme rivers roll away in restful curves where once such bitter struggles were fought and so many men were killed. The two women stand at the top of the steps and look down at the orderly scene.

It is Penelope who breaks the silence. 'I realize I can't imagine what it's like to remember nothing of one's parents, but I would like to try. You've never given me that chance, you know, never talked about your own childhood at all, even when pressed.'

'I wanted you and Ronald to have the stability and security I lacked. I certainly didn't want my childhood to cast a shadow over yours. By telling you nothing about it, I suppose I could pretend it never really happened.'

'Was it really so bad? Knowing you were illegitimate, I mean.'

'Illegitimacy is a small matter in this, Penny. Nowadays, smaller than ever. Lady Powerstock did her best to torment me with it, of course, but she had a far more effective hold over me than that.'

They begin to retrace their steps. Instinctively,

Penelope knows better than to urge her mother on. She has herself no memory of Lady Powerstock and whenever Leonora has spoken of her – which has not been often – it has been with this same guarded bitterness. Now, however, it seems she is willing to say more. Sure enough, when they are clear of the Memorial, she resumes.

'I've wanted to come to this place for more than fifty years, ever since my grandfather told me it existed and that my father was commemorated here.'

'What stopped you? Finding out he wasn't really your father after all?'

Leonora smiles. 'You could say that was the reason.'

'You don't have to tell me if you don't want to, you know, but did you ever find out who your real father was?'

'Oh yes. I found out.'

The two women turn on to the gravel drive, their feet crunching on its surface, and move slowly away from the Memorial, back towards the entrance. This time, Penelope cannot restrain herself.

'Who was he then, my grandfather?'

'That, in part, is what I planned to tell you on this holiday. But I should warn you: it's a long story.'

'Don't worry. I've waited a long time to hear it.'

'And it's as much about me as my father.'

'I've waited a long time to hear that as well.'

They reach the taxi and climb into the rear seat. Monsieur Lefebvre starts back towards Amiens. He does not enquire if they have enjoyed their visit, nor does he trouble to listen to the older of his two passengers as she begins talking in her flat, suppressed, English voice.

'We've never had much time to spend with each other, have we, Penny, you and I? I sometimes worry

21

that I haven't been the mother a good daughter deserves.'

'I never wanted for anything.'

'Except the warmth that comes from knowing me for what I really am. Tony's death was a shock, of course, but it was something else as well: it was the end of a long pretence, a pretence that my life before marrying him did not exist. I persuaded myself that you and Ronald would be happier not knowing all there was to know about me – and in Ronald's case I'm sure that's true. But actually, of course, I was the one who wanted to forget. Now, I think, it's time to remember.'

Half an hour later, as Monsieur Lefebvre slows in traffic on the outskirts of Amiens, Leonora has not finished. He is dimly aware that she is still talking and that his other passenger has said nothing since they left Thiepval, but he pays her words as much heed as he does the wide and lazy river Somme where it passes beneath the road bridge. He speeds on, immune to the past, whilst Penelope, who is not, continues to listen. For Leonora has not finished. In truth, she has only just begun.

PART ONE

ONE

Childhood memories fit their own, intricate pattern. They cannot be made to conform to the version of our past we try to impose upon them. Thus I could say that Lord and Lady Powerstock and the home they gave me at Meongate more than compensated for being an orphan, that a silver spoon easily took the place of my mother's smile. I could say it – but every recollection of my early years would deny it.

Meongate must once have been the crowded, bustling house of a cheerful family, as the Hallowses must once have been that family. Every favour of nature in its setting where the Hampshire downs met the pastures of the Meon valley, every effort of man in its spacious rooms and landscaped park, had been bestowed on the home of one small child.

Yet it was not enough. When I was growing up at Meongate in the early 1920s, most of its grandeur had long since departed. Many of the rooms were shut up and disused, much of the park turned over to farmland. And all the laughing, happy people I imagined filling its empty rooms and treading its neglected lawns had vanished into a past beyond my reach.

I grew up with the knowledge that my parents were both dead, my father killed on the Somme, my mother carried off by pneumonia a few days after my birth. It was not kept from me. Indeed, I was constantly reminded of it, constantly confronted with the implication that I must in some way bear the blame for the shadow of grief, or of something worse, that hung over their memory. That shadow, cast by the unknown, lay at the heart of the cold, dark certainty that also grew within me: I was not wanted at Meongate, not welcomed there, not loved.

It might have been different had my grandfather not been the grave, withdrawn, perpetually melancholic man that he was. I, who never knew him when he was young, cannot imagine him as anything other than the wheelchair-bound occupant of his ground-floor rooms, deprived by his own morbidity, as much as by the lingering effects of a stroke, of all warmth and fondness. When Nanny Hiles took me, as she regularly did, to kiss him goodnight, all I wanted to do was escape from the cold, fleeting touch of his flesh. When, playing on the lawn, I would look up and see him watching me from his window, all I wanted to do was run away from the mournful, questing sadness in his eyes. Later, I came to sense that he was waiting, waiting for me to be old enough to understand him, waiting in the hope that he would live to see that day.

Lady Powerstock, twenty years his junior, was not my real grandmother. She was buried in the village church-yard, another ghost whom I did not know and who could do nothing to help me. I imagined her as every-thing her successor was not – kind, loving and generous

– but it did me no good. Olivia, the woman I was required to address as Grandmama in her place, had once been beautiful and, at fifty, her looks were still with her, her figure still fine, her dress sense impeccable. That we were not related by blood explained, to my satisfaction, why she did not love me. What I could not explain was why she went so far as to hate me, but hate me she undoubtedly did. She did not trouble to disguise the fact. She let it hover, menacing and un-spoken, at the edge of all our exchanges, let it grow as an awareness between us, a secret confirmation that she too was only waiting, waiting for death to remove her husband and with him any lingering restraint on her conduct towards me. There was an air of practised vice about her that was to draw men all her life, an air of voluptuous pleasure at her own depravity that made her hatred of me seem merely instinctive. Yet there was always more to it than that. She had drawn some venom from whatever part she had played in the past of that house and had reserved it for me.

My only friend in those days, my only guide through Meongate's hidden perils, was Fergus, the taciturn and undemonstrative *major-domo*, 'shifty' as Olivia described him and certainly not as deferential as he should have been, but none the less my sole confidant. Sally, the sullen maid, and humourless Nanny Hiles both went in awe of Olivia, but Fergus treated her with an assurance, bordering on disrespect, that made him my immediate ally. A cautious, solitary, pessimistic man who had expected little from life and consequently been spared many disappointments, perhaps he took pity on a lonely child whose plight he understood better than she did herself. He would take me on covert expeditions through the grounds, or down to the wooded reach of

27

the Meon where he fished of a quiet afternoon, or into Droxford in the trap, when he would buy me a twist of sherbet and leave me sitting on the wall outside Wilsmer's saddlery whilst he went in to haggle over a new bridle for the pony. For such brief moments as those, kicking my heels on Mr Wilsmer's wall and eating my sherbet in the sunshine, I was happy. But such moments did not last.

It was Fergus who first showed me my father's name, recorded with the other war dead of the village, on a plaque at the church. Their Name Liveth for Evermore, the inscription said, and his name – Captain the Honourable John Hallows – is all that did live for me. I would stare at it for what seemed like hours trying to conjure up the real living and breathing father that he had never been to me, seeing only those stiff, expressionless, uniformed figures preserved by photographs in back copies of the *Illustrated London News*, glimpsing no part of his true self beyond the neatly carved letters of his name.

As for my mother, of her there was no record at all, no grave, no memorial of any kind. Fergus, when I questioned him, prevaricated. My mother's grave, if she had one, was far away – and he did not know where. There were, I was to understand, limits to what even he could tell me. Whether he suggested it or not I cannot remember, but, for some reason, I decided to ask Olivia. I cannot recall how old I was when it happened, but I had followed her into the library where she often went to look at a painting that hung there.

'Where is my mother's grave?' I said bluntly, partly intending the question to be a challenge. All hatred is, in time, reciprocated and I had come to hate Olivia as much as she hated me; I did not then appreciate how dangerous an enemy she could be.

She did not answer in words. She turned aside from that great, high, dark painting and hit me so hard across the face that I nearly fell over. I stood there, clutching the reddening bruise, too shocked by the pain of it to cry, and she stooped over me, her eyes blazing. 'If you ever ask that question again,' she said, 'if you ever mention your mother again, I'll make you suffer.'

The mystery of my mother thenceforth became the grand and secret obsession of my childhood. My father's death, after all, had a comforting simplicity about it. Every November there was an Armistice Parade in the village to commemorate the sacrifice of Captain the Honourable John Hallows and the many others like him. Though not permitted to join the Brownie troop that took part in the parade, I was allowed to go and watch and could imagine myself marching with all the little girls who, like me, had lost their father. But, at the end of the parade, they went home to their mothers; I could not even remember mine.

Sometimes, though, I thought I could remember her. It was impossible, of course, if what I had been told of her was true, but Olivia had succeeded in making me doubt everything I had not personally experienced, and there was one, dim, early memory, seemingly at the very dawn of my recollection, to sustain what I so wanted to believe.

I was standing on the platform at Droxford railway station. It was a hot summer's day: I could feel the heat of the gravel seeping up through my shoes. A train was standing at the platform, great billows of smoke rising as the engine gathered steam. The man standing beside me, who had been holding my hand, stooped and lifted me up, cradling me in his arms to watch the train pull out. He was stout and white-haired. I remember the rumble of his voice and the brim of his straw hat touching my head as he raised his free hand to wave. And I was waving too, at a woman aboard the train who had wound down the window and was leaning out, waving also and smiling and crying as she did so. She was dressed in blue and held a white handkerchief in her right hand. And the train carried her away. And then I cried too and the stout old man hugged me, the brass buttons on his coat cold against my face.

I recounted the memory to Fergus one day, when we were returning from a mushrooming expedition. When I had finished, I asked him who he thought the old man was.

'Sounds like old Mr Gladwin,' he replied. 'The first Lady Powerstock's father. He lived here . . . till *she* sent him away.' By *she* Fergus always meant Olivia.

'Why did she do that?'

'She'd have had her reasons, I don't doubt.'

'When did he go?'

'The summer of 1920, when you were three. Back to Yorkshire, so they say. A proper caution, was Mr Gladwin.'

'Who was the pretty lady, Fergus?'

'That I don't know.'

'Was she . . . my mother?'

He pulled up and looked down at me with a frown. 'That she was not,' he said with deliberate slowness. 'Your mother passed away a few days after she had you. You know that. No amount of wanting is going to make you remember her.'

'Then . . . who was the pretty lady?'

His frown became less kindly. 'I told you: I don't

know. That Mr Gladwin, he was a close one. Now, look to that napkin or you'll pitch your breakfast into the lane – and mine with it.'

If the pretty lady wasn't my mother, who was she? What was old Mr Gladwin, my great-grandfather, to her? There were no answers within my reach, just the secret hope I went on harbouring that maybe my mother wasn't really dead at all, just . . . sent away, like old Mr Gladwin.

I, too, was shortly to be sent away, to preparatory school in North Wales. It was the junior wing of Howell's, which some of the girls found austere and rigorous but where I felt at home from the very start. There were no shadows at school, no unspoken secrets from the past threatening to overtake me. It was the holidays I came to dread, the times when I knew I would have to return to Meongate to find Olivia waiting for me with her menacing smile, to find my grandfather even more frail and uncommunicative than when I'd left, to find Fergus a little less forthcoming each time with the priggish young lady he thought I was becoming.

Being sent away to boarding school at the age of eight meant I knew virtually nobody in Droxford – of my own age or any other. That, I suppose, is why I did not learn sooner about the murder at Meongate, why I was ignorant for so long of that fragment of our family's mystery.

I think it was the Cribbins boy who first told me. He used to help with the gardening during the summer holidays and was one of the few village children I had anything to do with. One warm, overcast afternoon, Cook gave me a glass of lemonade to take out to him in the orchard where he'd been put to cutting back brambles. We stood talking while he drank it. He asked me what the house was like inside.

'Haven't you ever been inside?' I retorted, a touch haughtily, for Howell's had trained me well.

'No fear,' he said between gulps. 'My dad's told me.'

'Told you what?'

''Bout the murder.'

'What murder?'

'Don't you know, Miss? There were a murder done at Meongate, years ago. My dad told me.'

'Oh that?' I replied. 'Of course I know about *that*.' It wouldn't have done to let him see that it had been kept from me.

The obvious person to ask for information was Fergus. I found him polishing the silver in the pantry.

'Murder, you say? Well, maybe there was and maybe there wasn't. What would Cribbins know?'

'Stop teasing, Fergus.'

He laid down the knives he had been cleaning and stooped close to my ear. 'I'm not teasing,' he whispered. '*She'd* skin me alive if she heard me talking about it. It's a subject best left alone.'

He knew better than to think I would leave it alone. The following afternoon, I tracked him down on the riverbank, at his favourite spot for fishing, where I could be certain we would not be overheard.

'Well? You can tell me here.'

'Tell you what?'

'About the murder.'

He grunted and flicked his line. 'They're not biting today.'

'*Fergus!*'

'I can see I'll get no peace till I tell you. It was during the war. One of his lordship's guests. Shot in his bedroom.'

'Which bedroom?'

'Don't worry. It wasn't yours. It was one of those that are shut up.'

'Who was he?'

'I told you: a guest. I forget his name.'

'Who killed him?'

'They never found out.'

'Gosh. You mean it's never been solved?'

'Not to this day.'

'How exciting.'

'I wouldn't call it exciting.'

'You wouldn't call anything exciting.'

He smiled. 'Well, take heed of this: don't mention it to *her*. She'd not thank you for it.'

'Was the murdered man a friend of hers, then?'

Fergus chuckled. '*She* doesn't have friends. You should know that. Now, clear off before you frighten away all the fish in the river.'

I taxed Fergus several more times on the subject but learned nothing. I dared not even ask anybody else. Cook and Sally had been handpicked, it seemed, for their avoidance of gossip. Perhaps, in Olivia's eyes, it compensated for their other deficiencies. They, I felt certain, would not help me. Besides, only to Fergus was I prepared to admit how little I truly knew of my family's history. Hints and snatches of hazy memory were all I had to go on.

I must have been a plague to Fergus with all my endless, unanswerable questions. Which room was the one where the murder was committed? Which room was my parents'? Why were there no pictures of them? Where was my mother buried? What did she look like? Why was Mr Gladwin sent away? Who was the pretty lady? He would just tap his nose, say he couldn't remember or couldn't tell me, then distract me with one of his puzzles involving string and matchsticks.

Even the little he did give away would probably have ensured his dismissal had Olivia known of it. Returning from one of her trips to London, trips which grew ever more frequent as the years passed, she would first ignore me, then subject me to withering inquisitions. What had I been doing? Who had I been talking to? What books had I been reading? Occasionally, as I grew older, she would ask my opinion of a new dress she had bought, or of some sparkling addition to her jewellery. Sometimes, I would make the mistake of admiring the item.

'It looks well because I wear it well,' she would reply. 'On you it would be . . . wasted.'

I never noticed Olivia take any interest in art, as distinct from adornment, with the exception of the picture that hung in the library. She often went there and since she read nothing beyond fashion catalogues it can only have been to look at the picture. It was a dark, horrid, rather perverted piece depicting a man in chain mail entering a castle bedchamber to find a naked woman awaiting him, draped across the bed. Looking at it used to make me shiver.

I could never quite explain my aversion to it to my own satisfaction until one day when Olivia was away and Sally had the afternoon off. I crept up to her bedroom in secret, just for the pleasure of defying her by trespassing there.

I remember the blue velvet curtains were drawn against the sun but were stirring slightly in the breeze from the half-open window behind them. Their heavy movement moved blocks of sunlight across the wide bed and the dressing table, on which stood a vast array of perfume bottles and cream jars, tortoiseshell-backed brushes and silver-framed mirrors: all the paraphernalia of Olivia's preserved appearance. I wished only, in that moment, to be standing in my mother's bedroom knowing she would shortly return, the lipsticks and combs belonging to her, not to this woman I hated. But it could not be. Olivia was the only mistress Meongate knew and I was her enemy. I looked at the layer of dust and powder Sally had left on the mirror – and smiled grimly.

As I turned away from the dressing table, my eye was taken by a painting hanging on the opposite wall. I caught my breath. It was surely a copy of the one in the library. But no. When I inspected it more closely, I saw that, though the scene and characters were the same, they were differently arranged. The man was now also lying on the bed, caressing the woman, kissing one of her breasts while fondling the other. The woman was looking slightly to one side and her face . . . I jumped back, startled. The woman's face was Olivia's when younger, Olivia's when her beauty did not need the props it now relied on. In the painting, she lay naked, as I had never seen her, but her expression was one she often wore. It was her very own patented blend of boredom and hatred.

For what must have been several minutes, I stared at the picture, transfixed, struggling to fathom the meaning of what I saw, repelled yet drawn by all that was blatant both in its placement – there, in a lady's bedroom – and in what it depicted – the writhing, coupled limbs, the man's mouth pressed to the woman's yielding breast; above all by the sneering indifference of that face I felt sure I knew.

For days afterwards, I could not rid my mind of the

painted image of Olivia. When she sat opposite me over dinner, passing disingenuous remarks to Lord Powerstock between mouthfuls, all I could see was her naked pillaged form. When I walked into a room and found her there and she looked up to note my presence with a cool, reproving glance, all I could see was the averted, cynical gaze of the woman in the painting. And when I looked again at the picture in the library, I saw it in a new light.

Who was the artist, I wondered, why did he choose Olivia as a model? I could not ask even Fergus to tell me that. I could only add to it to the list of unanswered questions held in my mind.

Soon, besides, my curiosity found another target. I had felt no interest in the hexagonal gazebo that stood above the wing of the house – the door to which, reached by a flight of spiral stairs, had always been kept locked – until Fergus let slip one day that my father had used it as an observatory and that his telescope, so far as he knew, was still set up there. I at once became determined to see it. I badgered Fergus to give me the key and, at length, he yielded, on condition that I breathed not a word of it to anyone. I agreed: it would be our secret.

The observatory itself, when I crept up there, proved to be a disappointment. Just a few pieces of dusty furniture and an old brass telescope mounted on a pedestal. But what the telescope enabled me to do was quite a different matter. It let me escape from Meongate. When I'd learned to train and focus it, I could watch the squirrels as they climbed the trees in the park or the rabbits as they hopped warily across the paddock. I could study a shepherd moving his flock on the slope of the downs or, after dark, gaze endlessly at a sky dense with stars. I could sit there, safely hidden, imagining my father noting down the arrangement of distant constellations, wondering if he had been the one to leave the half-empty box of matches on the shelf, crying softly sometimes when all the doubts and sadnesses weighted me down and I wished for nothing but to be able to look through the telescope and see him, hand in hand with my mother, patrolling the lawns of his rightful home.

Wishing and dreaming was all I could do to bring them back. To my schoolfriends, I claimed that my father had been posthumously awarded the DSO and that my mother had died of a broken heart. I described her as the most beautiful woman I had ever seen. As far as I could tell, they believed me. Sometimes, I almost believed it myself. After all, at Howell's I could pretend whatever I liked. Only when I returned to Meongate did the pretending have to stop.

TWO

The first time I heard about Thiepval was a day I shall never forget. It was a Saturday in August 1932, a day of humid, oppressive warmth, thunder threatening but never arriving, a clammy air of menace thickening round Meongate as the day lengthened. Olivia was to give a party that evening. Previously a rarity, there had been several such events that summer, the guest of honour and Olivia's principal dancing partner on each occasion being Sidney Payne, the wealthy Portsmouth builder.

I was fifteen then, possessed of sufficient false airs and fragile graces to take a scornful view of this sudden introduction of raucous gaiety. The day of my return from Howell's for the summer holiday, I had been introduced to Mr Payne: an ugly, dark, puffy-faced man with slicked-down hair and a pencil moustache. I hated him from the first, not merely because of his sweaty vulgarity and greedy, pig-like eyes, but because I sensed Olivia had marked him out as the kind of none too choosy, moneyed man she might look to for support in her declining years. This rash of parties, this invasion of coarse strangers that came in their wake, was not for his benefit, though he might have thought it was, but for hers. Olivia was looking to the future.

That Saturday afternoon, I paid a visit to my grandfather. I would not normally have done so, but preparations for the party were in full swing. Lord Powerstock's secluded rooms offered me a refuge. My excuse was that I had not seen much of him since returning from Howell's and he, for his part, looked unusually pleased to see me. He was seated by the window in his wheelchair, a rug across his lap, his face grey despite the sweltering heat, his gaze vaguely focused on the pages of a magazine he was turning with the one hand he still had the use of.

'Hello, Grandpapa,' I said. 'What are you reading?'

He held up the magazine so that I could see the title. It was the *Illustrated London News*. When I went over and knelt beside him, I saw that he had it open at the front page. There was a photograph of the Prince of Wales, dressed in military uniform, inspecting a guard of honour in the company of a frock-coated, foreign-looking gentleman.

'Who's the man with the Prince of Wales?' I asked.

'That is the President of France. They're inspecting French troops at Thiepval. Do you know where Thiepval is, Leonora?'

'Somewhere in France?'

'More than that. It's the centre of the Somme battlefield. The Prince of Wales went there to unveil the new Memorial to the Missing.'

My eyes took in the two photographs on the facing page. The one at the top, taken from the air, showed a vast brick monument of arches, pillars and raised blocks looming above bare fields, the concourse before it crowded with onlookers and parked vehicles. The picture beneath had been taken at ground level from amongst the crowd. From there the tall, slender central arch of the monument was visible, at its head the British and French flags, at its foot a line of soldiers standing to attention. In the foreground, the crowd watched, some straining from vantage points with cameras, others huddling beneath umbrellas.

'What does it mean, Grandpapa – a Memorial to the Missing?'

'It is to commemorate the men who died in the Battle of the Somme and who have no known grave. All their names are recorded there.'

'But why is it so big?'

'Because there are so many names. See, it tells you how many there are.'

I looked at the script beneath the photographs. There, sure enough, was the number: 73,412 men with no known grave.

'Your father is one of those, Leonora. His name will be recorded there. One day, perhaps, I will take you to see it.'

It was, in its way, an absurd suggestion, considering his debility. But for him to have spoken my father's name, which he so seldom did in my hearing, was achievement enough. It emboldened me to ask him more.

'Does that mean my father doesn't have a grave?'

He frowned and set his jaw. 'Yes. I'm afraid it does.'

'What about my mother? Does she have a grave?'

The frown softened. 'Oh yes. Of course she does. Whatever made you ask that?'

'Then . . . where is it?'

He turned his face aside and squinted towards the window. 'It is . . . far away.'

'Won't you tell me where?'

'Perhaps . . . when you're older.'

'How much older?'

Her looked back at me. 'When I . . . think you're ready.'

We were no longer talking merely of the whereabouts of my mother's grave. I think we both knew that what he was promising me, at some undetermined future date, was an answer to all my questions. What he was promising me was what he, at least, felt I deserved.

'I'm tired now, Leonora. Leave me to sleep.'

He let me take the *Illustrated London News* with me. I went up to my room and lay on my bed, devouring every word of the article, studying every figure in the photographs. You've seen the Memorial now and so have I. Then I could only imagine what it was like, could only pretend to myself that one day my grandfather would keep his promise and take me there. I read and re-read the quotations from the Prince of Wales' speech until they were imprinted on my memory. Even to this day, I remember his words.

'These myriads of names must form no mere Book of the Dead. They must be the opening chapter in a new Book of Life – the foundation and guide to a better civilization from which war shall be banished.'

Fine words for 73,412 men with no known grave. And my father one of them.

As it grew dark, the house filled with people. There was laughter, a babble of conversation, a gust of jazz music from the gramophone. Car doors slammed as other guests arrived. Somewhere I heard Payne's loud, brutal voice, slurred by drink. It was too much. As soon as the light left the sky, I sought refuge in the observatory, knowing that there I could escape the noise, that there they could not find me.

I would probably have been content to watch for shooting stars and wait for the party to finish had not the lamps come on in one of the rear bedrooms of the main block. I was surprised to see Olivia standing in the uncurtained window, for it was not her room and the party was still in progress. Curious, and secretly pleased to have her at a disadvantage, I trained the telescope on her.

She raised her head and rubbed at her throat, as if feeling the heat. Then she eased the window down and took several deep breaths. She was wearing a clinging pink silk dress, decorated with lace. It showed off her figure to flattening effect.

She turned away from the window and, as she did so, a man came into view, crossing the room to meet her. It was Sidney Payne. He seized her by the waist and kissed her full on the mouth, the force of his lips distorting her face, then on the neck. Her head swayed back and she laughed. He ran his right hand down over her hip and thigh, then kissed the tops of her breasts above the low neck of the dress. I could see an ugly flush of greed on his face, but not on Olivia's, now Payne wasn't looking at her, there was something even worse: that same expression I had seen in the painting, that inimitable, weary loathing. Then, with awkward, staggering steps, they moved, still entwined, across the room – towards the bed, I supposed – at any rate out of sight.

I couldn't have stopped watching if they hadn't moved away, but suddenly I felt grateful that they had. Alone in the observatory, I began to cry, not because of what I'd seen but because of what it meant. Olivia had

42

given me a glimpse of the future, a foretaste of what life at Meongate would be like once she had sole dominion. I could have guessed what it would be like. But now I knew.

My suspicions were confirmed sooner than I might have expected. One afternoon in November of that year, I was summoned from the hockney field at Howell's and told to report to the Headmistress's office. She was customarily stern and autocratic, so her gentleness of manner on this occasion forewarned me. My grandfather had suffered a fatal stroke and I must return home at once.

Very early next morning, my housemistress drove me to Wrexham and put me aboard the express for London. She was, I think, rather puzzled by my evident composure, but I could not help that. My grandfather had never disclosed enough of himself for me to mourn him in any heartfelt sense. Yet my composure was in part a device. I was determined to steel myself against whatever changes would now follow, determined to deprive Olivia of the satisfaction of knowing that I feared for my future at her hands.

It was as well that I had prepared myself, because, at Meongate, I found Sidney Payne already in residence. Fergus told me that he was certain Payne's perpetual presence had hastened his master's death. We were united in hatred of an interloper who threatened us both. Yet we were also helpless. The Powerstock title had died with my grandfather, and nobility, literally as well as metaphorically, left Meongate with his funeral cortège.

After the burial, Mayhew, the family solicitor, accompanied us back to the house for the reading of the will. A sleek, spare man of few words, he declined an offer of sherry and read the document at a swift, expressionless clip. Olivia and I comprised his audience, though Olivia seemed scarcely to be listening as she strolled around behind him. I, on the other hand, listened intently to learn what provision my grandfather had made for me. I had already reasoned that whatever he'd left me would be placed in trust until I came of age. I would therefore have to wait six years for independence from Olivia. It would be unpleasant, I knew, but not unbearable.

Mayhew concluded his preamble. Olivia moved slowly behind his chair. '"I devise all my real estate and I bequeath all my personal estate after payment of my just debts, funeral and testamentary expenses to my wife Olivia and I appoint her sole executrix of this my will."'

There was nothing else, no mention of me, no provision of any kind for his only grandchild.

'"Lastly I revoke all former wills in testimony whereof I have hereunto set my hand this eighth day of May One Thousand Nine Hundred and Seventeen. Signed: Powerstock."'

I was speechless. How could he have ignored his granddaughter? He had made the will when I was two months old. Mayhew began to gather his papers. At last, I found my voice. 'I don't understand.'

Mayhew looked at me. 'Don't understand what, young lady?'

'You didn't read out my name.'

'It was not there to be read.'

'But . . . I'm his granddaughter.'

Olivia stopped in her tracks and looked towards me. She was by the window now, with the light behind her, so I could not see the expression on her face as she spoke. 'Edward has entrusted your welfare to me, Leonora.'

There was nothing more to be said in her presence. I rose and left the room. I went into the garden, paced the lawn and tried to marshal my thoughts. I was Lord Powerstock's only blood relative, the only member of his family left, yet – nothing! Meongate, my home, my family's home, was mine, was theirs, no more. I looked towards the window from which he had so often watched me, struggled to understand why he should have done such a thing. Is that what he would one day have told me, had he lived? I would never know.

Turning back towards the house, I saw Mayhew climbing into his car. I ran across to him, holding up my hand to attract his attention.

'Mr Mayhew!'

'Yes, young lady?' His expression gave me little confidence.

'Can you tell me . . . why my grandfather ignored me in his will?'

'I cannot.'

'But . . . it isn't right.'

'I witnessed the document myself. Lord Powerstock's intentions were unmistakable.'

'Aren't I entitled to anything?'

He thought for a moment before replying. 'You are entitled to contest the will. But, as a minor, you could only do so through your guardian – Lady Powerstock.'

So that was it. Mayhew drove away and left me, alone and at Olivia's mercy. Such rights as I had were hers to dispose of. Lord Powerstock had consigned to her the future and to me – nothing at all.

What that future might hold was not long in becoming apparent. When I returned to Meongate a month later, for the Christmas holiday, a party was in progress. I walked up alone from the station in the chill of a

December afternoon to find lights blazing from every window of the house, sounds of music and laughter wafting out into the dusk. Fergus greeted me with a warning that I should be prepared for the worst. Olivia had given instructions that I was to join the party as soon as I arrived.

There were a dozen or so guests, foregathered in the drawing room, logs piled and roaring in the grate, jazz blaring from the gramophone, gin fumes and cigarette smoke hanging in the air, Sidney Payne red in the face and laughing loudly at a joke he had just told. Some I recognized as Payne's business associates who'd been to Meongate before, hard-drinking, coarse-voiced men with women twenty years their junior goggled-eyed and giggling on their arms; others were newcomers. I don't think any of them noticed me come in.

Except Olivia. She had been reclining on a *chaise-longue*, smoking a cigarette in a holder, and rose now, arrayed in crimson silk, to greet me with a watchful smile. 'Welcome home, Leonora,' she said, loudly enough to arrest the conversation nearest her. 'You're just in time to drink a toast. Sidney, a small glass of champagne for Leonora.'

Payne stepped forward and handed me a glass, breathing cigar smoke over me as he did so. I did not look at him. My eyes remained fixed on the gloating triumph I could read in Olivia's face.

'Sidney and I have announced our engagement,' she said. 'I'd like you to drink to our happiness.'

'I'll be one of the family now,' said Payne, somewhere on the fringes of my awareness.

I drank – or, rather, sipped – and asked if I might leave, but Olivia insisted that I remain. So I sat, still in my school uniform, on a hard chair, clutching but never finishing the glass of champagne, and watched and listened as the party proceeded.

One couple began to Charleston in the centre of the room, another to kiss passionately on a sofa in the corner. Voices grew louder, faces redder, laughs more hysterical. Drinks were spilled, cigarettes trodden into the carpet. My eyes began to water, my ears to throb. And through it all Olivia remained where she was, drinking little and laughing less, watching me as I endured the flagrancy of her strangely joyless victory. For it was more than merely a party, more than an announcement of her engagement. It was a declaration of intent.

Towards the end, Payne became very drunk. I noticed him back one of the girls against the wall and whisper something in her ear which made her laugh. As I watched, he lifted the hem of her dress and slid a five-pound note into the top of her stocking. And she laughed again.

Then I looked at Olivia and saw that she too had been watching him. When her gaze shifted back to me, it bore the expression of the woman in the painting, as I so clearly remembered it. With no other hint of her reaction, she left the couch, walked over to me and took the glass from my hand.

'You may go now,' she said.

By Easter, they were married. Payne's son by his first wife served as best man. I was not required to come home for the ceremony, which took place at a register office in Portsmouth and was followed, so Fergus later told me, by a weekend-long party at Meongate.

In my self-centred way – for at sixteen who is not self-centred? – I convinced myself that Olivia had contracted a loveless and repugnant marriage simply to further her hatred of me. Looking back, I doubt that had much to do with it. Her extravagant tastes and Lord Powerstock's deficient financial management had probably rendered a remunerative union essential if she was to continue to live as she wished. Payne, for all his obvious faults, had made enough money out of the post-war building boom to ensure that she could be kept in the manner to which she'd become accustomed. Or so she must have calculated.

But the true consequences of their marriage went beyond anybody's calculations. If Payne, his odious son and their circle of acquaintances rendered me a stranger in my own home, I had at least an ally in Fergus and school, in term-time, to retreat to. So when Angela Bowden, a schoolfriend whose father owned a chain of estate agents along the south coast, told me that Payne had been implicated in a building scandal, I thought little of it. When she showed me a newspaper cutting which talked of land subsidence beneath some new houses he had erected on the slopes of Portsdown Hill, just outside Portsmouth, I was at first merely amused. When I read the allegations of bribed building officials and corrupt City Councillors, I didn't really understand what it all meant. I simply reckoned that anything blackening Payne's name was to be welcomed.

The true significance of events dawned on me the day I returned to Meongate for Christmas in December 1933. It was exactly a year since Olivia's engagement party, exactly a year since she had, as she thought, sealed her prosperity for life. I walked up from the station wondering what I would find at the house, dreading every prospect that occurred to me yet never once guessing what truly did await me.

No party was in progress this time. No chandeliers

48

were blazing, nor fires crackling. There was not even Fergus to greet me. I went into the drawing room, where I could see a light was on, and encountered Payne, asleep in an armchair, snoring loudly and smelling of whisky. I dropped my bag heavily on the floor but he did not stir.

Growing puzzled, I rang the bell. After several minutes had passed, Sally appeared, looking more sullen and pinch-faced than ever.

'Where's Fergus?' I said.

''E's left us, Miss. Didn't the mistress tell you?'

'No. Where is she?'

'In the study, like as not.'

I found her where Sally had said, seated at what had been my grandfather's desk. She looked tired and much older than when last I'd been home. Her only greeting was an icy glare.

'Sally told me Fergus has left,' I said.

'Fergus was dismissed.'

'Why?'

'Prying once too often.'

'But he's been with the family—'

'Too long. Far too long. Old ways are changing here, Leonora. Fergus going is just one example.' She rose and crossed to the window. I noticed for the first time that her prodigious self-control had deserted her. She was angry, though for once not at me. 'My husband has declared himself bankrupt.'

'Bankrupt?'

'I thought you would have heard about it.'

'You mean those houses on Portsdown?'

'You *have* heard. Yes. The houses on Portsdown. My husband's prosperity, it seems, was as poorly founded as they were. He's a ruined man, facing criminal charges.

49

But that's a small matter. My concern is to avoid being ruined with him.' She turned to look at me quickly enough to catch a glimpse of my immediate reaction. 'And don't think you're not implicated, because you are.'

'It's nothing to do with me.'

'Oh but it is. You won't be returning to Howell's after Christmas. I can't afford the fees. I've just been writing to your headmistress.'

'Not . . . returning? You can't—'

'But I can, Leonora. I can.' She moved closer. 'As your guardian, I can do exactly as I like. Your education is now an unwarranted extravagance.'

'But what . . . what will I do?'

'With Fergus gone, there'll be plenty for you to do here. You can help Sally.'

No better than a servant, then, in my own home: that was her plan for me. I ran from the house and made my way down to the riverbank, where Fergus had so often fished. The overhanging trees were stark and bare, frost already forming on the grass. I draped my raincoat over a fallen trunk and sat there sobbing, confronting in all that bleakness the misery Olivia threatened to make of my life. No Fergus to confide in, no schoolfriends to return to, no hope of release. In the end, I dried my tears and resolved not to show any weakness to Olivia, not to give her any hint that she had the better of me. I would bide my time – and escape her yet.

In the months that followed, life at Meongate hung in a void of financial uncertainty and unspoken animosity. Payne drank away his days and waited for a court action that might add bribery and corruption to his acknowledged wrongs. Olivia busied herself in consultations with Mayhew that at least distracted her from me. Our only other visitor was Payne's son, Walter, a charmless thirty-year-old who needed but a measure of confidence to be a replica of his father. I avoided all of them and retreated into my private thoughts. When I could, I ventured into Droxford. There, in overheard conversations, I gleaned that Fergus was working as a lift operator in a Portsmouth department store (the post-mistress had seen him there) and that Payne's case would come up in April (his conviction was held to be certain).

On the fourteenth of March 1934, I was seventeen. At Meongate, the event was ignored by everyone except myself. Olivia had gone to Winchester, presumably to see Mayhew. Confined to the house by heavy rain, I entered the library in search of a book to read. I had made more use of it that winter than ever before. That afternoon, I made a new discovery. Pulling out a Walter Scott novel to look at, I noticed a book that had slipped behind the others at the back of the shelf. It was entitled *Deliberations of the Diocesan Committee for the Relief of the Poor of Portsea.* I opened it at random, thinking I would find it of little interest. But there, at the heading of a new chapter, was the title 'Squalor Amidst Plenty' and the name of its author: Miriam Hallows, Lady Powerstock. There was a dedication as well: 'Printed in memory of a fine lady who died as she lived, giving no quarter to complacency.' It had been written by my grandmother, Lord Powerstock's first wife, the woman Olivia had succeeded. I had looked at her gravestone in the churchyard often enough and wished she could speak to me. Now, here were her words before me.

I shut the book and hurried upstairs with it, seeking the privacy of my room in which to read what my grandmother had written.

I had sat down on my bed and was about to open the

book when, suddenly, Payne walked in. He was drunk, as always, face flushed and hair awry, collar loose, swollen lips forming uncertainly round his words. I could smell the whisky on his breath from the other side of the room.

'Olivia tells me it's your . . . birthday.' He tried to smile, but what emerged was an addled sneer.

'Yes.'

'You're growing up fast.' He swayed across the room towards me.

I closed the book and lowered my feet to the floor. 'I suppose so.'

He slumped down on the end of the bed; it sagged beneath his weight. 'Oh yes. Growing up fast.' He passed his hand across his face, as if to clear his sight. 'Growing up . . . into a . . . beautiful young lady.'

I smoothed down my skirt where it had ridden up beneath me and stared at the floor, hoping he might go if I said nothing.

'And it's your birthday. We should . . . should have had a party.'

'It doesn't matter.'

'Oh . . . it does.' He leaned across the bed and slapped his sweaty palm across my left hand where it was clenched in my lap. 'I'd like to . . . make up for it.' I felt the warmth of his stale breath on my cheek. 'How about a birthday kiss?'

I turned towards him to refuse, but he didn't give me a chance. He forced his moist lips against mine and pushed me down across the bed. I felt the stubble on his unshaven chin pricking against my face, felt his right hand pawing at my breasts. I tried to scream, but the weight of his body and his mouth prevented me.

My outstretched right hand was still resting on the

book. In desperation, I took hold of it and, with all my strength, swung it against the side of his head. The blow sounded louder than I'd expected. He slipped off me and the bed as well and crouched for a moment on the floor, shaking his head as if to clear it. Then he found his voice.

'You bitch!' he roared. 'You treacherous . . . bitch.' He lurched upright, grasped me by the shoulders and flung me, face down, across the bed.

For a moment, I was winded. Then I realized what was happening. He had pulled my skirt up around my waist and was stooping over me, breathing heavily. 'You bitch,' he said again. 'Mincing round here with your bloody airs and graces, looking down your nose at me. I'll show you . . .' I tried to turn over, but he forced my face down with his left hand against the back of my head, then dragged my knickers down with his other hand. I think I was too shocked to resist. When I felt the first stinging blow across my bare buttocks, I realized I'd taken his belt to me. The mattress bounced under the force of the blow. The first wave of agony came a moment later. Then I screamed.

What happened next I can't be sure. He hit me two or three times. Then there was another voice over his – Olivia's. Payne lurched up and blundered to the door, flinging his belt across the room as he went. The door slammed behind him. I knelt up on the bed and, for once, was glad to see Olivia. But in her face there was no mercy.

'You shameless little bitch,' she said. 'What have you done?'

'N-Nothing,' I stammered. 'He . . . he burst in here.'

'And you dropped your knickers for him. Like mother, like daughter.'

'Wha . . . what?' I couldn't understand what she was saying, couldn't think for the pain or see through my tears.

'It's what she did often enough. It's how you were conceived. So what else should I expect?'

'No . . . can't you see? He attacked me.'

'With a belt?' Her mouth curled with scorn. 'That's how your so pure mother liked it as well. That's how she amused herself while her husband was away, amused herself with my friends.'

'No. It's not true.'

'How would you know? Did you really think you were Lord Powerstock's granddaughter?'

'But I am.'

'Didn't they teach you arithmetic at Howell's? Find out when your so-called father died. Then you'll—'

She broke off. There was a knock at the door and Sally's voice, raised in urgency. 'Ma'am: there's been an accident. It's Mr Payne.'

Olivia flung the door open. 'What's happened?'

''E's lying in the 'all. Must've . . . fallen down the stairs. 'E's not moving.'

'Stay with Leonora.' Olivia swept past her and was gone.

Sally stepped uncertainly into the room and closed the door behind her. She said nothing, just watched in silence as I fumbled to rearrange my clothes. I rose unsteadily and moved to the dressing table, where I sat down and dabbed at my face with a handkerchief. I tried desperately to stop crying, tried vainly to stop shaking and sobbing. But I could not.

'Well, well,' she said at last. 'The mistress catch you up to something? Mr Payne could've fallen 'cos 'e was drunk, but 'raps he was upset . . . at being found out.'

I didn't turn round to look at her. Normally, she never spoke to me. Now, all the sour venom of her hostile glares came out in her words.

'Maybe you done us all a favour.'

Suddenly, in the mirror, I saw that she was standing immediately behind me.

'You've always thought me a fool, 'aven't you, Miss? But it's Fergus she put out on the street an' me as stays 'ere in comfort. That's 'cos I do as she says. So don't worry: I won't tell nobody about this.'

I was still staring incredulously at the reflection in the mirror of her hard, pinched face, when Olivia came back into the room.

'Leave us,' she said. Sally obeyed at once.

I looked down to avoid her gaze. In the struggle, I'd laddered one of my stockings: I noticed a large hole on my right knee. I stared at it and steeled myself not to look up. Olivia must have picked up Payne's belt, because I could hear the buckle clinking as she walked slowly round the room. Then it stopped, as she stopped, by the bed.

'What's this book doing here?'

'I took it . . . from the library.'

'There's blood on the spine. Whose blood is it?' I said nothing. Suddenly, she was standing beside me. She pulled my chin up sharply, forcing me to look at her. 'You hit him, didn't you? This is his blood.'

'Yes.'

'Then you should know: he's dead. Sidney Payne is dead.' She spoke of him impersonally, as if they'd never been married at all.

'It wasn't my fault.' I hoped she would see the pleading in my eyes, but, if she did, it was only as a sign of the weakness she would play on.

'There'll be lots of questions – an inquest, a coroner. But I'll keep you out of it. We'll say nothing about what happened here – on one condition. That, from now on, you do as I say. I'll keep you here and I'll keep your secret – on that condition. Do you understand?'

'Yes.'

'Otherwise, I'll have to tell the truth about your mother. How she did the bidding of any man who wanted her. How I can't even say which one of them fathered you. How you inherited her perversions and helped to kill my husband. Do you want all that to come out?'

'No.'

'So you do understand?'

'Yes. I understand.'

'Good.' She rose. 'Don't wash your face before the doctor comes. A few tears will impress him.' She went back to the bed and picked up the book. 'I'll keep this – in case it's needed.' She moved to the door, paused and looked back at me. 'By the way: happy birthday, Leonora.'

I had all that night, alone in my room, to think of what happened and what Olivia had said. Just a few minutes really – fifteen at the most. But they had been sufficient for Sidney Payne to die and my dreams, with him, of the parents I had never known. Not my father's daughter? It explained why my mother was never spoken of, why she died elsewhere and in disgrace, why my grandfather had disinherited me. It explained everything – and yet nothing.

Even in the depth of my despair, even in the grip of my shocked reaction, I knew that Olivia must have made it sound worse than it was. And why? Because now she had a way of holding me at Meongate. I had done nothing wrong, but I did not doubt that she could make it seem that I had. What would they do if they thought me responsible for Payne's death? A lunatic asylum – Olivia would make sure of it. Unless . . . I obeyed her in everything. We had played into her hands, Payne and I. There would be no scandalous court case now he was dead. There would be nothing I could do to resist her now she could threaten me with exposure as his murderer. A bloodstained book I had never read, a mother I could neither disown or defend, a father I could no longer claim. Her victory was complete.

The following morning, Sally told me that Olivia wanted to see me. She was in the study.

'I think it best that we understand each other,' she said, pacing the carpet by the window whilst I sat glumly beside the desk. 'You have no rights in this house – but I will allow you to remain. Indeed, should you attempt to leave, I will feel obliged to inform the authorities of the part you played in my husband's death. In return, you will do what I ask – in everything. Is that clear?'

'Yes.'

'Good.' She came and stood behind my chair. 'It occurred to me you might conceive the absurd notion that I had misled you concerning your parents. If so, you may be interested in the document in front of you on the desk. Read it.'

I picked up the small, crumpled brown envelope that rested on the nearest edge to me and drew out the contents: a telegram, addressed to Lord Powerstock, dated 4th May 1916.

'WAR OFFICE REGRETS TO INFORM YOU YOUR SON CAPT JOHN HALLOWS MISSING PRESUMED KILLED 30 APRIL.' So Olivia was right. He'd died more than ten months before I was born. He wasn't my father.

Perhaps she thought I would plead with her to tell me who my real father was, but I knew her well enough to judge she would never tell me, even if she knew. I replaced the telegram on the desk and walked slowly from the room, clinging to what little dignity was left me.

The inquest into Payne's death found that the fall downstairs had brought on a cerebral haemorrhage, aggravated by the amount of alcohol he'd consumed. The verdict was death by misadventure. Nobody seemed sorry he was dead, least of all Olivia. Even the odious Walter appeared largely indifferent, mouthing platitudes and glutting himself on sandwiches when he came back to the house after the funeral. Olivia made it clear to him that he wouldn't be expected to visit us any more. She'd even arranged for his father to be cremated, a rarity in those days, as if to ensure there would be nothing left of him, not even a grave, to attract attention.

I moved through that time in a trance, numbed by all that had happened and what it meant. I had lost the parents I'd dreamed of, been handed in exchange only desolate betrayal to explain my very existence. Such a past I could not face. I thrust the knowledge of it into a recess of my mind, along with the memory of my seventeenth birthday, along with all the other questions I'd once sought answers to but now forgot.

Angela Bowden wrote to me from Howell's, saying she'd heard of Payne's death from her father and was sorry I'd left the school so abruptly: would I like to visit her whilst she was at home over Easter? I did not reply. Not only would Olivia have forbidden me to go – I did not want to go. The world had shamed and assaulted me. So I hid myself from the world. I became, as time passed, more of a domestic servant than a daughter of the house. I exchanged, in other words, a role I no longer had a right to for one that Olivia imposed upon me. I grew, as she intended, timid, reclusive and introspective, above all obedient to her every demand.

Suborned by the threats Olivia held over me, I never once asked myself, far less her, why did she hold me there? It would have been easy enough to cast me adrift. The very passivity of her loathing for me suggested that an obvious course. But no. She wanted, almost despite herself, to keep me at Meongate, under her control, within her orbit. There was some motive for her domination of me that went beyond anything I so far knew. There was some purpose it served, rooted in the mysteries of that house.

In time, Meongate came to comprise our world. By seeing no one and going nowhere, we could both pretend – for different reasons – that Sidney Payne had never existed. Later, long after the most assiduous of village gossips must have abandoned the subject, our defences remained in place. Isolation had become a state of mind.

THREE

Only seven years after the Prince of Wales' speech at Thiepval, the Second World War came to contradict his brave message of peace. It came as a rare portent of change in the fixed and cloistered life we led at Meongate, yet, at first, it made little impact upon us.

Olivia received several official letters about the possibility of housing evacuees, but after she'd written to 'somebody who would remember her', the letters ceased. Sally took a job in a munitions factory in Portsmouth: Olivia did not replace her. When it reached her ears that, as a young, able-bodied, unmarried woman, I would be required to do some form of war work, she persuaded her doctor to write a letter saying that her infirmity necessitated my constant attendance on her. This was not a difficult fiction to sustain, since, without Sally, there was plenty for me to do and, besides, Olivia seldom left the house. Not that there was anything physically wrong with her. She simply hated the onset of old age and the loss of her beauty, which nothing could now disguise. Thus vanity drove her – and me with her – into a life of seclusion.

The war did not merely pass us by: it actually increased our isolation.

All that changed in the months before D-Day, 1944. The lanes around Droxford were lined with camouflaged trucks and tanks. Searchlights were set up on the downs. Troops were encamped in the fields. Meongate, I sensed, could not long remain immune.

One fine morning towards the end of April, returning through the orchard from an early stroll, I came upon a stranger in the grounds. I saw him from some way off: a tall, rather angular figure in army uniform – an officer, to judge by his cap. He was leaning against one of the apple trees, smoking a cigarette and gazing towards the house where it was visible beyond the rhododendron glade. He had his back turned and did not seem to hear me approaching, so, when I was about ten yards from him, I snapped a small twig off a low branch of the nearest tree. He spun round, clearly surprised.

'What the . . . Oh!' He smiled. 'Good morning.'

My first impression was that he was older than I'd thought. Handsome, undeniably, with a flashing smile, but there were touches of grey in his trimmed moustache. I identified him as a captain from the three pips on his epaulettes, assessed him, in that moment of first acquaintance, as just one anonymous representative of the military. What he made of me, in a shapeless old coat and walking shoes, clutching a handful of cowslips, I dreaded to imagine.

'What brings you here, Captain?' I said.

'Do you live here, Miss?'

'Yes.'

'Then allow me to explain. My name's Galloway.' He held out his hand and I shook it peremptorily. 'My battalion's moving into this area later today. The fact is

I'm reconnoitring for somewhere where they can camp.'

'I'm Leonora Hallows,' I said, as frostily as I could manage. 'My grandmother owns this house. She doesn't welcome visitors.'

'I was thinking we might tuck ourselves away down here – well out of your way.'

'Even so—'

'Actually, Miss Hallows' – he smiled again – 'strictly speaking, we don't require the landowner's consent. Obviously, we'd prefer to go where we're welcome, but . . .'

'I see. When will your . . . battalion . . . be arriving?'

'Around tea-time – as unobtrusively as possible.'

'I'll alert my grandmother.'

'I'd be obliged.' He looked back at the house. 'It's a fine building.'

I moved alongside him. 'I'm so glad you approve.'

'A good deal of history attached to it, I dare say.'

'My family has lived here for over a hundred years.'

'I noticed a Hallows on the war memorial in the village churchyard. Your father?'

I looked at him suspiciously. Such detective work suggested he had more than reconnaissance on his mind. 'As a matter of fact, yes.'

He returned my stare. 'Is that why you're reluctant to assist the military?'

I bridled. 'Who said I was reluctant?'

'Excuse me. I shouldn't have asked you that. Your motives are no business of mine.'

'No. They're not. Now, if you'll excuse me, I must go in. I'm sure I can leave you to find your own way out.'

'Of course.'

I walked away towards the house, moving quickly and without looking back, so that he could be sure I'd taken offence. I was determined not to let him see how confused I felt in the wake of our encounter. He was the first total stranger I'd talked to in years – courteous, good-looking and well spoken. I'd have been attracted to him even if I hadn't dreamt so often that just such a man might one day rescue me from my sealed and solitary life.

I conveyed the news to Olivia over breakfast.

'No choice, eh? Well, they can come – but they needn't expect a welcome. Be sure they understand that. I don't want to see them – any of them.'

'Won't that be rather difficult?'

'No. You will ensure they keep their distance.'

'Very well.'

'Not that it matters. In a few weeks, they'll all be gone – mostly to their deaths.'

Olivia's words recurred to me when, later, I stood at the front door and watched the cavalcade of canvas-backed trucks drive past the house and out across the park. The periodic thuds and thumps of bombing raids on Portsmouth had hitherto been our only direct contact with the war. Now there were callow young soldiers marching across our lawn to their last safe haven before . . . A jeep pulled up and Captain Galloway jumped out. He saluted smartly.

'No problems, I trust, Miss Hallows?'

'None as yet, Captain.'

'If there are, let me know.'

'I'll be sure to.'

There were no problems: he made sure of that by consulting me about every detail. Where their tents were to be pitched; how they might avoid ploughing up the lawns; whether the noise bothered Lady Powerstock: there was always some pretext for us to spend a few minutes strolling and talking. He was polite, punctilious and charming, as eager to hear me talking about the flowers that grew around their encampment as he was to speculate about what he might do in the post-war world. All my aloofness was demolished and soon I came to realize that I had made my first friend since schooldays.

One morning, when I was walking into Droxford, he stopped to give me a lift in his jeep and told me what impression Meongate had first made on him.

'I'm a Londoner, born and bred, but I've always dreamt what it must be like to live in a house in the country. I suppose I should have come straight to the front door when I arrived, but I couldn't resist looking around. You're very lucky to have such a home.'

'It's cold, isolated and lonely.'

'It didn't seem so to look at. When you surprised me in the orchard, I was wondering what you were like. I didn't expect to find out so quickly.'

'Why should you have wondered that?'

He smiled. 'Well, I took the liberty of asking a few questions in the village. They told me that you and your grandmother were somewhat . . . reclusive.'

'What else did they say?'

'That your father died in the last show.'

'And?'

'Oh, I forget.'

'I don't believe you.'

'All right, then. They said I'd find you unapproachable and uncooperative.'

'And you did.'

'Only at first.'

We had come to the village. He pulled up and I climbed out. I felt a sudden impulse to acknowledge

64

what he must have been told about me. 'I am all the things they say of me.'

'Now it's I who don't believe you.'

Why didn't he believe me – or the gossip about me? Later he would tell me how, appearing behind him in the orchard just as he'd been dreaming of Meongate and its younger occupant, I'd sown myself and my mystery in his mind, never to be dislodged. But if it is always difficult to understand how anybody as oneself can fascinate another, so it was impossible for me to believe, after all the barren years at Meongate, that I could discover affection – even love – as fortuitously as I had. That night, I looked at myself in my bedroom mirror and thought: No! It cannot be true. He sees in me merely an amusing way to pass the weeks he must spend here. I am deluding myself.

Yet we spent more and more time together, saw one another, ostensibly by chance, more and more often. He would meet me by the river, strolling before breakfast, or pass me in the lanes and offer me a lift in his jeep. He told me about his family, his early life, his work before the war, his plans for when it ended. Of myself, I said nothing and he asked little, as if he knew I was not yet ready to speak. What he could not know was my secret dread that, sooner or later, Olivia would tell him more than he could bear to hear, that she was only tolerating our friendship in order to heighten the pleasure of ending it.

There was, besides, another end in view: the unspecified but ever imminent date of the invasion, when Tony's battalion would embark for France and my hopes pass, with him, across the sea. One Sunday afternoon early in June, when we took a picnic up on to old Winchester Hill and sat on the sunny slope of the down, looking out across the valley towards Meongate, he spoke of our inevitable parting.

'The balloon will go up in a few days,' he said. 'On Tuesday, to be precise.'

'You mean the invasion?'

'Yes.'

It seemed incredible to think of it there, on the sheep-cropped turf, skylarks' song and heat haze rising about us, our picnic laid out on a chequered tablecloth, the Hampshire countryside nestling below.

'I could be shot for telling you as much.'

'Then why are you telling me?'

'Because I don't want to creep away like a thief in the night. As a matter of fact, I don't want to leave at all.'

'It was bound to happen.'

'The men are restless – keen to get it over with. But I wish waiting here could last all summer.'

'So do I.'

'Really?'

'Yes. You've made me happier than I could ever have imagined. And now it's goodbye.'

'But not for good. I intend to return.'

'You don't have to say that.'

'I mean it. I intend to return – and to ask you to marry me.'

'What?'

He smiled. 'I think you heard me.'

It was a dream of something I yearned for but feared could never be mine: the prosaic bliss of loving companionship. It was the happiness I had briefly known in those weeks projected into a future I had believed forever denied me. All these things he offered me – and all these things I still suspected Olivia could snatch away.

'Why are you crying?'

'Because what you promise me – what I so dearly want – can never be.'

'Why not?'

'There's so much about me you don't know.'

'There's nothing I could learn about you that would change my mind.'

'Isn't there? Isn't there really?'

'No, Leonora, there isn't. All you have to do is trust me. All you have to do is wait for me to return – and accept me when I do.'

So trust him I did, for me a more novel experience even than love. Two days later, on Tuesday, 6th June 1944, the villagers of Droxford awoke to find the trucks that had clogged their lanes and the troops that had camped in their fields vanished. Since hearing them roll down the drive at Meongate just before midnight, I had sat awake in my room, confronting the strange restored silence of Tony's absence. Only six weeks before, I could never have imagined any alteration to the sealed life Olivia had forced me to lead. Nor had it altered – save in the hope I had vested in him, save in the trust he had inspired in me.

'He's gone then,' said Olivia over breakfast.

'What do you mean, *he's* gone?' I replied. 'They've all gone.'

'You know what I mean.' There was sudden vehemence in her tone. 'You surely didn't suppose I was ignorant of your dalliance with the brave captain?'

So she had known all along. I replaced my cup in its saucer with deliberate precision and said nothing.

'What did he tell you? That he would come back for you? He won't. You may be sure of what. Whether to a

67

German bullet or a French whore, it makes no difference: you've lost him.'

Her words hurt me but did not sway me. I would not let her see how desperately I wanted to believe in him. Still I said nothing.

'Even if he did return, it wouldn't be for long, because then he'd have to be told the truth about you. So you see: you lose him either way.'

Then my hope betrayed me. 'How do you know I haven't told him the truth already?'

She rose from the table and walked to the window, then looked back at me, a cryptic smile at the edges of her mouth. I returned her gaze with as much composure as I could muster. Neither of us spoke. There was no need for words. In that house, between Olivia and I, silence had always been the stage for our bitterest encounters. It spoke loudly enough to me of her contempt and to her, no doubt, of my defiance.

In the months that followed, Tony's letters, arriving sporadically care of the village post office, became my most precious possessions, to be cherished and preserved, read and re-read until they threatened to fall apart at the folds, pulled from their hiding place and scanned whenever confidence threatened to desert me. They told me what Olivia sometimes made me doubt: that he loved me and would, one day, come to claim me.

What his letters did not tell me was whether he was in any danger. As to that, I had only the newspapers to guide me and the map Mr Wilsmer put in his shop window to chart the progress of the invasion. He must have wondered why I stared so often and so lengthily at the coloured pins he stuck in it and can have had no idea that I was simply trying to guess which pin was Tony's regiment.

As time passed and the war ground on, my anxiety faded. There was a sense in which, subconsciously, I did not want Tony to return, a sense in which the hope sustainable in his absence was preferable to the moment, however it arrived, when he learned the truth about me. The uneventful lapse of days at Meongate seemed strangely bearable now that I no longer thought I would remain there for ever.

Another spring came, but, with it, no battalion to camp in the orchard. The war in Europe ended. The danger was past but the waiting continued. Then, in early July, a telegram:

'AM HOME. WILL ARRIVE DROXFORD STATION NOON TOMORROW. ALL MY LOVE. TONY.'

He would be with me in less than two hours! I willed myself to show Olivia no glimmer of the consternation I felt. As far as she was to know, when I left the house later that morning, pannier basket on my arm, it was on the most trivial of errands. Yet when I sat waiting on the station platform, absurdly early, for Tony's train, I knew that it was, in truth, the most important of my life. My mind travelled back across twenty-five of my twenty-eight years to the same spot, waving goodbye then to a past I did not understand just as I was waiting now to greet a future I dare not hope for.

Suddenly, there he was, stepping down from the open door at the end of the train as it lurched and steamed to a halt. A slim, rather inconspicuous figure in an ill-fitting suit. At first, I didn't think it could be him. then he tossed away his cigarette in just the way he had that first time in the orchard and flashed me his greeting smile.

I should have hugged or kissed him. Instead, we halted a little apart and stared incredulously at each other.

'I'm back,' he said at last.

'You've lost weight.'

'I'll soon put it on again.'

'I expected you to be in uniform.'

'I stayed with my sister last night. This creation is courtesy of the government.'

'It's very . . .'

'Chic?'

Then we laughed and, suddenly, he was whirling me in his arms. Suddenly it was true: he'd come back for me.

We didn't head for Meongate. Instead we walked slowly, by the field path, towards Droxford, hand in hand in the midday heat. It should have been idyllic, but my anxiety, so long submerged, had re-surfaced and my torn mood did not escape him.

'Does your promise of last year still hold good?' he said.

'You know it does.'

'Then why so pensive?'

'Because I warned you then that there are many things you don't know about me. Now you'll have to know them. They may change your mind.'

'What things?'

'For one thing, the Captain Hallows whose name you noticed in the churchyard was not my real father. It was somebody else – I don't know who.'

'You did read my letters, didn't you?'

'Of course I did.'

'Then how can you believe such a thing would affect me? I love you, Leonora.'

I stopped and hung my head. Illegitimacy, after all, was only a pale rehearsal for what I had to tell him. 'There's more. A man called Payne—'

'I know about him.' He smiled. 'My first night in the White Horse, one of the local wiseacres gave me the gen on friend Payne. It's really of no consequence.'

'You don't understand.'

'I intend to marry you, Leonora. Invite a whole cupboardful of skeletons to the ceremony if you like. It won't make any difference.'

'My grandmother—'

'A dragon – I know. But you're over twenty-one. We don't need her consent.'

'It isn't that.'

Suddenly, he grasped me by both shoulders. 'Listen. I'll go up there now and tell her: I'm marrying you whatever she says or does.'

'But—'

'No! My mind's made up. You go on and wait for me in the White Horse. I shan't be long.'

Before I could speak, he'd set off back across the field. 'Tony! Wait!' I shouted after him. But he didn't stop.

I stood where I was for some minutes after he'd disappeared from view. I could have gone after him, of course, could have forced him to listen to my account of events, but I didn't. I had planned for a year how to put it to him and now I'd let the opportunity slip. I'd surrendered the stage to Olivia.

At length, I trailed into the village and went to the White Horse as he'd told me to. I bought a ginger beer and sat by the window, sipping my drink and gazing out at the street. This is the worst waiting of all, I remember thinking. Our love survived a year apart, but can it survive Olivia's few, well-chosen words?

I must have fallen into a reverie. Suddenly, sooner than I'd expected, he was standing beside me. He must have come in the back way, because he'd already bought a drink and was holding it up in front of him, as if proposing a toast. He was smiling broadly.

'What did she say?' I heard my voice break with the words.

'The question is: what do you say? I picked up a special licence in London. We could be married there tomorrow. My sister would be delighted to put you up. She's looking forward to meeting you.'

'But . . . what about Olivia?'

'I don't think she'll want to attend.' He sat down and chinked his glass against mine. 'What do you say?'

'What did she tell you – about Payne?'

'Nothing. I told her I intended to marry you and she said, "Do as you please". I wouldn't call it a blessing, but it was good enough for me.'

'She said nothing?'

'Other than that, not a word. So, is it on for tomorrow?'

My thoughts could not seem to grasp what he had said. Olivia had told him nothing, absolutely nothing. I had given her the chance to ruin me – and she had stayed her hand. It made no sense and yet, with Tony's smiling face before me, it seemed to make all the sense in the world.

'Leonora?'

'Tomorrow? Oh, yes, Tony. The answer is yes. Let's begin our future – tomorrow.'

Even now, I can hardly believe the speed and extent of the transformation the following days brought. Tony's sister Rosemary welcomed me to her home and family with the kind of natural, understated warmth I'd never previously encountered. She insisted that the wedding be delayed by a few days so that she could arrange some sort of reception and bustled me out to a

shop she knew to buy a dress. It seemed she had foreseen her brother's marriage longer than he had himself
and had hoarded ration coupons for the purpose.

Thanks to Rosemary, I was able to embark upon
married life in a state of bemused, unthinking rapture.
Nor did the changes stop there. Tony's best man, Jimmy
Dare, an army friend, offered him a managerial job at
his father's clothing factory in Wells in lieu of a present
and, within the week, we were house-hunting there. By
the time I next saw Olivia, we had bought the house in
Ash Lane where you were to be born.

We had returned to Meongate to collect the
remainder of my belongings. Already, I felt something
of a stranger there, unable to imagine, now that there
was so much more in my life, that it had once been
bounded by the walls of that house. To compound the
sensation, Olivia had hired a live-in nurse, a Miss Buss,
who received us coldly and left me in no doubt that she
would brook no interference in her management of
affairs.

After we'd loaded the car, I went back to bid Olivia
farewell. I found her in the conservatory, reclining
behind dark glasses, seemingly indifferent to our visit.

'I'm going now,' I said.

She did not reply.

'I just want to say . . . how grateful I am.'

She removed the dark glasses and looked at me
quizzically. 'What have you to be grateful for?'

'You could have tried to stop me. You could have tried
to make Tony think—'

'Think what?'

'I'm just grateful you didn't. That's all.'

'You needn't be.' She slid the dark glasses back on to
her nose, as if to deny me any glimmer of insight into

73

her unfathomable act of charity. I was grateful, but also suspicious, and she rewarded neither impulse.

'Miss Buss seems very efficient.'

Again, there was no response.

'Well . . . Goodbye then.'

Once more, no response. This, her implacably shielded gaze informed me, was the end of my servitude, but not an end I was to be allowed to relish. I walked slowly out of the conservatory and stepped free of the power by which she had held me, but the moment of my release was tinged with doubt. I was free, but no nearer understanding why.

Later, I began to think that Olivia might not have been as charitable as I'd supposed. By saying nothing, she had sown a secret between Tony and me. Perhaps she realized at the outset that its revelation would not prevent our marriage. Or perhaps she sensed that a secret between us would grow more threatening, not less, with the passage of time. Either way, I had been as prepared as I could be to tell Tony everything that had happened but, thanks to Olivia, had not needed to. I would never be as prepared again.

FOUR

Ronald's birth in 1948 set the seal on our marriage and gave Tony the son he so greatly desired. Jimmy Dare's father offered him a partnership to celebrate the event. For my own part, your birth in 1952 somehow meant more, simply because you were a daughter to whom I could be the kind of mother I had lacked myself. It was then, I suppose, that I finally if unconsciously decided to discard my past, not merely to forget it but to consign it to non-existence. In the world that Tony had made for me, doing so seemed not just possible but inevitable.

Olivia remained at Meongate. I did not visit her, nor she me. Periodically, Tony would go down to check that the house was in reasonable order. That was our only contact – and that was how I wanted it.

Early in January 1953, Miss Buss reported that Olivia's health was failing, a month later that she was not expected to live more than a few days. It was Miss Buss who suggested Tony should go down rather than me: she thought I might upset her patient. I didn't contest the point: I was grateful to be spared a final meeting. So it was Tony who was sitting at Olivia's bedside when she died. I stayed at home in Wells and played with my children.

I remember thinking, while he was away, of what Olivia's death would mean: the final sundering of my links with the past, the final proof that it no longer existed. I had succeeded in forgetting not merely the misery I'd endured at Meongate, but the hopes for some kind of vindication I'd vested in its many secrets. Now I wanted none of it. I'd manufactured a new life, embodied in you and Ronald, and had no use for reminders of the old.

As for Meongate itself, I wish now I'd scoured its rooms for relics of my family, reminders of my parents, tokens of my past, but all I felt at the time was an overwhelming sense of relief that a line could at last be drawn under that desolate phase of my life. I think I might not even have attended Olivia's funeral had Tony not insisted that I ought. He assumed I would inherit the house under the will and wanted to be on hand to arrange its disposal.

Old Mayhew had come out of retirement to act as Olivia's executor. She'd requested cremation, like her third husband, whose son was the only other mourner. I hadn't seen Walter Payne for nineteen years and was taken aback by the eerie, unwholesome replica of his father that he'd become. For all his efforts at ingratiation, I could scarcely disguise my revulsion.

Afterwards, we drove to Meongate, arriving before either Mayhew or Payne. Mentally, I was already prepared for this last visit to the house, for such I was determined it would be, but it was not enough to prevent my hand shaking as I opened the door and walked in. In the hall, a row of tea chests and packing cases stood, stacked to overflowing with the portable contents of the house. Miss Buss emerged from the passage and greeted us with cold civility.

'What's the meaning of this?' said Tony, gesturing at the chests.

'Mr Mayhew's instructions. I was to have everything ready for removal.'

'It seems indecently hasty.'

'I didn't feel it was for me to comment.'

'Mr and Mrs Galloway.' Mayhew came in behind us. 'I hoped to be here to receive you myself. Would you care for some tea? Perhaps you'd make some, Miss Buss. Shall we go into the drawing room?'

I meekly followed, shocked into silence by the echoes and associations that Meongate had preserved for me, my mind drawn towards a similar occasion more than twenty years before, when I'd learnt that Lord Powerstock had disinherited me. But Tony's mind was very much on the present – and he spoke for me. 'Miss Buss said you'd told her to commence packing everything up.'

'That is correct.'

'On whose authority?'

Reaching the drawing room, Mayhew ushered us in and closed the door. Retirement had not diminished the inscrutability of his thin-lipped, professional smile. 'Regrettably, Mr Payne is unable to join us. I thought we might therefore dispense with a formal reading of the will.'

Tony was growing angry. 'Do you mind answering my question?'

'I was merely passing on Mr Payne's instructions, Mr Galloway. He is co-executor – and sole beneficiary.'

'What?'

'Lady Powerstock left her entire estate to Mr Walter

Payne, her step-son and closest relative. The bequest amounts to this house and its contents, most of the capital being either exhausted or spoken for. I might add that the grounds have been considerably diminished by sales of land to neighbouring farmers.'

I was sitting on the sofa by now, letting my gaze flit around the furnishings of the room – left intact for our visit, I surmised – letting my mind recall the fire that had blazed in the now bare grate on the night of Olivia's engagement party. I could almost hear the deafening tones of the jazz they'd been playing on the gramophone, could almost taste the champagne I'd been forced to drink.

'Do you mean to tell me,' Tony was saying, 'that my wife – Lady Powerstock's granddaughter—'

'The phrasing of the will refers to the doubts surrounding your wife's parentage, Mr Galloway. That is why I thought we might leave it unread.'

My eyes stung again, as they had that night, as if once more the room was full of cigarette smoke, as if once more I could see Olivia watching me, watching her future husband . . . I rose from the sofa, determined to break the spell of Meongate for ever.

'I'm grateful for your tactful handling of the matter, Mr Mayhew.'

Tony looked at me in astonishment. 'Leonora!'

'I've no intention of contesting the will, Tony. Walter is welcome to everything. Has he signified his intentions for the house, Mr Mayhew?'

'The contents are to be auctioned. As for the house itself, I believe Mr Payne intends to refurbish and modernize it. He has spoken of opening some form of country club, of turning the grounds into a golf course.'

'I'm sure it'll be a great success.'

'There is one thing, however.' Mayhew cleared his throat. 'To describe Mr Payne as sole beneficiary was a slight exaggeration on my part. There was a minor bequest to you.'

'Why didn't you say so before?' snapped Tony.

'I go beg your pardon. It is extremely minor. Are you quite well, Mrs Galloway?' Mayhew had noticed me shiver and shot a piercing glance in my direction.

'It's rather cold in here, that's all.' I drew up the collar of my coat, but not to ward off the chill. I had shivered at the thought of what bequest Olivia could have devised for me. Suddenly, for the first time in years, I thought of the bloodstained book she'd taken from me the night of Payne's death. Had she destroyed it, as I'd hoped? And how much did Mayhew know? What had he gleaned from Olivia through the long years of their professional association? There was no way of telling from his blank, pinched, expressionless face.

A silence fell, as if he were judging whether I would ever summon the resolution to ask him what gift Olivia had left me. Nor did I. It was Tony who spoke. 'Damn it all, man, what is the bequest?'

'Lady Powerstock expressed the wish that Mrs Galloway should have something by which to remember her former guardian. It takes the form of . . . two paintings.'

'Paintings?' I spoke more from relief than surprise.

'Yes. I have them here.' He crossed to the far corner of the room, where a large rectangular shape stood against the wall, covered with a dust sheet. 'I gather they have no commercial value. They were painted by Lady Powerstock's first husband, a Mr Bartholomew. His work, I fear, is not in vogue.'

Tony walked across, tugged the dust sheet aside and

79

levered the two paintings apart to examine them. There was no need for me to see them, however. I knew which paintings they were, where they had previously hung and whose face we might find staring out of them.

'Were these typical of Bartholomew's work?' Tony asked.

'I cannot say,' Mayhew replied. 'I am not a connoisseur.'

'I don't want them,' I heard myself say. 'They can be auctioned with everything else.'

'If you're certain.'

'I am.' As Olivia must have been that I would not keep them. It was her parting gesture – defiant, distasteful, detestable.

Tony replaced the dust sheet and turned back to me. 'Hold on, darling. Never look a gift horse—'

'My mind's made up.'

Something in my expression must have told Tony I wouldn't be swayed. 'Right,' he said. 'Well, you heard, Mr Mayhew. They go under the hammer with the rest.'

So the deed was done. All the way back to Wells in the car, Tony vented the resentment he thought I should feel at Payne for the profit he would make from Meongate, for the fact that he who had never lived there should become its owner and I who was born there should receive only two unpleasant, unwanted paintings. I did not care. Payne was welcome to all of it. I had endured the final torment that Meongate held for me and would happily have paid any price to be able to turn my back on it for ever – as I believed I had done.

Three months passed, three months in which I cast off all shreds of the anxiety Olivia's bequest had momentarily inspired in me. It wasn't difficult. There was much to occupy my mind. The Queen's coronation had been fixed for the second of June and I found myself in the thick of planning for a street party to celebrate the event. I'd taken on more than my share of baking for the occasion and, by the Sunday before, had fallen badly behind. Noting my testy mood over lunch, Tony made a magnanimous offer.

'Would it help if I took the little 'uns down to Stoberry Park for the afternoon? With us out of your hair, you could make some headway in the kitchen.'

So I was left alone, which was, as a matter of fact, unusual, what with a husband, two children and Mrs Jeffries coming in every other day. It was the last day of May, soft, grey and windless, with the garden looking moist and somnolent through the kitchen window. I thought of Tony, puffing after a ball in the park when he would rather have been dozing at home over a newspaper, smiled and set to with the mixing bowl.

About half an hour later, there was a knock at the back door. A tall, sombre, rather shabbily dressed man was standing there. He apologized for coming to the back; there'd been no answer at the front. At first, I took him for a salesman: encyclopaedias, or sewing machines. I said I was busy.

Then he said: 'It's about your father.'

I looked at him and saw only a slightly down-at-heel stranger on a Sunday afternoon. But his words had sufficed to resurrect a buried life. I remember the thoughts that flashed through my mind as I confronted his impassive, imploring gaze. All the years through which I'd prayed in vain for some knowledge of my vanished father – and now, when at long last I'd learned to live without it, learned that it was better to abandon an impossible dream, now, when what would once have been so precious seemed merely untimely, now, whether I would or no, I was to hear of him.

'What do you mean?' I said. 'My father died many years ago.'

When he replied, it was as if he were reading an entry in a register, the same register you and I scanned at Thiepval. 'Captain the Honourable John Hallows. Missing, presumed killed in action, Mametz, 30th April 1916.'

'Who are you?'

'My name is Willis. I'm an old friend of your father. I saw the notice of Lady Powerstock's death. It prompted me to look you up.'

'I placed no notice.'

'No. A Mr Payne did so. He gave me your address.'

'What do you want?'

'A few minutes of your time – if you can spare it.'

'I told you: I'm busy.'

'Too busy – for just a few minutes?'

There was no threat or insistence in his tone. His manner was almost apologetic. Yet, welling within me, I could feel the contending forces of caution and curiosity, the reluctance of my new-found, mature, stable life struggling to suppress the child's lifetime quest for truths so long denied her. We stood in silence, whilst my mind raced around opposing notions: Olivia is dead, your father dead, Meongate lost, its contents sold and you are free: close the door on this visitor from your past. And yet, and yet, now may be the only chance you'll ever have, the only chance to know: hear his story.

'Come in, Mr Willis.'

He followed me into the lounge, declined an offer of tea and looked around awkwardly before taking a seat.

'My husband will be back shortly,' I said. 'He's taken the children to the park.'

'You have children?'

'A boy and a girl.'

He nodded. 'Well, I'll be gone by the time they get back.' He said it as if he intended to make sure he was. He glanced around again. This time, his gaze alighted on our wedding photograph, which I kept on top of the wireless. He stared at it for several moments. 'Your wedding, Mrs Galloway?'

'Yes.'

'I don't see Lady Powerstock in the group.'

'She didn't attend. So, you knew my grandmother.'

'Yes.'

'And my father?'

'I served with him in the Army. Through him, I met your mother and stayed at Meongate: There I met Lord and Lady Powerstock.'

So he knew them all. The names of people and places who clustered in my earliest recollections, spoken casually by a stranger: it was unnerving.

'I've had no contact with your family since 1916,' he continued.

'Why now?'

'Because, with Lady Powerstock dead, I'm free to tell you what I think you ought to know: the truth about your parents and your grandparents, the truth about Meongate and what happened there thirty-seven years ago. Above all, the truth about your father.'

Who was the pretty lady, Fergus? Where is my mother's grave? What murder? The answers might tumble like a stone down a slope. Once released, its progress could only be watched, not attested. Once the truth had been set in motion, we could no longer intervene. This was the choice laid before me by any quietly spoken, uninvited guest.

'What is the truth, Mr Willis? What have you come to tell me?'

'It's a long story. But one you should hear: one you're entitled to hear. Could you spare me an hour or so . . . some time soon?'

'Why wait?'

'Because your husband will be back shortly. You said so yourself. If I'm to tell you this, we mustn't be interrupted.'

'You've chosen a bad time.'

'The time chose itself. I'm staying at the Red Lion in the High Street. Could we meet there?'

'I'm very busy at the moment. The coronation, you see . . .'

'I can stay till Wednesday.'

Even as he put a term on his availability, I knew I would see him again. I couldn't walk away from what he had to tell me. 'Wednesday then. Not the Red Lion, though: I know the proprietor. The gateway leading from the Market Place to the Bishop's Palace. It's called the Bishop's Eye. Ten o'clock, Wednesday morning.'

So it was agreed. After he'd gone, I began to doubt my own word. He wouldn't turn up, or I wouldn't. Somehow, our next encounter couldn't really happen. When Tony brought you two back from the park, tumbling and clamouring for tea, I began to think I might have imagined Willis's visit altogether, might have fashioned his very existence from my desire to know the truth.

Yet I knew it was not so. I knew pretending I wouldn't see him was only an excuse for telling Tony nothing. Not that Tony would have forbidden me to meet Willis. It was not fear of his reaction that made me keep it from him – it was fear of my own. To want something so badly, so hopelessly, for so long, to convince yourself at last that not only can it never be yours but that you no longer truly desire it anyway, then to have it offered you, unlooked-for, unheralded, unsought: I could only cope with the prospect if I kept it secret.

I went through the street party on Coronation Day in a trance, a trance that did not end until ten o'clock the following morning. I'd arranged for Mrs Jeffries to come in all day so I could be free. I walked down Milton Lane through the warmth and sunshine of a placidly ordinary day in June. The neighbours I nodded to had no idea of the appointment I was about to keep. In the Market Place, workmen were up ladders taking down bunting from the day before, stallholders were setting out their wares. And, in the turreted shadow of the Bishop's Eye, Willis was waiting for me.

'I'm glad you came,' he said. He looked gaunter still, and more sombre, in the bleached morning air.

'Did you think I wouldn't?'

'No. I knew you would.'

We walked through to the Bishop's Palace and began to follow the footpath round the moat.

'To begin with,' he said after we'd gone a few yards, 'I should tell you that Willis was not always my name. My real name is Franklin. I don't suppose it means anything to you. The reason I no longer use it lies at the heart of my story. And what I'm about to tell you I've never told anyone else, nor ever will.'

We walked round the moat, then up Tor Hill and back, then round to the cathedral. We walked and talked for hours. His story was, as he'd warned me, a long one. But I didn't mind listening, didn't even notice how tired I was becoming. He had come to me from the padlocked past and now I would follow wherever his words took me.

PART TWO

ONE

What shall I tell you about your father? Shall we descend together the spirals of his soul? Alas, we cannot. All that I can do is tell you what I know.

What I know, of course, is not the same as what other people may know. What I know is one man's knowledge of another, a facet, a view, a flawed memory of that brief time when we walked together in this world; a memory, for all that, of the finest man I ever knew.

We met as fellow officers in the Great War: in a time and place where all beauties save friendship were ground into mud and blood, where there was no hope save what men like your father preserved for men like me.

For I was not exceptional. I cannot claim foresight or wisdom beyond my years, then or now. The war was a great adventure, something not to be missed. Just imagine believing that, as I did, in 1914. I was a fool, but what twenty-two-year-old man is not? Did foolishness deserve such a reward? I think not.

So let me tell you about the war – and about myself. I'd just come down from Oxford when it began and I was spending the summer at my uncle's house in Berkshire. He was a chartered accountant, a tedious but prosperous man who funded my education after my father deserted us and my mother broke down. I never forgave my uncle his generosity, nor he my fecklessness. I remember him taking me every week – with his unsmiling sense of duty – to visit my mother at the asylum in Reading. Every week she was worse. Every week I wanted to see her less.

A scholarship to Oxford seemed a merciful release from all that: a breath of fresh air. I was easily intoxicated, easily taken in by the glamour and bombast. I suppose it was a wonderful time to be male, clever and British. But, God, I paid a heavy price for it. We all did.

My mother died during my second term at Oxford and when I came down there was nothing – except my own lack of means – to tie me to my uncle. When the war came in early August, it was a godsend. I remember going up to town when the news came and celebrating – yes, celebrating – with some college friends. I'd been in the OTC at Oxford, so I was confident of getting a commission, and one of my uncle's friends was a retired colonel in the Hampshire Light Infantry, which made them the obvious choice. My uncle put in a good word for me – I think he was pleased to see me go.

Not that going was quite as quick or simple as I'd anticipated. It was the autumn before I had my lieu-tenancy confirmed and then there were six months' training at Aldershot. I was worried at times that the war would be over before I got there. Amazing, isn't it? How could I be so naïve? There was no hurry. The war would wait for me. Meanwhile, an officer's pay gave me plenty of ways of passing the time and the newspapers gave me all the false confidence I needed.

I got my embarkation orders just after Easter 1915. I'd spent the holiday in London and got back to the officers' mess in Aldershot on the Tuesday evening to find my name posted for France. Some other subalterns congratulated me and I enthused about seeing some action at last. Looking back, I can't believe I did so without reservation, without even a hint of irony. But I did. The following Monday, I was on a troop ship sailing from Southampton. Most of the chaps had tearful farewells to bear. I had only a dutiful wave from cousin Anthea. Perhaps that helped me to be glad to go.

Le Havre, a big bustling town full of troops and movement, was my introduction to France. Most of the men went straight on down the line, but we subalterns were told to report to the divisional depot at Rouen and await orders. We kicked our heels there for a couple of weeks while only rumour reached us. One of our battalions was having a bad time at Ypres. Something strange, something new the Germans had used, something about poison gas. We didn't know what to make of it. Till I was assigned to escort a troop train, that is, going back to Le Havre to meet a hospital ship. Bullet wounds I'd expected, but dozens of the men were physically unmarked. Their coughs – and the yellow pallor of their skins – filled me with dread. For the first time, I began to understand what war really was.

In the middle of May, another shipload of our regiment arrived from England. I was allotted a platoon and given my orders to join the third battalion at Béthune. It was a twenty-four-hour train away but, this time, the boredom and the endless card-playing had an edge: this time we really were on our way and this time

I had an inkling of what we were on our way to.

For the present, though, Béthune was another stopping-off point. It was a comfortable little town about seven miles from the Front: for the first time we could hear the guns and see the flares of shell fire by night and here we were instructed to await our company, which was in the process of withdrawing from Ypres. I was billeted with a charcutier and his family near the railway station, could see, every day and every night, the troop trains load and unload, men disembarking fresh-faced and prick-eared, jumpily eager for the unknown, while passing them, back from the Front, came files of grey-faced, silent, sullen figures, grim with the weight of my foreboding. Why was I there? What exactly was I so slowly and inexorably being sucked into? I did not know. I paced the cobbled streets of Béthune and waited to find out.

Battalion HQ was a tall, green-shuttered house on the edge of the town. There, one mild morning towards the end of May, I was summoned to report to my company commander, who'd got in the night before. It was your father: Captain the Hon. John Hallows. I'd expected some hard-faced veteran, I suppose, somebody in the image of Colonel Romney, of whom we subalterns went in awe. But he wasn't like that, not at all. I found him smoking and staring out of a window, a distracted but strangely calm man not much older than me – five years, in fact. He was about my height, a touch broader, with a moustache and a slightly studious expression. He turned from the window to acknowledge my salute, then shook my hand.

'How was it at Ypres, sir?' I said.

'There's nothing I can say to you, Franklin. It was how it was. I wouldn't want to taint you with my impressions. You must find out for yourself. We must all do that.'

'I'm looking forward to getting to the Front.' It was the sort of stupid thing I felt obliged to say.

'Really? Well . . .' His gaze drifted back to the window. 'I suppose I did once.'

'Have you been out for the duration, sir?'

He smiled. 'No. Since February.'

That shocked me. Three months had sufficed to give this weary cast to his voice and looks.

He was right. I did find out for myself. The company spent two weeks in a rest camp near Béthune, then moved up the La Bassée canal to take over a trench sector near Givenchy. In that time, I got to know Hallows better, as did we all. I'd taken him at first for a regular officer, but he soon disabused me out of that. Just an amateur, like I gathered he'd taken over the company in March, when the previous captain had been killed by a sniper. They'd moved into the salient round Ypres and been lucky to escape the worst of the gas when the Germans released it for the first time on April 22nd. Of that he spoke as if restraining his true thoughts. 'What's happening here is not what you'll have expected – not what you'll have read about at home.' Already, I did not doubt the truth of his words.

The trenches of the La Bassée sector were home for us that summer. It is odd to speak of such a grim and dangerous place as home, but so it became: the crafted labyrinth of trench and dug-out, sap-head and fire-step, was our abode, reached from Béthune through a landscape of smashed roads and ruined villages. To me it was new – and wholly awful – to see a summer land laid waste by man, but to many others it was, God help them, what they had become used to. Army life does not encourage too much contemplation. The mind concentrates on survival. At least for a while. And the mind of a young officer – even in such dismal surroundings – turns to thoughts of adventure and a little personal glory. My platoon were a glum collection, so I felt obliged to set a debonair example. Those summer nights near La Bassée I did more than my share of patrols and won for myself a properly warlike reputation. Hostilities were muted at the time and the risks I was running were greater than I knew.

As for Hallows, I became a little suspicious of him. His quiet efficiency and softly spoken fatalism were not what I had expected. Always grateful for intelligence, he seemed indifferent to what I considered my daring displays and at times discouraged too much night work. I put to him once a hare-brained scheme for a raid on the German line at its closest point: my idea was to ginger things up a little. He dismissed the idea, kindly but firmly. 'Remember, Franklin,' he said, 'we are responsible for men's lives: they are precious commodities, whatever this war might suggest to the contrary.'

I took his caution for want of spirit and thought the less of him for it. I did not see how sitting on our hands would bring the breakthrough we all desired. But Hallows had already despaired of a breakthrough, already seen it for an illusion sustainable only in the rarefied atmosphere of GHQ. For him, the welfare of his men was now paramount. He would risk it only at the insistence of others. Insistence came soon enough.

By early September, rumours of a big Franco-British push were rife in our sector and there was a good deal of optimism about the outcome. New drafts of men, replenished reserves of shells, a chance to turn the gas on the Germans. Victory seemed suddenly within our grasp. Victory, of course, was the greatest and grossest illusion of all. The high death toll kept it alive, perversely, because deluded newcomers always outnumbered the dwindling survivors who knew better.

Our preparations were impressive – to me. Each day saw consignments of gas cylinders being taken up to the front trenches. Each day rumour congealed into fact. On September 21st, heavy bombardment of the German lines began. It was held there would be few left alive in them to resist us. In reality, our artillery was merely serving notice of our attack, notice which the Germans were not about to disregard. On September 23rd, Hallows came back from battalion headquarters with our orders. He gathered the platoon commanders in a dug-out, distributed maps and read the detailed orders for an attack to be launched at dawn on September 25th, preceded by a discharge of gas. Our objectives were impressively detailed; their very precision filled me with hope. Until, that is, Hallows' summing-up.

'Those are our orders, gentlemen. Candidly, I must tell you that our chances of fulfilling them are negligible. The enemy is expecting us. Nothing I have seen of the gas companies makes me think they will manage an effective discharge. The wind conditions on the morning of the 25th will be all-important, but how can we guarantee that they will be the same all along the Front? I put that question a few hours ago to Colonel Romney. I received no answer. God help us all.'

September 25th dawned grey and damp. There was no breeze to speak of, though speak of it we did. Privately, I had criticized Hallows for his defeatism. Now his words came back to me. History books have since told me more of the Battle of Loos than I knew at the time, but all they have done is vindicate Hallows. I now know that the gas company commander refused to discharge in our sector because of the still conditions until General Gough directly ordered him to do so. What I knew at the time from the relative safety of a support trench was that a terrible commotion ahead represented the chaotic certainty of failure. Dozens were stretchered back past me, yellow-faced from our own gas. Those who escaped its effects were gunned down by ungassed Germans. When my platoon moved up to join the second wave, we found the front line a scene from Hell: corpses piled and fallen, gas hanging and drifting in pockets, German guns still firing, figures still flitting and voices shrieking out across the shell holes. On that day, in that place, the patriotic adventure ended for me. This was carnage, refined by military science into an obscenity of slaughter. This was something in which I wanted no part.

Yet a part I had still to play. And, true to the conditioning of Army discipline, I would have led my platoon into the poisoned air of sacrifice without, or at least despite, hesitation, had Hallows not called a halt. He came down the trench towards me, his face full of anger at generals far away.

'There'll be no second wave, Franklin. Secure this section but do not advance.'

'Have our orders changed, sir?'

'No. But I'll send no more men into that.' He gestured towards no man's land. 'I've sent to Romney for definite instructions. Meanwhile, we wait.'

As he moved off, my sergeant, who'd overheard, whispered to me: 'Reckon he's saved us from the high jump, sir.' He was right. Now word came from HQ. A further attack was postponed. We busied ourselves moving the wounded, then waited.

The waiting continued for ten days. Looking back, I am surprised I could have tolerated such a spell – without proper shelter – in that foul slaughter-ground. Sporadic bombardments continued. A few successful gas discharges were at length managed, but the advances they encouraged were swiftly repulsed, with heavy losses. Our own company remained in cautious occupation, as if Hallows' mood was known and not to be tested. By night, he led rescue parties to bring in the wounded. By day, he comforted and cajoled us. This was a different man from the one whose weariness and cynicism I'd distrusted earlier, or rather, the same man seen through my changed eyes. This was the John Hallows who became my friend.

I recall standing with him at the junction of a communication trench just after stand-down one morning – the first of October – looking out across the cratered field of death towards the German lines. I asked – almost rhetorically - 'Why are we here?'

'Haven't you heard what the men sing, Franklin?' he replied. 'We're here because we're here because we're here.'

'But that isn't enough.'

'For them, it has to be. For you and me, reason is scarcely appropriate. Whyever we came – duty, honour, *noblesse oblige* – won't measure up to this butchery called battle. Will it?'

I shook my head. 'No. But there's no way out – is there?'

'None. We are trapped in the mechanical insanity of a nation at war.' Then he laughed. 'Excuse me. I never thought to hear such words from my own lips. Like you, I dare say, I thought enlistment was the right thing to do. I did not understand, you see. And now it is too late.'

We talked often in the days ahead, as if to talk was an antidote to what we saw around us. I suppose Hallows was glad of an educated ear and I was glad, I know, of his confidence. He told me of his home in Hampshire, his father – Lord Powerstock – who would be appalled to hear his view of warfare, and his young wife, who would not be. He told me what he thought of the high command and their prosecution of the war. He told me what he made of a beautiful world which could permit such ugliness. He told me, in short, of himself.

In the middle of October, our battalion was withdrawn from the front line for Divisional Rest near Abbéville. It was a three-day march away, but we were all happy to go, happy to leave the war behind – at least for a while. We were billeted in the village of Canchy and could afford, at last, to relax. There, in leisurely surroundings, Hallows and I had many a philosophical debate over a bottle of wine in the cosy *estaminet* of M. Chausson, many a soulful tramp over the fields towards the Forest of Crécy, where another band of Englishmen had once fought – and won – a famous battle. Hallows told me that in his village church in Hampshire there stood the tomb of a knight who had fought at Crécy all those centuries before.

'I went and looked at it the day before enlisting last year,' he said. 'As the son of the squire, I was expected to join promptly and I didn't resist, but I went to see that Plantagenet knight beforehand for some kind of . . . benediction. I wondered how it had been for him. I wonder still. And do you suppose he ever wondered . . . how it would be for me?'

'Hardly.'

'No? Well, maybe you're right. But, then again, the

past is closer than you think in a place like this. There was a trench sector near Ypres where the German lines were only about thirty yards away and, every day, we could see them moving amongst their workings: grey, glimpsed figures not unlike the wolves in winter that knight of Crécy must once have been taught to fear.'

Wolves in winter: strange thoughts for such as us, thoughts we'd been led to by the exigencies of war. For that Hallows made me grateful. The war, whatever else it did, expanded us, made him more than just a smug and landed son, made me more than just a priggish young man. In France, we encountered the elemental. In France, we began to question what we'd been trained to expect of life.

Wolves in winter: appropriate images, since winter was indeed drawing in. by the end of November, we were back at the Front. A different sector this time, further south, beyond Albert, but much the same, in many ways. Trench warfare was still horrible, but no longer novel. I adjusted to the grimly cold trench tours interspersed with withdrawals to the relative cosiness of a nearby farm; adjusted, if you like, to the business of war. Not that it ever became easy. Snipers and night raids continued to take their toll. Though Hallows taught me to be careful care was not enough. Sudden death – above all, the sight of death – became commonplace.

Just before Christmas, Hallows went home on leave. I saw him off on the train to Le Havre, knowing how badly I would miss him. He'd become for me a guide in the dark, a reassuring presence, above all a friend. And friendships forged in war are made of strong stuff. Not that I was alone in missing him. The company had come to rely on him. They grew nervous in his absence, as if his physical presence alone made them safe. About this time, I emerged at the other side of my adjustment to the war. Its initial shock had faded. Yes, it was possible for men and nations to do this to each other. Now tolerance faded also. I'd been in France for nine months, long enough to learn that what was happening there was neither patriotic nor even necessary: it was merely criminal.

When Hallows returned at the end of January, I saw that he too had changed. It wasn't merely the usual post-leave depression. No, that wasn't it. Something else, something back home, had got to him. Others had told me how devastatingly fatuous the domestic view of the war was. I knew he'd been prepared for that, prepared to say nothing of the truth because the truth, by a fireside in England, would seem incredible. So that wasn't it either. What it was he wouldn't say – not even to me. But Christmas at home had worried him. That much was obvious. And worries like that were often fatal in France. They made a man careless.

Hernu's Farm, on a mild day towards the end of February: an innocent day of deceptive warmth. It shines now in my mind like a jewel. The men were resting in the barns and fields. Corporal Quinlan was throwing sticks for old Hernu's dog and Hallows was sitting in a wicker chair in the watery sun, smoking a cigarette and reading a letter which had recently come with a valentine from his wife. A couple of roosters were pecking at his feet for corn. Guns thumped lazily at the edges of a still afternoon. I rested on the shafts of a hay cart and tried to lighten my friend's mood.

'How is your wife?' I asked conversationally.

He looked up. 'Very well, I gather.'

'She must miss you.'

'Yes. As I do her. Count yourself lucky to be single, Tom. At times like this, it's best. I often think of what might happen to Leonora if I died out here. Perhaps I should say: *when* I die out here.'

'You must cut that out.' Mine was a good-humoured rebuke, but he had offended an unwritten battalion rule: speak of death if you must, but not your own. That was held to be self-fulfilling prophecy.

He smiled wryly. 'Sorry. It's just that sometimes I think this might go on for ever.'

I said nothing. I had thought the same myself.

'Perhaps the Americans coming in would tilt the balance. Do you think they will?'

I shrugged my shoulders. 'If the *Lusitania* wasn't enough, what could make them?'

'I don't know. The Americans are . . . strange people. Without history, without . . . obligation.' His point eluded me, as he seemed to notice. 'Sorry.' So many apologies were uncharacteristic, 'We had an American houseguest at Meongate over Christmas. He gave me one or two . . . two insights.' His concentration seemed to drift, then he looked at me intently. 'There's a big push coming this spring, Tom. I'm certain of it. Should I not . . . come through, would you be prepared to visit my family – tell my wife what happened?'

'Of course. But must we be so gloomy on such a fine day?'

'I suppose not. But remember – this is what they call a false spring.'

How right he was. Winter returned to Picardy and we with it, to the frozen trenches. In early April, I was given a month's home leave. I said goodbye to Hallows at the company dug-out one morning of scattered snow. He left off trying to coax a stove into life and walked out with me down the track towards Albert. His farewell was a jaunty one, but still there was that undertow of a bleak mood I couldn't catch.

'Take care,' I said, shaking his hand.

'Safe journey,' he replied, as if to deflect my sentiment. 'Bring me back an Easter egg – and some spring weather.'

'I'll do my best.'

Then he was gone, back into the dug-out.

Home leave wasn't the joy it should have been. The train to Le Havre and the crossing to Southampton: they were the best, because they represented – in their prosaic way – freedom, at least for a while. But being back in England? That was a different matter. It no longer seemed like home, it no longer seemed to be a place I could understand. The newspapers were fighting a different war from the one I'd been in and nobody wanted to hear the truth from my lips. I argued with my uncle, prowled the Lambourn Downs and wrote to Hallows, telling him how I felt. In London it was no better – if anything, worse. I began to wish my leave away, much as I knew that, as soon as I was back in France, I would regret it. The war had made me homeless.

In May 1916, just over a year after my first arrival, I was in Le Havre again. Another long train journey, clanking me back across a rain-sodden Normandy towards a fate that waited patiently. At least I was looking forward to seeing Hallows again: I really had brought him his Easter egg.

The battalion had moved to billets in the village of Louvencourt. I located the command post in an old granary and reported to Colonel Romney.

'Welcome back, Franklin,' he said stiffly. 'You'll rejoin C company, of course. You have a new CO.'

'New, sir? Captain Hallows . . .'

'Bought it down the line. Didn't you know?'

I said nothing. I saluted limply and walked out into the street. Hallows was dead and I hadn't known. To Romney it meant nothing: just another name, another casualty. I couldn't believe it, couldn't imagine that Hallows was gone. I had that absurd gift – an Easter egg – in my pack, but he would never taste it now.

I got the full story later from the CSM. They were to have pulled out of the Mametz sector on the first of May. The night before, Hallows had gone out with Sergeant Box to check the wire: he wanted to leave it in good order for our successors from the Surrey regiment. Neither man returned. There were gunshots heard in their reach of no man's land and a couple of flares went up. It was assumed they had run into a German patrol. Certainly the Germans started letting fly at something, which ruled out a rescue party that night. There was no sign next day and then the battalion had to withdraw. A couple of days later, news caught up with them in Louvencourt: one of the Surrey patrols had found a corpse half-submerged in a flooded shell hole. They couldn't bring him in, but they'd taken his pocket-book and now sent it on to us. It was Hallows'. The CSM still had it, stained with blood. He told me the men had been very upset. 'They've took it 'ard, sir. Very 'ard.'

Not as hard as me, I felt sure. With Hallows went my faith even in the nobility of survival. We were set there – under the perversely brightening skies of spring – on the grinding road to certain death. Whether it came suddenly, literally out of the blue, or stealthily by night, or in the lumbering schedule of some set-piece slaughter, seemed not to matter. The new company commander, Captain Lake, transferred from the first battalion, was too optimistic by half about the pending offensive. He had little time for me and I less for him. I wrote a long letter to Hallows' widow and made sure it was on its way before we moved to our trench sector by the banks of the river Ancre. I wondered if I ever would keep my promise to Hallows about visiting his family; on the whole, I rather doubted it.

June wore on. A long bombardment commenced to soften up the German lines, a prospect I viewed with all the scepticism of a veteran of Loos. Zero day was fixed for June 29th, then put back – on account of bad weather – to July 1st. Lake's briefing, hedged around with none of the warnings Hallows would have given, airily anticipated seizing the ridge east of Thiepval as part of the big push. Those of us who knew how well defended that ridge was knew also that our number was up.

July 1st dawned bright with a promise of roasting heat. Lake led us over the top at 7.30 a.m. The men had been instructed to walk steadily across no man's land towards lines whose occupants were by then supposed to have been shelled out of the way. Naturally, they had not been. Instead, they were ready and waiting to machine-gun the bunched ranks of slowly advancing troops. Round Thiepval, the sloping ground compounded our plight. I was hit before I had gone ten yards. Ahead of me, I saw Lake go down, and dozens more with every moment I watched, shorn like wheat by the scything fire. Surprised to find myself still alive, I crawled back to our trench. You could say I was lucky. Lucky to be hit before I'd gone far and to finish with nothing worse than a smashed shoulder. Yet no man who fought on the Somme that day should be called lucky. Ill fortune attended all our parts. With Hallows gone, I am not sure I much cared whether I lived or died. Perhaps that is why I survived.

A week later, I was in a hospital bed in London. England, in the summer of 1916. That, I suppose, is where my strange tale has its true beginning.

TWO

I was not in bad shape. Towards the middle of August I was transferred from hospital to a guest house in Eastbourne, taken over for convalescent officers. We were an odd collection, glad to be recovering but reticent about returning to France. Things had been going badly on the Somme – there was no other way they could go. The daily roll of honour read like a petition against inhuman generals. I picked my way along the seafront past old ladies and young men in Bath chairs, thinking – sometimes – that I could hear the guns across the Channel. Who, in the brightly painted charm of an English seaside resort, could believe that it was really happening?

Cousin Anthea paid me several visits. What was I going to do? Spend some time in Berkshire? Discussing the Somme with my uncle was a ghastly prospect, yet I would have to make up my mind: my shoulder was healing well and I would soon be discharged.

Early in September came salvation: a letter – unsolicited – from a benevolent society for injured officers, whose patron, the Countess of Kilsyth, arranged, so I gathered, for victims of the war – provided they were of suitable breeding – to be farmed out to the country houses of her titled acquaintances for rest and recuperation. I sat in a deckchair on the guest house balcony reading the letter with some relief, relief which became surprise when I turned to the attachment, a note from the particular household I was invited to join. The vellumed letterhead read: *Meongate, Droxford, Hampshire*. It was from Lord Powerstock: 'Having heard so much of you from my late son, I am hopeful that Lady Kilsyth will send you to us.' And she had. I was to keep my promise after all.

I reached Droxford railway station in the late morning of a fine Indian summer's day. No other passengers got off on the raked-gravel platform, though the train waited whilst crates of watercress were loaded. I walked out through the booking hall in a state of trance. Behind me, a whistle blew and the train moved out. A ticket collector, red-faced from doubling as a porter, caught me up and took my ticket with a smile and a comment on the weather. Then I was alone on the forecourt, wondering what to do next. I'd been told I would be collected, but there was no sign of anybody. The train chugged off along the valley and silence began to settle around me in the heat. A swarm of gnats hung beneath the carved eaves of the station building. Somewhere, a dove was cooing.

Then, along the lane, there came on the gentle breeze a jingle of harness and a clopping of hooves. A pony and trap came into view, making fair speed, and wheeled into the yard. It stopped beside me, the pony pulling up with a stamp that raised some dust. Dust that hung and drifted, a little like gas . . . but settled more quickly. I looked up at the driver: a stout, barrel-chested old man in faded blue frock coat and pale breeches, straw hat shading a white-whiskered face flushed with rather more than just the heat of a summer's day.

He greeted me with patrician good cheer. 'Good morning, young man. You must be the famous Lieutenant Franklin.'

'Hardly famous. I . . .'

'Spare me the false modesty. I'm too old for it. Haven't I come to collect you rather than leave it to a servant? Come. Hop aboard.' His twinkle-eyed humour was infectious. He wasn't at all what I'd expected.

I stowed my bag and climbed up beside him. 'Forgive me, but . . . are you Lord Powerstock?'

'Bless you, no.' He loosed a rumbling laugh, then twitched on the reins and started us back down the lane. 'What do you think of Lucy's bells?' He gestured towards the pony's head. There were little silver bells fastened to the bridle, tinkling as we rode. It was the same sound I'd heard on his approach – a puzzling sound, some-how out of place in the Hampshire farmland.

'Very nice,' I said lamely.

He laughed again. 'They're troika bells. From Russia. A personal gift from the Czar.'

'Really?'

'No. Not really. But they are from Russia. I did business there once.' He looked at me and winked. 'When I was your age. A long time ago.' He paused and bowled along the lane without speaking for a while. Then he began again, as if remembering something he'd been about to say. 'Lord Powerstock? That's a good one. No. I'm a skeleton in his cupboard, though a fleshy one, as you see. Charter Gladwin's the name: a sort of relic of family history.'

'For a relic, you manage this pony well, sir.'

He laughed again, as he did often, with ease, unforced and bubbling, like wine overflowing a recharged glass. 'Always defer to age, young man. It's an excellent policy, though I never followed it myself. After all, who else in these parts is likely to be able to remember the old Queen's coronation?'

'Nobody – I imagine.'

'Exactly. But you'll be wanting to know what I'm to do with young John – Captain Hallows. Well, I'm his grandfather. My daughter was his mother. Now they're both gone. Just me left. Comical, ain't it?'

'Well, I hardly . . .'

'No. You're right. Not comical. A damn shame. I liked John. A fine young man. Good few of 'em being lost out there, I dare say.'

'Yes,' I said grimly. 'There are.'

'Poorly equipped, badly led, sadly wasted. Ain't that the size of it?'

'You seem well informed, sir.'

'Not at all. It's what they said about the Crimea. I didn't think much could have changed.' He laughed and, this time, despite myself, I laughed with him.

The lane was rising now, taking us between high hedges over the swell of a gentle down and away from the line of the railway. We were leaving behind the water meadows of the curving Meon and climbing through sheep-cropped pasture and shady hangers of oak.

'The house will be in view soon,' the old man announced. 'I'll try to be on my best behaviour when we get there. You'll have to do the same.'

'I'll try not to offend anyone.'

'It's just there's been a black mood hanging over the place since John died. Not that I'm saying he should be forgotten, but it's been four months now. Edward – Lord Powerstock – don't seem able to pull round. As for Leonora . . .' He tailed off in tongue-clicking disappointment.

I recognized Leonora as Hallows' wife. 'She's bound to have taken it hard.'

Gladwin grunted at that and set his face to the road. We had reached the other side of the down now and were following a straight lane beneath arching chestnut trees. To the left of us ran a high brick wall, breached and patched in places. From the trap, glimpsed between thickly leaved trees, I could see a large house set in its own grounds. A few minutes later, we wheeled off the lane between open wrought-iron gates and up a curving drive through patches of sunlight and shade, then emerged from the trees and crossed open parkland towards the house itself.

'Welcome to Meongate,' Gladwin muttered. 'Hope you like the place as much as I do. Between you and me, it's why I let my daughter marry into the family.'

It was easy to see what he meant. Meongate stood gracefully in its park, well proportioned without being grandiose, an L-shaped structured of brick and flint, the drive leading past the main frontage of the house whilst a cross-wing at the far end ran away behind the building to form an angle enclosing an ornamental garden. Halfway along the roof of the wing, standing as high as its tall, slender-stacked chimneys, was a single glazed turret supporting a weather-vane. Sun caught the vane's gilded figure, warmed the brickwork of the house and lit the ivy-framed windows. Here were all the comforting English rural virtues cast in stone and leaf; here – little knowing what awaited me – I came home in Hallows' place.

We drew up before the open front door and Gladwin heaved himself down with a great shudder of the trap. A man appeared from the porch to take my bag and Gladwin bellowed good-naturedly at him.

'Not bad, eh, Fergus?' He flipped open a fob-watch. 'There and back in just over the half-hour.'

'You've been driving her too hard,' Fergus muttered as he went in with my bag.

'You're an old woman,' Gladwin boomed after him. He winked at me as I climbed down and Fergus reappeared. 'Lucy likes a run – which is more than you do.'

This time, Fergus only grunted as he led the pony away. We turned towards the house, where a woman was now standing in the doorway to greet us.

'Brace yourself,' Gladwin said to me from the corner of his mouth. 'It's her Ladyship.'

'Her Ladyship?'

'The second Lady Powerstock. The painted lantern of his Lordship's later life.'

As in everything, Gladwin exaggerated. The woman I was looking at was an elegant, Italianate beauty not many years past her peak, dark hair drawn up from a classical, high-cheeked face, a floral-patterned dress with a hint of silk shaping itself to a figure that conceded nothing to what I took to be her age. Was there, withal, something – something in the icy edge of her smile – to warn me? I cannot say.

'Lieutenant Franklin,' she said, holding out her hand in a way that made me bow as I took it. 'How wonderful to meet you.' Even while I was saying how pleased I was to be there, she was glancing towards Gladwin and hardening her tone. 'I understood that Fergus was to meet you.'

The old man did not respond directly. He grunted and looked at me. 'I'll not come in with you, Franklin. One or two things to attend to. Olivia will look after you. We'll meet again later.' He plodded away, hands defiantly grasping his lapels and head tossed haughtily back.

As soon as he was gone, Lady Powerstock led me through the porch into the hall, suddenly dark after the daylight and heavy with the polished wood of a vast, decorated fireplace. A broad split stairway led to a circular landing, from where sunlight seeped down and played in shifting patches on richly patterned carpets and wall-hung oriental rugs: touches of exoticism amid the stillness of a slowly ticking clock.

'I'll have your bag taken up to your room, Lieutenant,' she said. 'Unless you want to go straight up yourself, I'm sure my husband would like to meet you.'

'As I would him.'

'Then please come with me. He'll be in his study at this time.'

We made our way along a passage leading from the hall towards the wing of the house. I attempted some light conversation. 'Your house seems a million miles from the war.'

She smiled. 'You're not the first to say that.'

'No?'

'Thanks to Lizzie Kilsyth, we've been able to entertain many young officers who feel the same way. There are two others here at the moment. You'll meet them later.'

'I'm sure they feel as privileged as I do.'

'Perhaps. As a matter of fact, in your case it is we who feel privileged.' We had come to a turning in the passage. She paused by the door facing us and knocked. 'My husband has been greatly looking forward to meeting you.' Then she smiled again. 'As have I.'

She opened the door and I went in. The study, wood-panelled and book-lined, was at the corner of the house and its high windows looked out across the park to one side and a sunken lawn to the other. Facing the lawn windows was a desk and from this Lord Powerstock now rose and turned to greet me.

He was a tall, grey, stooped man with a lined face in which sobriety had since stiffened into sombreness. His son had been for him only one of the certainties war had swept away. The Victorian age had vanished and left him, beached and bereft, in a world he no longer understood, where grief was merely a metaphor for all the sensations of his loss.

'My dear boy: you are most welcome.' His hand trembled slightly as I shook it. 'How are you feeling?'

'Recovering well, thank you.' As I spoke, he glanced towards his wife, but already the door was closing behind her: we were alone together in a room where I sensed he was always alone.

'Glad to hear it. My son spoke of you often.'

'John spoke often of you too, sir. He missed his home and family keenly, I think.'

Lord Powerstock nodded slowly and moved to a cabinet near his desk, where glasses and decanters stood on a silver tray. 'Would you care for a drink, Franklin? I can vouch for the malt – if whisky's your poison.'

'I confess it's become so of late.'

He poured me a generous measure, then some for himself. 'You'll go a long way these days to find the equal of this.'

'Then, if you don't object, sir, here's to an honourable peace.' I added the honour for his sake.

He drank and mused on the toast. 'Is that the Army speaking, Franklin?'

'I can only speak for myself.'

'I'll wager it is, all the same, John said as much often enough.'

'I wouldn't want to pretend it's anything other than a ghastly business.'

'I'd think the less of you if you did. Since we subscribed to the Kilsyth Foundation, we must have had a couple of dozen officers here. Most of them are brave men who've been asked to do too much.' He walked to one of the windows and I followed. 'Take young Cheriton, for instance.' He pointed to a figure patrolling a border path beyond the lawn, a thin, pensive figure smoking a cigarette, whose every jerked movement spoke of jangled nerves.

'The trouble is, sir, that, if the war goes on much longer, too much will be asked of all of us.'

'Is that what happened to my son?'

'No, it wasn't. John could cope with anything. He gave strength to others – including me. The men looked on him as a talisman. And they were right: their good luck ran out after he died.'

Powerstock nodded gravely. 'That's something. In the manner of a death . . . there may be some comfort. Perhaps that's all that's left to us.' His free hand moved uncertainly to a gilt-framed photograph on the desk: a Victorian wedding portrait. He tilted it towards us.

'John's mother?'

'Yes. At least she's been spared this.' His words came ever more slowly, as if his mind were travelling through his past and finding only dismal ruin. 'Poor Miriam . . . Such a waste . . . And now our son.' Then he seemed to remember that I was there. 'Her father still lives with us.'

'Yes. He picked me up at the station.'

'Did he now?' He almost smiled at the thought. 'Dear old Charter. Bit of a curmudgeon, what?'

'I wouldn't say so.'

'No. Perhaps not.' Again, the slow, distracted delivery. 'My father didn't approve of the match . . . The Gladwins were in trade . . . Not that that saved me going up to Whitby to meet old Prospect Gladwin . . . Blood like tar, he said, from all the ships he'd sailed . . . All the ships . . .' He wrenched himself back. 'Excuse me. You'll be able to hear Charter's tales from his own lips. I dare say you're ready for some lunch.' He paused to push a bell by the fireplace. 'I shan't join you, I'm afraid. Not much of an appetite these days. But we must speak again later . . . about my son.'

'I'd like that.'

'It's all I can do now . . . Talk about him.'

Then a maid came and showed me up to my room.

It was a fine, airy room with a view of the park and a vase of freshly cut chrysanthemums in the window, a four-poster bed deep in pillows and starched linen and an adjoining bathroom where thick towels hung from warming pipes and the cavernous tub had feet cast in the likeness of a lion's paws: all the signs and fitments of leisure where I could forget . . . if I could ever forget . . . a frozen bivouac in Flanders . . . a trench after battle, smelling of burnt flesh and vomit and gas. I sniffed the chrysanthemums and, yes, it was still summer and Meongate and far from the war. I was safe, as Hallows could never be. Did he think of this place – did he see this park – as he stole across the rank-pooled hummocks of no man's land with faithful Sergeant Box that last night of April? Did his thoughts wander here – as well they might – and distract him for some final, fatal moment? Who could say? The past turned up its greatcoat collar and I went down to lunch.

Lunch was a strange affair. In the dining room, a side-table had been laid for four in the bay window, looking out over the clipped yew hedges and rose beds of the ornamental garden. Awaiting me I found the still nervous-looking Lieutenant Cheriton and the other resident officer, who introduced himself as Major Thorley of the Ordnance Corps. We were left to help ourselves from the sideboard and sum each other up.

Thorley I did not take to: altogether too chummy talkative in a patronizing kind of way, keen to broadcast his opinions of the household which was generously accommodating him. 'Rum lot here, Franklin,' he said, mouth full of cold chicken. 'Old Lord Powerstock goes round with a face like a coffin lid while his wife gives me the glad eye and starts me wondering what she really means by "make yourself at home". Take my drift?' I affected not to, but it did not deter him. 'There's some crazy old uncle, as well, and a daughter-in-law you hardly ever see. Still, who's complaining? Better than barracks, eh?'

At length he took himself off with a significant limp and I was left with the pallid young Cheriton, who had much less to say – and nothing at all about the circumstances which had led him to Meongate. These were clear enough to me from his halting speech and facial tremors, but, in avoiding a clearly painful subject, it was difficult to find a congenial substitute.

'How long will the Major be with us?' I enquired with transparent meaning.

'Oh . . . yes.' Cheriton managed a strained smile. 'But . . . overbearing, isn't he?'

'You could say that.'

'Look . . . Don't mind my mentioning this, but Thorley tells me you're not a stranger here.'

'The good Major has garbled the facts, I fear, as one might expect. I served in France with Lord Powerstock's son.'

We were back, inevitably, on disagreeable ground. 'Ah . . . yes.' He did not go on to say what he clearly already knew of Hallows' death.

'Tell me, how did Thorley come by the information?'

'Oh . . . Mompesson, I expect.'

'Mompesson?'

'An American . . . in business over here . . . Friend of Lady Powerstock . . . Visits often.'

I remembered my conversation with Hallows at Hernu's Farm six months before: he'd spoken then of an American houseguest at Meongate. Now I was to understand that the man was still a regular visitor and evidently more knowledgeable about me than I was about him.

On one point I agreed with Thorley. Where was Leonora? She was the one person I'd expected to meet at Meongate and the one person I hadn't. In a strange way, I felt slighted. I'd written to her after Hallows' death and she'd written back, briefly but graciously. I was vaguely hurt that she hadn't made an effort to see me.

As it happened, I didn't have long to wait. I took a nap in my room – a convalescent's custom – then went for a turn round the grounds. At closer quarters, there were signs here and there that they were not as well kept as once they had been: only in such small things as a straggling hedge, I reflected, can the war be detected here.

It was a warm afternoon. Thorley was aimlessly thumping a ball round the croquet lawn and would have caught my eye if I'd let him. Instead, I cut through the ornamental garden – where a dry fountain with tarnished cherubim testified to another touch of austerity – into the conservatory.

And that is where I found her. Where vine and clematis trailed amongst the tracery of a glazed roof, where lilies and hydrangeas splashed their potted colours about a tiled floor and musty pink geraniums lined the sun-baked windowsills. Where a cat lounged sleepily amongst the vigilant cacti and Leonora Hallows took tea with a private, sad serenity.

She wore a blue skirt and cream blouse, with a black neck-tie and a wide-brimmed hat. Her hair was straw blonde, her face calm and delicate like the porcelain on her tray. She looked up at me with blue, implacably tranquil eyes – and knew me, at once.

'Good afternoon, Mr Franklin. My husband said you would come.'

It was a disconnecting greeting, almost as if Hallows had just spoken to her. I mumbled some more formal introduction of my own and bowed as I held out my hand. She took it and squeezed it slightly as she did so. This, it was imparted, was a special token for the friendship her husband had given me.

She asked me to sit beside her and poured some tea. 'What did you mean?' I stumbled. 'Your husband said I should come?'

'In his last letter to me. He said that, if anything happened to him, his friend Lieutenant Franklin would find his way here.'

I blushed. 'I must tell you that, had it not been for

118

Lord Powerstock's letter to me, I doubt I would have done.'

She smiled. 'Never mind. Circumstances often intrude upon intention. However late or fortuitous, your visit is more welcome than I can say.'

'I am glad to be here, Mrs Hallows, and sorry also – for the reason I am here. Your husband was a fine man.'

'Indeed.' Her glance shifted a little. 'I always thought so.'

'Above all, a fine friend. I am honoured to have known him. All that I said in my letter to you . . . was true.'

'Thank you.' Then she deflected the subject, as if it were too painful to dwell upon. 'How do you find us at Meongate?'

'Such restfulness . . . is delightful.'

'Restful? Is that how it seems? Do we not strike you as a strange household?'

'No. Certainly not.'

'Perhaps we should. We four that are left are none of us tied by blood. Is that not . . . unusual?'

'I suppose . . .'

'Forgive me. I do not mean to embarrass you. I know that Lord Powerstock broods on the thought: the end of his line, the extinction of his name. He wonders what will become of us. He wonders if he has brought us bad luck.'

'Bad luck?'

'The Powerstocks have always been so successful – until now. My father-in-law's first marriage was not approved of. His wife gave him a son, of course, but she did not live to see him grow into a man.'

'How did she die?'

'It's one of the few subjects dear Charter won't talk

about. John told me she was an active member of a society for the relief of the poor. She devoted more and more time to her adopted families in the slums of Portsea and there she contracted smallpox. She died more than ten years ago. But sometimes I think my father-in-law still mourns her.'

'Surely his second marriage . . .'

She stopped me with an eloquent glance. 'Now, in a way, it's happened again. John and I had only been married for three months when the war broke out. Since then, Lord Powerstock has lost his son too.'

'Obviously, this is a sad time . . .'

'But things will get better?'

'We must believe so.'

'Only if it's true, surely?' Then she smiled again. 'I'm sorry. I shouldn't be putting such gloomy thoughts in a soldier's head.'

'That's all right. There are plenty . . .'

'Why, Lieutenant Franklin.' It was Lady Powerstock, materializing behind us. The hothouse heat, where others had to cool and shade themselves, seemed suddenly her particular environment. 'I see you've met Leonora. Has she been entertaining you?'

Leonora answered for me. 'We've been discussing the war, Olivia – and its effects on this house.'

'You will find the house a little neglected, Lieutenant, it's true. We're short-staffed, you see. The war must come first.'

'Naturally, I didn't . . .'

'But I do hope you haven't tired Leonora. The doctor has suggested lots of rest . . . in the circumstances.'

I took her hint. 'Of course. I mustn't intrude any longer. Perhaps you'll excuse me, Mrs Hallows.' I rose and took my leave.

Lady Powerstock followed me into the house. 'Thank you for being so understanding,' she said in an undertone as we crossed the morning room. 'Leonora was beside herself when she heard about John. The doctor had to prescribe a course of sedatives and sleeping draughts. She still tires very easily and can become upset . . . quite suddenly . . . for no reason. I'm sure you understand.'

'Of course.'

In truth, I did not. Leonora had seemed to me neither drugged nor hysterical and the letter she'd written to me at the Front had reflected the same measured composure that I'd now seen. Still, I had no wish to interfere in some mild piece of family friction. Except that, as Leonora had said, they weren't really a family at all.

I was already feeling fitter under Meongate's benign influence than I had amongst the invalid and elderly of Eastbourne and, as I settled into a comfortable if sometimes curious routine, I began to ponder the mystery that hinted and hovered at the edges of all that household's leisurely doings.

The occupants of Meongate pursued lives that seldom seemed to intersect. Lord Powerstock scarcely ventured beyond his study, though I was several times invited there to talk of military life and his son's prowess as a company commander; that seemed to comfort him. He even volunteered a little more about his own life, including the poignant facts about his first marriage which Leonora had already divulged. Of his second marriage he said nothing. Perhaps he thought it spoke for itself and perhaps he was right: no children, a twenty-year age gap, an opulent beauty turning to ... areas I didn't care to explore.

Leonora had been right. Powerstock was a man in mourning – for his whole life, not just his son. But why – if she knew this – did she seem to do so little to comfort him? That I couldn't understand, or even, more pompously, forgive. She pursued her claim, detached course, neither shunning nor seeking my company. I dug out the letter she'd written to me in France, acknowledging my condolences and saying what consolation there was to be had in speaking to her husband's friends. Odd that, now the chance was here to speak to me, doing so seemed a matter of indifference. Perhaps, after all, I thought, she just doesn't like me.

Thorley and Cheriton, meanwhile, went their contrasting ways. Thorley's took him regularly and lengthily to the White Horse Inn in Droxford, where I was blearily invited to join him, but did not. Cheriton – whose nerves a drink might have steadied – haunted the house, a wan and awkward figure who started at slammed doors and paced in the footsteps of a shattered dignity. I felt no affinity with either of them. Thorley was just a khakied windbag and I was as helpless to solve Cheriton's problems as he was himself: the war lay in wait for all of us, in dreams of mud-mangled death which for Cheriton – and sometimes for me – didn't end with morning.

Charter Gladwin offered a welcome beam of age-sprung joy amidst so much grief, with his tales of childhood in Whitby, of old fishermen who remembered Captain Cook, of shipping timber from Gothenburg and courting White Russian princesses, of marrying the daughter of the Mayor of Scarborough and raising the prettiest girl in the North Riding of

Yorkshire. But then Charter Gladwin was, as he often said, a survivor from another world and no real help in this one. Or so I thought.

Dinner was the only occasion which drew together the residents of Meongate. We officers wore uniform and took our respectful places at a table where Lord Powerstock presided with all the tattered observances of landed propriety. Leonora would join us in a simple dress and willingly consent to be overshadowed by Lady Powerstock, who wore daring Edwardian gowns and dominated the conversation. Sometimes guests would be present who followed her lead and bestowed upon us their ill-founded opinions of the progress of the war. Others – whose husbands were often still where we had lately been – said less and deferred more. I waited for one of the strangers to announce himself as Mompesson, but I waited in vain.

One day of soft September rain I strayed into the library in search of idle reading matter. As I might have guessed, the contents were scarcely for the frivolous reader, which is all that I was: so much leather-tomed anonymity gathering the duty of lordly neglect. If Lord Powerstock had ever frequented this place, he did no longer. The davenport stood empty by the mullioned window and the books unread on their shelves.

The strangest feature of the room was not its books, but the large oil painting on the one wall not shelved in: a scene from some medieval fantasy, vaguely Pre-Raphaelite in style with slashes of a more sensual purpose, bathed now in aqueous light from the window, arresting, even arousing, in its depiction. The curtained, stone-walled bedchamber of a castle. A naked woman, well formed and wantonly draped across the bed, yet looking over her shoulder in evident alarm at the door; it stands open to the chain-mailed figure of a man, who is unbuckling his sword-belt and gazing at the woman with obvious intent.

It was an unpleasant picture, not merely because of its voyeuristic effect but also by its placing, there in the library where culture might seem to excuse such explicitness. But that was not all. As I peered at the face of the woman, her painted image streaked by the rain-refracted light, I felt, for an instant, that I knew her. And, if I did, it could only be one person, though years younger and far removed from her present station. It could only be Olivia, Lady Powerstock, as I had never thought of her.

The following evening, after dinner, the ladies left us and Cheriton reluctantly consented to a game of billiards with Thorley, who always played against odds and always won. Lord Powerstock for once lingered in the drawing room, sitting with his brandy by the fire; he seemed to need its warmth for all that it was a mild night. Gladwin sat between us, puffing at the cigar which was his present topic of conversation.

'They must mix rhubarb with the tobacco these days; tastes bloody awful . . . Finest cigars I ever had were a gift from Count Nogrovny in St Petersburg . . . to seal a bargain over some sable pelts . . . What a daughter he had . . . I fought a duel for that girl, you know . . . Or for the sables . . . I'm never too sure which it really was . . . Winter of '61 . . . The river was frozen solid . . .'

Before his reminiscences could progress much further, he was asleep. Powerstock smiled indulgently and I took the opportunity to ask a question that had long been in my mind. 'Your son referred once to a

124

houseguest here named Mompesson. Am I likely to meet him?'

Powerstock frowned. 'Mompesson? Oh yes. A friend of my wife.' He swallowed some of the excellent brandy with apparent distaste. 'She has many admirers, you know. Something of a celebrity in society before we married.'

'Really?'

For once, he didn't hold back. 'Yes. A handsome woman, as you'll have noticed.'

'Indeed.'

'In her youth, she modelled for some of the foremost artists of London and Paris.'

So I'd been right. 'The picture in the library: is that . . .'

'What picture?' He seemed vexed. 'Couldn't say. Never go there . . . As to Mompesson, yes, you'll be seeing him. Due at the weekend . . . so my wife tells me.'

I thought I saw everything then. An elderly husband deceived by a younger wife. It was not unusual. Perhaps it accounted for Hallows' preoccupation when he returned from Christmas leave. If only that had been it. But the Meongate mystery was of another order. Quite another order altogether.

I woke early the next morning, after one of those nights all too familiar to me then, when dead, dismembered comrades returned to salute me. A tramp round the grounds before breakfast was my usual antidote, but that morning – being earlier and brighter than most – I decided to venture further afield.

September had chilled with its mists a summer's dawn, but a feeble pastel sun filtered through to gild the dewy lawns as I walked down the drive of Meongate and took in the airy promise of the day. I set a good pace along the lanes towards Droxford and passed not another soul on my way. Nearing the village, I cut down through a wood to the river, crossed it by a narrow bridge and so came by a muddy footpath to the church. There, where I'd attended morning service with Lord and Lady Powerstock the previous Sunday, I turned in to pursue a point I'd had not time for then. Some sheep grazing amongst the gravestones scattered in panic and a rook made its cawing flight from the roof, but they were the only signs of life.

Inside, the strengthening sun was shafting into the dim interior, catching the dust in its perpetual swirls and eroding the damp accumulations of closed night air. I prowled amongst the pews and pillars, eyeing stones and plaques, until, in a small side chapel behind the choir, I found what I was looking for: a canopied stone tomb with clinging shards of paint and the worn effigy of a knight, resting in armour upon a pillow. The inscription was faded and in shadow; I stooped to read it. It was rendered in Latin, most of it beyond me, but the name and dates were clear: WILLIAM DE BRINON, KNIGHT OF DROXENFORD (1307–1359), with a mention of Crécy in the dedication. There was no doubt. It was the tomb Hallows had told me about.

As I rose from my haunches, there was a startled cry from the choir. I looked across in alarm and there, beyond the decorated wooden screen, stood Leonora, with her hand to her mouth.

'Oh . . . Oh my . . .,' she said. Then, recovering herself: 'Mr Franklin. You startled me.'

'I'm sorry. I was just reading an inscription.'

'Of course. It was just that . . . Well, I don't know.'

By now, I'd joined her in the choir. 'You didn't expect

anybody else to be here? Actually, neither did I.'

'I often come down here at this time of day . . . to be sure of some solitude.'

'I'm sorry to have invaded it.'

'Nonsense. You have every right. It's simply that that tomb has . . . associations.'

'With John.'

'You know then?' She looked towards me and moved slightly as she did so, stepping unconsciously into a waiting portal of granular sunlight. And as she did so, in her felt hat and simple grey cape. I realized again how beautiful she was. What would I not have given then to be Hallows, come back to lift her veil of loss?

'He spoke of it once, when we were based near Crécy.'

'I see.'

'Would you like to be left alone?'

'No, no.' She smiled. 'In fact, why don't we walk back to Meongate together?'

I readily agreed and we set off back the way I'd come, down to the river and up through the wood. For once, Leonora seemed eager to talk.

'I'm sorry if we haven't seen much of each other since you arrived,' she said.

'Lady Powerstock explained that you had to take things easy.'

She laughed, with little humour. 'I'm sure Olivia told you what she thought you ought to hear. I dare say all the officers who come to stay are fed the same line. Sedatives to prevent hysteria . . . isn't that it?'

'Well, not exactly.'

'Since you were my husband's friend, Mr Franklin, you should know that his stepmother is a congenital liar.'

'I see.'

'I wonder if you do.'

'Since, as you say, I was your husband's friend, won't you call me Tom . . . as he did?'

'Very well . . . Tom. No doubt you're embarrassed by the friction in John's family.'

'No. It's just that . . .'

'You don't know who to believe.' She laughed and stopped to lean back against a tree trunk. 'I see your difficulty.'

'What I was going to say was that, as a guest of the house, I've no right to question how it's run. But I don't have any difficulty knowing who to believe.'

'Thank you.'

'John loved you very much, I know.'

She looked down sharply, as if upset.

'I'm sorry. I shouldn't have . . .'

'It's all right.' She smiled stiffly. 'Despite what Olivia says, I'm very self-controlled. I think of John always of course. As a matter of fact, when you appeared in the church, I thought . . . for a second . . .'

'That it was him?'

'Yes. Absurd, isn't it?'

'No. It's only natural. If there's anything I can do to help, I . . .'

'There's nothing.' Suddenly, her face was stern. She walked on quickly ahead and I followed. For the first time, the thought was forming in my mind that maybe there was a way of lessening Leonora's desolation along with my own, a way of doing so together. For the first time, the war was holding out to me a prospect – a distant, uncertain prospect – of something good.

THREE

That evening, Mompesson came. I was in my room when I heard the throaty roar of a high-powered sports car coming up the drive. I looked out of the open window as the car drew to a halt in a spray of gravel and the engine growled into silence. I knew it must be Mompesson: a tall, square, good-looking man in a loud check cap and dark travelling coat. He jumped down on to the drive and flung a bag at Fergus, then strode towards the door. There was somebody waiting for him there: Lady Powerstock.

'Ralph: it's good to see you.'

'Naturally. How's my Olivia?' He bent to kiss her hand and murmured something else as he did so. Her laugh was almost a giggle.

I was introduced to Mompesson before dinner. He was wearing evening dress and downing Scotch and soda in the drawing room with Thorley and Lord Powerstock. When I walked in, he rose and shook my hand.

'It's Franklin, isn't it? I'm Ralph Mompesson. Pleased to meet you.'

'I think I heard you arrive earlier, Mr Mompesson.'

'Call me Ralph. The motor is a mite noisy, I know. Frightens the peasantry, I'm told.' He laughed, a touch loudly, and Thorley joined in – unnecessarily, I felt. I wasn't warming to this glad-handed American with the flashing smile and dark, lacquered hair.

'Have you come far?'

'From London. 'Less you mean originally, in which case I'd have to own to New Orleans. As you'll have guessed, I've no part in this European war.'

'Then you're a fortunate man.'

'Reckon so.' He leaned closer. 'It was rough about John. I liked him.'

'So did I.'

If Mompesson really had liked Hallows, I suspected the feeling hadn't been mutual. I could have attributed his excess of charm to the American character and my reaction against it to pure prejudice, but there was some edge to his remarks – some hunter's stealth in his eyes – which told me the charm was only a front. I instinctively mistrusted him.

Over dinner, my instinct strengthened. Olivia sat next to Mompesson and laughed at his jokes with shrill indecency. She wore more jewellery – and a lower-cut dress – than I'd seen before and drank with unladylike enthusiasm. If Powerstock noticed, you couldn't have told from his drawn mask of a face. As for the rest, Thorley revelled in the more exuberant mood of the occasion, whilst Cheriton retreated into the shadows of his troubled thoughts. Leonora said little, though she responded to Mompesson's remarks with measured politeness. Gladwin was conspicuous by his absence, pleading a chess-playing engagement with a neighbour, so for light relief we relied upon Mompesson's lubricated wit. And wit indeed there was, though little humour. Just what sort of a joke he thought the war to be became swiftly evident.

'Zeppelin dropped a bomb awful near the Stock Exchange last week,' he drawled. 'Otherwise, we neutrals have been left pretty much alone lately.'

'How long will the US remain neutral?' I asked, remembering that Hallows had asked the same question.

'For ever, I hope.'

'Going to leave us to it, are you?' put in Thorley, who was too drunk to take offence.

'You bet,' Mompesson replied. 'The people who win wars are those who sit them out.'

I asked him what he meant by that.

'I'm a man of business, Lootenant, and war is good business. 'Course, I appreciate you gentlemen couldn't choose to stay out, but once was enough for me. I served in Cuba under Roosevelt in '98 and learned all I need to about war. Glory for the generals and death for those who loyally follow. It doesn't even pay well.'

A silence fell. We were embarrassed, I suppose, not so much by his frankness as by his chilling accuracy. But what could we say, obedient still to the stilted public image of patriotic duty? I was no longer taken in by it, of course, but it was about the only thought likely to comfort Hallows' grieving family and I for one didn't have the heart to dispel it. Why did they like him, I wondered, why did they invite him to their house? A well-mannered wit to amuse Lady Powerstock and brighten the dinner table? There had to be more to it than that.

I had a further opportunity to probe Mompesson's character after dinner, over brandy and cigars. Cheriton

131

and Lord Powerstock had left us and Thorley had fallen asleep, snoring inelegantly in a corner. But Mompesson remained agile and alert, strolling about the drawing room with none of the deference a guest might be expected to display.

'It's sad to think,' I said, 'that this house has lost its heir.'

'That's not peculiar to Meongate, is it?' he replied. 'It's a universal condition. This whole war is Europe's surrender of its birthright.'

'Is it?'

'Of course. What you're caught up in, my friend, is the death agony of an era, the end of Europe as the centre of Western civilization.'

'And you think your country will inherit that role?'

'In part – the British part, that is. And we'll be better at it, because we're a younger, more vigorous people. We're not shackled to our past.'

'It's an interesting point of view.'

He smiled. 'It's very British of you to take it so well. As for this house, it will survive, though to do so it may have to pass into new ownership.' Then he smiled again and left me to guess at what he really meant.

I was still sitting there after Mompesson had gone to bed and Thorley had hauled himself away, when Gladwin returned, shortly before midnight, with a great crash of the front door.

'Still up, young Franklin?' he said, striding in to warm himself by the dwindling fire.

'Just about. Mulling over my first meeting with Mr Mompesson.'

'So he got here, then.' He grunted and said no more.

'How was the chess?'

'We adjourned. I'm not sure I'll live long enough to finish this game.' He glared down at the fire. 'You might have kept this in for me.'

'Sorry. Is it cold out?'

'Cold and fine. Clear as a bell. It was on nights like this that John used to take himself up to his observatory to study the stars. No one goes up there now. I've not been since the comet in 1910.'

'That's the turret on the roof of the wing?'

'Yes. Didn't you know John was our resident astronomer?'

'I'm not sure he ever mentioned it.'

Gladwin grunted again and looked doleful. The memory of Hallows as an enthusiastic astronomer seemed to depress him. He plodded to the door. 'I'm away to my bed. Sleep well.'

I went up a little later. The house was dark and silent now, though, when I looked out of my window, I saw that, as Gladwin had said, it was a fine night, moonless and velvety black, the stars thickly sprinkled across the sky's impenetrable dome. I felt wide awake: Mompesson prophecies had left me restless. Inspired by the night and Gladwin's recollections, I decided to take a look at Hallows' observatory.

The guest rooms were on the first floor of the main building, facing the drive. The family rooms were in the wing of the house where the stairs to the observatory were, and so I felt something of an intruder as I made my way there, careful to make as little noise as possible, anxious not to disturb anybody. The house seemed wholly at rest as I located the spiral stairs and began my ascent.

It was a wasted journey. The door at the top, leading

to the observatory, was locked. Not surprising, I supposed, in the circumstances. Stifling a vague annoyance, I retraced my steps.

As I reached for the foot of the stairs, a figure moved swiftly past in the darkness. I stopped short, taken aback by this silent manifestation, then looked out into the passage. It was Mompesson, I felt certain, padding noiselessly and swiftly away from me and evidently unaware that he had been seen. At the end of the passage, a line of light beneath a door seemed to mark his destination. I watched as he reached it.

He turned the handle and pushed the door open. It was a bedroom, richly furnished and softly lit. I could see for certain now that it was Mompesson and, as he took a step into the room, I could see that he was expected. Lady Powerstock rose from her chair by the dressing table and turned to face him. she wore a pink, full-length silken gown and – to judge by the hugging fit of the material – nothing else. Her long hair fell freely in dark tresses over her shoulders. She spoke and Mompesson replied, but I could not make out what was said. Then she turned away. As she did so, Mompesson released the door and it swung slowly towards me, narrowing the angle of my view to Lady Powerstock's retreating figure. She pulled loose the sash of her gown and shrugged it casually from her shoulders. She was naked beneath. The gown slid down her back, clung momentarily to her hips, then fell to the floor. What she was offering Mompesson was clear in every mature and sensuous curve of her body. And, on what she was offering, the door in that moment clicked shut, leaving me in the dark, with only a remembered glimpse of her body.

*　*　*

134

Even as I stole back to my room, my reaction began to appal me. I felt no outrage on behalf of a dead friend of his betrayed father, rather a keen and self-centred resentment. Why, after all, should an arrogant, uninvolved American be able to walk into a war-wounded house and make free with its luscious mistress? Why were those of us who'd suffered months of torment and denial to be left to spectate as he came, and took his fill, and went? It was too much. Even sleep – when it came, fitfully and late – did not assuage my anger, nor relieve the awful, unconfessed desire that lurked behind it.

As is the way of restless nights, dawn brought slumber and it was mid-morning when I woke suddenly, roused by the clopping of horses' hooves on the drive. I rose and stretched and walked to the window.

I suppose I'd expected it to be Fergus, leading out Lucy, but no, it was two horses I'd not seen before, one a tall black hunter with Mompesson in the saddle, cutting an imposing figure in top hat and long coat. Aboard the other – a smaller, quieter animal – was Leonora, in black riding skirt and cape, with a grey scarf around her hat. There was, in her dress and bearing, an observance of mourning, but why was she out riding with Mompesson? All I'd learned of her since first coming to Meongate would have led me to expect her to refuse such an invitation. Yet, there they were, heading away together across the park. I thought of what I'd seen the night before and of Hallows' widow associating with a man who held in contempt both Lord Powerstock and the cause for which Hallows had died. There was something wrong, I knew, something awfully wrong.

* * *

I bathed and dressed and went downstairs. The house was in a lull of refracted mid-morning sunlight, quiet in the way of waiting rather than of rest; too quiet, in the way Sergeant Box may have warned Hallows that spring night in France, may have done, without being heeded, any more than I heeded whatever there was to be gleaned as I followed the threat the wrong way, into the labyrinth.

There was a chink of fine porcelain and a scent of coffee from the morning room. I followed it to find Lady Powerstock entertaining Cheriton, of all people, over the silver tray and ancestral service. She wore pink and seemed – I dreaded the thought – invigorated beneath her years, drawing even from Cheriton a snatch of nervous laughter. As I came in, she looked at me with her deep, far-seeing eyes, as if . . . Then I cursed myself for displaying a hint of embarrassment and accepted her invitation to join them.

'Ralph has taken Leonora out riding,' she said airily as she filled a cup for me.

'Yes. I saw them go.'

'I'm sure it's good for her to get . . . some fresh air,' Cheriton put in.

'Quite.' Olivia smiled. I looked at her – the charming, attentive hostess with her younger guests, conversing politely over morning coffee – and thought, for one moment, that I must be mistaken, that somehow I'd misconstrued . . . But no. What I'd seen couldn't be misconstrued.

I decided to test the water. 'Mr Mompesson evidently has little respect for the war effort.'

'It's not his war,' Olivia replied.

'Or yours?'

Her brow darkened just a little at that, but her

voice gave nothing away. 'We women do what we can.'

'That's not what I meant.'

'No? Well, what do you think, David?'

Cheriton flushed as she turned towards him. I'd not realized they were on first-name terms. To judge by his reaction, nor had Cheriton. 'I . . . I don't know.' Olivia smiled a mixture of triumph and placation. 'Matter of fact, think I'll . . . get a breath of air myself.' He rose jerkily from his chair. 'Lady Powerstock, Franklin: excuse me.'

After he'd gone, Olivia refilled our cups and timed her pause to make me think she would change the subject. But she didn't. 'Ralph's been a great help to us at this sad time.'

'Really?'

'I have the impression you don't like him.'

'I wouldn't say that. How did John get on with him?'

'I couldn't say. John was not a man who displayed his feelings. Perhaps you saw a less reticent side of him.'

'Perhaps.'

Her clothes rustled in the stillness of the room as she leant forward to replace her cup on the tray. 'Lord Powerstock tells me you admired the picture in the library.'

'It's very . . . striking.'

'My first husband painted it.'

'I'm sorry. I didn't know you'd been married before.' Everyone in that house, it seemed, had a past.

'Yes. He died young. A long time ago.' She smiled. 'There's no reason why you should have known.' Nor any reason why I shouldn't have been told before. But I hadn't been. 'This war, of course, has made early death tragically commonplace.'

'Yes.' She'd disarmed me with her recollected

137

widowhood, defied me to impute any dishonour to the model in the picture.

'It is such a shame, when there is so much pleasure to be had from life.'

Now I was the one eager to change the subject. 'It's for fellows like Cheriton that I feel especially sorry.'

'We try to do what we can for all our officers – while they're here.'

'While they're here.' My stay at Meongate was beginning to afford me little pleasure and less rest. I felt myself a spectator at a sport I didn't understand; I wasn't even sure who the players were, and the rules seemed made only for breaking. That weekend – so outwardly calm and comfortable, an embodiment of country house life – tested my nerves with all the undercurrents of its way-ward passage. Mompesson's swaggering presence cast its smirking shadow across the people and the place. Guests came to dinner that Saturday evening, laughed at his jokes and contributed to two enthusiastic foursomes at bridge. Leonora consented – without demur – to partner Mompesson and I had to watch from the side-lines as they played, while one of the visiting bridge ladies' husbands told me about his son's reports of a quiet time in Mesopotamia. It was as much as I could do to remain polite.

Sunday was a warm and cloudless day. Mompesson had brought a note of positively Edwardian gaiety to Meongate and few but I could resist. So, moodily, I shunned the afternoon party on the croquet lawn and went for a walk in the park. At the far end, where it met adjoining farmland, there was an apple orchard, and there, in a folding chair he'd set up amidst the blossom and fallen fruit, I found old Charter, well lunched and sleepy in his sunny corner.

'Ah, Franklin,' he said, doffing his straw hat.

'Sorry to disturb you.'

'Don't mention it. High jinks on the croquet lawn not to your taste then?'

'Not really.' I turned over a box that had been used to collect some of the apples and sat on its base. 'It might be more accurate to say that Mr Mompesson is not to my taste.'

He gave a rumbling laugh. 'You must realize, Franklin, that in a world of old crocks like me and wounded soldiers like you, fellows like Mompesson are apt to dazzle the ladies.'

'What would you say if I told you I found his familiarity with Lady Powerstock repugnant?'

'I'd agree with you, but I'm biased. Olivia and I are the firmest of enemies.'

'She mentioned to me yesterday that she'd been married before.'

'Did you not know?'

'No. Who was he?'

'Artist – so-called. Name of Bartholomew. You'll not have heard of him. Died three years before Edward met her. That's all we were ever told.' But there was a twinkle in his eye.

'You look as if you know more.'

'Matter of fact, I do. Made enquiries when Edward showed he was set on marrying her. Not that what I found out swayed him a jot. He was too far gone by then.'

'What did you find out?'

'Mr Bartholomew drowned. Lost overboard from a cross-Channel ferry in October of 1903. Bizarre, ain't it?

139

As to whether it was an accident or suicide, who knows? With Olivia for a wife, anything's possible.'

'You really don't like her, do you?'

'No, young man, I don't like her. Partly because she's not a patch on my Miriam. But there are other reasons. And I think you know what they are.'

'Not a worthy wife for Lord Powerstock?'

He grunted derisively. 'If she was my wife, I'd know how to deal with blighters like Mompesson.'

'Oh yes?'

'But she isn't, so, damn it, it's no business of mine.'

Nor of mine, strictly speaking. I left Gladwin to doze in the sickly sweet air of the wasp-lazy orchard and made my way disconsolately back towards the house. There was nothing for it, I'd decided, but to brave the croquet lawn, so I cut through the rhododendron glade in its general direction.

Halfway through, along its winding path, I saw two figures coming in the opposite direction: Mompesson and Leonora, deep in conversation. I could have hailed them, but something stopped me. I stepped off the path and positioned myself behind one of the rhododendrons. They could not see me as they approached.

'I'm sure you'll appreciate,' Mompesson was saying, 'that you really have no choice.' His tone was affable, with a steely edge.

'You think not?' Leonora: cool and defensive.

'When there is a choice between the distasteful and the disgraceful, I know what to expect from a well-born young Englishwoman.'

They pulled up not ten yards from me. Leonora turned to face Mompesson. 'I don't understand you.'

'Yes you do. It's just that you can't believe what you understand.'

'It is hard to believe anyone could be so . . . vile.' She spoke almost dispassionately.

'You have a week to get used to the idea. I'm going back to London tomorrow. I shall return on Friday. I shall expect our bargain to be honoured then.'

'How can you call it a bargain?'

'Because that's what it is to me. Something fine – at a cheap price.'

At that, Leonora's self-control snapped. Her jaw set in an angry line and she raised her right hand to strike him. Then, before the blow could fall, she stopped. For a moment, she stared at him and at once I saw why: he was smiling, calmly awaiting in such an act her admission of defeat.

Such satisfaction she denied him. She returned her hand to her side, glanced away, then spoke again. 'If John were here now . . .'

'But he isn't, is he? That's why you'll be waiting for me next Friday.' He touched his panama hat, then turned and strode back towards the lawn. Leonora stood watching him go, then took a couple of steps and hung her head. I thought I heard her sob. I longed to rush out and comfort her, but caution held me back: as the eavesdropper, I had to remain hidden. Then Leonora decided the issue for me. She sighed and walked slowly away.

I couldn't face being on hand for Mompesson's departure next morning, so I struck out early to walk off my depression. The day held misty portents of autumn and, halfway down the drive, I met the postman cycling up. I asked him if he had anything for me and, after leafing through the bundle for Meongate, he handed me one letter. I recognized the Army envelope at once and ripped it open. News from the Front held a strange comfort for me in that moment.

But there was no comfort in the contents. It was from Warren, sergeant of my old platoon, who'd promised to keep me in touch. 'The lads have been badly knocked about lately, sir, and no mistake. I have to tell you that, of your fellow subalterns, none of those who were here when you left is still with us, and most of them won't ever be again, if you take my meaning. To be honest, sir, I don't think things have been the same since Captain allows bought it. That was a sad day . . .'

I crumpled the letter into my pocket. Poor Warren, and the rest of them, still mourning Hallows for the spirit he'd conferred on them and which had gone along with him, still out there somewhere, where the guns boomed and the shells whined, far from this smug, serene landscape where I was hiding but could find no peace. I walked on slowly, seeing about me not the soft curves and green fields of Hampshire but the grey streaks and blackened stumps of a smashed land. And I a stranger in both.

A car horn split my reverie. I swung round with a start. It was Mompesson, leaving earlier than I'd expected and coasting up behind me in his sports car to cheat me of eluding him.

He grinned broadly. 'Good morning to you, Franklin. Can I take you somewhere?'

'I was only going into the village.'

'Well, hop in.'

'I'd rather walk.'

'I'd appreciate a word before I go. And you can always walk back.'

What did he have to say to me? Curiosity overcame

my distaste; I climbed aboard. 'Making an early start?'

He grinned again as we moved off through the gates at the foot of the drive. 'You said it. Sorry if I made you jump back there.'

'It doesn't matter. I was lost in thought, that's all.'

'Reckon you military men have plenty to think about.'

'Yes, we do.'

He glanced at me. 'You resent me because I'm not involved in this war, don't you?'

'I wouldn't . . .'

He held up a gauntleted hand. 'Stow the courtesies. You do. It's understandable. Maybe I would in your shoes. I'm a rich, free foreigner and no target for kraut bullets. But is that my fault?'

'Of course not.' We came to where he should have turned into Droxford. Instead, he turned right and began to drive up a rough lane towards the tops of the downs. 'This isn't the right way,' I said.

'It is for what I want to show you.'

'Which is?'

'What you need to understand. You see. I know why you resent me. It isn't just because the States are neutral. It's also because you think I'm too much at home at Meongate, too familiar, too popular.'

'I don't know what you mean.'

'Yes you do. You think I'm intruding on Hallows' property. Isn't that how it is?'

I wasn't about to give him the satisfaction of knowing he was right. 'Not at all.'

He pulled off on to the grass verge and jerked on the brake. Beyond the hedge, the ground sloped steeply away and we had a clear view across the escarpment towards the yew-fringed summit of Old Winchester Hill. Mompesson let the engine die and the tranquillity of the place disclosed itself in the silence that followed.

'Why have you brought me here?' I asked.

'So we can talk, man to man. Hallows once told me that hill was used as a fort by men thousands of years ago. You can still see the earthworks.'

'I dare say.'

'Hallows was hot on that kind of thing. Not that it did him much good.'

'What do you mean?'

'The trouble with your country, Franklin, is that it's immersed in its own past, surrounded by it everywhere it looks. This hill, the house we've just left. Everywhere. That's why you're in this crazy war. That's why Hallows died. That's why Meongate needs to be saved from itself. And I'm the man to do it.'

'You?'

'Why not? Unlike you British, I understand that you have to change with the times. My family learned that the hard way. The Mompessons owned land in Louisiana from way back. All that changed after the Civil War. It broke my father, but I saw where he'd gone wrong. In this life, you get nothing unless you go all out for it.'

'And what are you going all out for?'

'I intend to marry Leonora.' He must have read my expression as incredulity. 'I'm only telling you because you were her husband's friend and I wouldn't want you to misunderstand the situation. I'd be good for her. And for Meongate.'

So that was it. Olivia was just an amusing pastime. Leonora was the real target, one I suspected he already knew I'd considered aiming for myself. Our chummy drive on to the downs was a warning-off. Had it not been for the conversation I'd overheard the day before, I'd have been thunderstruck, but now his exchange with

Leonora made a disturbing kind of sense. It spoke of some kind of hold he had over her, some way he had of forcing her to comply. Otherwise, I felt certain, he'd never have told me so much. I tried to control myself when I spoke. 'And what does Leonora say about this?'

'I haven't asked her yet. Not straight out. But when I do, she'll agree. Never doubt it, my friend.'

I looked at him and saw the face of a man whom doubt never visited. 'It's good of you to have been so frank.'

He smiled. 'Don't mention it. I wouldn't want you to make a fool of yourself.'

Abruptly, I climbed from the car. 'Thanks for the ride. I'll walk back from here.' It was time to go, before I said too much. I set a brisk pace along the lane and did not look back. A few minutes later, I heard his car start and move off in the other direction, down towards the London road.

As I walked on towards Meongate, I wondered if, on his last home leave, Hallows had somehow sensed that Mompesson would try to usurp him, if that had been what he was driving at during our discussion at Hernu's Farm. Maybe he had. Maybe he had hoped that, if it came to it, I would intervene, if only for his sake. But was I equal to the task? Unlike Mompesson, I carried doubt with me like a pack on my back. He'd have said it was the Englishman in me. And he'd probably have been right.

FOUR

Later that morning, I sought out Lord Powerstock in his study. He was reading *The Times* with grave concentration, back turned to the window and the world. But he seemed passingly pleased to see me, offered me whisky and said he regretted how little time we'd had to talk during my stay.

'I think Mr Mompesson has attracted most attention of late,' I said pointedly.

He ignored the reference. 'Encouraging reports in *The Times* from France – have you seen them?'

'No sir.'

'They've come up with some secret weapon called tanks. Bringing great gains, apparently.'

Having served in France, I viewed newspaper reports with not so much scepticism as total disbelief. 'Too late for most of my comrades, I fear.'

He put down the paper. 'Like my son, you mean.'

'He asked me to come here, you know – in the event that he died. He was particularly concerned about Leonora – what would become of her.'

'Naturally.'

'What will become of her?'

'We will continue to look after her.'

'She has no family of her own?'

'Her parents are in India; her father's a civil commissioner in the Punjab. But she doesn't want to go back there. We want her to stay here.'

'In time, I suppose, she might re-marry.'

He looked as if he had never considered the idea. 'She might, at that.' At least I knew that Mompesson had said nothing to his lordship so far. 'After all, I did myself.'

'On that subject, I ought to apologize for misunderstanding you when you told me of Lady Powerstock's contact with the art world.'

'Mmm?'

'I hadn't appreciated that she was married to the painter Bartholomew.'

'You've heard of him?'

'Slightly.'

'Few people have.' After that, he lapsed into a silence that gave fair notice he was not to be drawn on the subject of Mr Bartholomew, artist and drowned man.

The more I found out, the less I understood. Perhaps what happened the following morning should have told me that I was not alone in that.

Dawn came steathily, trailing my awakening with its grey, silent tendrils. The room was still and quiet, the birdsong beyond reassuring me that I was yet safe, for another space of hours, from the kind of day to which I had too often woken.

I rose and pulled on a dressing gown. Then my sense of refuge was shattered. A livid scream from the room next door, three thumps in succession on the wall and some other choking sound. I hurried out into the passage and listened at the door: it was Cheriton's room. Silence reigned again, throughout the house. I tapped on the panelling.

'Cheriton – are you all right?'

No answer.

'Cheriton?'

Again, no answer. For a less obviously nervous man I would not have been so concerned; I did not imagine myself to be alone in suffering bad dreams. But dreams might not be all. I knocked again and went in.

Cheriton was sitting up in bed, holding his head in his hands. He looked up as I entered and in his face I saw the expression of a broken man.

'Franklin!' He visibly recovered himself. 'What's the matter?'

'I was going to ask you that. I heard a scream. You didn't answer when I knocked.'

'Sorry. Must have been a nightmare. You know how it is.'

'Yes. I suppose we all get them from time to time.'

'Do we?' The thought seemed to give him some small comfort. 'Do you ever . . . dream you're back in France?'

'Often. Except when I'm there. Then I dream of England.'

He shuddered. 'I'm to go before a medical board at the end of the month to see if I'm fit to return.'

'And are you?'

He looked straight at me. 'I don't know, Franklin. All I know is that I can't go back. It's unthinkable.' He reached for a cigarette and lit one. The match trembled in his hand.

'We all feel that. It won't be so bad once you get out there.' He said nothing, just drew grimly on the cigarette. 'You should try to enjoy life here while you can.'

He frowned. 'Enjoy? God, sometimes I think this place is no better than the Front.'

'What do you mean?'

He seemed to have second thoughts. 'Never mind. Sorry. Talking out of turn. As you say, it was just a nightmare. I'm sorry to have disturbed you. I think I'd better take a bath: clear the head, what?'

'I'll leave you to it, then.' I turned to the door.

'Franklin.' I looked back. 'I'd be awfully grateful if you . . . didn't tell anyone else about this. The Powerstocks, I mean. Wouldn't want them to think they'd got a loony on their hands.'

'They wouldn't think that.'

'Even so . . .'

'I'll say nothing. You have my word.'

'Thanks.'

I closed the door behind me, wondering just what Cheriton's nightmare had been. The war, with its commonplace horror? Or something closer to home, but no less horrible?

Leonora customarily took tea in the conservatory on fine afternoons, alone save for her cat, her books and her thoughts. It was the best chance I had of speaking to her privately, so it was the chance I took.

I walked in, almost apologetically, by the garden door. 'May I join you for a moment?'

She put her book down. 'Of course. Would you like some tea?'

'No, thank you.' I sat down opposite her.

'Then to what do I owe this pleasure?'

'We didn't seem to see much of each other over the weekend.'

'I was here all the time.'

149

I feigned a smile. 'Well, I think I was overshadowed by our American visitor.'

'I wouldn't say that.'

'Riding. Croquet. Bridge. He certainly took you out of yourself.'

She frowned. 'Do I take it from your tone that you do not approve of Mr Mompesson?'

'Not exactly. But let me ask you this. Did John approve of Mr Mompesson?'

There was the hint of a flush in her countenance. 'I do not think John would disapprove of my being entertained socially.'

'Of course not. But, to judge by certain things he said to me, Mompesson worried him. He made a point of it after he came back from leave last Christmas.'

Her brow furrowed, though whether from irritation or surprise I couldn't tell. 'I didn't know that.'

'Though I think now it may have been Mompesson's friendship with Lady Powerstock that really worried him.'

'What do you mean?'

'I can't believe you don't know what's going on. That's why I . . .'

'Enough!' The command was incisive. 'I didn't expect to hear this kind of thing from you, Mr Franklin, and I don't expect to hear any more of it.'

'You yourself said . . .'

'I have said all I intend to say on this matter.'

I couldn't fathom her sudden loyalty to Olivia but I couldn't outface it either. 'Forgive me. I didn't mean to distress you. I think I've got off on the wrong foot on this. All I really meant to say was that . . . if you are in any kind of difficulty at the moment . . . under any kind of pressure . . . and need my assistance . . . then I'd like to help.'

'There's no need.'

'John would have expected it of me.'

'Then, for his sake, let's pretend we've not had this conversation. Have some tea. Talk about something else – anything as long as it isn't about the war or Mr Mompesson.'

I surprised myself by accepting the tea rather than storming out. After all, what right did I have to choose her company for her? With Hallows gone, she was a free woman. My friendship with her husband conferred no rights upon me. I settled for the best I seemed likely to get: innocent conversation with a beautiful woman. We talked about our respective families and forgot the troubles of Meongate – imaginary or otherwise.

It didn't ring true, of course. I felt that Leonora liked me, even trusted me. She had been the first person to alert me to the strangeness of life at Meongate and had not bothered to hide her dislike of Olivia. So why the mock outrage on her behalf? And, if she really did know as much as I did, or more, about Olivia's relationship with Mompesson, why was she prepared to be cultivated by such a man? It made no sense. Or, if it did, a sense of which I had no inkling. And Leonora was clearly determined to offer me no enlightenment. Mompesson would return at the end of the week and offer her a marriage which she should, in all logic and feeling, reject outright. Yet, for some reason, that, I knew, was not how it would be.

Even I could tell that I needed a break from Meongate, a breath of air fresher than its atmosphere of over-ripe foreboding. The seaside seemed an obvious prescription. So, next day, I caught the first train from

Droxford down the line and went, by ferry, across the harbour to Portsmouth.

Not that Portsmouth took me far from the war that was waiting to reclaim me: the great, grey battleships anchored in the Dockyard and the bustling sailors on every wharf were there to remind me. But I turned south, away from the docks, and headed for the seafront at Southsea, where I'd spent the only holiday I could remember with my father and where, now, I shied pebbles on the deserted shore to test my shoulder and gazed out across the Solent. I forgot, for a while, the troubles of Meongate. What, after all, did they mean to me?

More than I pretended, as I was soon to find out. In the early afternoon, I retraced my steps to the harbour and made my way along the Hard towards the ferry. I expected to see nobody I knew but there, studying a tram timetable outside the entrance to the Harbour station, while a crowd milled past her from the ferry, was Leonora, slim and elegant in grey.

I crossed the road and touched her shoulder. She swung round abruptly and looked at me with a startled expression. 'Why Tom! What are you going here?' Her smile was stiff and uncertain.

'I'm on my way back to Meongate. I've been to Southsea – to take the sea air.'

'And how was it?'

' Very . . . refreshing. What brings you . . . ?'

'Shopping, of course. I have a weakness for the big stores in Southsea.' But the smile was stiff enough to hint that this was not the truth. 'One can feel terribly cut off at Meongate.'

'Well, I'm in no hurry to get back. Perhaps I could escort you round them.'

It was not what she'd planned: I could see it in her face. Yet how could she refuse? She accepted my offer with all the good grace she could muster.

I passed the afternoon in a state dangerously close to ecstasy. The reason lay not in what we did or where we went, but in the growing pleasure I derived from closeness to Leonora. I was no young innocent – indeed, the war had made me cynical beyond my years – so the symptoms I detected in myself could not be mistaken for a passing dalliance. Nor could they be written off as concern for a dead comrade's widow. The truth was clear and irresistible: I was falling in love.

What Leonora felt was, as ever, obscure to me. However different the afternoon was from what she had planned, she certainly did not appear to begrudge me her company. Indeed, as we sat over chicory coffee and flimsy muffins in a quiet tea shop, she seemed more relaxed and forthcoming than I'd ever known her, as if remoteness from Meongate and all its attendant anxieties could free her from the burden she carried – for a while at least.

What that burden was I still had no clue. I kept my bargain and made no mention of Mompesson as we returned, in early evening, to Droxford. Yet he was in my mind all the time, for as my affection for Leonora grew, so did my fear of my absent, confident, swaggering rival. We might talk as much as we liked – and I might dream as much as I dared – but none of it could erase the horrible conviction I felt that my love would count for nothing against the power he exerted. He was due back at the end of the week and I was still failing to find a way to forestall him.

On Thursday, I wrote a reply to Warren's letter and

walked down to the post office in the village to despatch it. As I was paying for the stamp, I glanced into the alcove housing the public telephone, only to see Thorley replace the receiver and turn towards me.

'Good Lord!' he exclaimed with a splutter. 'Franklin!'

'Hello, Major.' I might have looked at him quizzically, for there was a telephone at Meongate we were all welcome to use.

Thorley coloured. 'Don't like to use old Powerstock's blower too much, don't you know? Run him up a dreadful bill.'

'That's good of you.' I was suspicious; Thorley was not one to spare his hosts.

'Walk back with you to the house?'

I agreed: there was nothing else for it. I posted the letter outside and we set off back by the path past the church. Thorley seemed to have recovered from his momentary embarrassment.

'Not seen much of you lately, Franklin.'

'I've been about. Of course, our American visitor has had the house by its ears.'

'Bit of a card, what?'

'He plays a good hand at bridge, certainly.'

Thorley laughed rather too generously. 'Very good, that. Very good. Gather you don't like the fellow.'

'I wouldn't say that.'

'Can't stand him myself.'

'Really? You seemed to get on all right.'

'Ah well, it pays to butter these chaps up, you know.'

'If you say so.'

He fell silent as we filed along a footbridge across a rivulet of the Meon, then resumed. 'On a different track, Franklin, wonder if I could ask you a favour: man to man, as it were.'

'Go ahead.'

'Well, fact is, I'm a bit strapped for cash . . . just at the moment. Until the Pay Corps send through the next cheque, that is. I was wondering . . .'

It amused me: the worldly-wise major sponging off a second lieutenant. So I responded as he would have hoped. 'How much?'

'Could you spare . . . thirty pounds?'

I looked at him in amazement. 'I'm sorry, Major. I'd like to help if I could. But thirty pounds? I can't lay my hands on such a sum.'

He smiled ruefully. 'Sorry. Shouldn't have asked.'

'But . . . something towards it?'

'No. Not worth it, old man. Has to be all or nothing. Decent of you to offer. But let's forget it.' He threw back his shoulders and walked on ahead, reasserting his dignity.

It was Friday, September 22nd. An equinoctial gale had rocked the house all night and showed no sign of abating by day. The stately elms swayed and sighed in the park whilst dark, white-topped clouds billowed across the sky and early falls of leaves rushed and whirled on the lawns. I looked out at the scene from my window and thought how Warren and the others – bivouacked in steely Flemish rain – would envy me the private, cosy turbulence of Meongate. Then I tightened the window stay against the draught and went down to breakfast.

In the dining room, there was only old Charter to receive me, consuming a generous plateful of kedgeree with gusto and glowering out at the brief fury of a passing shower. I served myself from the sideboard and joined him at the table.

'Good morning, Franklin,' he spluttered.

'Good morning. Spiteful day, isn't it?'

'It'll pass.' Then he looked at me. 'If it's the weather you mean.'

'Of course. What else?'

'Couldn't say. But there's enough spite in this house to ply your meaning, I reckon.'

'I gather Mr Mompesson is to rejoin us this evening.'

The old man snorted. 'Much good we will have of that.'

'Won't you have to accustom yourself to his company on a permanent basis? He's made no secret of his aspirations to become . . . one of the family, as it were.'

He looked at me darkly. 'What aspirations?'

It was interesting to test how much he knew, though I fancied, by his reactions, that he was playing the same game with me. 'I have it from his own lips that he hopes to marry Leonora.'

His laugh took me by surprise: a deep, growling guffaw as he leant back in his chair. But, for all its seeming humour, it left no smile on his face. 'You must hand it to Mompesson. The man has nerve. Very little else, perhaps. But nerve, yes. He wants for nothing in that direction. Reminds me . . . No. Let that pass.'

'You don't seem unduly surprised.'

'I'm too old to be surprised by anything. But I fancy I know somebody who will be surprised.'

'As far as I know, he's not actually proposed . . . or even consulted Lord Powerstock.'

'He's not the man to do things the right way.'

'What I meant was that we mustn't jump to conclusions.'

'I'll not do that, young man.' He winked. 'Reckon I'll just take myself off to resume that game of chess with

156

old Jepson. Then at least I won't have to tolerate Mompesson's smirk.' He rose from the table. 'Excuse me, will you? I must be out and about. It's stopped raining.' He glanced back at the garden. 'That could almost be a rainbow . . . No. It's faded.' He smiled to himself and lumbered out.

I sat there, while the wind before another shower rattled the window, sipping coffee and wondering, with vague foreboding, why I'd told Charter, why I still couldn't detach myself from a dead friend's household and forget their troubles. Only it wasn't for Hallows' sake that I clung to his family. It was for my own. There was something wrong – in them or me – and I had to know what it was.

What drew me to the library I can't say: forgotten, book-lined vault, whose place had it been? Not Lord Powerstock's – he'd said as much. Then, his son's? Somehow, it seemed not. I thumbed along the dusty rows and found no clues. Until . . . less dusty than the rest, a slim volume in sombre board covers: its staid and formal title *Deliberations of the Diocesan Committee for the Relief of the Poor of Portsea* – a series of monographs, some religious, some medical, some social. Amongst the latter 'Squalor Amidst Plenty' by Miriam Hallows, Lady Powerstock. Printed, declared an introductory note, 'in memory of a fine lady who died as she lived, giving no quarter to complacency.'

'Do my husband's books interest you?' The voice came, softly, from behind me and for one second I could almost have believed . . . But it was Olivia. I replaced the book on the shelf and turned to face her.

'Just browsing.'

She smiled at me. 'Of course.' There was just the quiver of one eyebrow to suggest she knew what I'd been about. 'Although Edward tells me it's more likely to be the art in this room that attracts you.'

I stepped across to the picture on the wall. 'It's very fine, certainly. By your first husband, you said.'

'Indeed.' She walked across to join me, her dress rustling in the sudden silence. 'He would be better known, I think – had he lived.'

'Did you say this was his last work?'

'Not quite. There's a companion piece – unfinished, I fear.'

'A companion piece?'

'Yes: a sequel, if you like. The two pictures together tell a story. There was to have been a third.'

'A pity they weren't completed.'

'The second nearly was. You may see it, if you wish.'

I looked at her, so prim and restrained in her high-necked dress and drawn-up hair, and asked myself – as before – whether what I'd seen was real. But it was. The naked figure on the bed in the painting told me, by her smile, that I was not mistaken. 'I'd like to – if it's convenient.'

'Why yes. Of course.' She paused. 'I keep it . . . in my bedroom.'

It couldn't be. Not so simple a device. We were discussing a venue to view a picture. Nothing else. Yet I knew it was not so. The sun came out and splashed across the wall beside us. Suddenly, the body on the bed was floodlit, but Lady Powerstock paid it no need, merely smiled, seraphically, serenely, in the slow, secret satisfaction of a calculated moment.

'Shall we say . . . after tea – this afternoon?'

What could I do but agree? A refusal would have

signalled my suspicion that more than a picture was being offered. Besides, something else I didn't care to admit to drove me to accept.

'You know where my room is?'

'Ah . . . yes.'

She smiled again. 'Good. Until later then.' She moved away, as if to leave, but paused by the bookshelf where I'd been and plucked down the book I'd been reading. 'Have you seen the essay in this volume by my husband's first wife?' She must have known I had.

'Yes. I was looking at it when you came in.'

'I thought you must have been. Sad, isn't it?'

'Oh yes. Very much so. But it's good that you and Lord Powerstock should have been able to . . . make up for each other's loss.'

She replaced the book on the shelf. 'That's not quite what I meant. I think it rather sad that the Diocesan Committee should have put its name to this . . . convenient fiction.'

'Fiction? Surely the lady did work among the poor?'

'She was certainly a regular visitor to Portsea.' So saying, Olivia moved to the door and opened it. 'The question is: why?'

The sunlight faded from the wall and the room grew cold. Outside, the wind gusted a scatter of leaves across the flagstoned terrace.

I missed lunch and went for a long walk round the lanes to clear my head. The weather was in a washed-out, windless lull, though the dark clouds bunching over the downs to the west were ominous.

My return journey, perhaps inevitably, took me through the village. With my mind still on the book in the library and Olivia's dismissive remark about it, I diverted into the churchyard and ambled amongst the stones, in search of . . . what I knew I would find. A four-square, railed-off memorial to three previous Lords Powerstock and there, in its shade, a smaller, newer stone:

IN LOVING MEMORY OF MIRIAM ABIGAIL HALLOWS, LADY POWERSTOCK, DEAREST WIFE, MOTHER AND DAUGHTER, TAKEN EARLY TO HIS ARMS, 30TH MARCH 1905, AGED THIRTY-EIGHT YEARS – GREATLY LOVED AND SORELY MISSED.

Hallows had never spoken to me of her, yet how often must he, as a younger man, have come to look at this stone, one of the few reminders of his mother, and wondered . . . how it would have been had she lived? I turned aside and made for the kissing gate into the path that led towards Meongate.

As I did so, a figure emerged from the south door of the church and glanced towards me. It was Leonora, calm and regal in a plaid dress and dark cape. She smiled, but only faintly.

'We meet here again,' she said.

I doffed my hat. 'But this time *I* am surprised. May I walk back with you to Meongate?'

'Of course.' We went out on to the field path that led down towards the river. 'Were you examining the family plot?'

'I noticed it – in passing. The memorial to John's mother is very moving.'

'I think they all felt it so unfair that she should die as she did.'

'I imagine it must always be risky to work in such areas. Do you know Portsea at all?'

She looked at me. 'Not at all.'

'Surely we weren't far from it on Wednesday.'

'No. I believe not.'

We made our way down over the river and up through the woods to join the lane that bridged the railway line and curved east towards Meongate. There, still a mile or so short of our destination, we were caught in one of the heavy showers rolling in from the west. We took shelter in a Dutch barn just off the road and sat on two bales of straw watching the rain sheet across the fields beyond.

It was an opportunity I'd yearned for but also dreaded: a chance to offer Leonora some alternative to the proposition from Mompesson which she seemed unaccountably bound to accept. It was too soon, of course, too great a presumption on her bereavement, but her words in the rhododendron glade, echoing so often in my mind, had convinced me that unless she understood the depth of my feeling for her, she would soon be lost to me for ever.

I muttered some semblance of a casual remark. 'I don't think it'll rain for long.'

'Sometimes,' she said softly, 'I think it'll rain for ever.'

I looked at her. 'Do you miss him so badly?'

She glanced away. 'More than I can say.'

'For you it is bound to be worst. But it might help you to know that I miss him too. The men under his command mourn him still. One said as much in a letter to me recently.'

She looked back at me, her voice full of the tears she would not allow to flow. 'It's worse than you can possibly imagine.'

'I'd like to try to understand.'

'I realize that. But I don't think it's possible.'

'Why not? I hope I'm not being presumptuous when

I say that I think John would not have wanted you to mourn him . . . too long. Would not have wanted you to . . . abandon life.'

'No. He would not have wanted that.'

'This war won't last for ever. When it's over, we'll all have to rebuild our lives. Perhaps we should start now. Perhaps we could do so . . . together.'

It wasn't how I'd intended to put it, but Leonora had the good grace not to condemn me for that. Her response, instead, seemed weighted with the sadness which, for all her misfortunes, still seemed, at its core, unaccountable. 'You were my husband's friend, Tom, and therefore you are my friend. More than that I cannot offer.'

'Such things take time. I'm not trying to take John's place: nobody could do that. But I do think I could restore something to your life, as you could to mine. If you ever felt able to consider . . . matrimony, I'd be deeply honoured.'

She rose from the bale and walked slowly to one of the pillars supporting the roof, put one arm about it as she turned to face me as if to anchor her thoughts as much as her body. 'You are a good man, Tom. Too good for what is happening here. I can never marry you. Please understand that.'

I too rose to my feet. 'But that's precisely it. I don't understand. There's nothing wrong in the idea of a young widow . . .'

'I am pregnant.' She spoke the words softly but decisively, stopping my words and thoughts in their tracks.

'What?'

'I am three months pregnant. I presume I need not tell you what is wrong in the idea of a young widow

162

being three months pregnant when her husband is more than four months dead.'

I could not speak. I did not know what to say.

'I had hoped to spare you the information. I had hoped you would leave Meongate before concealment became impractical.'

Resentment flared within me. 'It's Mompesson, isn't it?'

'I have told you what I felt you were entitled to know. That is all.'

'He's already told me he intends to marry you. And now I've no doubt you will marry him, since you're carrying his child.'

She looked momentarily shocked by what I'd said, then recovered herself. She took a deep breath and looked straight at me. 'The subject is closed. Now please excuse me. I'm sure you'll understand that I would prefer to walk back to Meongate alone.'

It had stopped raining. She walked out into the lane and moved slowly away in the direction of Meongate. I did not follow, but shouted after her before bitterness could stem my anger: 'I'm glad John's not here to see Mompesson seduce first his stepmother, then his wife.' But Leonora did not look back. She walked on at a steady pace and passed from view.

I lit a cigarette and smoked it, leaning against the pillar where she'd stood. I had no wish to catch her up, no wish to be insulted again, as I felt I had been. It was not her fault that I'd hoped for so much, not her intention that I should have been made a fool of, yet, in my heart, at that moment of bleakest resignation, I blamed her for every facet of my humiliation. I forgot all the many things that were at odds with what I now believed about her and Mompesson. I remembered

163

only the friend I felt she'd betrayed and the vision of a future which was now denied me.

By the time I'd finished the cigarette and crushed it against the pillar, I was determined to be rid of Leonora and all the other occupants of Meongate who so fascinated and repelled me. It seemed the only way to preserve some vestige of my dignity, the only course by which I could still honour Hallows' memory. Swallowing the worst of my resentment, I headed back.

I reached Meongate in the middle of the afternoon. The wind had died and the house was in silence: a mood of siesta was upon the place. I went up to my room, glad of seeing nobody on the way, and lay on my bed, staring at the floral-patterned curtains and the washed blue sky beyond my window. I fell into a light and troubled slumber.

Something was crawling towards the bed: I could hear it slithering, slowly and painfully, across the carpet. With a clutch of panic, I knew that it was Hallows, blind and bleeding, dragging himself back from no man's land, as on that night when he did not return.

'Hallows?' I spoke his name as I lurched from the bed and stared, with waking eyes, at what had been only a dream. There was nothing there, except . . . a white envelope on the carpet by the door.

I moved across the picked it up. It must have been slipped beneath the door while I slept. I tore it open. A key fell out on to the floor and I was left holding the note it had been wrapped with.

'Tom: this is the key to the observatory. If you wish to understand what is happening in this house, go there at seven o'clock this evening. L.'

I slipped the key into my pocket and, almost without thinking, burned the note in the grate. I had not expected to hear from her again, but, now that I had my resolve to have done with her vanished before the frail hope that all could yet be made right: I would do as she asked.

I looked at the clock: it was a quarter to five. Then I remembered my appointment with Olivia. Why not keep it, I thought, if only to see Mr Bartholomew's famous picture and tell her that I was leaving.

I washed and changed and made my way to the wing of the house. Still, silence reigned. I passed the stairs to the observatory and came to the door where I'd seen Mompesson but a week before. I knocked, as he had not.

'Come in.' It was Olivia's voice, but muffled by distance.

I opened the door and went in. The room was empty. 'Lady Powerstock?'

'Is that you, Lieutenant?' Her voice came from an adjoining room, to which the door stood ajar. I took it to be the bedroom.

'Yes. You said I might see the picture.'

'Of course. It's on the wall facing the window. I'll join you presently.'

I turned to where she had said. It was unmistakably a companion piece to that in the library, its heavy gilt frame blending with the richly patterned bronze wallpaper. I walked across to study it.

A sequel, she had said, and she had been right. The same bedchamber of some mythic castle, the same sickly, morbid air of medievalist obsession, but gone a little further, sunk a little deeper into the mood of the place and the portrait of it. The woman on the bed had rolled over and now lay supine, one knee raised to preserve a hint of modesty. The man in mail had knelt

165

upon the bed and stooped across her, his head lowered to kiss her left breast. She had grasped his left hand and placed it over her other breast. It was a depiction of sexual conquest at once total and tantalizing, tantalizing because the woman's face was angled away from the man, gazing out of the picture with an air of abstracted superiority, as if she, as much as the artist, was merely a spectator, merely an observer of somebody else's deception. Was it Olivia? I looked at the face and knew I could never be sure, knew that that – as much as any brushstroke – was the painter's triumph.

'What do you think?'

I turned to see that Olivia had emerged from the adjoining room and stood looking at me, as intent upon my reaction as I was upon the picture. She wore a pale green, silken dressing gown, loosely tied at the waist, with her hair let down as I'd only seen it once before.

'I was resting after a bath. I'd forgotten you were to call.' The lie was as transparent as the gown hinted at being, where the sunlight shone through its shifting folds from the window behind her.

'I'm sorry. I didn't mean to disturb you.'

'It's no matter. Do you like the picture?'

What could I say? Blatancy silenced me with its hideous, unconfessed appeal. 'Your husband must have been a remarkable man.'

'But a troubled one. Deeply troubled, especially towards the end – as these pictures imply.'

She moved as she spoke, turned slightly so that the gown stirred and parted momentarily to reveal a bare and rounded thigh beneath. Our conversation was a sham, a mannered prelude to something I could not believe would happen and something she was determined

166

should not be hurried. 'He drowned – I believe.'

'Yes – as was fitting.'

'In what way?'

'Philip was a drowning man all his life.'

She moved closer and stood beside me, gazing at the picture with a rapt attention that hovered on the edges of declaring its falsehood. There was a heady scent in the air now she was near me, the perfume she wore blending its allure with the warmth of her body. I looked at her, not, the picture, at the proud and beautiful profile of her face, the long and haughty neck, the rise and fall of her bosom beneath the gown, the caressing touch of the silk where it moulded the unconstrained roundness of her breasts. I looked at her, as I was meant to, and fought desire with failing strength.

'You have not asked the question most people put to me.'

'Which is?'

'Am I the woman in the picture?' She glanced towards me, capturing and confronting the direction of my gaze.

'And are you?'

'What do you think, Lieutenant?'

'I don't know.'

'She is beautiful, is she not? And cruel also. Is that how my husband thought of me? Is that how you think of me?'

I looked at her in the long suspension of an absent smile. 'It might be.'

She clicked her tongue in teasing mockery. 'You disappoint me. I had expected you to be more decisive.' She tossed back her head and walked away towards the window. I watched her go, saw the material of the gown flex and slide around her hips as she moved, heard the faint kiss of the mobile fabric slip into my furtive mind and knew my indecision to be more appalling than she could guess.

She stopped between the window and the bedroom door and looked at me. 'What do you know of me, Lieutenant?'

I grasped at a chance to restore my dignity. 'More than you might think, your ladyship'

She smiled. 'That I doubt. The loose wife of an elderly husband throwing herself shamelessly at every young man who crosses her threshold. Isn't that how it is?'

'That is for you to say.'

'But you have been saying what you thought about it all the time you've been here – to my husband, to Leonora, to that dotard Charter. Why stop now?'

'I don't know what you mean.'

'Come, come. Why not admit it? You've been taken in by the false purity of Leonora and the hallowed memory of John's mother: the whole sham of family honour we practise here.'

'Is it a sham?'

'What do you think? The ghost of that woman drags her good works round this house till I'm sick of the sound of her name. And what did those works amount to? What you call shameless in me I call honest.'

Her bosom was heaving with controlled anger at all the reasons why she stood condemned, but she did know how right she was? Did she know the truth about Leonora? I dared not ask. I could only fend off my sense of guilt with an accusation of my own. 'I know all about you and Mompesson, Lady Powerstock. If there's corruption in this house, it's in this room.'

She laughed. 'Isn't that why you're here?'

Then I was angry. I advanced across the room towards

168

her. 'I'm here at your invitation.' I stopped a few feet from her.

'No. You're here to prove you're more than just a peeping Tom, more than just a carrier of tales.'

'Then why did you ask me?'

'To see if you're half the man Ralph Mompesson is.'

She stood between me and the light, between me and reason. Before I knew what I was doing, I had taken a step towards her and raised my hand to strike. But before I could strike, the gloating defiance in her eyes had stopped me. My hand fell to her shoulder, where the silken gown curved around her neck. It was too much – too lusciously late – for me to refrain. I slipped my hand inside the gown and cupped the large, firm breast beneath in my palm. I felt the nipple stiffen between my fingers. Then Olivia smiled and loosened the sash at her waist. The gown fell open: she was naked beneath. I saw my own hand fastened on her left breast and knew the horror I felt could not eclipse the pleasure I took from her offered flesh. She knew it too: the knowledge aroused her even more, I sensed, than my touch ever could.

'Perhaps, after all,' she said softly, 'I've under-estimated you. Perhaps you're more than half a man.'

'We're going to have to find that out,' I replied, my voice husky with nervous anticipation. I took my hand from her breast and slipped the gown off her left shoulder. The material glided, with fashioned leisure, round her back and, as she straightened her right arm, slid to the floor. She stood naked before me, the mature curves and lingering bloom of her body drawing me past the last moment when I might have called a halt.

'Then follow me.' She spoke the words softly: only her smile revealed the pleasure she took from being able to command me. She turned away and pushed open the door to the adjoining room: I could see the bed within, drawn back in readiness, as I should have known it would be. But I spared the fact little thought. My mind feasted instead on the vision it could not resist: Olivia Powerstock, stripping my desires barer than her own unfettered flesh, padding slowly across the carpet away from me towards the bed where I would certainly follow.

She reached the bed, propped one knee on the coverlet and looked back at me. On her face was the expression she had worn in Bartholomew's picture, the picture I understood now for the first time. The knowledge of her baseness was not enough. Still our minds succumbed – and our hands reached out to trace – the curving line of her propped thigh and proffered hip and half-turned back and profiled breast. I moved towards her.

As I crossed the threshold, a reflection of the room behind me slid across my gaze in the cheval-glass by the window. It was no more than a movement, no more than a passing shape, in the mirror's image, but yet wrong, at odds with what it should have been. I stopped in my tracks, watched for the split-second it took to resolve into a clear, discordant vision. The door from the passage – which I had certainly closed – stood open. And in its portal, framed and stern and staring straight at me, was Hallows. Only a flash, only a snapshot, of what might have been. Yet there he was. Captain the Honourable John Hallows, my dear friend, my forever absent host, stood watching me, expressionless but all-seeing.

I cried out and wheeled round. There was nothing. There was nobody. The door was closed – or closing.

Who could say the handle was not still faintly stirring? Not I. Not then. I'd dreamed vividly and violently enough of the war to know what tricks the mind could play, yet it had seemed, however momentary, a dreadful certainty that he was watching me and seeing what I was afraid to confront in myself.

I raced across the outer room and flung the door open. There was nobody there, no trace or sound in the passage that might have been a person. I closed the door and leant against it, feeling my heart pound and sweat start out on my forehead. The vision had told me what my reaction confirmed: in the house that had once been his home, I was Hallows' friend beyond any other tie. For me to give into the senses' snares of that treacherous place was to betray him as well as myself.

'What's the matter with you?' Olivia came out of the bedroom behind me, her face as hard as her voice, sternly fastening a hastily gathered robe around her waist.

'I can't . . .' I looked towards her but could not continue. The anger in her expression was moving swiftly towards contempt. She had seen nothing – beyond a sudden loss of nerve. I tried again. 'I can't . . . I can't stay.'

There was nothing to do but flee. I turned away from her withering look, opened the door and ran blindly down the passage.

I needed a drink – badly. I went down to the drawing room and poured myself a large Scotch. It didn't help much. Nor did a walk in the garden. The clouds were bunching and darkening again, presaging another stormy night. When I saw Cheriton heading towards me across the park, it made up my mind to return to the house.

I entered by the conservatory, hoping to see nobody, but, as I made my way along the corridor past the billiards room, Thorley hailed me through the open door.

'Fancy a frame, Franklin?' he asked. He was pacing around the table, pointing balls aimlessly.

I stepped inside the room. 'Sorry. Can't stop.'

He chuckled grimly. 'Know what you mean.' He missed a corner pocket. 'Know just what you mean.'

'Do you?'

'Oh yes.' He stooped over the cue again, then abruptly straightened up. 'Hear that?'

I listened. Faintly, through the high, blind-hung windows of the room, came the noise of a car engine. I knew at once it was Mompesson.

Thorley smiled and slammed the cue into the rack on the wall. 'It's our American friend. Time I made myself scarce.' He paused as he reached where I was standing by the door. 'I don't suppose . . . No. Forget it.' He walked quickly out.

I trailed after him and made for the back stairs. I had no wish to meet Mompesson. Already, I could hear a door slamming somewhere and Lady Powerstock trilling a greeting. Less than an hour before, she'd been . . . But my mind staved off the thought. What was the good of it? She'd taken from me my self-respect, but not yet all my honour.

I kept to my room till seven o'clock, wondering whether to obey Leonora's note or just quit that benighted house. The thought was a delusion: I knew all along that I would stay long enough to take up the veiled offer of a kind of truth. When the clock struck seven, the key was in my hand.

I made my way to the wing of the house, confident in

172

my assumption that Olivia would be downstairs, entertaining Mompesson over aperitifs the coast was clear. I don't know what I expected to find in the observatory. I think I had no idea. I think speculation had been erased by experience. Perhaps I hoped against hope that Leonora would have left evidence to exonerate herself; even, in some absurd way, to exonerate me.

I climbed the stairs in silence, reached the door and slid the key into the lock. And the door creaked slowly open on its hinges: it wasn't locked at all.

Three steps led up to the observatory proper: a tall, narrow, hexagonal room with full-length windows beneath the copper roof that supported the weathervane. An elegant brass telescope stood in the centre by a low stool. Otherwise, there was a cupboard, a small square table and a battered armchair: nothing beyond these sparse furnishings and scattered charts and pencil stubs to offset the impression of neglect that hung in the musty air. Not that the contents were what made the place, so much as the panorama it commanded, riding like a ship's look-out on the back of the house facing the surrounding fields and hills while the garden and grounds stretched themselves out beneath. Away to the west the setting sun was obscured by banks of cloud. Nearer to hand, I could look across between slender chimneys to rows of windows along the back of the house or down into the garden to see Cheriton still wandering the lawns amidst strewn leaves and rose blossom; the wind twitched at his greatcoat collar and rattled the glass in the observatory window. At night, it would have been a fine cockpit for viewing the stars. Now, at twilight, it was ideal only for studying Meongate. And that – I began to think – was why Leonora had named such a time.

I pondered her note. 'If you wish to understand what is happening in this house . . .' Where was understanding to be found in an abandoned observatory? It seemed to make no sense.

Then I looked at the telescope. Strangely, the glass was not capped. Stranger still, it was not trained on the sky, but angled down towards the house itself. I touched the shaft: it had been locked in position.

I leant forward and looked through the eyepiece. Sure enough, the telescope had been focused – and then locked – on one of the windows at the rear of the house on the upper floor. I peered closer.

It was Mompesson's room. He stood by the window, in a dark dressing gown, smoking a cigarette and gazing out at the garden, for all the world like a man relaxing after a bath. This, I told myself, could not be all I had been brought there to see.

It wasn't. He looked around suddenly and seemed to say something, either to somebody else in the room I couldn't see or to somebody who had knocked at the door. Then he turned back and ground out his cigarette in an ashtray on the windowsill: the gesture seemed exaggerated, somehow symbolic, as if for the benefit of another.

He propped himself against the sill and looked back into the room. I could see his lips moving, but still there was no glimpse of his interlocutor. The angle of the view meant I could only see about a quarter of the room; again, I questioned what the telescope had been trained on. Why Mompesson's window? Elaborate proof of Lady Powerstock's infidelity? If so, it was wasted on me, and, besides, Mompesson might at any moment join his companion in the obscured remainder of the room. The likelihood was that I would soon be looking at an unattended window.

As if to confirm this would be so, Mompesson pushed himself off from the sill and walked towards the centre of the room. But his companion came to meet him before he had gone far – and it wasn't Lady Powerstock. Leonora, dressed for dinner in a black evening gown, came into my view. She had known precisely when I should go to the observatory because she had planned what it was that I would see there. Mompesson paused by her right shoulder and took her arm as if to lead her elsewhere, but she stayed where she was and looked directly up towards me. She could not see me, of course, but she knew that I was there. And in her face I could imagine I read the message: 'Now you have your answer.'

Mompesson jerked at her arm – painfully, to judge by her expression – yet still she did not move. He turned and spoke to her and she replied without looking at him. her gaze was still to the window, angled fixedly towards me.

Mompesson stood behind her and placed his hands on her shoulders with no sign of gentleness. Again, there was an exchange of words. Then he began to unbutton the back of her dress, slowly, with an air of leisure, almost of familiarity. When he'd finished, he tugged the garment free at either shoulder. Leonora stood still and expressionless as it fell in folds about her feet, yet her gaze remained fixed in my direction.

What followed was frightening in its very inevitability, in its involvement of me – a mere observer – as a kind of participant. Because I knew that Leonora must know I was watching, because I sensed that between her and Mompesson there was nothing beyond a bizarre, carnal obligation, above all because I did not even try to intervene, I felt as defiled by my own inaction as by what I witnessed.

Leonora stood and waited – and calmly watched me – as Mompesson undressed her, freeing each garment with measured deliberation, savouring each parting of fabric from flesh. When he had finished – when Leonora stood naked before him and before me – the mystery of her mind was intact, for she had neither consented nor resisted, but in her body no mystery remained. In so slender a woman, the fullness of the breasts and stomach could not be mistaken: it seemed, somehow, to heighten the obscenity of her lingering exposure.

I could not stop myself watching, for what I saw was horrible and appalling, but something worse as well. In Leonora's implacable gaze there was a hint of an accusation I could not entirely refute: that some part of me enjoyed what I was seeing.

Then Mompesson moved out of my field of vision and, for the first time, Leonora released me from her look. She stepped clear of her discarded clothing and turned, with her back to me, in the direction that Mompesson had gone. In that instant, he reappeared, walking slowly towards her and smiling as he did so. In his left hand he held a leather strop. As I watched, some tremor ran through Leonora's body.

There was a noise behind me. I jerked back from the telescope and swung round. But there was nobody there. The door was closed as I had left it: I was alone save for my guilt, my fear that, more than ever, simply by spying and evading, I was implicated in the perversion and paranoia of that house. I turned back to the telescope. What would I see if I looked through the lens again? I closed my eyes and clenched my fists, determined not to look. In my mind, I still saw Mompesson swinging the strop, still saw the quivering

176

curves of Leonoras body as she waited. And then my resolve gave way. I had to know. I stooped and put my eye to the telescope again.

They had gone. There was the window, framed in the lens, and part of the room beyond. But it was empty. Mompesson and Leonora had moved out of sight, leaving only a bundle of clothing on the floor to prove I had not imagined it all. I watched, in growing torment, but they did not return. Was this – I wondered – Leonora's final reproof of me: to show me the distasteful prelude but deny me the unthinkable climax?

From such thoughts I could only retreat. I blundered down the short flight of steps to the door, wrenched it open and hurled myself down the stairs. Once again, I could only flee.

But not far. At the foot of the stairs, as I wheeled into the passage, stood Lady Powerstock. Grave and refined as I knew her not to be, decadently dignified in a low-cut evening dress and a necklace that glittered like her metallic smile.

'Running again, Lieutenant Franklin?'

I had lost all caution before the need to strike back at her. 'Who wouldn't run – from the depravity of this house?'

'Are you sure you aren't just hiding your own inadequacy in this tedious moralizing?'

'I don't understand you. I don't understand any of you. Are you two happy to share that man – for God's sake, like some hired stallion?'

She frowned. 'Which . . . two . . . do you mean?'

'I suppose you're too far gone to care. But why drag Leonora down with you?'

'Leonora?'

'Don't pretend you don't know.'

Her eyes flared. 'Know what?'

'This is pointless.' I pushed past her. 'I'll be leaving in the morning. I'll be relieved to go.'

'Nobody will try to stop you. We don't want you here.'

I walked on steadily, exerting myself to keep a seemly pace. When I turned the corner on to the landing, I felt the sudden relief of no longer having her eyes on me. I wanted nothing so much as to be away from her and her house. That, I thought, would be enough.

I struck out down the drive as dusk began to deepen into darkness, leaving behind the lights of the house and hurrying away past the swaying, wind-stirred elms, glad to be out where the cold air with its hint of rain lanced away the worst of my humiliation.

Only the wind, sighing in the leaves and branches, and one early, distant owl broke the silence that lay behind the determined trudge of my feet in the lane. Now the lights of Meongate had passed from view. Now, for a while, I was safe.

By the time I reached Droxford, the long way round by the road, it was quite dark, but there were lanterns hung in the windows of the White Horse Inn and cheery voices within to offer me the solace I'd hoped for.

I'd been in a couple of times during my stay, so received a passably warm welcome, ordered a jug of ale and retreated to a quiet alcove table, intending to drink myself into much-needed oblivion. But I was hailed from a chair by the fire. It was Thorley. He walked unsteadily across to join me, evidently several drinks the worse already.

'Couldn't face it, like me, I suppose,' he slurred.

'Face what?'

'Come clean, old man. Has he got you by the short and curlies as well?'

'I don't know what you mean.'

He gulped down some of his drink: it smelt whisky. 'I mean the bloody yank. Mompesson.' He was talking too loudly – a wizened old countryman by the bar sucked on his clay pipe and shot us a piercing look. 'That's why you're here, isn't it? To keep out of his way.'

I leant across the table towards him. 'Keep your voice down, Major. You're drunk.'

'Of course I'm bloody drunk. I intend to get drunker still. Who wouldn't? I thought this was a safe berth. Then Mompesson, with that syrupy, serpentine smile of his, pops up and gets me gambling for stakes I can't afford. Now he wants to cash in my IOUs.'

'Sorry to hear that.'

'Not as sorry as me.'

'What will you do?'

'I'm pushing for a medical board. At least if I'm back on active service, I'm out of his reach.'

'That seems rather drastic.'

'It's what he's driven me to. That's why I tried to touch you for a loan.'

'Sorry I couldn't help.'

'Never mind.' He paused. 'What's he got on you?'

'Nothing. I don't like him, that's all.'

'Have it your way.'

And I did. Sober as I was, or drunk as I later became, I had no intention of telling Thorley what I was reluctant to tell myself: that the Powerstocks had made a fool of me and possibly Hallows as well. Now all I wanted was to be rid of them. But, in the meantime, trading drinks with Thorley didn't seem so bad. None of what had happened had been his fault: both of us had had our weaknesses exploited. I was, I realized, no better than him, however objectionable I'd previously found him. we'd both been washed there by the tides of a war we were powerless to stop: it seemed almost a refuge to us. There are times – and that was one – when the world can seem dreadfully, unbearably unfair. If we'd been born twenty years earlier – or later – our nerves, our characters, our very lives would not have been called into question. Cometh the hour, cometh the men. But what about those who don't measure up?

So, in the false camaraderie of a drunken evening, swinging from mewling self-pity to coruscating contempt for ourselves and the world in general, Thorley and I helped each other through a few intoxicated hours, slurring and forgetting all the truths we'd rather not have known. Eventually, he fell asleep in the settle opposite me and I was left to drink on alone. Soon, I knew, the landlord would require us to leave and I would have to help Thorley back up the lanes to Meongate.

It didn't turn out as I'd expected. I remember looking at the clock over the bar around ten and glancing across at Thorley, who was too far gone to be stirred, but what happened next, in what order, at what time, waking or dreaming, I can't exactly say. Even now, I'm none too sure how much of it took place and how much I imagined. A drunken fool is a poor witness. But, for what it's worth, this is how it seemed.

I decided to strike out for Meongate alone, before I could be asked to take Thorley with me. I went out the back way, into the yard behind the inn, where some horses were whinnying gently in the stable. The cold night air failed to clear my head. My legs felt unsteady and the world refused to stop whirling before my eyes. I stumbled to a corner of the yard and vomited. That seemed to help. As I turned round, intending to make for the gate on to the road, I saw somebody – a dark, swimming shape – move across the yard towards me, from the direction of the stable. I tried to hurry ahead in order to avoid them.

I didn't make it back to Meongate that night. I suppose there never was much chance that I would. I should have stayed at the inn and taken a room. But I didn't. instead, sleep found me elsewhere and dreams whirled after me with all the giddy force that closed eyes could not withstand.

A cold drop of rain on the cheek roused me. I was awake instantly, with aching head and limbs, looking out from a bed of hay at the washed grey dawn of a September day. I had spent the night in a hay-filled barn, oblivious to all until the rain now sweeping across the fields had penetrated the leaking roof.

I struggled up and staggered outside. The barn was in the corner of a field, on the other side of which a gate gave on to the lane. By the fold of the land, I knew I wasn't far from Meongate, but I had no memory of getting even that close. I thanked the instincts of a drunken man and started across the field towards the gate. It had been a rough night, but I took comfort from the thought that I had only to collect my belongings from Meongate and I could be out of their clutches for good. That early, I judged there would be nobody about to see me come and go. The thought quickened my pace.

FIVE

But Meongate was far from quiet. As I walked up the drive, I could see a dark-coloured van pulled up short of the entrance to the house and, beyond it, a covered car. I didn't recognize either of them. As I came alongside the van, I noticed a coat of arms on the side and, beneath it, obscured by mud, the words HAMPSHIRE CONSTABULARY. Then I saw, standing by the open front door, a policeman. I recognized him as the ageing, friendly constable I'd seen cycling around the village several times. And he clearly recognized me.

'Mr Franklin, isn't it?'

'Yes. What brings you here?'

He didn't answer. 'The Inspector'll be glad to see you. Come along with me, will you, sir?'

I followed him into the hall. 'What's going on?'

'You'll find out soon enough.'

We turned into the morning room. There was another constable there, and a bustling sergeant, but no member of the household. Only, stooped over a table that had been brought to the centre of the room, sifting through the contents of a canvas sack open before him, a man I didn't know: grey, receding curls of hair fringing a ham-like face adorned with gold-rimmed half-moon spectacles, threadbare tweed suit beneath a shabby macintosh, large, ponderous hands picking at the sack, breathing asthmatically and humming to himself.

'Mr Franklin's turned up, sir,' the constable announced.

The man looked up and stared at me over his glasses for a moment, then idly pushed the sack to one side. 'Come in, Mr Franklin,' he said. 'Take a seat.'

'I'd like to know what's going on.'

'Wouldn't we all? Take a seat first.'

Reluctantly, I moved to the chair held back for me by the other constable. 'Who are you?'

'Shapland. I'm a detective inspector. We're here to investigate a murder. That's why I was anxious you should sit down, in case it came as a shock to you.'

I stared at him incredulously. 'Who's been murdered?'

He began to study his fingernails. 'An American gentleman: Ralph Eugene Mompesson. Some sort of businessman.' He took something from the sack and held it up: an American passport. 'Born New Orleans, 5th May 1879.' He let the booklet fall on to the table. 'Died Droxford, 22nd September 1916. It's a long way to come just to be murdered. Odd, don't you think?'

I was too taken aback to do anything but repeat the word. 'Odd?'

'I think it is.' He mused on the point. 'Born in the Deep South: all that passion and violence. Ends up here in sleepy Droxford – with a bullet through his head.'

'Good God.'

'Professionally done, if I may say so. With what you might term military precision.'

'You're not implying . . . ?'

183

He smiled his sleepy shopkeeper's grin.

'You were my prime suspect, Mr Franklin – until you came back here. Where have you been all night?'

'I had too much to drink at the White Horse. Slept it off in a barn.'

'Mmm. You look like that's true. See anything of Major Thorley?'

'He was with me at the inn. But we left separately.'

'Another barn, no doubt.' He looked up at the constable who'd brought me in. 'Check at the White Horse, will you, Bannister?' I heard the man clump away.

'Where's everyone else?'

'You can see them when I've finished with you. Did you like Mr Mompesson?'

'No. Can't say I did. But . . .'

'It wasn't a trick question. I'm just curious. What was he doing here? His lordsip's explained why the place is awash with young officers. But why an American businessman – if that's what he was.'

'A friend of the family.'

'Now, that was a trick question. I wanted to see if you would admit he was Lady Powerstock's . . . fancy man.'

'You've a damned impertinence . . .'

He held up his hand. 'Excuse me, Mr Franklin. I didn't ask for this case. Now I've got it, don't expect too many niceties. Like you, I'm just doing my bit for King and country. I retired three years ago, finished with this business, went off to grow my vegetables. Thanks to the war, I've been recalled. Ironical, don't you think?'

'In what way?'

'Because of the war, because of all that killing and shooting, we two find ourselves here discussing . . . just another killing, another shooting. But this one's different. This one we call murder. Or do we? Do you call it murder?'

'I don't . . .'

Suddenly, he rose from his chair. 'Come with me and see where it was done. Then tell me.'

Obediently, I followed him. For such a large man, Shapland moved quickly. He led the way back into the hall and up the stairs of the eerily silent house. As he went up, he continued to talk, in a piping, perversely cheerful voice.

'Murdered in his bedroom, but not as he slept. Apt fate, don't you think?'

'When did this happen, Inspector?'

'Last night, about eleven o'clock. He'd gone up to his room after dinner. That's where he was found.'

We were on the landing now, heading towards Mompesson's room. The enormity of what had happened began to sweep over me. Only the evening before, I'd spied on that room from the observatory. What awaited us there now?

Another constable was standing by the entrance to Mompesson's room: the door was open. Shapland went past him without a word and gestured for me to follow.

'He was found over here, by the dressing table.' He pointed to a dark stain on the carpet and the rough chalk outline of a corpse: the carpet's rich pattern subdued the starkness of the image.

'Found . . . by whom?'

'That depends who you believe. Ostensibly, Lady Powerstock and her maid.'

'Together?'

'Unlikely, isn't it? Lady Powerstock claims to have heard a noise whilst making her way to bed: possibly a gunshot, possibly not. She thought it came from this room. So, she fetched her maid and they investigated.'

'But you don't believe that?'

'Not for a moment. I believe she came to this room to keep an appointment with Mompesson, found him dead, then fetched her maid. The maid's obviously fearful for her job, so I shan't push the point. But I'm sure you know I'm right.'

'What makes you think I know anything about it?'

'Lady Powerstock was quick to accuse you . . . rather than an unknown intruder. I gathered she must have some reason to dislike you. The real question is whether you're cool enough to have come back here this morning knowing what you would find.'

'But I didn't know.'

He ignored my answer and stooped over the chalked outline on the floor, holding his glasses to adjust the focus. 'There's not much to be learned here. After the post-mortem, we'll know the calibre of the revolver. Do you have just the one we found in your room, by the way?'

'What the devil do you mean by . . . ?'

'It hadn't been used. That's a point in your favour.'

'I don't need any points in my favour.'

'Yes you do. Lady Powerstock says she saw you emerging from the stairs to the observatory shortly after seven o'clock yesterday evening. Do you admit that?'

I tried to think quickly. 'No.'

'We found the telescope in the observatory trained on this window. Somebody was spying on Mompesson, somebody who may have killed him later. Can you prove you weren't there?'

'Of course not.'

He moved closer. A tired old man going through the motions: like me, a refugee from war. But in his eyes

186

there was the look of a man who had seen too much human frailty to be deceived by anyone. 'Mr Franklin, who do you think killed Mompesson?'

'I've absolutely no idea.'

'But you won't miss him, will you?'

'No.'

He turned away and sighed. 'I don't think anyone in this house will. That's what I find so puzzling. A warmly received guest – but universally hated.'

'Surely not.'

'I think so. Even Lady Powerstock, I believe. It's as if . . .' He broke off and looked up as the sergeant came in.

'Bannister's telephoned from the White Horse, sir. Appears the Major took a room there last night. Left an hour ago, before breakfast. Said 'e was going to London.'

'How?'

'Didn't say, sir. But the train's the only way. 'E'll 'ave to change at Alton.'

Shapland took out his pocket-watch and glared at it. 'Then telephone the Alton station, man. We may be able to catch him there.' The sergeant bustled away. Suddenly Shapland dropped his stern expression and smiled at me. 'Is Thorley our culprit, Mr Franklin?'

'I don't think so.'

'We found various IOUs and bounced cheques in Mompesson's possession. Most of them were Thorley's.'

'Even so . . .'

'We shall see. You can go now. But don't leave the house without telling me.'

'I was planning to move out today.'

'Were you? Then change your plans.'

'Very well.' I turned towards the door.

'By the way, Mr Franklin: you said earlier that you and

187

Thorley left the White Horse separately. Now it appears Thorley didn't leave at all.'

'When I left, he was still there. I assumed . . .'

'Tut, tut. Assumptions are dangerous. Be sure you don't make too many. I'll see you later.'

I tried to walk past the constable at the door casually, without giving a hint of how I felt. Shapland had got under my skin. But he wasn't the only thing crawling there. Mompesson was dead, all his swaggering confidence brought down by one well-aimed gunshot. But whose? Thorley's? I hardly thought so and nor, I suspected, did Shapland. I knew I had to speak to Leonora, but knew as well that, more than ever before, I had to be cautious.

I went into the drawing room and there found Charter, dozing by the fire, as if he knew nothing of the murder inquiry going on about him. He opened his eyes at the sound of my approach and winked.

'Young Franklin,' he said, clearing his throat. 'I thought you were posted missing.'

I sat down in the chair opposite him. 'I'm afraid I got rather drunk last night and didn't make it back here.'

'I thought it must be something like that. This inspector they've dragged in took it as an admission of guilt. You've heard about Mompesson?'

'Yes. You seem to be taking it very calmly.'

'Good riddance, I say.' He smiled. 'But I don't say it in earshot of the police.'

'What would you say if I told you I did it?'

'Shake your hand.'

'But I didn't.'

'Never mind. Somebody did. That's all that matters. I beat Jepson in the end, by the way.'

'Charter, a man's been murdered. We've got to take it seriously.'

'I'll leave everyone else to do that.'

'And where is everyone else?'

'In their various bolt-holes.'

I rose and moved to the window. 'Do you know where Leonora is?'

'Gone for a walk, I think.'

'Perhaps you'll excuse me. I must have a word with her.'

I think he was asleep again before I reached the door.

I went out through the conservatory and saw her on the other side of the lawn, walking slowly, with head downcast, along the path beside the screen of maple trees that served as boundary between the garden and the parkland beyond. I walked across the lawn towards her and, when I was halfway, she saw me and stopped.

In her eyes, there was a look not of loss, though some might have read it as such, but of a further retreat, a concealed withdrawal from those who did not understand – of whom I was one.

When she spoke, her voice had some of the softness of the drizzle that hung in the air. 'Why did you come back?'

'I had no reason not to.'

'I didn't mean you to react so . . . violently.'

'React?'

'To what . . .' She looked away. 'To what you must have seen.'

'Leonora, I went to the observatory at the time you suggested. You know what I saw there. But that's all I did. I left the house afterwards, got drunk – stupid as it sounds – and came back this morning.'

'I thought . . .'

'That I killed Mompesson?'

She looked straight at me and the veil across her meaning dropped momentarily. 'I didn't mean to provoke his death. I just had to try to show somebody . . . why he had to be stopped.'

What she was implying seemed more incredible even than what I'd come to believe. 'You mean you didn't . . . care for him?'

She seemed taken aback. 'Of course not. Surely that was obvious. How much . . . did you see?'

'Enough. But not enough to make me kill a man. I've seen too much of that already. When Shapland told me, I thought you must have done it, must have been driven to it. Nobody could blame you.'

'You thought I . . .' She broke off. 'That's ridiculous.'

'Not really.' I held her eyes with mine and defied her to look away. 'It's what I wanted to believe. Remorse for ever having become involved with him. Horror at what he was somehow forcing you to do. If you did kill him, I think I could respect you for it.'

Still she did not look away. 'But I didn't.'

'Then . . . you *were* going to marry him?'

'No. I would never have done that.'

'But you are pregnant by him?'

'No. Despite all the reasons why you may suspect that, it isn't true. I am pregnant, but not by Ralph Mompesson.'

'Then . . . why did you let him . . . ?'

'I thought whoever killed him was trying to help me. And I thought that's what you'd done – for John's sake.'

'Not his alone.'

At last, she looked away. 'Perhaps not. But if you're saying you didn't kill him, I must think this through again. What you've said has worried me where you may have thought it would reassure. I must have time to think.'

She turned to walk on, but paused when I touched her elbow. 'I don't understand anything that's happened here, Leonora. You seemed to like me, yet it was Mompesson you favoured. Now you say you would never have married him and it isn't his child you're carrying. So what hold did he have over you? Did he know you were pregnant? Is that it? Was he threatening to tell people?'

'They'll know soon enough.'

'Yes, they will. But what else could it have been?'

She looked at me and in her face there seemed a yearning to tell me the truth, restrained only by overriding necessity. 'You must judge me as you see fit, Tom. I can answer none of your questions, much as I would like to. Yes, Ralph was threatening me. I felt nothing for him but fear and loathing. I didn't want him dead, but now that he is I'm not sorry. If only I could tell you all there is to know of his mind . . . all that he had planned. It was . . . horrible.' She broke off. 'But I can't. If you had killed him, I would feel I owed you the truth. If you did not, then I can't afford to tell you – I dare not.' Then she walked on hurriedly towards the rhododendron glade and I did not follow.

I went back to the house and made for my room. I needed time alone – like Leonora – to think. I slunk past the constable guarding Mompesson's room and closed my door on all that I could no longer escape.

A bath and a shave made me feel more human even if no more capable of dealing with events. Then I sat by the window, smoking a cigarette, thinking of Hallows and watching the arrival of a lumbering tow-truck, which the sergeant in charge directed towards Mompesson's car: slowly, his brash presence was being prised from our lives, but the manner of its going remained to trouble us.

There was a knock at the door. Reluctantly, I went to answer it: in the circumstances, I felt it would be unduly suspicious not to. But it wasn't the police.

Lady Powerstock stood smiling at me with a glittering falsehood apparently undimmed by the night's events. Her dark blue frock contrived to add voluptuous touches to a sombre façade and in her eyes and voice there was nothing to suggest she had been shocked – far less saddened – by her lover's dispatch.

'Why, Lieutenant Franklin. How good it is to see you back.'

With the constable at Mompesson's door in earshot, I could not speak my mind, as the tilt of her smile implied she knew. 'It wasn't my intention to stay away. I was shocked to hear what had happened.'

'It was a blow to us all.'

I decided to play her at her own game. 'I gather your maid was with you at the time.'

The smile stiffened. 'Yes. And where were you, Lieutenant . . . at the time?'

I lowered my voice. 'Not here – as you know. I didn't kill him.'

'No. I don't think you did. I don't think you're man enough to have done such a thing. And I'm in a position to know what you're man enough for – aren't I?'

'Are you?'

'But the police aren't. That's your problem.'

'Lady Powerstock, what exactly do you want?'

'Nothing you can provide. My husband would like to

see you. I can't imagine why. But I said that I would tell you. He's in his study.'

'Thank you for letting me know. I'll go down.' Then I closed the door before she had a chance to say more.

I didn't blame Shapland for thinking Meongate a strange household: it was. The prevailing calm was hardly what he can have expected after a murder. But the calm – as he seemed to suspect – was deceptive, in my case as much as any other.

And there were exceptions. As I made my way down the stairs a little while later, I met Cheriton coming up. He looked paler than ever and his hand on the banisters shock perceptibly. He stopped me on the half-landing and drew me into the angle of the wall beneath a large, drab oil painting of one of Lord Powerstock's Georgian ancestors.

'Franklin: thank God you've shown up.' His voice was as tremulous as his grasp.

'You're the first person to be glad to see me back.'

'What?' I saw that he was beyond any subtlety.

'I think the police had me down as their prime suspect.'

He grasped my arm. 'I don't . . . I don't understand what's happened, Franklin. One of us . . . somebody . . . has killed him.'

'So it would seem.'

'But . . . it's awful. I'm sure it must be . . . connected . . . that it must all be tied in . . . but how could . . . ?'

'Connected with what?'

He looked at me then with a desperate flare of hope. 'Could we . . . go somewhere . . . and talk? I need . . . I need to talk.'

'Sorry. I'm on my way to see Lord Powerstock. But . . . maybe later.'

The hope in his face crumpled and I felt sorry I could spare him no more time. 'Oh . . . I see. Right-o, Franklin. Maybe . . . I'll see you later.' He stumbled off up the stairs. I wasn't surprised the murder had tested his already strained nerves.

Lord Powerstock was waiting for me in his study, the grey light from the window behind him blurring the set and sombre lines of his expressionless face: the head proudly held but the brow sorely furrowed, as if only by a conscious suppression of the merest flicker of genuine feeling could he avert a revelation of the wreck his spirit had been reduced to.

His hand moved vaguely in some gesture of lordly greeting. 'It's good of you to have come, Franklin.'

'Not at all. I was appalled to hear what had happened.'

'Take a seat . . . and a drink, if you will. It's early, I know, but in the circumstances . . .'

I poured myself a large whisky. 'I hope the police haven't been too intrusive. I'm sorry I wasn't here to give a hand.'

'No matter, no matter.' He spoke slowly, as if dredging the words with difficulty from the slit of his pervading sorrow: a sorrow in which Mompesson's death was just one contributory grain. 'The police have . . . done their duty. It's hardly their fault.'

I sat down opposite him. 'Have they advanced any theories?'

He began to finger his tie-pin. 'Nothing was stolen. There were no signs of a forced entry. They conclude . . . Mompesson knew his murderer. I must conclude the same.'

'That's disturbing.'

'A member of the household . . . Shapland as good as said. We'd all retired for the night, so, as he sees it, it might have been any one of us.'

'I think he suspected me at one point.'

'If I did so myself . . . I would not have asked to see you. But you are my son's friend, Franklin. You . . . are the only one I can turn to.'

I was taken aback. 'Surely . . .'

He held up his hand. 'Do not trouble yourself to protest. It is so. They tell me Major Thorley is missing. If he should turn out to have killed Mompesson . . . all well and good. If not, what then?' He lowered his hand slowly, with an air of resignation.

'I don't know. Shapland can't be sure the murderer wasn't a stranger to us.'

'But we can be . . . can we not? You know how matters stood between Mompesson and my wife. Come, do not pretend otherwise – you are a perceptive man. And lately . . . I have begun to worry about Leonora. I think that you have done so also.'

There was a pain in the very tone of his telling: the pain of having known, all along, what he could have done to prevent his family's tragedy unfolding as it had. I had thought that he was merely, albeit culpably unaware, but now I knew it to be worse than that. This exile in his study was self-imposed, to keep the truth at bay. The world had taken his first wife and their only son and left him the tattered remnant of his good name. Before Olivia's threat to deprive him even of that, he had retreated into the shadowy sanctuary of his private thoughts. But, at dire need, a gentleman knows his duty and follows its prompting. That he was now trying to do.

'Lord Powerstock, did you know Mompesson

had it on his mind to propose marriage to Leonora?'

'Yes, though it was not he who told me, but Charter. At first, I could not believe it.'

'But later . . .'

'I came to see how it might be so.'

I moved towards the conclusion I felt he was willing me to draw. 'In the circumstances, killing Mompesson must have seemed . . . the right thing to do.'

He shook his head dolefully. 'Indeed it must. But not to me. I didn't kill him, though now he's dead I wish I'd had the courage – the resolution – to have done it . . . or done whatever was necessary to rid us of him. It was, after all, my responsibility. But no, I didn't. Nor did you. We carry decency too far, Franklin, you and I. We make it an excuse for not intervening in all the wrongs being done around us . . . and in our name. I fear . . . I so very much fear . . . that we left another to do what we should have done for John's sake. I very much fear . . . for Leonora.'

'Leonora?'

'She was the object of Mompesson's ambition. She was left . . . to find a way of thwarting it.'

'Could she not simply have refused him?'

He grew – if it was possible – grimmer and more hesitant still. 'My wife . . . has provided me with . . . certain evidence . . . that Leonora is in no position to refuse a proposal of marriage.' He looked down. 'I cannot . . . understand. But I am bound to forgive.'

So. He knew. Olivia had guessed – or discovered – that Leonora was pregnant and lost no time in wounding her husband with the knowledge. And now, in his despair, Mompesson's murder assumed a sinister colour. Torn between accepting a loathsome marriage and facing public disgrace, Leonora might – if driven beyond endurance – have ended her conflict of conscience with one violent act.

'I believe . . . she will talk to you, Franklin. See her. Learn what you can. Tell me what you learn – however unpalatable you think I may find it. I need to know. Above all, I need to be able to do my duty to my family. You understand?'

I felt I did. 'Yes, sir.' I rose to go. 'I'll do my best.'

He said nothing, but caught my eye as I turned at the door before going out. His one solemn nod was a consent – for me to do on his behalf whatever needed to be done.

In the hall, all was sudden bustle. The sergeant was making for the door while one of the constables followed him, bearing a bundle of Mompesson's possessions and a jumble of notes and forms. Shapland was watching them from halfway up the stairs. He grimaced at me with what I think was meant to be a smile.

'Good news, Mr Franklin,' he boomed. 'Major Thorley has been detained at Alton. We're going up there to question him. So you'll be left in peace – or whatever it is that prevails here. Constable Bannister will look in later, but you may not see me again until tomorrow. I have some enquiries to make.' By now, he had reached the foot of the stairs.

'I hope they prove fruitful, Inspector.'

'We shall see.' He turned towards the door. 'Don't worry. We shall meet again.'

So Shapland was gone – but not for long. And, in the poised uncertainty of his imminent return, life at Meongate stood still as we waited, all held suspect in our different ways, for news – of Thorley, or the post-mortem, or some revelation that might exonerate us.

None came that day, nor seemed likely to. So, as if to evade the guilt that hung implicitly over us, we kept ourselves to ourselves, sealed in our rooms, or pacing the lawns, or sitting distractedly at windows, conspiring, by our mutual silence, to pretend that nothing had happened.

But something had happened and, though I for one did not mourn Mompesson, the shock of his death and what it might mean could not be kept at bay. I lay on my bed as the afternoon slipped anxiously away, rehearsing in my chalked outline of the night's events. I clung, if only for comfort, to the plausible notion that many beyond Meongate might have had cause to hate Mompesson and one might, perhaps, have come to the house under cover of darkness and murdered him. Blackmail – in any form – had not seemed beyond him and, given his arrogance, he might well have practised it on somebody who was not about to give way.

Bannister returned from the village in mid-afternoon with no news from Alton and stood guard at the front door, though whether to keep watch on the residents or turn away visitors was not clear. Certainly, there was no word from Mompesson's friends or family, if he had either, though a shabbily dressed man did drive up – and was sent packing – who might have been a reporter. Otherwise, all eerily uneventful, as if Shapland were deliberately testing our nerves, waiting for something – or someone – to break.

From his point of view, I knew, none of us was to be trusted. Thorley, a drunkard in debt fleeing the scene of the crime, was, if anything, too obvious a candidate, though what he was blurting out even then was anybody's guess. Cheriton, it seemed clear, would run a mile at the sound of a shot, far less fire one himself. Among the resident officers, therefore, the three most accustomed to using a gun, I might seem the likeliest to have turned one on Mompesson. The fact that I could remember nothing after leaving the White Horse was bound to count against me and Shapland was not to know – as I did myself – that such a decisive act was beyond me.

What I could not deduce was how much Shapland knew – beyond his shrewd surmises – of Mompesson's relationship with the Powerstocks. His role as Olivia's lover was not in doubt, but why – after all this time – should Lord Powerstock have intervened? If he had not, then was this the fruit of some harboured jealousy on Olivia's part? She had failed in her advances to me. She might have followed me to the observatory and seen what was to be seen, might – in a rage – have murdered Mompesson if she could not have sole possession of him. But I had seen the unmistakable marks of her casual sensuality: pleasure, not possession, was her object.

Which brought me back – however I tried to avoid it – to Lord Powerstock's fear that Leonora had been driven to murder. She had denied it, but what I had seen from the observatory was either shameless and perverted, neither of which she was, or sadistic and suborned. I knew Mompesson to be the former; could Leonora have been the latter? If so, what pressure had he exerted upon her? Why was she bound to yield to his demands? The truth on that score might explain what so far had eluded me: why anyone would have had to resort to murder to be rid of Mompesson.

* * *

I had to speak to Leonora, had to make one more effort to persuade her that silence and denial were not enough. I left my room and went down to the conservatory at the time she customarily took tea there: but not that day. Only the cat was in his usual place.

As I retraced my steps, I met, in the hall, Sally, the maid, bearing a laden tea-tray towards the stairs. I asked her who it was for.

'Miss Leonora, sir. I'm 'oping she'll eat something.'

'Here,' I said, winking, 'let me take it up.' She hesitated. 'It's all right. I'll persuade her to eat some of the shortbreads – I promise.'

'I'm not sure as I should.'

'This business has been a strain for you, I imagine – being first on the scene.'

She blushed. Though too simple to convince Shapland or me that she and Lady Powerstock had discovered the body together, she was not so simple as to be unaware of that. 'As you say, sir.'

'So why not make yourself some tea while I take this?'

'Well . . . I could do with a bit of a sit down.'

I smiled. 'Off you go then.'

She was surprised to see me rather than Sally – and yet not surprised. She was sitting at a small table in the bay window, writing in her diary, with a vase of dahlias before her and a pink-curtained view of the park beyond.

'Hello, Tom,' she said simply, flipping the diary shut as she turned towards me.

'I brought your tea.'

'So I see. Won't you join me?'

'I was hoping you'd say that.' I set the tray down on a cabinet by the door. In front of me, on the wall,

200

there was a gilt-framed photograph of a wedding party: I recognized Hallows and Leonora in the centre. 'Though I expect you realize this isn't strictly a social call.'

'Only if it is are you welcome to stay.' Her face and her voice were determined, but not unkind. I looked around the room and saw there all the placidly pleasing touches that made it her particular haven: the simple but restful furnishings with a half-read novel left here and an intricate piece of embroidery there, a Turneresque landscape on one wall and an upright piano, with music in its stand, against another. There was no visible sign – beyond the wedding portrait – that Hallows had spent time there, but I could imagine him relaxing in one of the floral-patterned armchairs and watching, with quiet joy, his lovely wife jotting in her diary. At that moment, I too wished mine was just a social call.

'You know it can't be quite that,' I said, as I poured some tea and carried it over to her.

'Thank you.'

'Lord Powerstock's very worried about you. So am I. He knows, you see . . . about your condition.'

Suddenly, her tone was icy. 'You had no right to tell him. He would have heard it from me – when I judged it best.'

'As God's my witness, Leonora, I didn't tell him. I think Olivia must have guessed.'

She looked away. 'Of course.' Then back to me. 'I'm sorry. These days, I suspect . . . everybody.'

'So, I think, does Inspector Shapland. And that is why we're so worried about you.'

She smiled. 'You needn't worry for that reason. Whoever killed Ralph has my gratitude. But it wasn't me.'

I tried a guess. 'The father of the child you're carrying and the murderer of Mompesson: could they be the same person?'

The frank intensity of her look seemed to command me to believe her. 'I can't answer any of your questions, Tom.' I was to believe, then, that for the best of reasons she could tell me nothing. 'Please leave me to myself – at least for a while.'

'Very well.' There seemed nothing else for it. I moved towards the door.

'Tell Lord Powerstock not to worry – too much.'

'Won't you tell him yourself?'

'He would only be distressed by my inability to answer his questions.'

'They will have to be answered, sooner or later.'

'Then it must be later.'

'Shapland will be back by morning – with Thorley's testimony and the results of the post-mortem. What will you say then?'

'I don't know.'

'Leonora . . .'

She silenced me with a single, raised hand. 'It's no use, Tom. For our friendship's sake – for John's sake, if you like – give me time.'

I nodded in silent acquiescence and went out.

The afternoon lengthened into evening. Constable Bannister took a telephone call from Alton, then announced his departure, pending Shapland's return on the morrow. We at Meongate were left to brood.

Dinner was a strained and cheerless occasion. Leonora did not join us, sending a message via Sally that she would stay in her room. That left five of us to gather in the mannered charade of a communal meal:

Lord Powerstock was as set and stony as William de Brinon, Knight of Droxenford, whilst Lady Powerstock added a sinister silence to her sultry nocturnal presence and only Cheriton, with the quaver of his voice and the quiver of his hand, disclosed the tensions that were truly at play. To these old Charter seemed the most immune, his appetite holding up whilst others picked and sipped. And only he seemed prepared to speak – even obliquely – of what had happened.

'It'd never struck me before,' he remarked towards the end of the meal, brushing Stilton crumbs from his whiskers as he did so. 'But it seems a rum business having the police investigate so-called murders when all the armies of Europe are running the riot the other side of the Channel.'

Cheriton coughed and gulped down some water.

'I am not at all surprised,' Olivia responded, 'that the difference escapes you.'

'As you know my dear' – he smiled theatrically 'most things do . . . escape me.'

'But not all?' There was some serpentine purpose now behind her probing – and behind Charter's parries.

'Even blind and deaf old men see and hear some things – when those things are garish and loud enough.'

'It is reassuring to know that not all your senses are gone.'

Lord Powerstock brought his glass down on the table with just enough force to impose a truce. I attempted to divert the discussion.

'Should we take any steps to secure the house rather better, sir, in view of what's happened?'

'I've told Fergus to make sure all the doors are locked and windows latched.'

Olivia caught my eye with the candlelit glint of her

own. 'You truly believe then, Lieutenant, that Ralph was the victim of an intruder?'

Powerstock intervened. 'I had hoped we could avoid this kind of pointless speculation. When Inspector Shapland returns in the morning, we shall know more. In the meantime, please let us behave . . . with decorum.' There were nods of assent. 'I shall be attending morning service at St Mary's tomorrow as usual. Until then, I'll bid you all goodnight.'

He left us then and, having no taste for further sparring with Olivia or, on this occasion, the unstemmed flow of Charter's stray thoughts, I withdrew as well. Until the morning, solitude seemed the only bearable condition. I went out through the conservatory for a breath of night air, but, finding the garden door locked in testimony to Fergus' vigilance, I retreated in the direction of my room.

In the hall, I found Cheriton smoking a cigarette and walking up and down by the long-case clock beside the fireplace. I bade him goodnight.

'Oh, Franklin,' he said, 'could I . . . ?'

'Yes?'

Then he seemed to think again; he tossed the cigarette into the grate with a jerky, strangely decisive gesture. 'No. Never mind. Less said the better, what?'

'Probably. Goodnight.'

He said nothing, just smiled faintly: his face had the crumpled look of a man well aware of his own frailties. I'd seen such a look many times during the war, often in myself. Perhaps that's why I didn't look back as I climbed the stairs.

SIX

I surprised myself by sleeping soundly, at least until dawn. Then I was wide awake, pacing my room and squinting out of the window at the creeping light of a misty morning. I dressed and went downstairs, intent upon breathing some fresh air before Shapland came back and, with him, the fetid recollection of Mompesson's death.

With Fergus not yet about, I had to slip the latch on the front door and go out that way. I felt unduly conscious of the crunch of my boots on the gravel drive, amplified by the stillness and silence around me. The day was cold, with dew on the grass, but there was a promise of warmth and brightness later: the mist had a wispy quality of reassuring impermanence. I thought of France then, of waking in a dug-out after Loos the autumn before to find Hallows' batman frying bacon on the tiny stove only he could manage whilst Hallows himself stood at the sand-bagged door, greatcoat flung round his shoulders, drawing on his first cigarette of the day and straining to descry, by sight of intuition, what message the misty morning held.

I was going to walk round to the garden. But then I saw, at the edge of the grass beyond the drive, a break in the cobwebbed sheen of the dew, a footprint, a trail of footprints in fact, leading out across the park, curving away from the house and down towards the orchard. They could only recently have been made, otherwise the dew would have re-formed, yet who else could be about at such an hour? I began to follow them.

One of the elms in the park stood on a slight knoll, its thick roots stretching like a rib-cage beneath the dome of grass. There the trail of footprints led and there they ended. As I approached, I saw who'd made them. Cheriton was sitting at the foot of the tree, with his back to the trunk, cradled between the gnarled two shoulders of two descending roots and staring towards me and the house beyond.

I raised my hand in greeting but he did not respond. I glanced back at the house, its ivy-clad flint and brickwork emerging slowly from the mist, and saw how the view might have plunged him into reverie. I raised my hand again and called to him: 'Fine morning, isn't it?'

He didn't answer. And as I took one further step towards him, out of a shaft of misty sunlight into clear sight, I saw why.

Cheriton was dead. The certainty was there in the staring blankness of his eyes and the strange, stiff severity of his posture. It didn't need the clotted blood on his sagging chin or the splatter of it on the bark behind his head to tell me: he was dead and at peace. His legs were crossed, as a man's at ease might be. His right hand, which had held the revolver in his mouth, had slipped down his chest, but the fingers were still curled around the butt and trigger. His left hand was by his side, clasping an envelope.

I stooped over him and closed his eyes. It was the most and the least that I could do. I didn't feel any more moved than by all the other dead and strangely shocked young men I'd seen since the spring of 1915. Some of those too had taken their own life. But I did feel a pang of regret. Why hadn't I spared Cheriton the time he'd asked for – on the stairs, the day before? Later, when I'd been willing to talk, he hadn't been, as if, with the coming of night, he'd decided what to do. And this was it: death at the time of his choosing, a privilege the war had seemed to take from him, but now reclaimed with faltering dignity, drawing comfort from the tree, from the earth, from the dust, even from the bloody taste of ashes in his mouth.

I slid the envelope from his left hand. There could have been no more than a single sheet within. I turned it over in my hand. He had written on the front a single word, a name: *Olivia*.

I folded the word out of sight and slipped the envelope into my jacket pocket. Then I took it out again and stared at it. Should I open it? What had Cheriton said to her? And why her? I looked down at the slumped figure and wondered what it was I hadn't known about him. Had he too been led by Olivia to areas of desire he'd rather not have known about? Had he killed Mompesson? The letter might tell me, but the letter was addressed to her and, in his presence, I hadn't the heart to thwart his last wish by opening it. I put it back in my pocket. Then I began to walk slowly towards the house.

Only Fergus was up. I got him to telephone Bannister at the police station, then inform Lord Powerstock. I sat in the morning room, waiting for the shock to hit me, not of Cheriton's death, because I didn't know him well enough, but of what it seemed to mean: an implicit confession to Mompesson's murder that wrote a neat if scarcely happy *finis* to all the police probing and doubtful pondering. Except that I could already see the begged questions lining up for answers. Cheriton was no killer: that's why the war had caused him such anguish. If his death did explain all the mysteries, only the letter he'd left could tell me how. But the letter wasn't for me.

Charter came in, still in his dressing gown and Turkish slippers, white hair tousled and portly figure rumpled, his voice gruff from slumber. 'What's happened?' he rumbled.

'Cheriton's shot himself. I found him in the grounds.'

Charter slumped down in a chair. ''Pon my soul.' A look of pain passed across his face. 'Poor young fellow. Shot himself, you say?' And his great, grey old head shook slowly from side to side in mourning for the ways of youth he did not understand.

'I've asked Fergus to cover the body with a blanket. I've no doubt the police will be here soon.'

'This is a bad, sad business.'

'Is a suicide worse than murder?'

'In this case, young man, it is.'

'I suspect the police will see in it a solution to their problem: that of who killed Mompesson.'

Charter shot his eyes to the ceiling. 'No doubt they will. But you don't believe Cheriton did, do you?'

'No. As a matter of fact, I don't.'

'I must get dressed.' He hauled himself from the chair and ambled to the door. 'We'll speak again later.'

When I heard a ring at the front door, I guessed it would be Bannister and made my way to the hall. Lord

208

Powerstock was standing solemnly at the foot of the stairs whilst Fergus went to answer the bell.

'I'm sorry about this, sir,' I said.

'Not your fault,' Franklin. Nor anyone else's. Fitting, in a way: a soldier's death. Goaded beyond endurance, I suppose.'

'What do you mean?'

'By Mompesson, of course.' He seemed slightly irritated by my reservations. 'Isn't that how it was?'

'I don't know.'

He grunted, then made for the door, where Bannister was now announcing himself. 'Come with me, Constable. We'll show you where he is.'

They bustled out. I stood alone in the hall, almost on the very spot where Cheriton had stood the night before, wondering how Powerstock could be so suddenly decisive and certain. I didn't have to wonder for long. Offered a way out of confronting his suspicions about Leonora, he'd taken it, with all the excess of relief that betrayed the falsity of his confidence. He would escort Bannister to the place, he would take command of his battered but unbowed household, he would forget all the portents of a more sinister truth that he had been prepared to confront only the day before. That, I saw, was now his purpose.

I left him to it. There was something I had to do before Shapland returned. I hurried up the stairs and made straight for Lady Powerstock's room.

I went in without waiting for an answer to my knock. In the outer room, Sally was clearing a breakfast tray. She looked up in surprise. I heard Olivia's voice from the bedroom beyond. 'Who is that?'

'Lieutenant Franklin, ma'am.'

She appeared in the doorway, in a nightdress and

gown, all hints of the voluptuary suppressed: this was the dignified lady of means at the respectable conclusion of a restrained toilet. 'You may leave us, Sally.'

The maid gathered the tray and walked out past me. I closed the door behind her.

'What do you want, Lieutenant?'

'You've been told about Cheriton?'

'Naturally.'

'Then, what I want to know is why he should have left you this note.' I took the letter from my pocket.

Her eyes widened, for an instant. Then she restored the practised air of unconcern. 'I can't imagine.'

'He shot himself, you know. He put a gun in his mouth and pulled the trigger. And I found this letter in his hand, addressed to you, by your Christian name.'

She was unmoved by the details. 'Who else knows of this?'

'Of the letter – nobody.'

'And you've come to deliver it?'

'I was in two minds whether to open it at once or give you the chance of telling me what it says. I felt I owed it to Cheriton to do the latter.'

'How noble of you. But what makes you think I know what's in it?'

'Everything I know about you tells me you do. You drove Cheriton to this, didn't you?'

She walked slowly to the window, as if considering a philosophical point. 'I wonder sometimes if it is military conditioning which gives you young officers this special facility for blaming your own actions on other people.'

I tried to break free of her sarcasm. 'Lady Powerstock, two men are dead. And you had a hand in both deaths.

I know what you were to Mompesson: his whore. But what were you to Cheriton?'

She was as impervious to insults as to threats. 'I can only conjecture what's in that note. Perhaps he did become infatuated with me. Some men do' – she smiled – 'as you know. Perhaps he grew jealous of Ralph – for whatever reason – and killed him, then took his own life in remorse. Who knows?'

'We can find out – by reading this letter.'

'Of course. But consider: it may say other things. If I really was intimately involved with Lieutenant Cheriton, he might know what I know . . . of your amorous inadequacies . . . and peep-hole discoveries. He might know – and speak of it . . . in the letter.'

'That's preposterous.'

'Is it? Well, you may be right. But the Lieutenant Cheriton I knew was a young man of delicate sensibilities. I remember you speaking once of what you saw as the depravity of this house. If that was a valid perception, what if he entertained it as well? What if he saw what you saw from the observatory on Friday?'

That was her ace, played with the ease and artistry of a mistress of her craft. 'The observatory? How do you know . . . ?'

'Tut, tut, Lieutenant. Are we to be obtuse as well as absurd? Leonora's unconventional proclivities have long been known to me and have enjoyed free rein – if I may use the word – since her husband obligingly got himself killed. But I can only guess what effect a knowledge of her practices would have on a shy young man not without aspirations for the hand of an attractive young widow.'

'Cheriton? How could he possibly . . . ?'

'He may have been shown.' She smiled. 'I may have

211

thought him entitled to know. The letter may tell me what he discovered. It may tell anyone who reads it.'

'Is this true? Did you really do that?'

'Once that letter is opened, it becomes public knowledge. The beautiful young widow of a fine gentleman who died for his country shames his memory in perverted couplings with an American fortune-hunter – and is pregnant into the bargain. It would be a feast for the newspapers. But what about you . . . and Leonora . . . and my husband? What would there be left for you?'

In that moment I forgot how impossible it was to believe that Cheriton had killed Mompesson as a prelude to killing himself. In that moment, Olivia convinced me. She plucked the letter from my faltering grasp and tossed it into the grate, where the fire Sally had recently laid was crackling into life. Bright young flames began to lick around the sealed white envelope. I watched, transfixed, as the last words of a reticent man went up in smoke.

I walked downstairs in a daze, not sure where to go in the aftermath of what I had allowed Olivia to do. Fortunately, I wasn't to be left to my own devices. Bannister was waiting for me in the hall.

'I've been looking for you, Mr Franklin. The Inspector's here. Wants to see you right away.'

Without a word, I followed him into the morning room. Shapland was slumped in one of the wing-backed armchairs, sending up clouds of acrid smoke from a fat-bowled pipe.

'And so, Mr Franklin,' he said, without getting up, 'we meet again. This isn't how I'd planned to spend my Sunday morning.'

'Nor any of us, I imagine.'

'They tell me you discovered the body.'

'That is so.'

'Then, show me how.' He lurched from the chair and led the way back into the hall. 'Absent when Mompesson is murdered – first on the scene of Cheriton's suicide. I'm not sure whether to compliment you on your timing or sympathize with your bad luck.'

'Neither is necessary.'

'If you say so.' We came to the front door, where Bannister stood back to let us pass. 'Did you come out this way?'

'Yes.' I blinked in the sudden brightness as we stepped out on to the drive. 'I hadn't slept too well and decided to take a stroll before breakfast.'

Out in the sunlight of the day, with the last of the mist burned away, Shapland looked more rumpled and seedy than ever, but still artful and dogged enough to see through most deceptions. 'Why come out this way?'

'Since the . . . murder, all the doors have been locked at night. I knew I could lift the latch on the front door.'

He nodded and gazed down the drive. 'And why did you head across the park rather than stick to the gravel?' He ground his heel in it. 'Unless it was too noisy for your purpose?'

'It's true I didn't want to disturb anybody – but there's nothing sinister in that.'

'Let me be the judge of what is and isn't sinister, Mr Franklin.'

I exerted myself to remain unruffled. 'Very well. I'd probably have struck across the park anyway, but then I noticed footprints in the dew.'

'Where?'

I walked to the spot at the edge of the grass. 'Here.

Footprints leading away from the house. Quite distinct in the dew, which meant . . .'

'They were recently made, probably since dawn.' He joined me on the grass. 'So you followed them?'

'Yes.'

'Why?'

'I didn't know anybody else was up. I was curious – and worried; it might have been an intruder.'

'Unlikely, if the footprints only led away from the house.'

'So I thought.'

'Lord Powerstock's servant is adamant he put the catch down on the front-door latch last night. Is that how you found it?'

'I don't think so. I think it was up already. But I can't be sure.'

'He moved ahead of me across the grass and I followed. 'If it had been an intruder – or even if it hadn't – you might have found yourself alone with Mompesson's murderer.' He stopped and looked at me. 'Did that worry you?'

I stopped alongside him. 'Not unduly. I didn't think of it in those terms.'

'No. I suppose not.' We went on again, aiming un-erringly for the elm on the knoll where I'd found Cheriton. 'So what did you expect?'

'Somebody else who couldn't sleep. That's all.'

'And was Lieutenant Cheriton a sound sleeper?'

'Invalid officers seldom are, Inspector. As it happens, since my room was next to Cheriton's, I'm in a position to know that he suffered a good deal with nightmares.'

Shapland nodded. 'No doubt.' We topped the knoll and rounded the bole of the tree; I was relieved to see that the body had been removed, though string between a couple of stakes had been used to mark off the spot. 'And you found him here?'

'Yes.'

'Describe how he was – if you will.'

'Surely you've seen . . .'

'I'd like to hear it from your own lips, Mr Franklin. Please.'

So I told him, in as much detail as I could, omitting only the note I'd removed. As I went through it all, Shapland crouched on his haunches by the string, sucking on his pipe and glaring back occasionally at the house. When I'd finished, he remained silent for some time, then tapped his pipe out on one of the tree roots and rose to look at me.

'The condition of the body as it was shown to me – and as you've described it – leaves no room for doubt. He took his own life. But why?'

'Who can say?'

'You could hazard a guess, Mr Franklin. Yes, I think you could do that. Lord Powerstock hasn't hesitated. He takes it to be an admission of Mompesson's murder. He tells me that Cheriton was often taunted – or felt taunted – by Mompesson about his war record. His Lordship tells me that it was touch and go whether Cheriton would be sent here to convalesce or be court-martialled for cowardice. He thinks Mompesson may have got wind of that and used it against Cheriton. What do you think?'

'I think Lord Powerstock would know better than I. I've not been here as long as Cheriton. And I wasn't privy to the reasons why he came. But what you've told me doesn't seem out of character – for either Cheriton or Mompesson.'

'How would Mompesson have come by such information?'

'I imagine somebody must have told him.'

'By implication, Lady Powerstock?'

'That's your inference, Inspector. I'm implying nothing.'

He turned back to the marked-off space at the foot of the tree. 'Laying Mompesson's murder at this poor young wretch's door solves everybody's problems, of course. The Powerstock family name is left intact and you and I can go our separate ways and forget all about it. It's altogether too convenient for my liking.'

'Surely you shouldn't rule it out on those grounds.'

'I don't. But nor do I come easily to the conclusion that a nerve-shattered young man unable to cope with the pressures of war could summon the resolution necessary to murder Mompesson.'

'Perhaps he just snapped.'

'Perhaps. But he'd have needed a cool nerve to sit tight in his room till the body was found. And I didn't get a whiff of that when I questioned him yesterday. He seemed nervous, yes, but about going back to France, not my enquiries. Do you know when he was due to resume active service?'

'He told me he had a medical board at the end of the month.'

'And how did he seem to be facing up to the prospect?'

'Badly. He didn't want to go back. But none of us does, believe me.'

'I do, I do.' He began to wander down the far side of the knoll, as if finished with the place. As before, I followed. 'I'll tell you what troubles me, Mr Franklin. Suicide for fear of going back to the Front fits everything

I've seen. It's just that the timing's wrong. Why so soon after the murder? I don't like coincidences – they make me restless. That's what supports the idea that Cheriton was the murderer. Except that I don't believe it was in his nature. Do you?'

'I can't say.'

'A suicide note would have convinced me. A confession in his hand. I'm surprised he didn't leave one. These young, sensitive types usually do. But you found nothing?'

I steeled myself to sound expressionless. 'Nothing.'

'That's odd.' We went on in silence for a while, taking a vague route between the spaced elms towards the orchard. Then he resumed. 'It's especially odd in view of the position of his left hand. Did you notice it?' He looked at me with a smile.

'I don't think so.'

'It was placed neatly by his side. And the fingers and thumb were held just so' – he held up his own hand to depict the gesture - 'as if he'd been holding something in that hand – holding it there when he died. Yet you saw nothing.'

'There was nothing there.'

'Unless somebody else had removed it.'

'There were no other footprints in the dew. Nobody else had been there.'

He smiled at me. 'No. I don't suppose they had. Shall we go back to the house?' He wheeled in that direction without waiting for an answer. 'You haven't asked, by the way.'

'Asked what?'

'About Thorley.'

'I felt sure you'd tell me – if you wanted me to know.'

He laughed, so warmly I could believe he was

genuinely amused. Very good, very good. Well, we caught up with him at Alton and he corroborated your account of Friday night – as far as he could. Then we released him.'

'Just like that?'

'I have his address in London. And we're keeping an eye on him. But I don't regard him as a serious suspect. He had some kind of motive and he definitely had the means and opportunity. But he doesn't have what it takes to kill a man in cold blood. Nor did Cheriton.'

'What does it take?'

We paused at the edge of the drive. 'It takes what you've got, Mr Franklin: not the hot-blooded fury of the warrior or the half-crazed frenzy of the coward, but the finely controlled turmoil of a man at odds with himself.'

I tried to outface him. 'You've mistaken your man, Inspector.'

'You may be right. I've made plenty of mistakes in my time. It's an occupational hazard. If you want my candid opinion, I think my superiors will settle for the Cheriton version. It's much neater and it'll keep Lord Powerstock happy. But I shan't make it easy for them. I shan't let them forget the inconsistencies.'

'Such as?'

'Such as the calibre of Cheriton's revolver: standard army issue. Whereas the post-mortem reveals Mompesson was shot with a smaller, quieter weapon. Almost, you might say, a lady's weapon.'

'What do you conclude from that?'

'I conclude you know more than you're telling, Mr Franklin, and that, perhaps, you're protecting somebody – or yourself. I don't blame you for letting suspicion fall on Cheriton. It can't hurt him now, after all. But you needn't think I'm taken in by it – not for a moment.'

'There's nothing to be taken in by.'

'Perhaps not.' He made as if to walk away, then turned back to face me. 'There is one more thing that's puzzling me, though. You said the footprints in the dew looked fresh.'

'Yes.'

'But you heard no gunshot?'

'Not consciously, though I suppose it might have been what woke me. Still, my window was shut and he was some way from the house.'

'His bed hadn't been slept in, you know.'

'Are you suggesting he was out there all night?'

'The post-mortem will tell us that. But it seems unlikely. Rigor mortis hadn't set in when I saw the body.'

'My impression was that he'd been dead not much more than half an hour or so. That would fit with first light. I can't imagine him going out there in the dark.'

'No. Nor can I. Which suggests nobody – apart from you – could have removed a note, if there was one.'

'But there wasn't.'

He nodded slowly, though the expression on his face drained all the assent from the gesture. 'Well, we'll talk again later . . . I have no doubt.' Then he slouched away across the drive and disappeared into the house. I watched him go, cursing myself silently for all the lies I'd been forced to tell by that one concession to Olivia's threats, that one act which went so far to confirm Shapland's suspicions that I could almost believe them myself. He'd warned me of his tracker's instinct for complicity in a crime and still I'd gone ahead and done enough to prove him right for all the wrong reasons. Now he was on my trail.

*   *   *

How I envied Thorley as that long, absurdly sun-splashed Sunday slipped painfully away at Meongate. For reasons of his own, Shapland had let Thorley go, but I was required to remain, expected to wait patiently whilst all I knew was a seething restlessness of body and mind. Perhaps that was Shapland's hope that in some sudden release of the tension I would reveal the truth he thought I possessed. Little did he know that for me as much as for him that truth was still only a shifting, uncertain shape in the darkness glimpsed from the corner of the eye, never there when you looked in its direction.

I didn't wait for the police to leave, but took myself off for a long walk round the lanes, reasoning that physical exhaustion was about the only kind of comfort I could hope for. I could never now hope to know what Cheriton's note contained, but I couldn't stop trying to guess. That, I realized, was the measure of Olivia's cruelty in persuading me to give it up. I had escaped one kind of seduction only to succumb to another.

I did not return to Meongate until early evening. An uneasy quietude that might have seemed at any other time merely peaceful hung upon the place. There was no sign of the police, nor, indeed, of anyone else. The ticking of the clock in the hall was magnified by a background of silence and immobility. Cheriton was no longer there to pace and fret, nor Mompesson to smile and swagger. There was no click of balls from the billiards room to signal Thorley passing an idle hour. In different ways to different ends, they'd gone.

I was about to go up to my bedroom when I heard something, a slight and delicate rustle from the morning room: somebody was there after all.

I went in and found Leonora, seated in a corner reading a book: it was the turning of a page that I'd heard. She looked up without smiling and put the book down on a side-table.

'Hello, Tom,' she said gravely.

'When I came in, I thought the house was deserted.'

'Lord Powerstock was unable, for obvious reasons, to attend morning service, so he's gone to evensong instead. And Olivia's gone too. She wouldn't want him to be seen there alone. I've not seen Charter since this morning. Nor you, till now.'

'I've had a lot to think about.'

She looked directly at me for the first time. 'I was so very sorry to hear about Lieutenant Cheriton. To take his own life . . . It's awful.'

I walked slowly over to the cabinet and poured myself a Scotch. 'I'm not sure it is awful.'

'What do you mean?'

I went back with the Scotch and sat opposite her, hunched in my chair. 'He'd probably have been killed when he went back to France anyway.'

'That's hardly . . .'

'And when I found him, he looked somehow more peaceful than he'd ever seemed here.'

'Why should he have done such a thing?'

'Maybe because he killed Mompesson.' I swallowed some of the whisky. 'But I don't think he did, do you?'

'No.'

I wanted to tell her then that I'd given away the only evidence Cheriton had cared to leave, but instead I drank a little more whisky and told myself to believe that the note had never existed. 'I don't suppose the truth of it will ever be known.'

'Perhaps not.'

I set the glass down and rose from my chair. 'Leonora . . .' I struggled for the words with which to approach the issue between us.

'Yes?'

'How well did you know Cheriton?'

'Hardly at all. He kept himself to himself, perhaps too much so for his own good.'

'It's just that . . .' As I looked down at her, my eye was taken by the book she'd been reading. It lay face down, but on its spine was a title at once familiar to me: *Deliberations of the Diocesan Committee for the Relief of the Poor of Portsea*. Why that, of all books, at such a time? I stared at it in puzzlement.

'Is something wrong?'

'This book . . .'

'You know it?'

'Yes. I saw it in the library. But . . .'

She seemed strangely defensive. 'Why should I not be reading it?'

I went back to my chair. 'No reason. No reason other than . . . How is it possible, after all that has happened, with two men dead, with your home in uproar, for you to sit here, quietly reading an obscure volume of social research?'

'I'm sorry if I disappoint you.'

'You don't. You baffle me. This book is dedicated to John's mother, isn't it? She wrote part of it. Yet there seems more to it than that. Olivia called it a convenient fiction. What did she mean by that?'

'She meant she resented Miriam's memory.'

'Of course. But why read it now? Something with so little bearing on the present. It seems . . . heartless.'

'Think that if you must.'

'Unless . . . it has a bearing.'

She seemed about to say something. The form of a word hovered on her lips. I could believe, in the half-light of descending evening, that she was about to vouchsafe a secret. Then something stopped her. She looked abruptly towards the french windows that led to the conservatory and by the sharp intake of her breath I knew that somebody was there.

It was Shapland. A ragged, slope-shouldered, apologetic figure framed in the doorway, cast in crepuscular shadow. I jumped up.

'Inspector . . .'

He scratched his head and smiled as he advanced across the room. 'Sorry to disturb you. I came round through the garden. The scent of the lavender is . . .'

'Spare us the botany, Inspector. What do you want?'

'Don't take on so, Mr Franklin. I didn't mean to interrupt. Why not let Mrs Hallows continue with what she was saying? Something with a bearing on my enquiries, perhaps.'

Leonora smiled disarmingly. 'It was nothing, Inspector, I assure you. We were merely discussing a book we've both read.'

Shapland stooped and tilted the book so as to read its title. His brow furrowed. 'Portsea? You surprise me, Mrs Hallows.'

'Why?'

'Hardly an edifying subject for a fine lady. I served my time as a constable there forty years ago, before the Diocesan Committee took much of an interest, I'm afraid. I gather the first Lady Powerstock picked up the contagion that killed her there – and I can't say I'm surprised.'

'You seem well informed about my family.'

'I've learned a little – but not why murder or suicide

should have come to this house. Nor what bearing the first Lady Powerstock's good works in Portsea have upon the case.'

'As I've told you: none at all.'

At that, I intervened. 'Inspector, what can we do for you? It's late for unannounced arrivals.'

He grinned at me. 'I was hoping to see Mr Gladwin. He's the only member of the household I've not questioned.'

'I doubt he can tell you much.'

'Nevertheless . . .'

Leonora rose abruptly and crossed to push the servants' bell by the door. 'I think you'll find him resting in his room, Inspector. I'll have you shown up.'

'Thank you.'

'I hope you'll bear in mind that he is very elderly.'

'Aren't we all? Don't worry, Mrs Hallows. I shan't keep him long. Like Mr Franklin, I don't expect him to tell me anything that will alter my conclusions.'

'And what are those conclusions?'

'Officially, I'm inclined to go along with the theory that Cheriton killed Mompesson and then killed himself. Unofficially, I don't believe a word of it. But, since everybody wants me to plump for that, who am I to resist?'

At that point, Fergus came in and, at Leonora's request, showed Shapland up to Gladwin's room. I watched him go with relief, but, if Leonora felt the same, she didn't show it.

'He thinks I had a hand in this,' I said after a while.

'So did I, at first.' She had resumed her seat and that same look of wisdom beyond my reach.

'But not now?'

'No. Not now. Now I think it is you who are

224

suspicious of me. And for that I cannot blame you.'

'I only want to help. You know that. Everything you seem to be, everything I feel about you, is contradicted by all I've seen in this house.'

'I realize that. I wish it were not so.'

'Was Shapland right then? Are we all condoning a presumption of Cheriton's guilt to hide our own?'

'Tom, you must believe I know nothing of what drove Lieutenant Cheriton to kill himself.'

It was too much. This time, I had to tell her. I poured myself some more whisky. 'Cheriton left a note. I destroyed it without reading it. Shapland knows nothing about it.' I had not dared to look at her as I spoke, but, when I turned towards her, her expression was unaltered.

'Oh, Tom. You shouldn't have done that.'

'Believe it or not, I did it for you. I believed the note might contain some evidence linking you with Mompesson.'

'What made you think that?'

'Olivia . . .'

'What has she to do with this?'

'The note was addressed to her. She persuaded me to let her destroy it – for everybody's sake.'

She shook her head slowly. 'She has deceived you. It can have served only her ends.'

'I know. But she convinced me that Cheriton knew as much as I did. And I couldn't let that knowledge reach Shapland. I was afraid – am still afraid – that Cheriton might have visited the observatory before or after me.'

'How could he have done? He had no key.'

'That's just it. When I went there, at the time you specified, the door was unlocked.'

She looked down. 'Oh God.'

'What's wrong? What does it mean?'

'It means that what I most feared has happened – and I don't know what to do.'

'Then let me try to help. I think John would have wanted you to let me.'

A smile hovered on her lips. 'Yes. I think you're right. But I can't speak of it now . . . with Inspector Shapland upstairs and Olivia due back at any moment.'

'What then?'

'Tomorrow. We'll go for a ride in the trap, get away from this house. Then I'll tell you all that I can.'

'Very well.'

'Now I think I'll go to my room. I don't want to be here when Olivia returns.' She rose. 'I'll ask Fergus to get the trap ready at ten.'

'I'll look forward to it.'

'I'm not sure you should.' She moved to the door. 'Good night, Tom.'

She went out quietly, closing the door behind her, and leaving me to ponder in the failing light what she could not tell me till morning. I crossed to the table and picked up the book she'd been reading. The pages fell open, as if from frequent use, at Miriam Powerstock's posthumous contribution. I lit the oil lamp beside the chair, sat down and began to read.

'Squalor Amidst Plenty' was very much what I'd expected: a measured but compassionate plea for attention to be given to the material and moral welfare of the people of Portsea . . . good, civilized, tub-thumping prose. I could easily imagine Hallows' regard for the mother who wrote and felt such things. 'There is a regrettable tendency to expect little of the humblest and oldest quarter of a dockyard town beyond the poverty and prostitution, the drunkenness and degradation, that we actually find there. With that complacent attitude this essay and this writer have no sympathy. Too long have we tolerated this slur upon our conscience. Too long have we ignored the misery and misfortune of those whose tragedy is that they know nothing beyond the mean alleys and diseased dwellings of Portsea.'

It went on in much the same vein. The late Lady Powerstock proved by the depth of her review that she knew the people and places she was describing well enough to justify her conclusion: that without the respect and help of their betters, the inhabitants of the area could not hope to escape the disease and squalor which made them notorious. Of the barefoot children and ragged, drunken men, the scabbed harlots and carousing sailors, the labyrinth of drinking dens and decrepit tenements, she wrote evocatively. She was brave to have visited them and braver still to tell others what they did not want to hear. But, as I and others knew, it had done her no good. Living words from a dead woman: they meant little enough to me at the time. Little enough indeed, for I had not the eyes to see what Leonora had truly been reading.

Noises from the hall alerted me to Lord and Lady Powerstock's return. Having, like Leonora, no wish to see them, I slipped out of the room and headed for the back stairs. As I went, I heard Shapland explaining his presence to Olivia; evidently, he'd finished with Charter.

I slept well that night. Somehow, the thought that Leonora would at last tell me the truth that lay behind those weeks at Meongate was comforting. It kept my hope alive that her account would leave my respect for her intact and the way to love still open.

I took breakfast with Charter, who was, for once, more sombre than me, picking at his kipper with the air of a preoccupied man.

'I hope the Inspector didn't give you a hard time last night,' I said, in an effort to lighten the mood.

He shook his head where normally he would have smiled. 'It would take more than that fellow to give me a hard time. Matter of fact, I think it was rather the other way about.'

'It's just that you seem a bit . . . down.'

'I don't like to see young lives wasted, that's all. It depresses me.'

'You mean Cheriton?'

'Of course.'

'Lord Powerstock seems to think it resolved matters in the best way we could hope for.'

'Edward's a good enough man. It's a pity he doesn't sometimes have a little more imagination.'

'So you don't . . . ?'

I broke off at the sound of running feet from the hall. Sally burst into the room, flushed and breathless.

'What's the matter, girl?' said Charter.

'Oh sir, I'm worried.' She caught her breath. 'I took a tray up to Miss Leonora's room – and she wasn't there. Bed not slept in, nor nothing. But . . . there was this note, left where I couldn't miss it.' She held up an envelope. 'It's addressed to Mr Franklin.'

I rose and took it from her trembling hand. Already, I shared her foreboding.

'What's it say, man?'

I opened the envelope and took out the note inside, scanned it, then read it aloud. 'Tom: I am sorry to break our appointment, but, in the circumstances, feel bound to do so. There are certain matters which I must confront and I cannot share the responsibility for doing so, much as I would like to. Accordingly, I am going away this morning by an early train. Please tell Charter and Lord Powerstock not to worry. I hope to be back within a few days at most. Until then, I must ask you to be patient. Leonora.'

Charter stared at me with a little of the incredulity I felt myself. 'Gone away? Gone where?'

But I could give him no answer.

When Lord Powerstock was given the news, he asked to see me in his study. To my surprise, Olivia was with him, patrolling the carpet with regal severity whilst Powerstock sat, crumpled and forlorn, at his desk.

Olivia allowed no scope for niceties. 'What do you know, Lieutenant, about this melodramatic disappearance?'

I was too troubled myself to disguise my dislike of her. 'As much as you, Lady Powerstock – and as little.'

Her eyes flashed a look of simmering rage; apparently, this latest turn of events did not suit her plans. 'The note was addressed to you – and referred to an appointment.'

'We had planned a ride in the trap. That's all.'

'How do you think this will look – just when the police seemed satisfied that there was no more to investigate?'

'I should have thought Leonora's welfare was of more concern than appearances.'

'Then, what can you tell us? Inspector Shapland mentioned last night that he had found you together in the morning room, which means you were the last to see her. What did you discuss with her?'

'Nothing – of any relevance.' I turned in desperation to her husband. 'Lord Powerstock – you must realize I had no part in this.'

He cast a wan glance towards me. 'My wife fears, as do I, that Leonora may have sought . . . medical treatment.'

'What?' I swung back to face Olivia.

'Must we spell it out, Lieutenant? An abortion.'

'That's absurd.'

'In the circumstances, I should have said it was the only sensible thing she could do, if she pays any heed to those "appearances" for which you have such contempt. Unfortunately, she may also have been so foolish as to contemplate using an unqualified practitioner in the interests of secrecy.'

Was it possible? Olivia had turned the knife in the wound of my suspicion. 'That's a monstrous suggestion.'

'Possibly. But it is what we believe is in her mind. And yours.'

'Mine?'

'Perhaps you thought it chivalrous to agree to cover her tracks in this way.'

'This is ridiculous. Lord Powerstock . . .'

But he had been persuaded – or suborned – to take her part. 'I have assumed, for all our sakes, my boy, that Cheriton shot himself out of remorse for killing Mompesson, but it is possible that he was actually driven to it by the knowledge that he was responsible for Leonora's . . . condition. There is the note to consider, after all.'

'The note?'

'Naturally, Olivia has informed me of its existence.' He cast a sickly smile in her direction. 'The fact that it was addressed to Leonora . . .'

'Leonora?' I looked from one to the other of them and realized at once that protest was useless. Now that the note was destroyed, I could never hope to convince Powerstock that it was addressed to his own wife. By confiding in him so falsely and so soon, she had out-flanked me. And now Leonora's flight seemed to confirm all her vilest implications.

Even as the thoughts went through my head, Powerstock resumed his vein of craven credulity. 'So you see, my boy, that we really must ask you to tell us where she has gone. Otherwise, how can we help her?'

My thoughts whirled on without him. Olivia knew full well I had no means of divining Leonora's whereabouts, which could only mean she did not want to find her, whilst appearing, for her husband's benefit, to be full of concern. It began to make a horrible kind of sense.

'I have no idea where Leonora may have gone, but I'm sure she wouldn't even consider what you're envisaging.'

There was a sneering curl to Olivia's mouth. 'We do know her rather better than you, Lieutenant.'

I attempted to retaliate. 'In that case, I suggest you inform Inspector Shapland and ask him to trace her.'

'You know very well that we cannot do that.'

'Why not?'

Powerstock intervened in stricken tones. 'If the police were to discover Leonora's circumstances, they might misconstrue the situation completely. We need an end of police investigations.'

'Then you must trust in Leonora's judgement.'

'It is doing that,' said Olivia, 'that has caused this problem.'

'All we are asking,' Powerstock continued, 'is that you be frank with us.'

'I doubt you'd like it if I were. My recommendation stands: go to the police.'

Olivia moved to her husband's side in a gesture full of the concern she did not feel. 'If Leonora comes to any harm, Lieutenant, we will hold you responsible.'

'Then I'll solve your problem for you. If Leonora hasn't returned by tonight, I'll go to the police myself.'

'You wouldn't do that.'

I moved to the door. 'Wait and see.' Then I left, before Olivia had a chance to find some chink in my resolve.

It may have sounded like an ultimatum. If so, it was as much an ultimatum to myself as to Lord and Lady Powerstock. With Leonora gone, the revelation she'd promised me had been snatched away, leaving me with a craving for truth beyond all other considerations. Now I had to know, had to understand all that had happened. Nothing less would do.

I struck out from the house at once: aimless walking drained me of the anger that threatened to spill over into senseless action. That morning, as I neared the gates at the foot of the drive, I saw a canvas-topped car pull up in the lane and recognized it as the single cab old Taylor ran from the garage in Droxford. A slight figure in a black overcoat and Homburg, looking over-dressed for the warmth of the day, climbed down, paid him off and walked slowly in through the gates as the cab pulled away.

'Good morning,' I said.

He drew up sharply, as if he hadn't seen me till then. 'Oh . . . yes . . . good morning.' A blinking, mild-faced little man with the etiolated look of a clerk far from his office.

'Can I help you?'

'Is this . . . Meongate?' His voice was low and hesitant.

'Yes. It is.'

'My name is . . . Cheriton. George Cheriton.' Then, of course, I knew who he was and why he was there.

'You must be David's father.' He nodded. 'My name's Franklin, Mr Cheriton.' I held out my hand. 'Please accept my condolences. I knew your son only slightly, but yours must be a great loss.'

He shook my hand weakly. 'It's good of you . . . to say so. It's come as a great shock . . . naturally. It's not how we had . . .' His voice tailed off, then recovered. 'Mrs Cheriton is very upset. I've come . . . to collect David's belongings. If I may.'

'I'm sure Lord and Lady Powerstock would like to see you. They're both in. Why not go up to the house?'

'Thank you. I will.' He moved past me at a vague, shuffling step and I watched him proceed, with painful slowness, up the drive. This, I thought, is the real cost of Cheriton's suicide: an elderly, unassuming parent reduced to numbed despair, a stain of shame on his wreath of mourning, a death we thought of little account magnified by one mans' obscure grief. This, I thought, is why I must find out the truth. It was the least I owed him.

I passed the day wandering aimlessly the hills and lanes that rolled west from the Meon valley towards Winchester: a landscape ignored by war, the trees thickly leafed and stirred by gentle breezes, rabbits scurrying in the corners of corn-stooked fields and geese screeching in distant farmyards, a homeland made strange by the conflict I'd known – and still knew, as it stalked me, down the peaceful afternoon, back to Meongate.

* * *

I returned late, after a detour for supper to an inn at West Meon, far enough from Droxford to escape attention from local gossips. Dinner was over, as I'd hoped, and only Charter was still about, seated by the fire and straining his eyes over a leather-bound book. As I entered, he plucked off his pince-nez and peered through the drawing room gloom towards me.

'Franklin: where have you been hiding?'

'I've been walking. I couldn't stay here. Has Leonora returned?'

I already knew the answer before he gave it. 'No. Did you expect her to?'

I sighed. 'No. Not really. I . . . hoped.' I slumped into the armchair opposite him.

'Not enough, my boy, not enough. Where's she taken herself off to? That's the question. Olivia seems to think you know.'

'That's just for Lord Powerstock's benefit. I've no idea where she is. We were going for a ride in the trap. Instead – this happened.'

'Then what's to be done?'

'I think we must go to the police. I'm sure Shapland could find her.'

'Edward wouldn't hear of it. It would revive the scandal just when it's dying down. Shapland's been here today and told him he's recommending no further enquiries.'

'On the assumption that Cheriton killed Mompesson?'

'That's the size of it. It'll break his father's heart. He came here today, you know.'

'Yes. I met him as I was leaving. And I agree: it will break his heart, if it hasn't already. But our first

234

consideration must be Leonora. If she's not back by morning, I'll go to Shapland.'

'I think you should, my boy. I think you should. But, for now, you look as if you need some rest.'

He was right. A more than merely physical fatigue was creeping upon me. I rose to leave him and, as I did so, he re-opened his book. 'What are you reading?' I asked as I moved past him. The book was plainly bound, with no title visible.

'This? Oh, jottings of my own, you know.'

'Really?'

'Yes. I kept a diary when I was younger. I had some of them bound up when I felt I was getting too old for my days to be worth recording.' He winked at me. 'I like to refer to them from time to time. It's amazing how much an old fellow like me forgets. This one covers five years in the 1860s.'

'What were you up to then?'

'I went wherever my father's business took me. And that was anywhere a cargo was to be had – the Baltic, the Mediterranean, the Caribbean. Great days, great days.'

'When I'm less tired, I'd like to hear about them.'

I'm not sure I really meant it. I felt this was no time – if there ever was a time – to be immersed in Charter's interminable reminiscences. I was only surprised he felt able to concentrate on them himself. So I made my way up to my room without heeding what he might have been trying to tell me.

Nothing had changed by morning. The house stood enveloped in the cool, grey indifference of another day, and of Leonora there was still no sign.

I knew then that I was right: we couldn't leave her to

her own devices any longer. Wherever she'd gone, whyever she'd gone there, we had to follow.

I decided to dodge further debate on the issue by cutting breakfast and going straight to the police station in the village, there to make contact with Shapland. But it wasn't to be as easy as that. As I came down the stairs, I saw that Olivia was waiting for me in the hall, disdainfully perusing the morning's copy of *The Times*. She looked more arrogantly feline than ever in an orientally patterned dress and casual pose: a coiled, carnal threat and a flashing glance up the stairs towards me.

'Lieutenant Franklin. I'm pleased to see you up so early. Have you given any further thought to our discussion yesterday?'

I said nothing until I'd drawn level with her at the foot of the stairs. 'You may fool your husband, but you don't fool me. I should never have let you have Cheriton's note.'

'It was your decision. You agreed that it was for the best.'

'I didn't know you were going to lie about it later.'

'Then obviously you're wrong. I do fool you.'

'No more. I understand you now. It was just that, before, I couldn't believe anybody could be so heartless as you undoubtedly are.'

'We must all protect ourselves.'

Now that my mind was made up, I was determined to spare her nothing. 'That's not good enough. If the war's taught me anything, it's that we must protect others as well as ourselves. The fact that Mompesson was your lover isn't so bad in itself. It's that you felt nothing for him. Or for Cheriton. That's what's beneath contempt. It's that you're happy now to bury their deaths under a fiction that persuades nobody except

Lord Powerstock simply in order to preserve the husk of your good name. And that's all it is: a husk. The core's been eaten away by your own depravity.'

'Tell me, Lieutenant, what do you think gives you the right to talk to me like this?'

'That decrepit old man who came here yesterday to collect Cheriton's belongings. The picture in the library and the one in your bedroom. They remind me of my obligations to dead men. One whose last words I let you destroy unread and one whose last painting I understood too late. They're what give me the right to do this.'

'And what is it you're going to do?'

'I'm going to see Shapland and tell him everything I know. Everything that may enable him to find Leonora.'

'I can't stop you, of course, but I think I should warn you: once you involve this man Shapland, there'll be no end to it. He'll root out everything there is to be found – not all of it to your credit.'

'You won't sway me this time.'

'It'll be the excuse he needs to re-open his murder inquiry.'

'I have nothing to fear from that.'

'Really?' She drew closer, with a hint of menace. 'Once it's established that Cheriton didn't kill Ralph, the question will be: who did? Imagine all the good reasons why the answer might be Leonora. Then ask yourself if going to the police now is really in her interests.'

'You might be trying to distract attention from yourself, Lady Powerstock. Imagine all the good reasons why a link between Leonora and Mompesson could be thought to have made you murderously jealous.'

She drew back slightly. 'The Army has trained you too well, Lieutenant. You think only in straight lines. You still do not understand. Neither of us knows what the other knows save this: that we stand or fall together. If you try to destroy me, you may succeed. But it is certain you will destroy yourself. That is the truth which you claim to desire.'

'Too late. My mind is made up.'

'You overrate your own decisiveness. I know you for the equivocator you really are. Look at this.' She thrust the newspaper towards me, folded open at the roll of honour. A tightly packed column of dead officers' names marched across my gaze: the daily consignment of futile, epauletted sacrifice. 'You can end up like those without the slightest difficulty. John did it easily enough. You can make a fuss about one fellow officer who died here rather than in France and, maybe, blacken our name. Then you can go back out there and be killed in your turn. Is that what you really want?'

'I'm aware of the bleakness of my prospects, Lady Powerstock. What I want now is the truth.'

'That is a luxury we can ill afford in times of war. If you could bring yourself to realize that, your prospects might not be so bleak.'

'Oh?'

'Lord Powerstock and I have influential friends in the War Office. It would not be difficult to arrange for you to be posted somewhere where your prospects of survival – not to mention advancement – would be greatly enhanced.'

I looked straight at her. 'In return for my silence?'

'It is a simple enough service to render. John felt obliged to follow his regiment to France and where is he now? Will you make the same mistake?'

'I've already made too many mistakes. This time I shall do what I know to be right. Excuse me.' I made for the door. I'd been stung into refuting her implication that I could once again be swayed, but already I sensed she was not entirely in error: somewhere the claws of her corruption still clung to my sense of self-preservation. I wanted to be out of her sight before she could tighten her grip.

'Be sure you know what you're walking out on, Lieutenant.'

I wasn't sure, not sure at all. But I kept on walking.

Droxford police station was a solid, two-storey, red-brick building down a side turning off the main street of the village. I entered the outer office and found Shapland sooner than I'd expected. He was seated at a low desk behind the counter, sifting through some documents jumbled in a shoe box, whilst a wall clock behind him beat time to his deliberations and stale tobacco mixed in the air with the scent of polished wood and old linoleum.

Shapland looked up at the sound of the door creaking shut behind me. 'Well, Mr Franklin. Do step in.'

'I hoped to find you here, Inspector.'

'You were lucky. There's not much left for me to do here. Now that my enquiries have finished.'

'Finished?'

'Didn't they tell you? The Chief Constable's considered my report and our official conclusion is that Cheriton killed Mompesson, then killed himself. Subject to the findings of the inquests, of course. They'll be held next week: Tuesday the third of October. You'll be required to give evidence about Cheriton, so I'm afraid I'll have to ask you to be available until then.'

'This conclusion: is it yours?'

'Of course not. But the Chief Constable's not inclined

to pursue the matter on the basis of my unsubstantiated suspicion. Not where a peer of the realm's involved.'

'Frustrating for you, I imagine.'

'Not a bit of it.' The communicating door from the police house swung open and Constable Bannister entered, bearing a tray. 'Ah, here's breakfast. Do you want some?'

'No thanks.'

Bannister eased past me and placed the tray on the desk in front of Shapland, who snatched away a paper he'd been studying. Bannister cast me a sheepish look and retreated. 'Not even some tea?'

'I don't think so.'

'Please yourself. George fries bacon just the way I like it: plenty of grease.' He seized the sandwich from the plate and began eating. 'You don't mind me going ahead?'

'Not at all.'

'So what can I do for you?'

'I just wanted a quiet word.' I moved round to his side of the counter. 'I didn't want you to think I was avoiding you.'

'Never crossed my mind.' He went on chewing enthusiastically: a thin rivulet of grease had seeped to his chin but he didn't seem to notice. 'I think you killed Mompesson and you know I'm right – obviously. But nobody else does, so don't worry: you're in the clear. Judging by these papers, Mompesson's no great loss to the world.'

'Those are his possessions?' I pointed to the shoe box.

'Yes. They're what he had with him at Meongate. Cheque book, passport, cash, IOUs, an address book containing several titled ladies, I'm afraid, odd scraps and letters: nothing much. Nor did the Metropolitan

Police find anything significant at his London flat. No family that the American Embassy can trace. In fact, something of a mystery man. He lived well, had good connections, dealt profitably in shares, held a lot of stock in American railways, attracted despairing letters from married women and had the nerve – or the foresight – to keep them all. No. Not a nice man at all.'

'If it's all so straightforward and the inquiry's closed, why are you sifting through his stuff?' I was still trying to find a way to approach what I really wanted to tell him, still delaying – as long as I could – a fateful move.

'Because it's only straightforward in the official version. Cheriton couldn't have killed a mosquito, leave alone Mompesson. You did it – and I want to know the reason.' There was no melodrama in his statement. He had finished his sandwich. Now he slumped back in his chair and sipped tea from a chipped 1911 coronation mug.

'I can't give you the reason for something I didn't do.'

'Then try something else. Here . . .' He rifled through the pile of papers by his elbow, pulled out one torn sheet and tossed it across the desk at me. 'From the stamp pouch of Mompesson's wallet. Just a scrap – but what does it mean?'

I picked it up. A few lines scrawled on a half-sheet of cheap, lined notepaper, jaggedly torn at the base: 'Since 13th June: Room over 7 Copenhagen Yard, off Charlotte Street.' I shrugged my shoulders.

'It's an address in Portsea.'

'It means nothing to me, Inspector.' But that wasn't quite true. My mind was racing to make connections, yet had no way of testing them. An address in Portsea, where the first Lady Powerstock had worked with the poor. Her memoir of it studied by Leonora the night

241

before her disappearance. An address known to Mompesson – since 13th June. It meant less than nothing, but it was more than I had to go on before.

'A prostitute, I surmised.'

'You could be right.'

'But the writing isn't Mompesson's.'

'So?'

'It's just another inconsistency, another oddity. You and Mrs Hallows were discussing Portsea on Sunday evening, weren't you?'

'In passing. It's where the first Lady Powerstock . . .'

'I know. But that was more than ten years ago and Portsmouth's a big city. So it means nothing . . . does it?'

'As you say, Inspector. Not a thing.'

He gulped more tea. 'Until the inquest, I've a chance to catch you out, Mr Franklin. The murder weapon's still missing. New evidence could persuade the Chief Constable to re-open the inquiry. One of these scraps' – he gestured at the pile - 'could make all the difference.'

'I can't help you, I'm afraid.'

'Then why did you come to see me?'

'Simply to say that. I would help you if I could, but I can't.'

His brow furrowed and he stared at me over the rim of his mug. His doggedness – which I'd arrived intending to put my trust in – had become inconvenient. Now that I had a clue of sorts to follow, I wanted only to be rid of him.

'I must get along.'

'The Coroner will write to you formally about the inquest. You'll still be at Meongate?'

'If not, I'll let you know.'

'Do that. And if you want another chat before the inquest, you know where to find me.'

But I had drawn back from the brink. I no longer needed to turn to Shapland and I didn't intend to. At last, I had something to go on.

SEVEN

I went straight to the railway station and waited for the next train down the line. There, where the troika bells on Lucy's harness had first summoned me, unsuspecting, into Meongate's taut enactment of a private war, I began at last to trace the path I'd overlooked till then. I was the only passenger on the platform, waiting in the brooding stillness while the affable old porter manoeuvred a trolley in the shadow of the station canopy: nothing else moved, nothing stirred, nothing verified the sensation I nevertheless felt – I wasn't alone, save by the trick of time, wasn't free of others who'd begun a journey there. Nor, now, were they free of me.

When the train duly came, and I boarded it, the sensation grew. It chugged and clanked southwards, its lurching progress became a metaphor in my mind for the reluctant approach of an uncomfortable truth. I shared a compartment with a child and his demure governess, who was at constant pains to prevent him asking why I wasn't in the Army. I was wearing mufti and they weren't to know, but even her embarrassment didn't stir me, didn't break the mood of uncertain, fatalistic familiarity. As on that first long train journey across Normandy to the Front, I had no idea what was growing ever and slowly nearer, only a presentiment, a shade of a suspicion that it was worse than I thought yet, in some strange way, exactly what I had expected.

At Fareham, I changed to another train, full of boisterous sailors returning to Portsmouth. Once again, I was immune to their mood, alone in my world of motionless turmoil. While they swapped cigarettes and loud jokes, my mind was afloat. The grey mudflats of Portsmouth Harbour and the glowering keep of Portchester Castle, canvas biplanes assembled on the airfield at Hilsea and the green-bowered gravestones of Kingston Cemetery: other places, other faces overlaid, glimpsed like passing reflections in the sooted glass of the carriage window – Hernu's Farm with Hallows, Meongate without him, Leonora's calm yet questing countenance and Miriam Powerstock, long dead but daguerreotyped on our memories and our lives, fixed by some chance or significance, there, at the heart of the mystery, waiting peacefully to confront me.

Portsmouth Town station: high-roofed and crowded, echoing with shouts and whistles. I asked at the book-stall for directions to Charlotte Street and was given them with a straight look. The road outside was a jumble of vehicles and people, horns sounding and dust billowing from a tarpaulined gap in the row of build-ings opposite. 'Zeppelin raid last night,' a newsvendor told me. 'Aiming for the Dockyard. They caught us a wopper instead.'

I made my way through the ruck as best I could, then tried my luck down a side-turning: a maze of back alleys and dingy terraces, opening out as I pressed on into a motley spread of market stalls, peeling shopfronts and grimy taverns opening for business – a smell of fish and stale hops, dirty water standing in cobbled runnels and a parrot squawking at me from a petshop cage. All so far – so very far – from the rural grace of Meongate. And yet some strand linked the two.

I asked for more directions at a whelk stall: the way to Copenhagen Yard was gestured with a thumb. It lay down a cobbled alley with a central gutter where a dog was sniffing at a grating. The dog didn't move at my approach, just bared its teeth and watched me pass. Stained sheets long past washing hung across the alley on a line. Beyond them, the yard opened to my right, where several tenement stairways shared a narrow space with the lean-to of a woodyard. A grubby child without shoes regarded me blankly from a doorway. From the stairs behind him came the sound of two slurred female voices raised in argument: he paid them no need.

'Wot you want, mister?' the child said without expression.

'I'm looking for . . . the room over number seven.'

He pointed to a door at second-floor level above the woodyard, reached by rickety stairs that bridged the lean-to. 'You sound just like 'im.'

'Who?'

'The bloke wot lived there.'

'Is he there now?'

'Dunno.' He turned abruptly and disappeared into the house.

I took the stairs two at a time, for all their ominous creaks. The door at the top was plain and unmarked, its paint peeling. There was no bell, not even a letterbox, just a keyhole and a padlocked hasp that told me nobody was in. Nevertheless, I knocked several times and strained across the railings at the top of the stairs to look in at the window. The thin curtains were drawn: through the gap between them all I could see was a sparsely furnished kitchen.

'What do you want?' An adult voice, from behind me. I swung round. At the foot of the stairs stood a burly figure in a flat cap and working clothes, his apron smeared with grease and wood shavings.

'I was looking for the occupant of the room over number seven.'

'That's the room. But there ain't no occupant.'

I walked down the stairs towards him. 'Are you the owner?'

He squared his shoulders. 'You could say. Who're you looking for?'

'As I said – the occupant.'

'The room's empty.'

'Has it been empty for long?'

'Mind your own business. I've already 'ad the police sniffing round 'ere. Now you.'

'What did you tell them?'

'Same as you. Nobody lives there. It's been empty for months.'

'Since 13th June, perhaps?'

'Maybe. Maybe not.'

'Do you know a man called Mompesson?'

'Never 'eard of 'im.'

'It's hard to believe a room would stay empty for months in a place like this.'

His lip curled. 'Believe what you like.'

I decided to try one method the police couldn't have used. I took a sovereign from my pocket. 'All I want is some information. Who was the last person to live up there?'

He looked at the coin in my palm. 'Double it and I'll give you something.'

'What?'

'A name. That's all.'

'The name of the occupant?'

'Not exactly.'

I had no choice. 'Very well.' I handed him the sovereign and took out another.

'Dan Fletcher: friend o' mine. 'Is sister keeps the Mermaid in Nile Street.'

'Thank you.' I gave him the other coin and walked away. Another name was all I needed – another clue to follow. Besides, the name of the pub struck a chord. The Mermaid. As I made my way out of the yard, I trawled my memory of 'Squalor Amidst Plenty', Miriam Powerstock's posthumous plea for action. That's where I'd heard it before. 'The police raid on the Mermaid Inn meeting of 26th November 1904, justified on the grounds of supposed seditious links with Royal Naval personnel, has done much to undermine local confidence in the good faith of the authorities . . .'

Behind the flapping sheet strung across the alley, the boy from the yard was waiting for me. ' 'Ello, mister. Joss tell y' much?'

'About what?'

'The bloke from the top room. Y' know.'

'A little.' I made to move on.

'It weren't Dan Fletcher. I know 'im.'

I turned back and stooped to his level. 'Then who was it?'

'Wot's it worth?'

'Half a crown for his name.'

He drew the ragged cuff of his shirt across his nose. 'Dunno 'is name.'

'What do you know?'

'More 'n Joss told you.'

'Tell me.'

''E weren't like Dan Fletcher. 'E were more like you. Moved in a few months back. Didn't see much of 'im. Went out at night. Ain't seen 'im since last Thursday.'

I gave him the half-crown. He turned towards an open doorway in the wall of the alley. 'What did you mean . . . like me?'

He stopped and thought, just for a moment. 'Like you look. Like a soldier.' Then he was gone.

Nile Street was only a short step away, but it took me long enough to find it through the maze of alleys. The Mermaid Inn stood on a corner, a green-tiled alehouse with smoked-glass windows, the words BRICKWOOD & CO.'S BRILLIANT ALES blazoned over a central door giving on to a dim, cavernous interior. It was not yet noon and still quiet inside, one or two mournful figures gazing into cloudy glasses while a broadly built, aproned woman stood behind the bar, polishing it. It wasn't as bad as I'd expected, not as dirty, not as hostile. Not then, anyway.

The woman was stern-faced, with grey hair tied back. Once, she might have been good-looking. Now, her vitality had turned to gauntness. I ordered a whisky, then broached the subject.

'I'm looking for Dan Fletcher.'

She put my drink down in front of me. 'Who wants him?'

'My name's Franklin. He doesn't know me.'

'Then why are you looking for him?'

'It's about the room in Copenhagen Yard.'

She stopped polishing the bar. 'Wait here. I'll see if he's in.'

She disappeared from view and left me to look around at the low, tobacco-stained ceilings, the bare tables and alcoves, the pinched, absent looks of the solitary drinkers. One was a woman, with matted hair and a tight dress: I avoided her eye.

The landlady came back, by a door from the passage to my side of the bar. 'Come through,' she said. I followed her into the passage. 'It's at the far end.'

I walked ahead while she returned to the bar. The door at the end of the passage stood ajar. I knocked and went in.

The room was not what I'd expected. Small and lit only by one window looking on to an enclosed yard, it was nevertheless spotlessly tidy, carpeted in some fashion, with a couple of fraying armchairs, a bureau by the window and several well-stocked bookcases. A budgerigar in a cage hung in one corner and there were red geraniums in a window box. The place had a wholesome, homely air.

In one of the armchairs, a square-shouldered, lean-faced man with thinning grey hair and much of his sister's gauntness sat smoking a pipe and reading a book, a strangely restless, muscular figure at odds with his quiet back-room surroundings. He didn't get up when I walked in, just closed his book and sucked on his pipe.

'Franklin – my sister tells me.'

'That's right.'

'I don't know you.' His tone was guarded but neutral, a touch more cultured than the man at the woodyard. 'What do you want of me?'

'I gather you can tell me who lives in the room above number 7, Copenhagen Yard.'

'What makes you think so?'

'I asked around.'

'Are you from the police?'

'No.'

'Then why do you want to know?'

'Have you heard of the murder recently at Meongate, near Droxford? A man named Mompesson.'

'I read of it.'

'Did you know the man?'

'No. Did you?' He had a direct, straight-eyed defiance about him: he was not to be rattled.

I walked over to the window to be out of his flinty gaze. 'Slightly. Amongst his possessions was a note recording the address in Copenhagen Yard. And a date: 13th June.'

He frowned. 'I can't help you, Mr Franklin.'

'But you do know who lives there?'

'I didn't say so.'

'Yet when I mentioned the address to your sister, she brought me to you straight away.'

He smiled. 'She was trying to be helpful. That's all.'

I glanced at the yard beyond the window – narrow, whitewashed walls, empty barrels in one corner, a scent of geranium through the open sash. 'It's tenuous, Mr Fletcher, I agree. But there's something wrong here, I know. The police have given it up, but . . .'

'You haven't?'

'I can't. I'm in too deeply.' My gaze shifted to the bureau, its flap open on an orderly array of books and papers, a well-used blotter, ink in a stand. Almost more of a study than a pub back-room, I remember thinking. 'I have a dead friend, you see, whom I owe a debt.'

'This man Mompesson?'

'No. Another man. A friend from the Army.' There was a gold pocket watch acting as paperweight for some letters in the bureau. I followed its coiled chain with my eye, snaking round the edge of the blotter . . . to a photograph, a sepia miniature in a silver, oval frame. 'He lived at Meongate, you see. His name was . . .' The photograph was of a lady, dark-haired, in a high-necked lace blouse, whose face I'd seen before, in Lord Powerstock's own study, in a portrait of his own wedding. I lifted the picture from its place and stared at it in disbelief.

I hadn't heard Fletcher move, but, suddenly he was beside me, snatching the picture from my hand. He stood awkwardly, putting most of his weight on a stick, but on his level stare there was no hint of weakness.

'His name was Hallows.'

'That photograph . . . is of his mother.'

'It may be.'

'It is. She worked in this area before her death. She even wrote about this pub. The police broke up a meeting here twelve years ago. And you keep her picture in your bureau.'

'You know a great deal, Mr Franklin.'

He was wrong. I still didn't know enough. 'You knew Lady Powerstock, didn't you?'

'Yes.' He replaced her picture in the bureau and reached past me to raise the lid. 'What of it?'

'And Mompesson?'

'I've never heard of him. I was acquainted with Lady Powerstock. She was a fine woman. But she's been dead for eleven years. I have no connection with her family.'

'Did you know the late Captain Hallows – her son?'

'No.'

'Or his wife – Leonora?'

'No.'

'Now missing.'

252

'What?'

'She left Meongate early yesterday morning and has not been seen since. She's been somewhat distressed since the murder – and the subsequent suicide. I'm worried about her.'

He turned and limped back towards his chair. 'I told you, Mr Franklin. I can't help you.'

I followed him. 'Have you seen her? Has she been here?'

I couldn't decipher the expression on his face as he looked at me. 'What business would she have with me? There's no reason for her to have been here.'

'I think there is. I think the reason is connected with the photograph of Lady Powerstock you keep by you. The sort of photograph that might be kept by . . . an admirer, let's say.'

He turned then to confront me. I could tell by his simmering look and tensed muscles that he was angry, but still composed. 'Tread carefully, young man. Since you claim to be looking for a lady who's missing, I'll attribute your insolence to concern on her behalf. But I shan't have Miriam Powerstock spoken of disrespectfully. By Heaven I shan't.' I could see that I'd hit the mark. 'Don't let this limp fool you. I started work on ships when I was fourteen. It makes a man strong – strong enough to break your arm if I want to.' He reached out and seized my left forearm with crushing force. I winced. 'See what I mean?' Then he released me.

'I've no wish to speak of anyone disrespectfully,' I said after a moment. 'Mrs Hallows is missing from home. I'm bound to do all I can to find her.'

'Suppose she had been here. Suppose I could tell you she was well. Would that satisfy you?'

'If you know where she is . . .'

'Exactly. It wouldn't satisfy you, would it?' He moved back towards the bureau. 'There'd never be an end of questions. About me, about Miriam, about all the things people like you just can't leave alone.' He turned the key in the bureau lock. 'So the answer to your question is no. I don't know Mrs Hallows. I've never seen her.'

'I'm not sure I can believe you, Mr Fletcher.'

He looked out into the narrow yard beyond his window. 'Well, that's your problem, isn't it?'

'If you know anything, it's your duty to tell me.'

He turned to face me. 'Don't talk to me about duty. You're too young and I'm too old. I know my duty – and it isn't to help you.' He paused. 'You carry your shoulder stiffly. Is that a war wound?'

'As it happens, yes.'

'Then you should know better than to lecture me about duty. Doesn't what's happening in France sicken you?'

'How would you know what's happening in France?'

'I read the newspapers. But, unlike most people, I read between the lines. If you're involved in this war, you have my pity – but not my respect.'

'You're a hard man, Mr Fletcher.'

'Life's made me like that. I thought once I could help others, that together we could win a better life, some of the privileges people like you enjoy. But that was before this.' He slapped his stiff right leg.

'And before Miriam Powerstock died?'

'That's none of your business.'

'Whatever you think of me, you must understand that I'm only trying to help Mrs Hallows. It's vital that I find her.'

'Why?'

'You may as well know. She's expecting a child. With her husband dead, I'm not sure she's responsible for her own actions.' It wasn't true. I may have doubted Leonora's word, but never her level-headedness. If Fletcher had met her, he would know that.

He was clever enough not to challenge the point. He nodded slowly, as if absorbing the implications of what I'd said. 'That certainly explains your concern, Mr Franklin. The family doubts paternity, I suppose.' Then he seemed to think again. 'Unless . . .'

'Unless what?'

'Captain Hallows has been dead longer than his wife's been pregnant. Is that it?'

'Now it's my turn to say that's none of your business.'

He limped back towards me, musing as he did so. 'Your tone confirms it.'

'Perhaps you can at least understand now why I must find her, before she does anything . . . irresponsible. She shouldn't be left to wander . . . in an area like this.'

'This area is my home, Mr Franklin. Be careful how you speak of it.'

'Surely you can see . . .'

'What I can see is a pampered young man meddling in things he doesn't understand. Unlike Lord Powerstock, I'm not a man of property: I live under my sister's roof, on sufferance. But my past is one possession I don't intend to give up, certainly not at your say-so. I know nothing of your friends. I want to know nothing of them. I met the first Lady Powerstock when she worked in this area – a long time ago. But that's all.'

'That's not good enough.'

'It's all you're getting. And now I think it's time you left.'

I could see further argument was useless. Fletcher looked then as I always now think of him: bleak and unshakeable, like some outcrop of rock on a windswept moor. Despite my concern for Leonora, I felt his secret drawing me past his implacable hostility. A resentful old dockyardman with mind and body twisted by an unfortunate past? Even then, I could see there was more to him than that. He was too subtle, too lucidly intelligent, for the image to fit. There was something else, something more in his proudly set face, his books and his bureau, his one, treasured picture of Hallows' mother, that told me I'd found, in him, the missing link between what I knew and what I sensed in the Powerstock household. Yet still he was right. Still I did not understand.

I left the Mermaid in a rage. I had no way of forcing Fletcher to tell me anything, but I knew – or sensed – that he could tell me everything I needed to know if only I could find some way past his well-prepared defences. I went to the nearest pub, a tiny alehouse in the shadow of the Dockyard wall, crowded with workmen, and drank quietly in a corner, trying to reason out what, so far, seemed inexplicable.

Later – none the wiser – I retraced my steps to the Town station and telephoned Meongate. It was Fergus who answered and confirmed there was still no news of Leonora. I warned him that my own return might now be delayed. I had no intention of leaving Portsmouth until I'd gleaned more than Fletcher hoped I would.

It was mid-afternoon and quieter on the streets. I made my way to the Guildhall in gathering drizzle and found, at its rear, the public library. There, in a drab chamber where old men in frayed coats stood at boards reading newspaper accounts of the latest triumphs, an attendant brought me back copies of the local evening paper for November 1904.

I skimmed through the bound and crinkled pages to the date I wanted: Monday, 28th November. There was no missing the headlines above a right-hand column: DISTURBANCE AT PORTSEA TAVERN – POLICE BREAK UP SEDITIOUS MEETING – 8 ARRESTS, ONE CONSTABLE INJURED. I scanned the report.

'Prompt police action brought to an abrupt close on Saturday night a riotous gathering at the Mermaid Inn, Nile Street, Portsea, and, with it, the disruptive movement amongst HM Dockyard personnel of which this so-called public meeting was the culmination.

'Recent months have seen a number of groups spring up in the locality allegedly seeking to improve living conditions in Portsea, groups which, it now transpires, have also been motivated by revolutionary political objectives. Disaffected members of the Dockyard labour force and others of the unemployed have succeeded in recruiting support from well-intentioned and well-connected philanthropic circles for a sustained campaign for better living and working conditions in the area. That this seemingly laudable endeavour concealed more sinister political aims was never more evident than in the groups' contacts with Royal Naval personnel, some of whom were present at Saturday's meeting – and others before it – where some of the more inflammatory speeches could only be interpreted as an incitement to mutiny.

'This last factor alone obliged the police to take action, which they did in exemplary fashion. The meeting was broken up with the minimum of damage and injury, although one constable was cut about the face with a knife and is now recovering in hospital. The ringleaders were all arrested, amongst them Donald Machim, notorious for his violent role in the engineers' strike of 1897–98, and Daniel Fletcher, for long a thorn in the flesh of the Dockyard management as a formenter of unrest. Machim, Fletcher and three others were brought before the magistrates this morning on charges of conspiracy, sedition and incitement to riot. They were remanded in custody until 5th December.'

So there it was. Miriam Powerstock had written of the disrupted meeting in tones which left no doubt of where her sympathies lay. And Daniel Fletcher, who kept her photograph by his side eleven years after her death, had been arrested that day. I asked for the following months' copies and went through them until I found the trial report. On 23rd February 1905 the five defendants had all been found guilty as charged and sentenced to various terms: five years for Machim, two for Fletcher, eighteen months for the others. And the judge had spared a coruscating word for the conspirators' philanthropic supporters.

'It has been profoundly depressing to hear that several members of the cloth and of the aristocracy at one time placed their faith in the likes of these wretches to improve society when, in fact, their true and abiding intention was to undermine it in every way that they could.'

So much for that. Even as the judge recorded his words for unyielding posterity, Miriam Powerstock had been carrying the virus that later killed her. Now I could begin to understand what Fletcher meant, what made him as bitter as he was: her death at Meongate, a sacrifice – as he might see it – for his bankrupt ideals, while he sat in a prison cell, or still sat – with the memory of what it meant – in a pub back-room in Portsea.

I left the library and wandered out into the grey, un-caring light of late afternoon. The street past the Guildhall was busy with homeward-bound traffic, the pavement thick with raincoated figures, who knew little of the war I'd returned from and even less of a twelve-year-old drama still fresh in my mind.

I followed a tunnel beneath the railway embankment that led to a park where unexpected quiet reigned, where drizzle blurred the edges of my indecision. I sat on a bench and watched dusk gather about the war-geared city, cranes still working and a hooter blaring in the distant dockyard. The silence around me was sufficient to admit the smeared patter of the rain, the moist stillness to absorb the lone, passing figures. There I waited for darkness to fall.

Night came: inky black in the park, the city's lights shrouded against air raids. I made my way back towards the railway station and called in at a nearby picture house to watch a jerky newsreel from the Somme. Strident music and bombastic commentary couldn't hide, from me at least, the truth behind its choreo-graphed mockery: forced smiles from the tired faces of men who would never come home.

By the time I left, it was late enough for my purpose. I followed the same route as before to Charlotte Street, where now the pubs were full and noisy, the naphtha touches above the eel and pie stalls lighting the faces of drunken men and shabby women, a barrel organ crank-ing somewhere its mechanical overture to the night's excess.

I cut down the alley that I knew led to Copenhagen Yard. The noise of the street faded behind me till only the odd shriek and smash of glass caught up with my footsteps. The day's rain smeared the cobbled margins of the alley, where a cat hissed and retreated through the sundered boarding of a narrow door. This was the place I had been before, but changed by night, its squalor rendered sinister by the cloak of darkness; changed, perhaps, as much by my reasons for being there as by its own, shifting, deep-shadowed nature.

I turned into the yard. This time, no staring youth was there to meet me, only the blank, rain-dewed tenement walls and black, socketed windows. Water dripped irregularly from a sagging gutter on to the dully echoing lean-to roof. Nothing stirred.

I crossed to the wooden stairs and paused. Still there was nothing. It seemed safe enough to climb them. From the narrow, railed platform at their top, I scanned the yard beneath me: it was deserted.

I had brought a stone with me from the park. Now I lifted it from my pocket in a gloved hand and brought it down against one of the panes of the kitchen window. A sharp crack of glass split the silence. But there was no reaction: such a noise, I judged, was not unusual. I tapped out the loose shards of the pane with the stone, then reached in and pushed back the latch. I prised up the sash till the window was half-open, then climbed on to the railings and eased myself across on to the sill. A scramble and I was through, dropping down on to bare boards where broken glass crunched beneath my feet.

I lit a match. The flare of light showed a mean, stripped kitchen, bare but for a stove and sink in one corner and a table in another, lath and plaster walls behind sagging paper. But I was in luck: on the table was a butt of candle in an enamel saucer. I put the match to its dwindled wick. By its wavering light, all I could see was what I might have expected to see: a drab, deserted garret. Nothing more.

I went out into the passage. There a strip of linoleum covered the boards. To my right, two more doorways opened on to empty rooms. To my left, the passage ran to the entrance door. And there the flickering light showed a pale shape on the floor: a letter. I stooped and picked it up: a thick vellum envelope incongruously lodged amidst the dust and scattered plaster. I held it up to read the name: *J. Willis, Esq.*

That was all. But not all. I knew the precise, elegant hand. The writing was Leonora's. I hurried back to the kitchen and replaced the candle on the table, then tore the letter open. Inside was a single, folded sheet. I held it in the pool of faltering light and began to read. It opened abruptly, without address or salutation.

'I must speak to you. It is more important than I can say that I should do so. If you receive this letter, I beg you to make contact. I have seen Mr Fletcher and he will know where I can be found. Leonora. September 25th.'

I stared at the brief, charged message. The date was the day before: the day of Leonora's disappearance. Now I knew for certain that she too had followed the trail which led to Fletcher and an empty garret in Portsea, a trail whose end she knew but I still did not.

Metal chinked against metal, somewhere close by. I jerked upright and strained my senses for some sign of what it might mean. Sure enough, there it was again. Somebody had released the padlock on the front door and slipped the hasp, somebody who must know, by the candle I had lit, that I was there. I snuffed out the flame and thrust the letter into my pocket. At once, though too late, the glimmer of an electric torch reached me from the stairway beyond the window. I was discovered.

There was no time to hide or flee. I made for the passage, hoping, I think, that there was a bolt on the door I could slide across to deny access. But it was a vain hope. As I swung into the passage, I heard a key turn in the lock. An instant later, the door burst open and a dazzling torchbeam met my panicky advance.

'Stop where you are!' The voice was abrupt and authoritative. Instinctively, I obeyed.

'Who's there?'

'Surely you know me.'

'Fletcher?'

The torch snapped off. Now I knew by his outline in the less intense darkness of the doorway that it was indeed Fletcher; I could see the drop of his right shoulder where he leant on his stick. 'What are you doing here, Mr Franklin?'

I tried to talk away my sense of guilt. 'I might ask you the same question.'

'Hardly. I rent these rooms from the owner of the woodyard. So I have every right to be here.'

'Earlier, you denied any connection with this address.'

'But you didn't believe me.'

'No.'

'Then who else did you expect to meet here?'

'Maybe the real tenant. Maybe Mr Willis.'

'I see. You know about Mr Willis, do you?'

'I know of his existence. And that Mrs Hallows was trying to contact him – at this address.'

'How do you know that?'

'Now you're the one asking questions. Why should I be any readier to answer them than you were mine?'

He chuckled. It surprised me, this show of

light-heartedness from someone who'd hitherto seemed only grim and unyielding. 'There are many reasons why you should answer me, Mr Franklin. Not the least of them is that I see now you will not be deterred by mere silence. Something more is required to satisfy you.'

'Only the truth.'

'Only?' He chuckled again. 'Wait here.' He walked past me and moved into one of the other rooms leading off the passage. There, he switched on his torch again. I heard him open a door and fumble with something, then strike a match. There was a brief whiff of gas in the closed air, then a flood of light as he adjusted the lamp.

I followed him in. The room was in no better repair than the kitchen, bare-boarded and unfurnished save for a truckle-bed, a crude dresser with enamel jug and bowl standing on it, a frayed easy chair and a thin coir mat beside the bed. Fletcher crossed to the window and drew a stained canvas curtain across it, then turned back to face me.

'What do you know of Mr Willis?' he said.

'I found a letter addressed to him – in Mrs Hallows' hand.'

'And you opened it?'

'Yes. It's a plea for him to contact her. But he doesn't live here any more, does he?'

'Breaking and entering. Reading other people's letters. That doesn't seem appropriate behaviour for an officer and a gentleman.' The sarcasm was undisguised but mild: there seemed a weariness even in his hostility.

'You left me no choice. I have to find Leonora. All other considerations are secondary. And you know where she is.'

'Do I?'

I crossed the room and handed him the crumpled

letter. He scanned it briefly. 'Do you mind if I sit down, Mr Franklin? This is the only chair.'

'Go ahead.' I saw him wince and put a hand to his right thigh as he released the stick. 'Does the leg bother you?'

'Somewhat. Especially when I have to turn out at night on a fool's errand.'

'A dockyard accident?'

'No accident. But let that pass. You think this letter proves I know where Mrs Hallows is.'

I sat down on the truckle-bed and faced him across the room. 'I'm not interested in proof. I know it to be so. This man Willis lived here, presumably at your invitation. Why you should rent rooms here in secret, rather than have him lodge at the Mermaid, I don't know. Unless he's a political crony you don't want to be seen with.'

'Political?'

'Perhaps you were in prison together.'

'You know about that too?'

'I looked up back copies of the local paper. The seditious gathering at the Mermaid in November 1904 is reported in detail. As is your subsequent conviction.'

'If it's truth you're after, you won't find it in a local rag that says whatever the Admiralty tells it to.'

'Then why don't you tell me the truth?'

'Because I'm finished with politics and delusions about changing society. Because I'm finished with the past.'

'Yet you keep Miriam Powerstock's photograph in your bureau. She belongs to your past, doesn't she? She must have died while you were in prison.'

At last my words reached some part of his secret self. 'Yes, she did.' He looked around the room, as if assessing the bleakness of our surroundings. Somewhere outside, a bottle smashed: there was a shriek, then silence again. 'But my grief is my own. It's none of your concern.'

'I'm afraid it is. Leonora is looking for Willis. I'm forced to conclude that he's the father of the child she's carrying. She came to you to find him. Why? Your only connection with Powerstock family is your friendship with the first Lady Powerstock. So it must amount to something more than private, forgotten grief. Mustn't it?'

He nodded slowly. 'Mrs Hallows came to see me yesterday, in search of Willis. I gave her this address, though I warned her that he'd probably already left it. As you can see, I was right. When you told me she was pregnant, I thought, like you, that Willis must be responsible, so I came here to see if there was any trace of him. All I found was a broken window – and you.'

'Where has she gone? She says in the letter that you know.'

'I know how she can be contacted. She told me in case I saw Willis before she did. From what I've seen of her, she's in no danger. You need feel no concern for her welfare. But I promised to tell her family nothing if approached by them. I'm bound by that promise. As a gentleman, you should understand my position.'

'I'm not a member of the family.'

'You amount to the same thing. You're of their class: that's why you're their guest. I owe them nothing. I owe you nothing.'

'Isn't Leonora one of their class as well? Yet you seem to owe her something.'

He leant forward in his chair. 'You're a clever young man, Mr Franklin, though not as clever as you think. So take my advice: leave it alone. You spoke of grief. That's all this chase will bring you. That's all there is waiting for the Powerstocks. In finding me, that's all you've found.'

'I told you before. I'm in too deeply to stop now.'

'Then don't say you weren't warned.'

'I won't. But if you won't tell me where Leonora is, at least tell me what sort of a man this Willis is. Not much of one, to judge by what I've seen.'

'Unworthy of her, would you say?'

'I would.'

'Well, who wouldn't be?' A smile hovered on his lips. 'If you really want to know about Willis, then I'll tell you. But not here. This room' – he looked around it – 'makes me feel uneasy. It's obvious he's not coming back here. Let's go somewhere else.'

'Very well.'

He levered himself from the chair and reached up to turn out the lamp. No more was said as we made our way out. I stood beside him as he padlocked the door, then followed him down into the yard. He was panting from the effort by the time we reached the foot of the steps, but didn't pause before turning into the alley.

'Are we going back to the Mermaid?' I asked.

'No. Another pub, where I'm not known. You can be anonymous in a crowd, anonymous and safe.'

We turned down a side-alley and already I was lost. It was a narrow, cobbled path threading between the backs of jumbled terraced houses, heading vaguely northwards. Water trickled down a central gutter and Fletcher's stick troubled him on the slimy cambered stones. Nevertheless, we made good time.

A rat darted across our path at one point and Fletcher pulled up sharply. He began glancing round at the rough walls of the alley and the dark spaces beyond.

'Is something wrong?'

'No.' He looked back at me. 'Where did you pick up your shoulder wound, Mr Franklin?'

'The Somme.'

He nodded. 'How long were you out there?'

'Just over a year. Since the spring of last year. Long enough.'

'But you'll go back?'

'Of course.'

'Why?'

It was a strange question to be asked: unheard-of in respectable circles. From Fletcher it didn't seem odd at all. But I had no intention of revealing my doubts about the war to him. 'Duty, Patriotism. The war still has to be won, you know.'

'You really believe that?'

'I believe there's no alternative.'

He moved so suddenly I didn't know what was happening, far less have time to resist. I was pinned against the wall beside me by the weight of Fletcher's body, my left arm trapped and my right held behind my back. His strength was as formidable as he'd said. As he tightened the arm lock, my wounded shoulder protested and I cried out. I heard his stick clatter into the gutter, then the flash of a blade before my eyes silenced me.

For a moment, there was only the cloud of our panting breath in the air between us and the knife held beneath my chin. I forgot the pain of my shoulder and thought instead of the absurdity of cheating death on the Somme only to meet it in an alley in Portsea.

Then he spoke, his voice a whispered rasp in my ear. 'I could kill you now, Franklin, as easily as they gut fish on the dock. I could kill you and leave you here and nobody would ever know.'

The irony of it all emboldened me. 'Then why don't you? I couldn't say I wasn't warned.'

His grip tightened. The knife drew nearer. I closed my eyes, expecting in that moment that he would do as he said.

Then I was free. Fletcher released me and I nearly pitched forward on to the cobbles with the shock of it. I looked towards him but he had swung round and cried out and flung the knife down the alley in a sudden frenzy. It rattled to rest somewhere in the darkness. Then he lurched against the wall, felt for his stick, found it and pushed himself upright.

It was raining. I remember noticing the sheen on the stones for the first time, feeling the drench of it mingling with the sweat on my face, seeing Fletcher turn towards me through the mist of its falling.

'I'm sorry,' he said.

I felt strangely calm, strangely unmoved by the proximity of death. 'Why did you do that?'

'You wouldn't be stopped. You said so yourself. There were only two choices: to kill you or to tell you. And to tell you is to kill something in me – a love, a memory, an illusion. So let it die.' He moved towards me and stopped as I drew back. 'Don't worry. I have no more weapons. We'll go on to the pub. You'll feel safe there – and so will I.'

I kept my distance as we proceeded. Slowly, my nerves began to settle. I said nothing. This time, Fletcher did all the talking.

'It would have been easier if you'd meant what you said. But you didn't. You're no more the dutiful patriot than I am, though no doubt you were, before you saw what it meant. For me, prison and a game leg. For you, war and a smashed shoulder. We've drawn much the same in the lottery, I reckon.'

We went on a little way in silence. Then he began again. 'You said there was no alternative. Maybe you're right. Maybe I was a fool for ever trying to find one. But life plays tricks on you, as you'll discover. It doesn't let you be sensible – all the time.'

We came to the end of the alley and joined a narrow street, curving past the high walls of the Dockyard. We walked on the other side. Fletcher glancing up at the wall opposite as he went.

'That's where it began,' he said after a while. 'His Majesty's Royal Naval Dockyard – Her Majesty's then. It should have been just a job of work. But it became something more, something worse.'

'How long did you work there?'

'Nearly thirty years. It sounds a long time, doesn't it? Sometimes, looking back, it's like it hardly happened. Seven years' apprenticeship as a shipwright. Another five to become established. Then a charge hand. I'd have made it to foreman in the end.'

'But you didn't?'

'No. Because I met Donald Machim. He came down from Clydeside after the engineers' strike collapsed in '98. He had a trade they wanted, but I don't think they knew what they were taking on. He soon saw I had something he could work on: intelligence, restlessness, call it what you like. I read too much to make a respectful dockie for life, you see. And Machim was amazed by how docile the workforce was. Unions had never got a look-in at the Yard and the Admiralty wanted to keep it buttoned up. Machim was determined to end that and brought me round to see it his way.'

We'd passed several pubs already, but still we kept on along the road tracing the Dockyard wall. And Fletcher kept on too, tracing his past as we went. 'Pompey was even worse then than it is now: disease, poverty, squalor. Grafting for sixty hours a week you didn't have time to think about it. But Machim did. And what he thought made sense.

'His chance came in 1904. A lot of men were laid off that autumn, but he'd heard talk of a huge new battle-ship to be built the following year. So he reckoned that was the time to strike, when the men were discontented and the Admiralty couldn't afford a prolonged dispute. Not that it ever came to that. The meeting at the Mermaid was to have been the start. Instead, it was the finish. There were some naval artificers in the audience – so it was said. That gave the police the excuse they needed to break it up and charge us with sedition.

'I never saw Machim again after the trial. I spent two years in Winchester Gaol, then came back to Portsmouth. By then, the Yard was busier than ever before, building Dreadnoughts to fight the Germans. I was a marked man, regularly turned down for work. Eventually, I was taken on when the *St Vincent* fell behind schedule, but there were men who'd worked under me years before who hadn't forgotten their grudges, others who'd been set back by the trouble after the Mermaid meeting and still blamed me for it: it was the opportunity they were waiting for. One dark night in February 1908 they took their revenge. I was making my way to the gate at the end of my shift when they set on me. I never saw who they were. They threw me into Number 15 Dock, which was drained and empty. That's how I injured my leg. That's how they made sure I never worked in the Yard again.'

'It seems drastic.'

'It was. But I'd committed the cardinal sin.' He smiled. 'I'd been proved right. Or, rather, Machim had. When work started on the first of the Dreadnoughts, the Admiralty introduced a new bonus system. But it was a fraud. For all their hard work, the dockies ended up worse off than ever. They should have listened to us.'

We turned abruptly off the road past the Dockyard wall and headed down a busier, noisier street, towards a brightly lit alehouse.

'This is Prospect Row,' said Fletcher. 'You'll find plenty of your brave fellow patriots in uniform in the houses along here.' His meaning was obvious: shabbily dressed girls lolled in doorways, drunken sailors came and went. We hurried past them and turned into the pub.

'The Fortune of War,' Fletcher announced. 'As you can see, it's well named.'

It was a low-ceilinged, smoke-filled barn of a place, crammed with carousing groups of soldiers and sailors, filled with their gabbling and singing. A piano was thumping out a sea shanty and a bemused young soldier, girl in tow, brushed past us as we entered. Too much laughter, too much drink, too much false, tinny jubilation: I knew what lay ahead for so many of them, didn't begrudge them their snatched consolation. But even without Fletcher's gaunt shadow at my shoulder, I couldn't have felt part of it.

A barmaid came past with a tray of empty glasses. Fletcher caught her eye and ordered some drinks. We took them to an alcove table away from the worst of the noise and smoke. Above us, on the wall, was a black-bordered portrait of Lord Kitchener, around us the seething, desperate unawareness of many who would share his fate.

'Why have we come here?' I asked.

'It's a popular pub with the Forces: matelots waiting for a ship, tommies waiting to cross the Channel. I wanted to see how much you're really a part of it. The answer is hardly at all.'

'You said you'd tell me about Willis. Where does he come into all this?'

'You'll know soon enough. I've never even tried to kill a man before. You have to understand why I might have made an exception in your case.'

'Very well then. You've spoken about Donald Machim. What about Miriam Powerstock?'

'That's where it begins and ends. You know that. You've already guessed. I met her at Father Dolling's Parsonage in Clarence Street. Trafalgar Day, 1894. I used the gymnasium he ran next door, sometimes went to his lectures, argued with him about politics. That Sunday he invited me to tea before evensong. Not that I went to his services, as he well knew. But Dolling was a good man: he disliked the cosy conventions. That's why they got rid of him in the end.

'And Miriam came to tea too that day. Dolling had introduced her to the parish after they met at a garden party the Bishop of Winchester gave. Her Christianity was like Dolling's: uncompromising. She helped him run the Sunday school. It was, she told me, her attempt to give something back. She never told me how her husband felt about her Sundays in Portsea, but I'll bet he didn't like them.'

'You and she became friends?'

'Yes. Let's say that. We became friends. At first, I thought she was just another titled lady slumming it. But after they pushed Dolling out, she changed. She began to understand what I'd known all along: that there were plenty of people who wanted Portsmouth to stay as it was. Her own husband, for instance. He was on the board of Brickwood's, the brewery that owns the Mermaid. Still is. Ironical, don't you think?'

'Did he know you were acquainted with his wife?'

'Not till I was arrested. Besides, I wasn't really, not at first, not for a long time. But, in the end, before the end . . . you could say I loved her.'

He stopped speaking. Through the din behind us of laughter and smashing glass, his silence echoed down the desolate years. He had loved her. And I did not doubt that she had loved him too.

'I last saw her a few hours before the Mermaid meeting in November 1904. She warned me it was a mistake. She didn't trust Machin. She thought him too much the unfeeling revolutionary. And she didn't think the authorities would let us get away with it. She was right on both counts. I should have listened to her. I wish I could listen to her now.

'She wrote to me in prison, of course. But Powerstock wouldn't let her visit me. Besides, she was ill by then, though I didn't know it. Smallpox – picked up in some stinking tenement, working to help people who weren't even grateful. Such a waste. A waste of a life. Rather like my own, I suppose. Her father wrote to me telling me she was dead. Otherwise, I might never have known.' He broke off, seemed, with a physical effort, to wrench his thoughts back to the present. 'But you want to know about Willis.'

'Yes. I do.'

'Franklin! Christ, what are you doing here? – in mufti too.' A figure blundered into my chair and leant unsteadily over me: khaki greatcoat, glass in one hand, cigarette in the other, drunken cast to the face, lock of hair tumbling over his forehead. I struggled for recognition. 'Thought you'd bought it.' He slumped down in an empty chair beside us and slammed his glass on the table. 'Who's your chum?'

Now, at last, I recognised him. It was Marriott, a platoon commander when I first joined the regiment in France, invalided home before Loos, one of those shallow, arrogant young men whom the war seemed unable to touch, with a resilience founded on lack of thought. I made some faltering introductions, he and Fletcher eyeing each other suspiciously.

'I'm in barracks down the road,' Marriott said, visibly excluding Fletcher from the remark. 'I didn't know you were in town.'

'I'm not – officially. I'm still convalescing: came home in July with a shoulder wound.'

'Bad luck. Can't wait to get back, I'll bet.'

'Is that what you're doing – going back?'

'Yes and no. Bit of a swine, actually. I'd like to be back in the thick of it, of course, but the powers that be have other ideas.' He tweaked back the lapel of his greatcoat to display a green gorget-patch on the tunic beneath. It was the tab worn by staff intelligence officers. I winced inwardly at the thought of Marriott having a hand in strategy, but clearly he was untroubled by such reservations. 'Experience is what they need at GHQ these days, I suppose.' I nodded sagely. 'Reckon you'll be fit soon?'

'I should think so.'

'I could have a word with the MO if you like. We can't afford to have fellows like you sitting things out. Not now we've broken through.'

Fletcher interrupted. 'What do you mean, Captain – "broken through"?'

Marriott turned to him with a patronising smile. 'Don't you read the newspapers?'

Fletcher's mouth was set in a sullen line. 'I do, yes. But do you?'

Marriott too was becoming nettled. 'What did you say your occupation is?'

'I wait – for the country to come to its senses and realize the sacrifice of thousands of lives isn't worth a politically fraudulent objective. By which I mean what you would call victory.'

Marriott looked as though he would choke. He glared at me as if I were responsible for what Fletcher had said. 'You're mixing in strange company, Franklin. What's this fellow to you?'

'A friend.' The words came almost unbidden, but easily, as if they were waiting to be spoken, waiting to test me by what they implied.

'You should choose your friends more carefully.' He thought for a moment, whilst Fletcher regarded him calmly. 'But then you always did have some unsound acquaintances.'

'What do you mean by that?'

'You hung around with Hallows a lot, as I remember. A disgrace to the regiment, with all his defeatist talk. Look what happened to him. There's a lesson to be learned . . .' He had been raising his glass to drink when Fletcher leant across the table and seized his forearm.

'If there's a lesson to be learned, Captain, it'll be wasted on a fool like you.' The glass fell back on to the table with a clatter and nearly toppled over. Suddenly, there was another man standing beside me: a young army officer, stockily built, with an earnest look.

'Is everything all right, Guy?' he said to Marriott.

Fletcher released Marriott's arm and rose awkwardly

from his seat. 'Everything's fine,' he muttered. Then he seized his stick, brushed past the man and headed for the door.

I made to follow him, but Marriott rose abruptly and blocked my path. With Fletcher's departure, he seemed to have recovered his confidence. 'What the devil are you doing drinking with a blighter like that, Franklin? The man's some sort of pacifist.'

'Is it really any of your business?'

'Yes, it damn well is. He could be a German spy for all I know.'

'Don't be ridiculous.'

'I've a good mind to fetch the police.'

Marriott's friend came to my rescue. 'Forget it, Guy. He was probably just squiffy. Come and have another drink.'

With a reluctance that was mostly show, Marriott brushed at his sleeve, picked up his glass and moved out of my path. 'All right. But I won't forget this, Franklin. I think I will have a word with the MO about you.'

'You do that.' I paid him no more heed. I hurried to the door, was momentarily blocked by an incoming drunken trio, then gained the street. I looked up and down, but there was no sign of Fletcher. Unless – yes, there he was, standing by a lamp post back the way we'd come. He saw me, then moved on, not waiting for me to catch up, and, before I could, he crossed the next street and turned down a side-alley.

I had no need to worry: he didn't mean to lose me. The alley led between two warehouses and, at its end, I could see a narrow wharf giving on to a reach of the harbour. There, reclining against a bollard and gazing out at the calm water, I found him. The night was wind-less but still wet, the rain turned to gathering mist. It was quiet on the wharf, with only the wailing sirens of distant craft in the harbour to break the silence. He looked up at the sound of my approach and nodded in acknowledgement.

'Why make a scene like that?' I asked. 'There was no need.'

'There was every need. His kind sicken me.'

'Aren't I his kind?'

'No more than Willis.'

'Willis?' I remembered then what the boy in Copenhagen Yard had said. 'Is Willis in the Army too?'

'He's a deserter.'

Then I thought I understood. 'So you hired those rooms to shelter him. Hence all the secrecy. But why what is he to you?'

'I felt I owed it to him.'

'And how did he come to be acquainted with Leonora? The Powerstocks know nothing of him.'

'Don't you understand yet, Franklin? Willis was in your regiment.'

'I've never heard of him.'

'Yes you have. By his real name. Hallows. Captain the Honourable John Hallows.'

I stared at him, not in disbelief but in awe of my own reaction. Hallows' face in the cheval-glass in Olivia's bedroom was there, calmly watching me, at the edge of the waters that lapped in lazy mockery about the wharf. He was not dead. Somewhere, he still lived and breathed and kept his counsel. And somewhere too my sense of loss was stung by something worse: if he lived, he could not be the man I thought I knew. If he lived, he was diminished, and I with him.

'I didn't want to tell you,' Fletcher continued. 'I don't think I would have told anyone else. I wish it had been

277

someone like Marriott who came looking instead of you.'

'Hallows is alive.' I could only voice the thought, inadequate, shallow, awesome as it was.

'Yes,' said Fletcher. 'Hallows is alive. Dead to his family, his country, his regiment. Yet stubbornly, inconveniently alive.'

'But . . . how?'

'That I can't tell you. He came to me in June and I agreed to shelter him under a false name in those rooms I rented on his behalf. He said that he had deserted, but was presumed dead: that he just wanted time to think, to be alone. I gave it to him. It didn't seem much.'

'Why did he come to you?'

Fletcher smiled. 'Of all people, you mean? That's the strange thing. He was still at school when Miriam died and I'd have thought he knew nothing of me. But it seems she confided in him where she couldn't confide in her husband. It was a secret he intended to keep for ever – would have done, but for the war and whatever drove him to cut and run. Alone and frightened in the country that had once been his home, I suppose he turned to the only other . . . exile . . . he knew, or knew of. He must have reckoned that, for his mother's sake, I wouldn't turn him away, must have judged by what she told him of me that I wouldn't hold desertion in the face of this war against him. And he was right. I think he was surprised to find me still alive, still living at the Mermaid, still waiting for him.'

'Waiting?'

'Yes. When he walked in from nowhere, when he explained who he was, when he confessed with relief what had brought him to me, I realized that I'd been waiting for him ever since Miriam died. For eleven years

278

I'd waited for some message from her. Then, suddenly, her message was standing in front of me.'

I walked to the edge of the wharf, moving slowly to stem somehow the flood of consequences that Fletcher's words had released. 'Leonora has known this all along. She is pregnant by her own husband, but her husband is meant to be dead. How did he contact her without the rest of his family knowing?'

Fletcher's reply came from behind me as I gazed out across the gloomy, turbid water. 'I don't know. He claimed nobody but me knew he was alive. Had I thought otherwise, I'd have been more anxious. As it was, I calculated that nobody would be looking for a dead man. Even so, Copenhagen Yard was only a temporary berth. I advised him to leave Portsmouth, head north, lose himself in some big city. He was too near home here for peace of mind – his or mine. Now I think he wanted it that way. He told me the war was too awful to bear, and that was easy to believe, but now I think there was more to it than that. There was some purpose to his flight beyond a horror of war.'

Swiftly, I was discerning what that purpose might have been. 'When did you last see him?'

'Friday the fifteenth. I went round there once a week to check how he was. I advised him again to leave Portsmouth. He said that he would but I didn't believe him. Last Friday, when I went, he wasn't there. It was unusual. He never went out during the day. But I didn't think too much of it until I read in the evening paper on Saturday about the murder at Meongate.'

So now we had come to it. 'You think Hallows did it?'

'All I know is that a man was murdered at Meongate and Hallows disappeared. Make of that what you will.'

'If the police knew Hallows were alive, they would

suspect him. he could well have had reason to kill Mompesson. And . . . there are other things.'

'Yesterday, Hallows' wife came to see me. I had no idea she knew of me, far less that Hallows had been in touch with her. I linked her anxiety with the murder. I told her where she might be able to find her husband. But we know now that she was too late. And we also know why she was so anxious to contact him. Perhaps she'd not told him she was pregnant. Perhaps . . .'

I turned back to face him. 'Where did she go? Where can I find her?'

'She said she was hoping to stay with a friend on the Isle of Wight – a schoolteacher there. I have the address. You're welcome to it. Maybe you know why she wasn't going back to Meongate.'

'I think I do. She would have been forced to name the father of her child. And she could not give that name if she was to keep his secret.'

He pushed himself upright and moved closer. 'I didn't know I was sharing a secret. What I did wasn't for Hallows, of course, or his wife. It was for . . . someone else.'

'For Miriam?'

'For her sake, for her secret, I'd have killed you in that alley.'

'What stopped you?'

'She did. She wouldn't have wanted that. No secret can be kept for ever. That's why you found me, in my buried life. That's why you'll find Hallows. Not because of a murder. Nor because you'll know where to look. But because, eventually, he won't want to stay hidden. There's no comfort in hiding, my friend. Nor much in revelation. But, at least, there's the honesty of being in the open, of seeing the enemy, of looking him in the eye, squarely, without flinching.'

'Who is the enemy?'

'I wish I knew. For a while, I thought you were. But now I see you're just another victim like me. Like Hallows.'

Fellow victims. That was our shabby fellowship, our share of whatever Hallows' fate was. We walked in silence back to the Mermaid. Too much had been said for further speech. And, as we went, I trawled my memory of all that had happened for some clue to explain it. Hallows' papers had been found on a corpse in no man's land. Had he, then, planned his escape? If so, why had he encouraged me to go to Meongate after his death? What thoughts ran through his head as he lay on the truckle-bed in Copenhagen Yard? When did he and Leonora meet? If there was a clue, it was in my compulsion to know, the compulsion Hallows had fed, and primed, and left to find its target. If he had planned my pursuit, its end was already known to him, wherever he was, waiting for me to find him.

At the Mermaid, Fletcher's sister brought us beer and some supper in the back room. I was hungry and tired after the night's events, but not too tired to tell Fletcher some of what I knew about Hallows' family. Late into the night, long after the pub had fallen silent, we sat and talked about Mompesson, the hold I thought he must have had over Leonora, the part I feared Hallows might have played in his death. It was the least I owed Fletcher: some part of what I knew. By the time I'd finished, I was certain Hallows had killed Mompesson, that he had foreseen what would happen to his home and his family without him, what mischief Mompesson would work with them, had foreseen it all and resolved to prevent it.

Yet, when I woke the next morning in an upper room of the inn, I knew it didn't make sense. Desertion and murder would hurt Hallows' family more surely than his death. The price of thwarting Mompesson was worse than the evil he might have wrought.

I had resolved to go at once in pursuit of Leonora. She had written where she might be found on a scrap of notepaper and left it with Fletcher: 'c/o Miss Grace Fotheringham, East Dene College, Bonchurch, near Ventnor, Isle of Wight'. I stared at it morosely as Fletcher's sister served me breakfast in the tiny kitchen.

'This is very kind of you,' I said, to break the silence.

'It's kind of Dan,' she replied, without smiling. 'He's too kind. Always has been. That's his trouble. I never met her' – I knew at once who she meant – 'but that was the start. He lost everything because of her.'

'Then he's fortunate to have a sister like you.'

'My Bill was dead by the time Dan came out. The brewery wouldn't have let me keep this place without a man to help me. I've done him no favours. But this I will say.' She leant over me. 'Your type bring him nothing but bad luck. Leave him alone. That's all I ask.'

Fletcher walked down with me to the Hard, where I was to catch the Isle of Wight ferry. The sun was shining, though it did not soften the stark streets of Portsea. To our right, as always, loomed the Dockyard wall.

'Your sister wants you to be left alone,' I said as we passed the Main Gate.

'We can't all have what we want. You should know that.'

'Sheltering a deserter is a serious offence, especially for somebody with a previous conviction.'

'We're both taking risks. I wonder if you realize how great they are.'

'I think I do.'

'For instance, I don't expect you're aware that we're being followed.' I made to swing round, but he restrained me. 'Don't look. Take my word for it, I saw him hanging round the Mermaid this morning and I've brought here by a roundabout route, which he's followed every step of the way.'

'Who is he?'

'A policeman, I reckon. Do you know why they should be after you?'

'I told you Shapland's no fool. But can you be sure?'

'Sure enough. We'll put it to the test, though.'

We walked down the jetty to the ferry pontoon. There I bought a ticket and waited with Fletcher on a bench where we had a good view of the other passengers. Fletcher nodded towards a thickset, overcoated man in the ticket queue.

'There's your man. And this is what we'll do. He'll have instructions to follow you, not me. So you'll wait until the last possible moment before boarding the ferry. He'll do the same, of course, to be sure you don't trick him. But I'll prevent him getting aboard.'

'How?'

'Leave that to me. And don't worry. The worst he can do is arrest me.'

When the ferry came in – a chugging, compact little steamer – the other passengers bunched near the gangway, but I hung back and, true to Fletcher's prediction, so did the man in the overcoat. He seemed to glance anxiously towards us, trying to guess what move we would make. After the passengers had gone aboard, some freight was loaded, but still the three of us stood where we were. By then, the other man must have known we had his measure.

It was as the crew were raising the gangplank that Fletcher twitched at my sleeve and I lunged forward. Already, the ferry was easing away from the pontoon as I jumped aboard. The deckhands gave me straight looks, but I was only interested in what was happening ashore.

The man in the overcoat had evidently tried to follow me. He and Fletcher were still entwined, the other man gesticulating and mouthing words I couldn't hear above the ferryboat's engine. A porter bustled over to placate him, while Fletcher said something – probably an apology – and glanced in my direction with a half-smile. The ferry was well away now, white water churning behind it as it manoeuvred out into the harbour mouth. Shapland might have been too clever for me, but not for Fletcher.

EIGHT

There was a breeze getting up in the Solent. I sat on desk as we buffeted across, looking back at Portsmouth as we left it, then ahead at the green mass of the island.

From Ryde, I took a train across the island to Ventnor on its south coast, a holiday resort emptied by the war but still genteelly picturesque, a scatter of white-faced buildings fringing the sea at the foot of a steep, wooded slope. At the railway station, I asked directions to Bonchurch and followed them, out of the town to the east, where the houses became larger and less congested, leisured villas tucked away in thickly leafed parks.

The village of Bonchurch was a cluster of mellow cottages round a pond overhung with willows. At the post office, I was told how to find East Dene College. It lay down a winding, rhododendron-lined drive, at the head of which a sign declaimed: EAST DENE COLLEGE, ACADEMY FOR YOUNG LADIES. Not that any of them were in evidence as I approached. The courtyard was deserted, the greystoned building in silence amidst the swaying trees. But, as I neared the entrance, a stern-faced lady in a black dress emerged, snapped shut the book she was reading and cast me a sharp look.

'Good morning,' I said. 'I'm looking for Miss Fotheringham.'

The look hardened. 'Miss Fotheringham will be teaching at this time. What is the nature of your business?'

'I'm sorry. It's a matter of some urgency. Might I see her for just a few moments?'

'Your name?'

I gave it. She led me into the entrance hall and directed me to a small waiting room with windows looking back down the drive. There was a photograph of the college staff and students, dated September 1901, above the fireplace, but no trace of Miss Fotheringham in the list of names. Three girls in ankle-length white dresses ambled past the window, carrying tennis rackets. One glanced in at me, but seemed not at all abashed.

The door opened behind me and I turned round. A woman of about Leonora's age stood there, dressed, like the girls, all in white. Perhaps she too had been playing tennis. She was dark-haired, with a dimple to her cheeks that suggested a cheerful disposition. But, on this occasion, she wasn't smiling.

'I'm Grace Fotheringham,' she said. 'What can I do for you, Mr Franklin?'

'I'm sorry if this is inconvenient.'

'It's certainly irregular. But I was told it was urgent.'

'It is. I'm looking for Leonora Hallows. I believe you know where she is.'

She walked past me and gazed out of the window. 'Leonora has told me about you, Mr Franklin. How did you know where to come?'

'Does it matter? Can I see her?'

'She needs rest, time alone, away from her family.'

'I'm not a member of her family. And you may as well know that I shan't leave until I've seen her.'

She looked at me for a moment, as if seeking to confirm what I'd said. Then she spoke in an undertone. 'She's staying at my cottage in the village. Sea Thrift. In Shore Road, just beyond the post office. She'll be there now.'

'Then I don't need to bother you any more, Miss Fotheringham. I'll bid you good morning.'

'One thing . . .' I stopped at the door. 'Leonora is my friend, Mr Franklin. I don't want her upset any more than she already has been.'

'Tell me, how much has she told you?'

'If you mean do I know she is with child, the answer is yes.'

'As to the identity of the father?'

'That is none of my business. As far as the locality is concerned, her husband has only recently been killed.'

'You are a friend indeed, Miss Fotheringham. I am pleased to have met you.' I meant it: I could see why Leonora had turned to her.

I retraced my steps to the post office, then turned into Shore Road. Sea Thrift was a small, thatched stone cottage behind a flint wall surmounted by a straggling hedge flecked with red valerian. The entrance was a wrought-iron gate set in and shaped to a stone arch in the wall. Through its bars, I could see a well-kept garden of trimmed grass and brightly stocked flower borders beneath canopies of pick cherry and green lime. To one side, a wicker chair had been placed beneath the overhanging eave of the house and there, reclining in the late-morning sunshine in a lilac dress, was Leonora.

287

There was nothing in the world, or the place, or her pose, to tell of the turmoil she must have felt.

She looked up at the first creak of the gate. A King Charles spaniel by her chair pricked up its ears but did not so much as yap.

'Good morning,' I said lamely. Then I saw that she was suddenly breathless. 'I'm sorry. Did I surprise you?' I closed the gate behind me and walked into the garden. Still she did not speak. I stood awkwardly in front of her. 'Fletcher told me where you were. I've just come from the school.'

'I thought I could trust Mr Fletcher,' she said at last, her face strangely expressionless.

'You can. He had no choice but to tell me.'

'How much do you know?'

'Everything. I know John is still alive.' Still no change of expression, but a faint catching of the breath. 'I think you should have told me sooner.'

'How could I? You must know what it means.'

'May we talk? About what it means?'

'I see that we must.' She rose from the chair and, for the first time, smiled. 'I'm sorry, Tom, for deceiving you. I hope you don't think too badly of me.'

'No.' I tried to smile as well, but the expression froze as it formed. It seemed, somehow, too banal for the moment. 'There is much that I still don't understand.'

'Let us walk a little.' She led the dog into the house through some french windows, then closed them behind him. He regarded us mournfully from a foot-stool as we walked away. 'I have taken Swinburne out several times already. Like his namesake, he is not noted for his energy.' She closed the gate behind us as we emerged into the lane. A dog-cart clopped by, with a plump, red-faced parson at the reins. He raised his switch in acknowledgement.

'I think I see what sort of a refuge this place is. But you can't hide here for ever, Leonora.'

'I shan't try to. Indeed, they have now heard from me at Meongate. They should have had a letter this morning telling them I am safe and well, though not where I am.'

We turned down past the post office. The butcher in the shop next door raised his boater. Leonora smiled at him and spoke to me in an undertone. 'As you see, I am already known and welcome here. Bonchurch is a tight-knit, friendly community sympathetic to my plight. You will appreciate that, if the truth were known to them, I would once again be an outcast, and would disgrace my friend, who has risked a good deal by taking me in.'

'There need be no question of it. But is that what you feel from Meongate – an outcast?'

'Entirely. I could not remain there, for all manner of reasons. Though I am sorry to have left in the way that I did. Here, for the moment, I am safe. I am Grace's war-widowed friend, sadly with child. Respectable and plausible. But what of you? How did you find me so soon?'

As we went on past the gates of East Dene, down a sloping, even rougher track towards the sea now visible beyond the trees, I told her of the sequence of events that had led me to her. None of it seemed to surprise her, perhaps because, in so many ways, she'd been there before me.

By now, we were on a path that led through the grassed and shrub-strewn hummocks of some long-ago landslip, the sea below us to our right, sucking at the shingle of a hidden shore. Behind us, across the fields, the gables and roof-trees of East Dene were clearly visible. There, I imagined, in some tall-windowed classroom, Miss Fotheringham would be teaching French with distracted refinement, wondering the while how her friend was faring.

'I do not begrudge you the truth,' Leonora said. 'I want you to know that. John had no right to deceive you as he did. Alas, I cannot account for all that he has done – or may have done. I do not fully understand him any more.'

'But you have seen him. You have known for a long time that he is not dead.'

'Yes. For a month, I thought him so. The news came from France in early May. There was a memorial service at the church. You wrote to me and I wrote back. Then it happened.

'It was a Saturday: June the tenth. Mompesson was staying at Meongate for the weekend. He'd become an even more frequent visitor since the report of John's death. And it was apparent to me long before then that he wanted somehow to become a member of our family. I don't mean by being Olivia's lover. That was distasteful but not unusual. No, he wanted Meongate, a hold on the title if he could not have the title itself. As soon as I became a widow, I presented an attractive target. At first, I was too distraught to notice, or to care. At worst, his attentions distracted me from my grief. Olivia came to hate me then, I believe, to fear she would be set aside for a younger woman. As a matter of fact, I doubt he would have felt the need to forgo her even if I had agreed to marry him. But let that pass. To all of this I remained oblivious, until that night.'

I interrupted to stem the flow of her account. Suddenly, I didn't want to know too soon. She had held back so much for so long that I was ill-prepared for its revelation, all of a piece, as we stood on the sloping, uneven ground above the sea. 'Wait. All of this I've only been able to guess at. You speak of Mompesson wanting some way into the family. Why? What for? What was he after?'

'I too can only guess. He didn't confide in me – or anyone else. I dare say. But his own family had land and wealth in Louisiana before the Civil War took it all from them. Was he jealous of us because of that, do you suppose? He had a talent for making money, but talent alone couldn't give him social status. Is that what he wanted from us?' She turned and took a few paces down the slope. I didn't close the gap, sensed instead that it was necessary if she was to tell me what had happened.

'That Saturday night, I went to bed early. I usually did when Mompesson was visiting us. The strain of being polite to him exhausted me. I fell asleep more quickly than I had done in weeks.

'When I woke, I thought I was dreaming. John was there, above me, his hand over my mouth to prevent me crying out. An illusion, a nightmare: what else could it be? But then he spoke and I knew that he really had returned. And when he spoke, I knew that something had changed in him. The husband I had thought dead was still alive, but yet not whole, not restored to what he had been.

'"I am not a ghost," he said, "and I am sorry you should ever have been led to believe I was dead." He sat on the bed and took his hand from my mouth. I did not cry out, though I could have done, for joy at his survival. I thought – in so far as I thought at all – that there had been some absurd mistake which he could now put right. He told me he had entered the house secretly.

Nobody but I knew he was there, or still alive. It was, he said, how he wanted it. And all that mattered to me in that moment was that my love had been returned to me. When I held him in my arms, I held a miracle.' She turned round and looked at me again. 'Can you imagine what that meant to me, Tom?'

'Did he tell you what had happened, how he had survived?'

'Later. I had slept a little and woke to find him standing by the window, smoking a cigarette and watching dawn break over the park. I saw him then more clearly than before: rough clothes, unshaven, no uniform, no luggage. With a shock, I realized he had the look of a fugitive. And something in the way he looked at me – the instant before he noticed I was awake – made me realize something was wrong.

'"I'm going to have to leave you again," he said. "Officially, I must remain dead." The he told me. His death was no bizarre misunderstanding, but a fraud. He had deserted. He said that he had thought of doing so often, that the war was an ugly, brutal farce he could no longer tolerate. When the opportunity had come, he had taken it. Cut off in no man's land, he had left his papers on a dead companion and stolen away from the battlefield. He wouldn't go into details, wouldn't say where he'd been since then. He had come to me in the hope that I could somehow absolve him of the guilt that he felt, somehow divine what it was that he should do.

'But I couldn't. That was when I failed him, at his time of greatest need. I love him and he loves me. I was – I still am – overjoyed that he did not die in France. But it isn't as simple as that, is it? Doesn't some part of you resent him as a traitor? Wouldn't the whole world condemn him as a coward if they knew how he'd cheated death?'

What she'd said was true and I could only admit it. 'John's right: the war should not be allowed to continue. But, as long as it does, it will demand its due. It isn't cowardly to seek a way out. In fact, it takes a special kind of bravery. But you're right too: the world wouldn't understand such an act.'

She sighed. 'That's what I told him. that, sooner or later, he would be found, that what would happen then would be worse than to lose him in the war, however dreadful, however pointless.'

I thought of the punishment meted out to deserters. 'It is so. It may still be so.'

'I urged him to go back to his regiment. Then he might have some chance of talking his way out of a charge of desertion. He said he didn't think it would work, that they wouldn't believe whatever story he invented. So I asked the question I most dreaded putting to him. If he did not give himself up, how could we remain together? If he was to stay in hiding, how long must I go on pretending he was dead?'

I expected her to continue, but she did not. A silence fell, clarifying the rustle of the grass in the breeze around us. She seemed to need some prompting. 'What was his answer?'

She shook her head. 'He had none. He said that he saw the sense of what I was proposing, that what I'd told him only confirmed what he'd so often told himself. Yet something seemed to hold him back, something beyond mere indecision. It wasn't as if he was hesitant, or nervous, or even much afraid. There was a calmness about him, a detachment I found more disturbing than anything else.

'Then he said he'd have to go. It was beginning to grow light: he couldn't risk being seen. I tried to win from him some promise to do as I'd advised him, or, failing that, some agreement to meet me again, but he said he could guarantee nothing, beyond his love for me. Before he left, he mentioned you.'

'What did he say?'

'He'd spoken of you before, of course, so your name wasn't new to me. "Franklin may come to see you," he said. "If he lives. If he remembers. Keep the truth from him at all costs. But trust him. He deserves that." He was right: you do.'

'Maybe. But I've been no help, to either of you.'

'That's because John can only help himself. He left that Sunday morning and I've not seen him or heard from him since. I saw him slip into the trees at the edge of the park after one backward glance and I prayed then that he might not stray too far from me. I felt sure he would, after all, give himself up. Instead . . . nothing. No news, no word from him. To the world he remained dead. As the days passed, so did the tension of waiting. I began, at times, to think I'd only dreamed his return. But it was not so. My own body gave the lie to it. When I realized that I was pregnant, I realized also the impossibility of my position. I could not keep John's secret without seeming to have betrayed him. I could not sustain his family's belief in him without destroying their belief in me. And the one man I needed most to confide in – whose mind might have been changed by my news – I did not know how to find.'

'As you say: an impossible position.'

'But about to become worse. At the beginning of August, Mompesson showed his hand. He had often asked me to go for a drive with him. I had as often refused. This time I had no choice. "I wish to speak to you about your husband's supposed death," he said. "Would you not rather do so in private?" My blood ran cold. He knew.

'He drove out along the Winchester road and stopped near the golf course. There he told me. He had seen John leaving Meongate that Sunday morning in June. He knew he was alive and that I also knew. Now, he had had him traced to an address in Portsmouth. He would not give it to me, but this he made clear: unless I co-operated, he would go to the authorities. John would be seized and shot as a deserter. He left me in no doubt of it. Unless, as I say, I co-operated.'

She turned away again and looked out to sea. 'What choice did I have? I couldn't call his bluff, because he wasn't bluffing. I couldn't warn John, because I didn't know where he was. I could confide in no one. I was obliged to meet the terms that Mompesson set upon his silence. They were more severe than I'd imagined. He did not want money. He wanted me. You know something of his ways – I shall not speak of them. He wanted to use me as he would have done the slaves he felt were his birthright, denied him by history. For John's sake – for no other reason, I promise you – I agreed to let him have his way.

'That was not the worst. There was a heavier penalty still. He wanted to marry me. It was absurd, yet horribly cunning. We would know it was a bigamous marriage, of course, but nobody else would, so long as the secret was kept. And how could I not keep the secret? How could I not agree? When he found out – through Olivia, I think – that I was pregnant, he was delighted. Everyone would assume he was the father: he would make it his business to ensure they did. So the marriage would hurt Lord Powerstock just as it pleased Mompesson.

'At heart, though, he still wanted Meongate more than he wanted me. I began to see how he might have planned it. To marry me was only the start. Posing as the innocent, he could then expose John and ruin both of us. Such a blow would kill Lord Powerstock, clearing the way for Mompesson to marry Olivia and acquire the estate and privileges he desired. By keeping John's secret, I was only serving Mompesson's ambition. Perhaps you think it fanciful, but that is how it seemed to me.'

'It sounds all too likely.'

'Shall we walk on a way?' She moved off and I followed, trailing slowly along the overgrown path. Three girls, carrying butterfly nets, seemingly bound for East Dene, passed by and bade us courteous good mornings. When they'd gone, Leonora resumed. 'I didn't know what to do. There seemed no way out, no one to turn to. When you came, with your gentlemanly offers of friendship, it only made matters worse, only reminded me of the bitterness of my plight. I feared it might be so when Lord Powerstock said that he'd recognized your name on one of the lists Lady Kilsyth circulated, but I didn't try to stop him inviting you. Besides, time was running out. When Mompesson next came, he set a term on my compliance. I was given until last Friday to surrender myself to him.' She shuddered visibly in the warm air. 'That was to be followed by an announcement of our engagement.'

'I had some inkling of it. I overheard part of your discussion with him in the rhododendron glade.'

She stopped and glanced at me. 'But you could not have guessed what lay behind our words.'

'Only that he had some kind of hold over you.'

She nodded and moved on. 'As truly he did. I think he enjoyed giving me so much time to contemplate what would happen.'

'Before he left, he boasted that you would agree to marry him.'

'A measure of his confidence, and a warning to you, no doubt. After he'd gone, I racked my brains for some way to defeat him. it seemed to me that my only hope was to contact John. All I knew was that he was somewhere in Portsmouth. But why? A naval town seemed a strange place for a deserter to hide. I thought about all that he'd said, went over it again and again. There was nothing in it to suggest why he'd gone there. Then, out of the blue, it came to me. Charter happened to say something about John's mother. That wasn't unusual. But it reminded me of her work in Portsmouth. It made no sense, but it was John's only connection with the town. I resolved to go there, in search of a clue as much as of him.'

'But I met you off the ferry and spoiled your plans.'

'Not exactly. I didn't have any plans. Meeting you made me realize how futile my journey was. I still had no idea where to look. When we returned to Meongate, I was no better off.'

We had come to the end of the path. It faded away amongst some gorse bushes where the sloping ground steepened towards the clifftop. We stopped and looked at each other. 'When I made my own foolish proposal, I now see you had no alternative but to reject it as you did.'

She smiled faintly. 'None, Tom. None at all. I'm sorry. Shall we go back the way we came?' We began to retrace our steps. 'I felt that unless I made the rejection conclusive, you would persist, which could only have hurt both of us. So I told you I was pregnant and left you to jump to the obvious conclusion: that Mompesson was responsible. For me, it was only a fore-taste of what everyone would think.

'But it solved nothing. I was left to keep my appoint-ment with him that evening, with all that it entailed. I had run out of time and hope. So, as a last, desperate throw, I slid a note beneath your door. I went to the observatory and trained the telescope on Mompesson's window. I hoped that you would go there, that what you would see might make you understand that I was his victim, not his mistress, that it might prompt you to save me from him.' She glanced at me. 'But I suppose that's not how it looked.'

I felt shamed by the faint hope she'd placed in me. 'For someone as trustworthy as John said I was, it might have been enough. But no, it's not how it looked. Not to me.'

'When I heard that Mompesson was dead, I thought I'd gone too far, that I'd driven you to murder for my sake.'

'Nothing so noble. A drunken night in a barn is all I was equal to.'

'Then a different suspicion formed in my mind.'

'That John killed him?'

'Yes. At first, it seemed absurd, but, after all, who else? Was that his real purpose in coming back – to protect me from Mompesson?'

'I'm certain he saw Mompesson as a threat.'

'As I am. When you told me that the observatory had been unlocked, I felt sure it must be so. I had locked it after setting the telescope. There was only one other key, which I'd last seen in John's possession.'

'Why should he have gone there?'

'Because he knew he would be safe there, able to monitor the comings and goings of the house, able to spy on Mompesson. Maybe he saw something that night that finally convinced him Mompesson had to die.' She paused and, in the space before she began again, I imagined what he might have seen.

'More than ever, I had to speak to him. And, at last, I guessed where he'd gone. I read his mother's chapter in the Diocesan Committee Report – and knew it was the connection I'd been looking for. You almost guessed your-self – until Inspector Shapland interrupted us. I'm sorry I had to deceive you in order to make my departure, but I couldn't afford to explain what I was doing.'

'I understand that now.'

'I made my way to the Mermaid Inn. There I met Mr Fletcher. When I told him who I was, that I knew John was alive, hiding somewhere in Portsmouth, he seemed to soften towards me. He told me where John had been living, but warned me that I was too late: John had gone. And so it proved. I left the note in the hope he might yet return.'

'It doesn't look as if he will.'

'Grace is my oldest friend. She is the only person in all the world I could trust with such a secret. And I could no longer bear it alone. So I came to her and she did not disappoint me.'

'She knows everything?'

'Everything I know. We have invented a convenient fiction for the ears of her neighbours. It has won me peace, for a while.'

'And John?'

'I cannot bring him peace if I cannot find him. and where now can I look?'

'Where indeed?' Wherever he'd gone, this time, he'd left no clues, no trail for us to follow. 'If he did come back to save you from Mompesson, he's done what he set out to do.'

'But at what cost?'

Her words hung in the reflective, salt-soaked air. Our steps began to skirt the village church nestled in its hollow behind overgrown stone walls. Its offered age-old absolution struck at me across the centuries. Hernu's Farm, so long ago, when Hallows had reached, with faltering grasp, towards loyalties and loves that eclipsed the war we were caught in. I'd not known then what promptings he would follow, what battle he was really fighting. And now? How much did he know of all the ways I'd failed him? Meongate – his home and my entrapment – had seen a more certain parting than any distant battlefield.

Leonora turned off the path and went down through the narrow gate into the churchyard. I did not follow as she entered the church; felt, instead, wordlessly excluded from her unanswered thoughts. What had she done, after all, but keep faith with her husband as the Church's vows required? But they would not under-stand, no pious congregation would defend, the lengths she'd gone to. Hers could only ever be a secret confessional.

I stood with my back to the porch, gazing past the ancient, crooked gravestones and the brambled hedge towards the sea. What I felt was self-reproach leavened by doubt. I should never have believed what I had of Leonora in her dealings with Mompesson, could never have done had I not known what desires Olivia awakened in me. I had judged another as I would have feared to be judged myself. But the doubt remained, a dark corona was Hallows, as it always had been, from first encounter to last, oblique farewell. I had failed him, in the test I never knew he was setting. What test had he also failed?

'I think I'd like to go home now.' I jumped at the words: Leonora had emerged from the church in silence and materialized at my elbow.

'Yes, of course. Let's go back.' We made our way out on to the path. 'If you're sure that's what you want.'

'What else can I do?'

'Come back with me to Meongate. I feel I've wronged you. If I'd been less suspicious and more trusting, this might have been avoided. Now I'd like to make amends.'

'Don't blame yourself, Tom. We're all accountable. If John felt driven to kill Mompesson, it's because we left him no choice. But I can't come back with you, not if I'm to keep John's secret. And it must be kept, mustn't it?'

'I hope it can be.'

'Tell Lord Powerstock you found me, but not how. I don't think he'll quibble with my reasons for remaining here. Since I cannot tell him the truth, he will have to believe the worst of me.'

'What about Shapland?'

'Tell him as little as you need to.'

'He may call you as a witness at the inquest.'

'He has no reason to. But if he does – so be it.'

'You realize that the likeliest verdict will be to pin the blame on poor Cheriton?'

'I do. But what choice do we have?'

'None.' I shook my head at the hollowness of the word. There was, as Leonora had said, no choice: no choice of falsehoods once the truth had been suppressed; no choice of roads that would not lead to bitterness and ruin.

Ahead of us, the path widened into a metalled track past the entrance to East Dene. There, walking slowly towards us down the drive, was Grace Fotheringham. She glanced anxiously in our direction. 'Is all well?' she called.

'As well as can be,' Leonora replied. She looked at me before continuing. 'I believe Mr Franklin and I have said all there is to be said – and that he is now content to leave.' I hung back as she moved ahead to meet her friend.

Nobody spoke in the interval that followed, but I sensed in the silence an air of conclusiveness, almost of dismissal. Now that they stood together, I felt excluded by their friendship, become once more the unlooked-for stranger. I walked past them down the lane, then stopped and turned back to face them. 'Goodbye then,' I said, and, even as I pronounced the words, I knew it was just that: a final leave-taking. I would never see Leonora again.

'Goodbye, Tom,' she said. The breeze had died. The lane was still, in the unique, mellow, passing stillness of early afternoon. I wondered for an instant how the scene might look to any vaguely curious passer-by. Then Leonora stepped forward and kissed me on the cheek. 'Go with my blessing,' she said, so softly I could believe Miss Fotheringham had not heard, nor had been meant to.

I took her hand, awkwardly, uncertain what she might take the gesture to mean. Some hint of the closeness we might have known? Some fellowship with her for sharing John's secret? What did it mean, after all, that moment now passed when we might have become more to each other than we ever now could? Nothing, beyond a curtain unopened, a corner unturned.

I released her hand. She looked at me gravely, the sad, open greyness of her eyes forever forbidding the tears we might once have shared. There were no words left. I turned and walked away from them, down the broadening lane between the thatched cottages. I didn't look back until I'd passed the post office and the turning that led to Sea Thrift. And when I did look back, they were but two shapes, blurred by distance and growing strangeness, two symbols standing for all that I still did not understand.

The bell on the post office door rang as a customer emerged and broke the spell: a stout lady, dressed in black, cradling a Pekinese dog in her arms. Banality was all about me, more certain than any shadow. I walked on down the lane and, this time, did not look back. This time, the curtain closed and I turned the corner.

What was I to do? The question wouldn't leave my head as the little train jolted back across the island, was still with me as I stared from the ferry rail at the seagulls wheeling behind the boat. Now I knew Leonora's secret, I was as helpless as her, bound to Hallows by love or loyalty but left to guess the role he'd played in all that had happened.

We drew into Portsmouth Harbour past the towering grey flanks of anchored warships and I glimpsed, swaying at its mooring further ahead, Nelson's *Victory*, patched and painted remnant of another war in another time. England had expected too much of her soldiers in my war and I no longer knew where my duty lay. Once the ferry had docked, I headed straight for the Mermaid. There was nowhere else to go.

I was back – sooner than I might have expected – in the room where Fletcher lodged his secrets, with the budgerigar and the geraniums in the window-box. The bureau was open again, the photograph of Miriam unconcealed. Fletcher lit his pipe and poured me a glass of rum. He listened, patient and undismayed, to my account.

'Do you think you can handle the inquest the way she wants?' The question was simple and direct, unvarnished by doubt or scruple.

'Probably, now you've got the police off my back.'

'I haven't. They'll have seen you come back here.'

'But they won't know where I've been and, even if they did, it wouldn't help them. We couldn't tell them where Hallows is and they've no reason to suspect he's even alive. We must keep it that way.'

'For how long?'

'At least until after the inquest. Then . . . well, I don't know. What are you suggesting we do? Turn him in?'

'No. But you must have asked yourself: Where's he gone? What's he doing?'

'I don't know.' This was the true sum of the mystery. Abandoning the war in order to protect Leonora, even if it meant murdering Mompesson: that much I could understand. But what next? To stay hidden for ever was worse than . . . My gaze shifted to the window, sought its middle distance in which to frame my projection of what he'd done. What had Leonora said? 'A calmness about him, a detachment.' It had been no accident. He had planned it all, even to my following him to Meongate. It was his purpose we had served every step of the way. But what was his purpose?

'I see you're thinking the same as me.' Fletcher's words

snatched my attention back from the window. 'If he killed Mompesson to save Leonora, how can he save himself? And if he can't, what will that do to her?'

'He loses every way. We all do. If he returns to her, he will face a charge of desertion, maybe murder too. If he doesn't, then what was the point of it all?'

'I don't believe he will come back, or stay in hiding. Nor do you.'

Fletcher had touched the heart of my suspicion. Suddenly, I felt cold. 'No. Not really. It is as you say.'

Neither of us spoke. We had arrived at the end of our ponderings. For Hallows, we both felt certain, there was no way back. Whether he died in France, brutally, in the gruesome night of no man's land, or later, at a time of his choosing, keeping faith with the people he loved, made, in the end, no difference. There, in that back room of the Mermaid Inn, as Fletcher watched me solemnly through his pipesmoke, I guessed how it was for Hallows. Whilst Mompesson was there to threaten us, his covert, secretive life was justified. Now, with Mompesson gone, honour could be found only in death.

Fletcher let me out the back way, into the alley behind the yard. 'One thing,' he said, as he unbolted the gate. 'Since you mentioned his name last night, it's been bothering me: Inspector Shapland.'

'What about him?'

'I know him. He gave evidence at the trial: Machim's and mine. Nothing crucial. He'd run to earth some of our associates. Dogged, efficient. I'd have thought him retired by now.'

'Recalled for the duration, I gather.'

Fletcher nodded. 'Then it fits. As you say, no fool. He'll remember me.'

'There's still nothing for him to go on.'

'No. But be careful. Don't come to see me again.'

He meant it, in his guarded, dispassionate way; meant that, whatever secrets we shared, they bestowed no intimacy. Once I'd shaken his hand and he'd closed the gate behind me, our association ended. The past retreated into the shadows of his silence.

NINE

I reached Droxford as night was falling and booked into the Station Hotel: brick-built, ivy-clad, run-down and empty, some distance from the village and as far from Meongate. An obscure location suited my purpose.

Next morning, the confrontation couldn't be deferred. I walked up to Meongate through the lanes, remembering my first arrival but a few weeks before, when Charter had met me and bowled me along in the trap. There had been that day a note almost of gaiety. Now it was gone for ever.

And Charter wasn't there to meet me that morning. Only Fergus, straight-faced as ever. He told me I would find Lord Powerstock in his study.

He didn't seem surprised to see me. He might, I reflected, have sat there in his chair all the time I'd been away, preparing his look, not of disapproval, but of perpetual disappointment.

'Have you seen her?' he asked in a voice bereft of expression. 'We have received a letter.'

'I've seen her. She is well, but does not wish to return.'

'So the letter said. And perhaps it is better so.'

'It will certainly solve some of your problems.'

'You did not go to the police, then.'

'No. It wasn't necessary. I found her without them.'

'And what do you intend to do now?'

'I intend to leave this house, Lord Powerstock. Until the inquest, I cannot leave the area. But as soon as I'm able, I will remove myself from your lives.'

'I think that may be for the best.' In his reticence, there was no diminution of his bitterness. His beleaguered family pride was about me, like an acrid presence in the air. I had not done as he had wished. But, to have done so, I would have needed to be as blind as he had made himself.

I stood before him a moment longer, teetering on the edge of some further remark, some reference, however fleeting, to where I'd been and what I'd found there of the wife he'd once adored but had somehow failed to know. But it was useless. I could tell by the set lines of his face: he would not admit such knowledge. Without another word, I turned and left the room.

I intended, without further ado, to collect my belongings and go. But, in the hall, I paused to sift through some letters left on a silver tray to see if any were for me. There were three, but only one looked urgent. It had arrived that morning; a thin War Office envelope. I tore it open.

Marriott, it seemed, had been as good as his word. It was a curt summons to a medical board in Aldershot the following Monday. And, though Marriott might have thought it would come as a blow, he was wrong. For the first time, a return to active service had its attraction.

I pocketed the letter and made for my room. I packed hurriedly, eager to be away now that I knew more than

I wanted about those who lived – or had lived – at Meongate. I went into the bathroom to wash before leaving. As I raised my face, dripping, from the basin, I was aware of a presence in the room behind me.

I wheeled round, towelling the soap from my eyes. There was nobody there: I cursed my own nerves. But then a shadow cast by the light from one of the bedroom windows, the window I couldn't see through the doorway, moved, a dark, shifting patch on the patterned carpet. I caught my breath and stepped forward.

As I did so, Olivia came to meet me. She stood, framed by the doorway, smiling placidly with that hint of a sneer so peculiarly, so perpetually hers. She was wearing a cream dress, full-skirted but close-fitting about the bodice and waist, with her hair let down to her shoulders. She posed, not deigning to disguise her awareness of her own beauty, presented herself to me where the filtered sunlight played on her dark hair, where I could admire, despite myself, the lush maturity of her looks, where I could still, despite everything, be made to feel – and be seen to feel – the physical tug of her attraction.

'I gathered you had returned, Lieutenant.'

'Briefly. I'm moving out straight away. I shall stay in the village till after the inquest. Then you'll see no more of me.'

'We had a letter from Leonora, as you must know. She gave no address, but it was postmarked Newport, Isle of Wight. I recall she had a bridesmaid who went to teach on the island.'

'You could trace her if you wanted to. But do you?'

'No. Naturally not. I am, of course, glad to be rid of her.' She saw my eyes widen at her frankness. 'Let us dissemble no more. I take it from your assent to her

309

exile and your failure to pour out a torrent of allegations to the police that you are reconciled to the course we proposed before you left here, that you have come to heed my warning.'

'I shan't make any trouble for you, Lady Powerstock. I'm finished with you here. All I want to do is go away . . .'

'And die for your country? How noble.'

'I've seen enough nobility here to last me what remains of my lifetime. Now, if you'll excuse me . . .' I made to go past her, but she did not move aside. And I could hardly, with all that had happened, lay a hand upon her. I halted and refused to give best to the directness of her gaze. We were close enough now for me to catch the scent of her perfume, the same perfume she'd worn once before, and wore now to shame me.

'Tell me, Lieutenant: what did she do to win your silence? Did she offer you more of what you saw from the observatory?'

I made no move to strike her: to have done so would have been her victory. I said nothing: it was the only reply to her taunts. I knew at last that I was free of her; that, no matter what she said or did, I would have none of it. This time, I would simply walk away. No man could have defeated her: that I saw clearly for the first time. Perhaps Bartholomew had supposed he could suborn his young, wilful model, but he it was who had drowned. Perhaps Lord Powerstock had thought she would adorn his failing, feudal years, but she had imprisoned him in his own house. Perhaps Mompesson had thought he could play her false, but she was falser still. And Hallows? If he had escaped her, it was only to die.

At last, she moved aside. 'You are a fool, Lieutenant.'

She spoke softly as I went past her, almost clinically, without malice.

I thought of Cheriton, dead against an elm in the park, a note to her clutched in his hand. 'I have been a fool. It is true.' I picked up my jacket and bag. 'But no more.' Then I walked out on to the landing and she did not follow.

A few moments later, I was walking down the drive of Meongate for the last time. I did not look back. Olivia would have been watching and I was determined to show her no sign of weakness.

At the hotel, I unpacked again, then opened the other letters I'd collected from Meongate. One was from the Coroner's office, summoning me to be present at the magistrates' court the following Tuesday at 10 a.m., as expected. The other was from a firm of solicitors in Winchester: Mayhew & Troke, 'acting for Lord Powerstock in connection with proceedings shortly to be held before the Coroner for South Hampshire. Would I do Mr Mayhew the honour of calling at his offices before the week was out to clarify one or two aspects of the case?' I cursed silently: till the inquest was over, I could not be rid of them. Resistance, I knew, was useless. I walked into the village and telephoned Mayhew's number from the post office. A clerk who answered suggested two o'clock the following afternoon and I agreed.

I made my way back by a path that led past the water-mill. There, I lingered by the watercress beds and watched the millwheel lap the water in its lazy, foaming circles, watched its prosaic, mechanical beauty in the grey light of late morning and wondered whether, after all, Hallows deserved of me the perjury I planned.

I don't know how long I stood there, lulled into introspection by the rhythmic slush of the water, but the spell was only broken by the crack of a twig underfoot as somebody approached. I wheeled round to find Shapland smiling at me with genial curiosity, leaning on a walking stick that did nothing to lessen his look of a city policeman loose in the countryside.

'Good to see you back, Mr Franklin. I've just been up to the Station Hotel to see you. Why did you leave Meongate?'

'I didn't want to impose on their hospitality any longer. I'd have left Droxford completely if it weren't for the inquest.'

'And where have you been for the last couple of days?'

I hesitated, certain he knew the answer already. 'Here and there.'

He walked past me and leant on the railings flanking the watercress beds. 'Did you meet Cheriton's father while he was here?'

'Briefly, yes.'

'It was only natural he'd be cut up about the boy, of course, but it's tragic he should have to worry about an accusation of murder being added to the shame of suicide.' He looked back at me. This time, he wasn't smiling. 'Don't you think?'

'We are surrounded by tragedy, Inspector.' I looked at him blankly. I knew he'd had me trailed to Portsea knew now, with his talk of tragedy, what he was driving at: that Cheriton was our fall guy, the one scapegoat who couldn't complain. But for Hallows' sake, above all for Leonora's, I couldn't admit one grain of the shame I felt.

'I'll walk back some of the way with you.'

He was scarcely the company I wanted, but I couldn't

object. We walked past the mill and crossed a stile on to a path beside the stream that fed the wheel. I said nothing, but Shapland wasn't to be deterred.

'Police work has its share of tragedy, Mr Franklin, as I'm sure you can imagine. I thought I'd seen the last of it, but life plays tricks on you, don't you find?' I thought of Fletcher saying the same and still I remained silent. 'For instance, this isn't the first case I've investigated that involved the Powerstocks. Twelve years ago I had a hand in a sedition case in Portsmouth: quite a sensation in its time. One of the conspirators turned out to be a friend of the first Lady Powerstock.' He paused and I waited for his next attempt to draw me out. 'But that doesn't surprise you, does it?'

'Nothing about you surprises me, Inspector. I'm sure you know every twist and turn of the criminal mind.'

'Who said I was talking about crime? My theme was tragedy – not at all the same thing.'

'I'm not sure I see much difference.'

'Then let me explain. Lord Powerstock's first wife mixes in strange company and dies young. His second wife is unfaithful to him and she has his daughter-in-law appear to take an unhealthy interest in the same disreputable man. And, thanks to the war, he loses his son and heir. Finally, a young officer chooses to commit suicide on his property. Enough, I think, to comprise a tragedy.

'Crime, on the other hand, is altogether more specific. In the late evening of September 22nd, somebody enters Ralph Mompesson's room at Meongate and shoots him dead. Crime, pure and simple.'

We had come to a gate on to the lane that led to the hotel. I went through, but Shapland did not follow. He leant against the top bar of the gate and regarded me with quizzical scrutiny.

'My job is to investigate the crime, of course. But I've always tended to stray from the strict letter of my duties.'

'Is that wise?'

He began tapping the bars of the gate with his stick. 'Probably not. It may explain why I never attained a higher rank.'

'I must get back to the hotel. Are you coming any further?'

'No. You carry on.'

'Very well. Good day to you, Inspector.'

He said nothing. He may have nodded, but by then I'd turned my back on him. I heard his stick beating time to my steps on the gate and felt his eyes on me, all the way down the lane.

'It was kind of you to call at such short notice, Lieutenant. I do appreciate it.' Mayhew was speaking, Lord Powerstock's solicitor, a mild, modulated man, hair sleeked down and face professionally erased of meaning; yet, withal, there was something in his eyes, something veiled but minatory, that suggested he saw more clearly than his vapid pronouncements might seem to imply. 'The recent deaths at Meongate have greatly distressed his Lordship. He has asked me to protect his interests at the forthcoming inquest.' The room was wood-panelled and lawbook-lined, dusty with accumulated reticence. From the window, there was a view of the cathedral, its gothic stone as grey as the day, pigeons flapping mournfully at every carved device. 'These are, I trust, in tune with your own: that a natural reluctance to impute motive to one who has taken his own life should not deter us from connecting the two events.' I wasn't sure I still grasped his meaning, or why he'd wanted to see me, what it was they required

314

of me beyond a mute compliance. 'I therefore thought it prudent to seek from you some confirmation that any evidence you give to the Coroner will be consistent with such a conclusion.'

'Mr Mayhew, you should know there's nothing I could say to suggest who killed Mompesson. I can only speak – will only speak – of what I saw with my own eyes.'

He lowered his head and flattened his hand in some gesture of approbation. 'Precisely. Be factual – and frugal even in that.' He turned to his desk and handed me a sheet of paper, on which had been typewritten a passable summary of my account of finding Cheriton's body. 'Does this encompass what you intend to say?'

I scanned it. 'Yes.'

'Neither more nor less?'

'As you say.'

'One thing.' He leant forward intently. 'The police, I believe, have been disposed to query the absence of a note. A suicide note, you understand.' He smiled momentarily. 'You are sure there was none, are you not?'

His gaze was to the floor. I might almost have imagined, beneath the patina of professional discretion, some tremor of distaste for what he had been obliged to do in the service of Lord Powerstock's disorderly household. What, after all, might he have known of their varied failings? 'There was no note.'

'I need hardly say that any impression to the contrary, however created, would rebound to the substantial disadvantage of all concerned.'

I had come to Winchester to be suborned by softly spoken gravitas, to give this hired lawyer the assurances his master – and his mistress – had been denied. And all the way, along the city's cobbled streets and up the steps of Mayhew & Troke's steepling Tudor premises, I had sensed as much – and not resisted. 'There is nothing to fear on that score.'

'Splendid, splendid.' But there was no splendour in his voice. 'I am, as you must realize, Lieutenant, entirely in his Lordship's confidence. A comprehensive knowledge of his personal affairs is implicit in what I am about to say.' He paused, as if to allow me to object. But I said nothing. 'It seems to me that there is no good cause to make any mention at the inquest of the circumstances in which Mrs Hallows may find herself. Or, indeed, of any part you may have in those circumstances.'

I wondered idly what line Olivia had fed him, how she had depicted us, how much of it Lord Powerstock had brought himself to believe. And Mayhew? Belief was not his business. The law, with all its evasions, was.

Seeing that I still proposed to say nothing, he resumed. 'His Lordship tells me that he has now reconciled himself to the fact that, following Captain Hallows' death, he has no responsibility for Mrs Hallows. She may, as it were, go her own way. I am told the information may be of interest to you.'

Leonora too, then, had been thrown over in Powerstock's retreat from threatening scandal. Whatever view of events he had had distorted for him by Olivia, this was the gloss upon that distortion: they would not pursue Leonora if I did not pursue them. And the inquest was to be proof of my agreement. 'You may tell his Lordship, Mr Mayhew, that I entirely understand the position. He has nothing to fear from me.' Mayhew's eyes widened faintly: fear was an unprofessional concept. 'Now, since we are all at one on this issue, perhaps I may bid you good day.'

I spent the weekend at my uncle's house in Berkshire. For once, the brittle aloofness of my reception was welcome. With Anthea away nursing in France, I was left very much to myself, which is how I wanted it. Even my uncle's reflex endorsement of *The Time*'s condemnation of 'peace talk' failed to stir me.

On Monday morning, I reported to Aldershot for my medical board. An RAMC colonel and two manifestly bored regular officers conducted a desultory examination of my case.

'Three months since you were wounded, Lieutenant.'

'Yes, sir.'

'Thoroughly healed?'

'Yes, sir.'

'No reservations about returning to active service?'

'None, sir.'

'I gather you've to give evidence at an inquest this week. Young fellow from the Wiltshires who shot himself.'

'That is so, sir.'

'Well then, gentlemen,' the colonel said, turning to the other two. 'I think we are agreed that lieutenant Franklin is fit to resume service. Perhaps an initial three months at home?'

I wanted none of his indulgence, only to be rid of all the home front had brought me. 'Excuse me, sir, but I do feel fully recovered, able to undertake general service abroad without further delay.'

The colonel's brow furrowed: I can't have looked the heroic type. 'Very well, Lieutenant. General service abroad.' His pen began scratching an entry on a form. 'Report to barracks a week today.'

'Thank you, sir.'

* * *

An hour later, I was at Alton station, sitting aboard the Meon Valley train, waiting for it to pull out. We were already late, but I was in no hurry. At length, a labouring locomotive gathered steam and we clanked forward. At the last moment, a figure silhouetted in piston steam flung open a door and jumped aboard. He looked into my compartment and in instinctively glanced away: I didn't want to encourage company. To no avail, it seemed. The door from the corridor slid open.

'Franklin: so they've dragged you back too.' It was Thorley. He slung his bag on to the luggage rack above my head and slumped down opposite me, breathing heavily. 'God, this is a bind.' He didn't seem surprised to see me, nor as garrulous as his former self.

'You're wanted for the inquest?'

He nodded. 'Damned inconvenient. I'll be asked for my assessment of Cheriton's state of mind. But how do you assess a nonentity?'

'What about Mompesson?'

'I know nothing about that one.' He coloured and glared out of the window. 'Have you got a smoke? I hadn't time to buy any.'

I gave him a cigarette and lit it for him as the train juddered over some points and curved south away from the main line. 'You've got off lightly, Major, believe me. Compared with those of us who were there at the time.'

'I wasn't sorry to hear it'd happened. Got me off a bit of a hook, actually.'

'I know. You told me all about it at the White Horse that night.'

'Tongue ran away with me. Strictly out of order. By the way, who was the fellow you went off with?'

'Sorry? What fellow?'

'When I came to in the bar, you'd run out on me. So I took a look outside. Just in time to see you lumbering off in the distance, three sheets to the wind. Some fellow was helping you along.'

The passing landscape froze. There had been somebody in the yard behind the inn that night, somebody who left with me. But I had been alone come morning. I saw our faces – Thorley's and mine – reflected in the grimy window, saw another face – still beyond my reach – lodged in my memory.

'Something wrong?'

'I remember no such person, Major. So far as I can recall, I left alone.'

'He was there, large as life.'

'Have you mentioned this to the police?'

'I told them as little as I needed to. No sense queering your pitch. We've got to stick together in this.'

So another pact was silently concluded. Our train chugged south towards Droxford whilst I mechanically recited the events at Meongate that Thorley had missed. Behind my words, my mind strained after one night beyond recall, on which Thorley had cast the only glimmer of light. When, half an hour later, we disembarked at Droxford, Thorley headed for the White Horse, but I did not accompany him. We had reached an understanding, but that was all.

I had deliberately avoided Meongate for some days, so there was an element of shock in once again being in the same room as Lord and Lady Powerstock. This time, however, it was the small, stuffy courtroom adjacent to Droxford police station, musty with wartime disuse and suddenly crowded with coroner, clerks, police, jurors, witnesses and onlookers.

Towards the rear were elderly village folk not about to miss a *cause célébre*, towards the front those with an interest in the case. I avoided Olivia's glance and took my seat away from all of them. Yet still I could not keep my eyes from them. Lord Powerstock sat bolt upright and stared straight ahead. Mayhew leant across for the odd word with him, though Olivia appeared to do all the talking. Shapland was at the front, flanked by two constables. Of Charter there was no sign.

The coroner was a stout, bustling, impatient man. Perhaps the murder of foreign nationals in wartime struck him as of little account. At all events, he opened the proceedings briskly.

The police pathologist gave a clinical account of the killing. 'The deceased was killed by a single gunshot from close range just behind the right ear, which pierced the cerebellum and would have caused instantaneous death. The calibre of the bullet and the velocity on entry are suggestive of a small, wide-bored pistol. I examined the body where it lay shortly after three a.m. on Saturday, 23rd September, by when rigor mortis had not set in. I conducted a full post-mortem some six hours later. All the signs were indicative of death having occurred very shortly before the body was discovered at eleven-fifteen p.m. on Friday, 22nd September.'

Shapland gave a thorough if weary account of the police investigation and was asked what he had established of Mompesson's background. 'Very little, sir. He lived alone in a second-floor apartment in Wellington Court, off Knightsbridge, in west London. He was evidently a man of some means. He speculated successfully on the stock market, lent more money than he borrowed and part-owned a racehorse stabled at Epsom. He was a moderately well-known figure in

London society but seems to have had no close friends. The United States Embassy have been unable to trace any relatives.'

'You say he had no friends, Inspector. Would you say he had enemies?'

'It wouldn't surprise me, sir. He had in his possession a number of promissory notes, some outstanding.'

'We will leave you to pursue that matter, Inspector. Have you found any trace of the weapon described to us this morning?'

'No, sir. I examined a number of sporting weapons and military revolvers lodged at Meongate. None had been recently used and none fitted the description.'

The coroner consulted his notes. 'A small, wide-bored pistol. Would that be commonly known to the un-initiated as a derringer?'

'I believe so, sir.'

'A weapon more common in the United States than this country?'

'I believe so, sir.'

'Thank you, Inspector.'

Shapland cast a baleful look in my direction as he left the box, as if to warn me that, even if the coroner fell for an American connection, he wasn't about to.

Olivia's performance was, as I might have expected, impeccable. She entranced the court with her perfect imitation of the dismayed hostess. She had heard what might have been a shot at about eleven o'clock, had been concerned for Mr Mompesson when he did not answer her knock, had fetched her maid, had entered the room and had found, too awful to recall, what the court now knew.

'May I ask, Lady Powerstock, how long you had known the deceased?'

'Somewhere over a year. My husband and I had entertained him at Meongate on several occasions.'

'Did you ever gain the impression that he felt in any way threatened?'

'Not at all. Mr Mompesson was the most relaxed and carefree of men. Of course, we knew nothing of his business dealings. He was merely refreshing company and had done much to lighten my husband's sense of loss following the death on active service of his son.'

'The police found no evidence of a break-in, Lady Powerstock. Does this, to your mind, preclude the idea of an intruder?'

'Far from it. My husband is not – I should say was not – in the habit of locking any of the doors at night. An intruder would not have found it necessary to break in.'

'Quite so, Lady Powerstock. Thank you.' The coroner's mind seemed to be moving more and more in a direction that suited us all.

Then, suddenly, before I'd expected it, the case was over. No more witnesses were called. The coroner explained his reasoning to the jury. 'The business of this court, ladies and gentlemen, is to determine the cause of the death of Mr Mompesson. It is abundantly clear in this case that the deceased was murdered and I shall shortly direct you to return a verdict. It will then be for the police to continue their investigations into who may have committed that murder.'

And so it was. The verdict was brought in that Mompesson had been murdered by 'a person or persons unknown' and the court was adjourned for luncheon. The coroner departed, the jury followed him and, slowly, all the others drifted away. Thorley came across and invited me to join him at the White Horse. I declined. Nobody else spoke to me.

The court reassembled an hour later. The same jurors were sworn in to consider the next case: the death by gunshot wounds of David John Cheriton, second lieutenant. The same whey-faced pathologist presented his gruesomely dispassionate findings. This time, they only confirmed what I already knew. And this time I was the next witness.

'How did you come to be resident at Meongate at this time, Lieutenant Franklin?'

'I had been invalided home from France to recover from a shoulder wound sustained in action on the first of July. During the summer, I received an invitation to spend some time at Meongate, Lord Powerstock being in the generous habit of accommodating convalescent officers.'

'When did you arrive at Meongate?'

'Early in September.'

'Was Lieutenant Cheriton then also in residence – on the same basis.'

'He was.'

'From what was he convalescing?'

'I don't know.'

'Did he give any sign of having been physically injured?'

'No.'

'Did his malady, then, appear to have had a nervous origin?'

'There were some indications of that. But I didn't pry into the matter. He kept himself very much to himself.'

'Did he display any notable reaction to the death of Mr Mompesson?'

'I can't say I had the opportunity of discussing it with him.'

'Please now describe to the court what you found upon leaving the house early on the morning of Sunday, 24th September.'

I repeated my well-worn account. But the coroner didn't let me go without obliging me to convert omission into perjury.

'Was there a note or any other sign on the body to indicate why Lieutenant Cheriton might have acted so drastically?'

'I didn't search the body.'

'But there was nothing visible?'

'There was nothing.'

Shapland said his piece, then Lord Powerstock was called. Making his way to the witness box, he moved more slowly than usual, seemed shrunken and shuffling, reduced already to the pale shadow of a proud aristocrat.

'How long my Lord, had Lieutenant Cheriton been your guest?'

'Since the beginning of August.'

'Did you know the circumstances of his invalidity?'

'I was given to understand that he had suffered from what is commonly known as shell shock.'

'You knew nothing more specific than that?'

'Not until Mr Mompesson volunteered certain information to me during one of his visits.'

'What was that information?'

'Mr Mompesson had, by chance, met in London Lieutenant Cheriton's company commander from France, who was on leave at the time, he had mentioned to him that Lieutenant Cheriton was staying at my house. The officer expressed surprise and disclosed that, in his opinion, Cheriton had displayed sufficient cowardice in the face of the enemy to warrant a court martial rather than convalescence. Mr Mompesson said that he felt I ought to know this.'

'Did you take any action arising from this intelligence?'

'No. I did not consider it my business.'

'Did Mr Mompesson take any action?'

'I cannot say for certain. But there were indications that he confronted Lieutenant Cheriton with the accusation. I recall interrupting one heated conversation between the two when it was difficult not to construe that it had been the subject under discussion. Mr Mompesson, I should add, was proud of having been decorated for gallantry whilst serving in the Spanish–American War of 1898 and was not a man disposed to tolerate weakness in others. From about this time, Lieutenant Cheriton's state of mind seemed to me to deteriorate progressively.'

'When was this?'

'Towards the end of August.'

'And how did this deterioration manifest itself?'

'Moroseness. Reluctance to converse. A nervous tremor in the hands.'

Next, Thorley.

'When did you arrive at Meongate, Major?'

'A week after Cheriton.'

'What was your impression of him?'

'Frankly, I thought he'd lost his nerve.'

'Did you notice any sign of friction between him and Mr Mompesson?'

'Yes. Can't say it surprised me. Mompesson was a cocky fellow. He was like a cat with a mouse.'

'When did you leave Meongate?'

'Twenty-second of September.'

'Shortly before the murder of Mr Mompesson?'

'Yes. Strange coincidence.'

'Why did you leave?'

'I thought it was time to get back in harness. Too much moping around isn't good for morale.'

'When you heard subsequently of Lieutenant Cheriton's death, were you surprised?'

'Can't say I was. He had a medical board at the end of the month. I don't think he could face the thought of going back.'

'Did you connect his death in any way with that of Mr Mompesson?'

'Can't say I did. If Cheriton had had the nerve for that kind of thing, he'd have pulled himself together a long time ago.'

An army doctor was produced who stated that Cheriton had been diagnosed neurasthenic. He had detected no signs of clinical depression but had, on the other hand, not seen him since he took up residence at Meongate. The coroner then read a letter from Cheriton's commanding officer in France.

'Lieutenant Cheriton was an enthusiastic but highly strung officer. Had his temperament been more robust, I would have been more dismayed than I am at the suggestion that he took his own life. He was originally certified as neurasthenic on 23rd June this year and invalided home three days later. I cannot enlarge upon the circumstances of his illness. Captain Speight, who might have been more familiar with his case, was killed in action on 29th August.'

The coroner then addressed the jury on what he described as a 'clear case of suicide'. He said that it was for the police to determine whether there was any connection between the two deaths but that the very absence of a note might tend to suggest that there was. Without withdrawing, the jury returned its verdict that Cheriton had 'killed himself whilst the balance of his mind was disturbed'.

This time I didn't linger. I made for the exit, wishing to be away before there was either chance or need to speak to the Powerstocks. But Shapland – moving with that disarming speed of his – caught me up.

'In a hurry, Mr Franklin?'

'The cases are closed, Inspector,' I said as we emerged into the yard. 'What do you want of me?'

'You heard what the coroner said: police investigations will continue. That means I'll go on asking questions.'

'Not of me.' We turned out of the yard into the lane, made narrow by the throng. 'I'm to resume active service next week.' I strode past the police station towards the main road. He didn't follow and I didn't look back.

The first train to Alton was due at ten to eight. I was at the railway station by 7.30 on a cold, mist-fringed morning, a light frost clinging to the rails. It was as I wanted it: an early departure, a clean break, a final leaving. It seemed so much longer than a month since I'd stepped off the train from Fareham, so much longer for me and for others. I dropped my bag by a bench and sat down to wait.

I felt cold in the still air. I pulled up my greatcoat collar and lit a cigarette. A bell rang in the station building: train due. Then the door from the ticket office slammed and a figure walked along the platform towards me.

It was Charter Gladwin.

'Well met, young Franklin.' He smiled, doffed his hat and sat down beside me. 'On your way, I see.'

'I'm afraid so.'

'I take it ill you didn't come to say goodbye to me.'

'I'm sorry. I expected to see you at the inquest.'

'And I expected to see you when you came back last week. I wanted news of Leonora.'

'I understood she'd written to Lord Powerstock.'

'She had. But that's not my meaning.' I hadn't heard him so gruff before. I genuinely regretted having let him down, but an old man's consolation had seemed at the time of small moment.

'I am sorry, Charter. Since Mompesson's murder . . . it's been difficult.'

'But you have seen her?'

'Yes. I've seen her.'

There was a dull metal clank as a signal was raised. From the south, through the chill, motionless air, drifted the sound of a train whistle. 'Where are you off to now?'

'My uncle's place in Berkshire. Then, next week, I resume active service.'

'Glad to be leaving Droxford?'

'To be honest, yes. But I will miss you.'

He laughed, with some of his old guffaw, his breath misting in the air. 'Good of you to say so. But I think it's John you really miss.'

'Maybe it is.'

The train came into view with a sudden gout of noise and steam. It rumbled and juddered to a halt. 'Mind if I join you?'

'You're leaving as well?'

'No. But I'll run up to Alton with you. There's something I've been meaning to tell you.'

We climbed aboard and settled ourselves in a compartment. Charter lit his pipe and beamed across at me like some smug Pickwickian traveller. A whistle blew and the train drew out.

'John was born in the old Queen's golden jubilee year: 1887. He was a month old when the villagers and estate workers celebrated both his birth and the Jubilee. I came down from Yorkshire for the occasion. It was a grand day.

'He was a handsome, good-natured boy, a natural leader of men. You could have followed him to the ends of the Earth. But, even as his grandfather, I saw the signs of what was wrong.'

'Wrong?'

'I fear he was cursed with something most of us are spared: foresight. He knew what was going to happen. That's why there was always that sadness about him. He grieved when Miriam died, of course, but he didn't seem surprised. And the war? I think he knew it was coming. Not feared, or suspected, but knew.

'He loved Leonora, but even she couldn't make him happy. I don't think anything could. She could give him some form of contentment: that was all. It was the same contentment he got from gazing at the stars through his telescope or taking his dinghy out in Langstone Harbour.

'I've got through life by the skin of my teeth, not knowing what was going to happen next. But what if I had known? What then, eh? Can you imagine what that would be like?'

'No, Charter, Nobody can.'

His eyes drifted to the passing fields. He puffed at his pipe. 'How is Leonora?' He looked at me. 'And the Fotheringham girl?'

'You know about her?'

'I know enough to guess that's where she is. If I'm to see her again, I suppose I'll have to take a trip to the Island.'

'She asked to be left alone.'

'I don't think she meant by me, do you? Besides, I'll certainly want to be on hand . . . for the birth of my great-grandchild.' He smiled as he said it and blew a smoke ring to the luggage rack. And I stared at him and heard his throaty laugh mock all my subtle deceptions.

The sun was beginning to turn through the mist. It picked out the curving line of the downs and filtered on to Charter's white hair through the dust on the carriage window. Still he was smiling, waiting patiently for my mind to catch up with the implications of what he'd said.

'Did you think I didn't know? Old men don't sleep well. I wake early of a morning. Early enough to see who might be leaving the house at crack of dawn. I know he's alive, as, I imagine, do you.'

'Where is he, Charter?'

'I don't know. I was hoping you might have found him.'

'The trail went cold. He'd visited a man named Fletcher in Portsea.'

Charter ground his pipe stem between his teeth. 'So he went to Fletcher. I might have known.'

'Since then, he's vanished. He left his last known address the day before Mompesson was murdered.'

'Where do you think he's gone?'

'I don't know. I've no way of tracing him. And I'm not even sure I want to. If I did track him down, what would I find? And there's something else. You can't come back

330

from the dead, Charter. I think he may have come to understand that.'

The train shuddered to a halt at West Meon station. From down the platform came the scrape and thump of freight being loaded into the guard's van. Abruptly, Charter hauled himself from his seat. 'After all, I think I'll get off here.'

'You said you'd come as far as Alton.'

'I'll walk back from here. It'll do me good.' I followed him into the corridor. 'We've said all there is to say, haven't we?' He pushed a door open and climbed down to the platform, then turned round to look up at me. 'So – take care, young man.'

I pulled the window down and closed the door. 'You too.'

'I never did tell you about that duel in St Petersburg, did I?'

'No. You never did.'

'Well, it can wait now.'

The train lurched into motion. I held up my hand in farewell. Charter stepped back and raised his hat. As the engine gathered steam, the platform – and Charter with it – slid away behind me. My last sight of him was as a portly, silhouetted figure on the vanishing station, benignly waving his hat, for all the world a kindly uncle seeing off his favourite nephew.

TEN

So I went back to war. It had waited patiently, like some huge, dormant beast, waiting to claw me back. And now I went willingly, almost with relief. No Anthea to see me off at Southampton, no shocks awaiting me at Rouen. For I knew where I was going. Back to the third battalion, changed in all but name, still locked in the Battle of the Somme and entrenched now near the village of Courcelette, three miles east of where I'd left them as many months before. Three miles – for how many thousand lives?

I rejoined the third battalion at the beginning of November, by which time only the high command maintained the presence that the Somme campaign was still in progress. By the 16th, it had officially closed and we were left to spend the winter in flooded or frozen trenches.

There were few faces I recognized. Sergeant Warren, who'd written to me in September, had been killed the same month, probably before my reply reached him. Colonel Romney had been transferred to Egypt. Lake's successor, Finch, was a nerve-shattered alcoholic. As for

332

the men, they were mostly new to it but, by instinct or reason, grimmer than their predecessors. Despair hung upon us under the grey skies of wintry France. Hope was a stranger. And I no longer cared.

Christmas came and went. I declined an offer of home leave. The year 1917 opened dull and drear and found us, drained of spirit, cast on the frozen ramparts of a mindless, endless war.

I thought often of Hallows, and Leonora, and all that had happened at Meongate. But I wrote no letters and received none. It seemed somehow safer that way, as if, in some wasteland that was Picardy, there was at least some form of refuge, some consolation to be had in its blank and grinding ruin.

Rumour abounded that the battalion was to follow Colonel Romney to Egypt in the spring. I paid the prospect no heed. France, Egypt or the ends of the Earth. What, after all, did it matter? In February, I was promoted first lieutenant – reward, I think, for still being alive.

During March I had a long weekend due and arranged to spend it in Amiens. Cousin Anthea was in the area, having just returned from England, and I agreed to meet her in a café near the cathedral. It was a cold, grey afternoon with flurries of snow. I arrived first, sat at a corner table and ordered Cognac.

Anthea burst in late, with a gust of her irrepressible, ever-jarring good cheer. She was a bundle of energy and enthusiasm, with a schoolgirlish laugh and an undimmed conviction that all would turn out for the best. To the nursing profession, probably a godsend. To me, at the low ebb of my wintry soul, anathema. The café was dark, full of glum-faced, elderly customers rustling newspapers and saying little, wreathed in fumes of ersatz coffee and stale garlic. I wanted only to rest and retreat into the shadows of their unyielding company. But Anthea would have none of it.

'I can't stay long, Tom. We're terribly hard-pressed at present.'

I nodded. 'How are you?'

'Very well,' she said emphatically. 'Never better. I thrive on hard work.'

'How was England?'

'Everyone's in very good spirits. It seems certain now that the Americans will come in on our side.'

'So I'm told. What about the family?'

'Fighting fit.'

'Good.'

'Papa's taken a new gardener. He had to let Moffat go. He simply wasn't up to the heavy work any more. Oh, and apparently' – she leaned intently across the table – 'Charlotte's expecting again.'

I was momentarily nonplussed. 'Charlotte?'

'Your cousin, silly. In Keswick.'

'Oh yes, of course.'

'Didn't you stay with some people called Hallows last summer?' she said abruptly.

'Er . . . yes. Why?'

'There was an obituary notice in *The Times* the last day I was home. I thought I recognized the name – and the address.'

I felt my throat dry suddenly. 'What name?'

'See for yourself. I cut it out. I thought you'd be interested.' She reached into her bag and took out a folded piece of paper. I snatched it from her.

'HALLOWS: on 19th March 1917, in Ventnor Cottage Hospital, Isle of Wight, peacefully, after a short illness, Leonora May Hallows (née Powell), aged 25 years, of

Meongate, Droxford, Hampshire, beloved widow of the late Captain the Hon. John Hallows. Funeral service at the Parish Church, Bonchurch, Isle of Wight, on Friday, 23rd March at 12 noon.'

And so she was gone, her fragile beauty plucked and lost like a flower before the storm. As soon as I read it, I knew it was it was bound to be. I had loved her. Time was to show that she was the only woman I would ever love. Yet I had known her for such a short time. The first afternoon at Meongate – to the last at Bonchurch. Less than a month, so much less, than the lifetime for which I would remember her.

Anthea was no longer with me when, an hour later, sobered by grief beyond the reach of all the drink I'd consumed, I leant on the parapet of one of the bridges crossing the Somme and saw again, in my mind, Leonora's face, turned to look at me, her gaze travelling past me to the future she would never know. Nor was it only grief that caused the tears to well in my eyes. There was guilt, a wounding accusation of self, gouging at the centre of my loss. I should have saved her, should have found a way to protect her. Instead, nursing self-pity in the name of a love she could never return. I had left her to meet her fate.

I thumped the stonework of the parapet until my hand ached. I bowed my head and wept. And then I knew. It was too late for Leonora, but, for the sake of what I'd felt for her, I knew what I had to do. I had thought myself free of them, immunized by the futility of war, but now I knew: I must go back.

With the funeral already past, there was little point to such a journey and even less need for haste. But that isn't how I felt. Having refused leave when it was my due, I obtained it now at short notice on spurious grounds: an ailing parent. The battalion, I was told, would embark for Egypt in the first week of April. I would either have to follow them or join a different unit. Not that I cared either way. By the end of the week, I was back in England.

I walked down to Bonchurch from Ventnor on a bright morning – the last of March – and went straight to Sea Thrift. From within, the dog barked vaingloriously at my knock. Then Grace Fotheringham came to the door.

'I thought you would have come sooner, Mr Franklin.'

'I came as soon as I heard.'

'Won't you step inside?'

I'd not entered the house before and found it, now, as I might have expected: light, airy, femininely dainty, with the breeze stirring curtains at every open window, daffodils in slender vases sharing the brightness of the morning.

She led me into the sitting room, where french windows look out on to the garden. The dog sniffed suspiciously at me feet. 'You'll want to know what happened.'

'Yes.'

She gestured for me to sit down, then sat opposite me. 'It seemed a simple chill at first, then it turned to influenza. The illness was complicated by her pregnancy and the strain of delivery was too much for her. She contracted pneumonia and died five days after birth.'

'I'm so sorry.'

'The Powerstocks wanted nothing to do with the funeral. That's why it was held here. Only an elderly uncle attended: a Mr Gladwin. Her own family are in India, I believe.'

336

'And the baby!'

'She's still at the hospital. Premature, you understand. But she's going to be fine. I expect to be able to bring her home on Monday.'

'You'll bring her here?'

'Where else? I had a distasteful letter from a Mr Mayhew making it quite clear that Lord Powerstock felt no obligations to the child. I can hardly send her to India. I shall look after her myself.'

'Have you named her?'

'Yes. I've given her her mother's name. What else could it be?'

What else indeed? I could have walked the mile to the hospital and seen you then, I suppose. But I didn't. I'd come looking for another Leonora, denied me by loves and loyalties outweighing mine. And she wasn't there any more. So I thanked Miss Fotheringham and prepared to leave.

'Why did you wait so long to call?' she asked as she showed me to the door.

'I've only been in England since yesterday.'

She frowned. 'Come, come. That can't be. The sexton told me he'd seen a strange man at the graveside two days ago. Who could it have been but you? The description certainly fitted.'

I ran all the way up the hill to the church, a larger, grander affair than the old church I'd visited with Leonora: a stern monument to Victorian propriety, bounded by railings and an aura of pious rectitude.

I stepped inside the gates and paused to catch my breath. There were daffodils scattered gaily between the grim, upright gravestones, rooks cawing in the bare trees above me, an acrid scent on the breeze from a distant bonfire. Every clear, sun-etched line of stone and branch denied the mystery that I knew, now, was nearer than ever before.

There was only one new grave, the earth still mounded and un-turfed, one wreath left, the inscription on its card washed blank by recent rain, its scattered blooms flecking the grass around. I'd brought no flowers, could only stare, with sudden grief, as much at my own inadequacy as at this final confirmation that Leonora was truly gone.

There was nothing to do. Now I'd jumped to the instinctive conclusion, now I'd raced up the silent lane to this place of rest and found only what I might have expected, I felt cheated by my own need to believe that there was something beyond what I saw. I retreated to a bench beneath the eaves of the church, within sight of Leonora's grave, and sat there, waiting for disappointment to fade. I lit a cigarette and watched a squirrel nosing curiously amongst the stones. But it didn't help. All I felt was the creeping lassitude of an overdue despair. Two years caught in a war beyond reason had drained my spirit. I should, I knew, have stayed in France, or gone to Egypt, followed death's beckoning finger without resistance. Instead, I sat alone in an English churchyard at the brittle edge of spring and felt only the weariness of one who had already lived too long.

I fell asleep. A trance of sunlight and solitude and warm stone. The body took its pleasure where resolution had given way. I slept deeply, as tired men will do, dreamlessly, almost contentedly.

When I woke, he was sitting next to me. How long he'd been there, or what had stirred me, I couldn't tell. He might, I reflected, have been there for ever: quiet, ironic, overlooked. He seemed much more than a year older, reduced, somehow, in his drab civilian clothes, worn to a greyness of skin and spirit by whatever lie he'd lived. I looked at him and knew him, but only, as it were, as the brother of a friend: a certain family resemblance to the man I thought I knew.

'Hello, Tom.'

I said nothing. I did not know what to say.

'It's good to see you. Better than you know.'

It was still his voice, beyond any doubt of faded recollection, his authentic voice within an unprotesting stranger.

'I'd hoped you would come.'

Then I spoke. 'Why? Why did you do it? I don't understand – any of it – to this day.'

'Understanding is perhaps too much to ask. When it came to the point, it would have been easier not to go through with it. But it had to be. Do you believe in destiny, Tom?'

'I'm not sure – not any more.'

'I knew it would end when it did: in 1914. The world, I mean, my world. When I married Leonora that spring – three years ago – I sensed the need of haste, as if, slowly, imperceptibly, the life I'd lived so safely and securely was tilting beneath my feet, creaking inaudibly towards the moment when it would open and consume me. And so it was.

'It wasn't that I simply didn't fancy my chances of survival. I knew there was none. For destiny can't be dodged, can it? Not for long. I thought of what would happen after I'd gone, of Leonora alone at Meongate. And when I met Mompesson, I knew at once what would happen. Because he told me, not in so many words, but clearly enough. And I believed him.

'That's why I set out to dodge destiny, just to walk away from it, at a time of my choosing. Is that cowardice, I wonder? Or merely disobedience to fate? I planned it to coincide with your leave because I couldn't risk being swayed by friendship. I'm sorry to have deceived you.'

'I was told you'd gone out with Box to check the wire: that neither of you had come back. But your papers were found later on a corpse in no man's land. That was Box, wasn't it?'

'I'm afraid so. I'd intended simply to slip away from him, but he ran into an enemy patrol and got hit. So I went back and did my best for him. I put my tunic round his shoulders to keep him warm while we crouched in a shell hole and the German artillery let loose overhead. By the time it had quietened down, Box was dead. Then I thought: Why not leave my papers on him? I had no need of them and, if anyone took him for me, so much the better. So I did. I left Box where he lay and took off by a route I'd already reconnoitred. I headed south and cut through the lines where transport was heaviest, then doubled back to Hernu's Farm. I'd cached some money and clothes in an outbuilding and found it all intact. I was on my way. I walked all through the next day and, in the evening, caught a train at a place called Montdidier. It took me to Paris.

'There, with money and respectable clothes, it was easy enough to pass myself off as a journalist. I was able, after a period spent cultivating the right contacts, to obtain an excellent forgery of a passport in the name of Willis. With that, it was possible to return to England at my leisure. Once home, however, it wasn't so easy. Money was fast running out and, besides, I hadn't thought any further than seeing Leonora again. So I went to Meongate, under cover of darkness, and the joy of being with her again was enough.

'But only for a moment. Then I realized I'd gone too far: it wasn't possible for me to come back from the dead. Leonora tried to persuade me to give myself up, but that I couldn't do: it wouldn't have been fair to saddle her with a deserter for a husband. So I simply went away – and hid.'

'You went to Fletcher. And I know why.'

He smiled grimly and glanced down at the ground. 'You've done well, Tom. Yes, I went to Fletcher – and he sheltered me. I'd long wanted to see the man who meant so much to my mother. Odd it should have been when I had no choice. Or perhaps not so odd. Perhaps I recognized a fellow exile from the human race.

'At all events, Fletcher found me a room in Portsea and I stayed there, wondering what to do. Every weekend, I went to Meongate in secret and spied on the house from the woods to see if Mompesson was visiting. He usually was. One day, I saw you too. It came as a relief to know you were there. I hoped you might somehow protect Leonora. For all the melodrama of my flight from France, what could I do that wouldn't ruin her or break her heart?'

'But on September 22nd you did do something, didn't you?'

He looked up again. 'Matters couldn't go on as they were. Fletcher kept warning me to leave Portsmouth and he was right: I couldn't remain there. That evening, I entered Meongate in daylight, via the stables, and went up to the observatory: I knew I'd be safe there.'

'Because it was locked – and you had the key?'

He glanced at me and frowned. 'Key? No, I had no

key. It wasn't locked. But what I saw from the observatory that evening made me wish it had been.'

'What did you see?'

'My wife . . . and Mompesson . . .' Abruptly, he rose from the bench and took a pace forward. 'I shan't speak of it. All that I'd striven to protect – all that I'd deserted for – was taken from me in that moment. Since then, I've been what I am today: a man as good as dead.'

'What you saw may not have been as it appeared.'

He swung towards me. 'Don't you think I don't know that – now? At the time, it was too much for me. I fled the house. It was nearly dark by then. I went to the church, where it was empty and still, and prayed beside William de Brinon's tomb. But I found no absolution. I felt excluded – even there – by my own deceit. As I was leaving, keeping to the shadows as I went, I saw you pass by at the end of the lane, heading for the inn. I needed you then, Tom. I needed your friendship. At last, I felt ready to tell somebody the truth.

'I waited for you to leave the inn and, when eventually you did, I showed myself. But you didn't recognize me. You were drunk, too drunk to know me. It was the final irony. I tried to tell you the truth, as we tottered back across the fields towards Meongate, but you didn't hear a word. I left you sleeping in a barn. I didn't think you'd remember. If you had, you'd have thought it was just a dream.'

'I'm sorry. Truly sorry.'

'Don't be. If anyone's to blame for what's happened, it's me – or Mompesson.'

'I don't blame you for killing him.'

Hallows turned away again and gazed towards Leonora's grave. 'I didn't kill him, Tom. I never went back to Meongate. I walked through the night across the downs to Petersfield and caught the first train to London the following morning. I've not been back to Meongate from that day to this.'

'That doesn't make sense. It must have been you.'

He shook his head. 'No. It wasn't me. That afternoon, wandering the streets aimlessly, I saw, blazoned on a news-stand, an *Evening Standard* headline: COUNTRY HOUSE MURDER OF AMERICAN. So I bought a copy. And there it was. I didn't know whether to laugh or cry. Mompesson was dead. What I might have done – what I should have done – somebody else had done for me. And, at last, I understood how my destiny was bound by Mompesson's. Once he was dead I had to seem the same. I might have talked my way out of desertion, but from murder there was no escape. Even now, an unsolved crime waits to claim me the moment I declare myself. I'm trapped, Tom, more certainly than by the war. I'm trapped between a choice of deaths.'

I rose and stood beside him, where I could see his face. He continued to look away. 'When did you know she was pregnant?'

'Ten days ago. Her death too I learned from a news-paper. That's the price . . . of being a stranger.' His voice thickened. He looked back towards her grave. 'I came here at once and went to the hospital. I said I was a cousin. They told me there that she'd had a child. Suddenly, amongst strangers, posing as a dutiful but unconcerned relative, I learned that I was a father, a father who could not claim his child.' He broke off, then resumed in a faltering tone: 'Now, at last, I understand what might have forced her . . . to do as Mompesson required . . . why she should have come here . . . why she killed him. now I understand . . . what I left her to face . . . alone.'

'Where have you been since September?'

'It's better if you don't know. It would have been better if you'd gone on believing I was dead. Because that's what I am, or should be. But you could tell me what you've been doing since then. I'd like that.'

So I told him about the war I'd returned to, the war that had gone on without him. We walked as I spoke, trudging slowly round the gravel paths that threaded between the gravestones. A greyness was entering the sky and the day and, with it, a growing chill.

'When will it end, Tom?'

'Who knows? This year, next year? Three years from now? I can see no end to it.'

'So what will you do?'

'Go back – to Egypt or France. It hardly matters where. There'll be another big push this spring. I don't expect to see it through.'

'In a way, I envy you. I wish that I could face death on equal terms, with some semblance of equanimity.'

I couldn't forestall the trace of bitterness that entered my voice. 'Isn't that what you went to such lengths to avoid?'

'Not really. I wish I could make you understand. Every choice was bound to bring misery, or death – or both. And every choice – but this one – would have left Mompesson the victor.'

'Would that have mattered so much?'

'I thought so. Now I'm not so sure. Whatever we do rebounds on others. That evening, after I'd read of his murder, I went to Mompesson's flat in Knightsbridge. There was a policeman outside and a couple of journalists questioning a commissionaire. I stood on the other side of the road and watched them. It began to rain and any idle passers-by dispersed. One woman

344

remained, on the same side of the road as me, staring up at the block. Thirtyish, elegantly dressed. When I glanced at her, I saw that she was weeping.'

'Who was she?'

'Somebody from a secret compartment of Mompesson's life. What did we know of him, after all? A mountebank, a gambler, a fortune-hunter. He set his sights on my wife, my house and my name – and would have had them all. I was determined to stop him. That seemed to be all that mattered.'

'But you didn't stop him. You said so yourself. Somebody else did it for you.'

'Which proves Mompesson's point. He said the English were too old a race, effete, fatalistic, indecisive. In my case, it seems he was right.'

We had come full circle and stood now beside the bench where we had started. The shock of seeing Hallows again, after all the doubting and seeking, had given place to a sapping disappointment. He was only, after all, what I had perversely believed him not to be: a shabby fugitive hounded by his own sense of failure. After all the subterfuge and struggle, he had shirked the challenge, had walked away and left another to kill Mompesson for him. And now a newly dug grave gave the lie to his year of cheated life.

Hallows sighed and pulled his shoulders. 'So that's it, Tom. Bad, isn't it? I've been lodging at a guest house in Niton, posing as an amateur paleontologist with a weak chest. Secretly, I've been waiting for you. I've been here every day, hoping to see you.'

'Why me?'

'Because, if you came, I knew what it would mean. I knew it would mean you loved her.'

He had touched a nerve. 'What if I did? I thought you

dead, for God's sake. I did nothing . . .' My voice died in my throat as I thought of Olivia. 'Nothing . . . dishonourable.'

'Of course not. But, now you've come, for her sake, won't you let me do something for you . . . for both of us?'

'What could you do . . . now?'

'There is only one thing. You used to tell me you led an empty life. That you had no real family – or true friends. That the war was bearable because you had so little to go back to.'

'That hasn't changed.'

'But you don't want to die.'

'Of course not.'

'I do.'

I stared at him. His expression was intent but unmoved, serious but entirely calm. 'What?'

'I've had it, Tom. I've played out the string till there's no slack left. Leonora is dead because of me. I deserted to protect her – and all I did was kill her with my child. I couldn't even kill Mompesson. Do you understand what I'm saying?'

'I only understand that you're right: you can't dodge destiny.'

'You can. I can do it for you.'

'What do you mean?'

'You could wangle a transfer to another battalion, maybe another regiment – in a different sector. Couldn't you?'

'Yes. But to what purpose?'

'Who would know you there?'

'Nobody. I was hardly known in the third battalion by the time I got back last autumn. So many were dead.'

'We're about the same height. I could shave off my

346

moustache. Nobody would doubt that I was you. I'm sure you're right about another push this spring. Thousands will die. I want to die with them. I could do so in your name. You could go free, Tom. You could do what I dreamt of doing. You could walk away from this war. Mr John Willis of London has a healthy bank account now. He doesn't appear on any official lists, so the war can't touch him. He can do whatever he likes. When the war ends, he'll still be alive. You could be him. What do you say?'

'I say you're mad. It would never work.'

He grasped my left arm with sudden force. 'I'd make it work. I wouldn't come back – I promise you. I'm asking you to let me die for you.'

When I looked at him, in that instant, I believed him. He meant what he said. And my only objection told its own story. It would never work – but what if it did? My own reaction shocked me: I was tempted. A chance to do what he had failed to do: walk away from the war. Walk away from the past and achieve what life could never offer: a clean break, a fresh start. He was right, after all. We had killed Leonora and the war was without end. As John Willis, I could go anywhere, be anyone. It was the only thing Hallows had and the only thing he didn't want. A life for a life. The gift of a true friend.

'How long would it take you to arrange to go back?'

'A week at most.'

'You'd sail from either Southampton or Portsmouth.'

'I dare say.'

'You could write to me here – care of the village post office in Niton. If I knew where and when you were to embark, I could be there, waiting for you. We could slip away somewhere . . .'

'There's no need to spell it out.'

'You'd have to – in the letter.'

'There'll be no letter. I won't go down this road.' I turned from him. On the other side of the churchyard, a rook flapped lazily away from Leonora's grave. I closed my eyes and felt them sting with tears. It was absurd, unthinkable, preposterous, and yet . . .

Hallows spoke from behind me. 'I'll wait for a letter. I'll hope for one. It's all I have left to hope for.'

I turned back to face him. 'If you've not heard from me by the end of the week, forget it.'

'Very well.'

'That's all I'll say. That's all I can say. I must think.'

'Of course.'

'Goodbye, then.'

He held out his hand, but I did not shake it. To have done so would have implied not merely agreement but complicity. I walked away slowly down the path, wondering if I would ever see him again. At the gate, I looked back. He was still standing by the bench, gazing towards me, a distant, obscure stranger with no hint in his expression of the despair he felt or the hope he held out to me: a future unlooked for. I returned the gesture. Already, I knew I would see him again. But I walked away with a show of decisiveness, sustained by my own sense of disbelief.

I moved through the next few days as a man in a dream. I went back to Aldershot and booked into a commercial hotel, then drifted into regimental HQ one morning and took a step into the irrevocable. Meredith, a malleable administrator in Transport and Movements, couldn't understand my eagerness to return from leave. The battalion was, as expected, en route by leisurely train to Italy, there to take a ship for

Egypt. He had no transfers to other battalions to offer at present. As for other regiments, he would, if I insisted, see what he could do. I insisted. Already, it was merely self-deception to suppose that I could turn back. I could have used up my leave and waited my turn. But I had done neither. Hallows' offer had worked its way into my soul and found there a secret readiness to do as he suggested.

After my first visit to Meredith, I trudged down to the regimental playing fields and watched some new recruits contesting a rugger match with all the desperate energy they would later need in France. What was it, I wondered as I patrolled the touch-line, that Hallows was asking me to give up? The camaraderie of army life that was really only gallows humour and the fellowship of the condemned. A loving family that amounted to an absentee father, a dead mother and an emotionally retarded uncle. Even cousin Anthea would scarcely be inconsolable. Hallows had brought me the vicarious ties of his own tangled emotions and they had led us both to a fresh grave in Bonchurch. If I resisted, who would thank me? It would only be the conditioned reflex of a doubtful breeding, a breeding whose code would demand in the end, however skilfully evaded or bravely faced, the same pointless sacrifice.

A cheer went up from the smattering of spectators: a try had been scored. Players clapped one another on the back. I thought of Lake, shot down before my eyes the summer before; of Warren – dogged, touchingly faithful Warren, dead like so many of these players would shortly be; of Cheriton, driven by some demon of his own or Olivia's devising to end his life. I walked slowly away from the field and was sure now, for the first time.

*   *   *

The following day, I looked in on Meredith again. If I really wanted it, he could fix an attachment to a Northumbrian regiment stationed at Ypres, where there was a temporary shortage of officers. But I would have to set off within a matter of days. As if listening to the speech of another man, I heard myself agree without hesitation. I posted a letter to Hallows the same morning.

So we came to the appointed place and time. Southampton Town station, April 10th at the chill outset of a clear spring day. The long troop train had started from the Midlands the night before and I had boarded it at Aldershot as day was breaking. I was amongst strangers, most of whom were still asleep and would remain so until the train reached the docks. Nobody noticed me get off, or walk back along the platform and look up at a distant footbridge, where a single figure leant against the parapet and stubbed out a cigarette in confirmation that he had seen me.

We met in a deserted reach of the goods yard, where steps from the footbridge led down to my level. I followed Hallows in silence to an empty workmen's hut. There we exchanged clothes. Minutes later, we emerged, left the yard and made our way down a narrow road past the warehouses that flanked the station. Smoke billowed up above the sloping roofs as the troop train gathered steam.

'The SS *Belvedere* in Empress Dock. Due to sail in an hour. From Le Havre, go by train to Poperinge. Then on to Ypres. You're due with the 30th Northumbrians by tomorrow morning.'

'I understand.'

'How's the uniform?'

'An excellent fit. What about the suit?'

'Not so bad.'

'In the inside pocket you'll find the key to the flat in Praed Street. Everything you need is there.'

We came to a junction, where Hallows must have sensed I intended to leave him. We both stopped. 'You won't see me again, Tom. You realize that?'

'I think I do.'

'We might have joked, or laughed, or simply talked, at another time, another parting. But not today. Not this last time.'

'I'm sorry. There's so much to say, yet so little I can say. What are we, Hallows, you and I?'

'Friends, I hope.'

'Much more than friends, I think.' I shook his hand and turned to go, then stopped. At the last, I could not quite escape my own conscience. 'One thing. One thing I meant to ask you in Bonchurch.'

'Yes.'

'When you entered Meongate that night, last September, where else did you go, apart from the observatory?'

'Nowhere else. I went straight there, by the back stairs. I knew it was a safe route at such a time.'

'You didn't . . . see Olivia?'

He shook his head and seemed about to smile, but did not do so. Suddenly I sensed a secret advantage he had of me: how much he knew I could never quite be sure. 'No, Tom. I didn't see Olivia.'

'And the observatory wasn't locked?'

'I told you. It never was. I had no key. Is it really so important?'

'No. But this is. We could call a halt here, you know.

We could still step back into our separate lives. You don't have to go through with this.'

'I can't turn back now and I don't want to. Let it go, Tom.'

A cleaner had wedged open the doors of an inn on the corner of the street and was eyeing us now as she mopped the step. Somewhere nearby, a steam-hammer coughed into spluttering life. Then Hallows smiled and touched his cap and moved across the junction away from me. I watched him go without another word, down the straight road towards the docks; watched him as if it were me, as it could have been, in my uniform, my kit-bag over his shoulder, a receding figure slowly fading amidst the traffic of the day. Then the troop train lurched and juddered its slow length between us, where the rails crossed the street, and, when it had gone and its sluggish smoke dispersed, I saw that Hallows too had gone, vanished into a life of his choosing that carried with it my past.

The loss that I felt then, the keen, gnawing emptiness that swept over me as I turned my back on all he embodied, was also the shock of total uncertainty. The friend who left me there also took me with him. It was a different man who walked up the curving road to the floating bridge across the river Itchen and climbed the slipway on the other side, a different man about to enter an unchartered future.

It doesn't matter where I was, or what I was doing, when, four months later, I saw the long-expected entry in the roll of honour. 'Killed in action, 16th August 1917: FRANKLIN, 1st Lieut Thomas Blaine, aged 25 years.' Hallows had kept his promise.

PART THREE

ONE

We had returned to the Bishop's Palace and were standing by the low wall skirting the moat, gazing at the mottled reflections in the water of the palace walls and the trees beyond. Willis had finished his story, yet my thoughts remained trapped within it. Should I have been happy that my parents had been shown to be the faithful, loving people I had always wanted to believe? – or sad that fate and its sundry human instruments had laid waste their lives and for so long crippled my own? I could not tell. There was no answer in the face of the firm, surviving witness who stood beside me, nor consolation in the placid, slowly rippling water.

Willis had answered all the questions that had dogged my childhood: the identity of the pretty lady, the whereabouts of my mother's grave, the full story of the Meongate murder. He had given me back a real father and a loyal mother. He had exposed Olivia's lies. Yet it wasn't enough.

I felt disabled by his story, somehow paralysed, incapable of an ordered response. I had always wanted to believe that Captain the Honourable John Hallows was my father and Willis had assured me that he was. Yet the image of him as the unstained, incorruptible war hero was gone in return. To discover the real man behind a carved, respected name is, as I should have known, to view a flawed soul. And my mother? Acquitted at last of every one of Olivia's accusations, she had deserved and rewarded my love. Yet she was not the pretty lady I had waved goodbye to at Droxford railway station.

'Payne told me you'd grown up at Meongate,' Willis said at last. 'I don't understand why. I can't believe Grace Fotheringham would have abandoned you. So why did the Powerstocks take you back?'

It was true: the stone never stopped rolling. In dispelling one mystery, Willis had created another. 'I don't know,' I replied. 'I have no certain memory of Miss Fotheringham at all. I have no memory of a time when I wasn't at Meongate.'

'She was never mentioned?'

'Never. Nor was I ever told where my mother was buried. Olivia saw to it that the disgrace of my supposed illegitimacy was never forgotten.'

'She would have seen to it that nobody's sins were forgotten – except her own.'

'You hated her?'

'Oh yes. But my hatred rewarded her. She preferred it to indifference – even to worship, I suspect. She was . . .'

'An evil woman?'

'Perhaps. But you are better placed to judge her than I am.'

'I have no fond memories or her, if that's what you mean.'

'Yet she took you in. She cared for you even after your grandfather's death.'

'Technically, yes. But if you knew the kind of life I

356

endured at her hands, you wouldn't think taking me in was anything other than an act of cruelty.'

He swung round to look at me, suddenly disturbed; moved, it seemed, by my last remark more than he had been by his own story. 'I would like to hear of it, Leonora.' He pulled himself up and looked back towards the moat. 'If I may call you Leonora.'

'Of course.'

'Well then, if you can bear to speak of it, I would like to hear your story.'

Only the extent and candour of his own account can explain my willingness, indeed my desire, to tell him of my life. I had previously told nobody other than Tony as much as I told John Willis, the passing stranger, that afternoon in Wells. One secret, of course, I withheld from him as I had from my husband: my part in Sidney Payne's death. Otherwise, all the griefs and traumas of my years at Meongate tumbled into words as we walked and talked together.

By the time I'd finished, we were at Priory Road railway station; Willis was about to take his leave. He'd collected his bag from the Red Lion and walked with me through the crowded streets. The station itself was full of schoolchildren, capering and calling in the afternoon sunshine. We went to the far end of the platform, sat on a bench, and waited for the next train to Witham. There, I knew, he would join a main-line train, but, incredibly, I'd not thought to ask where his journey would end.

Willis himself was strangely silent. My story seemed to leave him as uncertain of response as his own had me. I looked at him, sitting erect beside me on the slatted bench, and struggled to see him for the two men he was: the young, sensitive, courageously confused officer plunged into the treacherous currents of life at

357

wartime Meongate – and the old, lean, anonymous man in gabardine and battered trilby, struggling against the habits of ingrained solitude to pay his due to a dead friend's only daughter.

'My parents have always been strangers to me, Mr Willis,' I said at length. 'It is the penalty of being an orphan. I never thought I would come to know them. Yet now, in a sense, you have brought them to me.'

'Only their story,' he said in a voice husky from long silence. 'Only the truth their daughter had a right to know.'

'Why did you wait so long?'

His reply seemed strangely defensive. 'Without that notice of Lady Powerstock's death, I wouldn't have known how to contact you.'

'Yet surely you assumed Miss Fotheringham had adopted me.'

'Then let's just say the notice pricked my conscience. The more so when Payne told me you were Olivia's ward. It made no sense. It still makes none. For that I'm truly sorry.'

'It's hardly your fault.'

'Your father died for me, Leonora. I could have tried to ensure his daughter was properly cared for. I simply assumed it could be left to Grace.' He smiled grimly. 'No pun intended.'

'I don't think you need feel guilty. I don't resent your acceptance of my father's offer. I believe he owed it to you. I'm glad he honoured the debt. It was a noble act.'

Willis swallowed hard. 'We owed each other . . . more than I can say.'

'Did you believe what he said about not killing Mompesson?' I was giving voice to a secret hope. I wanted to believe my father really had slain his enemy.

358

Willis's reply was uncompromising. 'Yes. I do.'

'He may have said it to make it easier for you to escape his offer.'

'I'm sorry, Leonora. He was telling the truth.'

'But if he didn't do it, who did? Who could have?'

'That's one question I can't answer.' He looked up. 'Here's my train.'

I hadn't noticed the train approach and, now, as it drew in, I realized for the first time that Willis really was about to leave me. My messenger from nowhere was about to return to his element. 'You've told me nothing about the life you've led since 1917,' I said in a rush, sensing it was already too late to hope that he would.

'There's nothing to say,' he replied. The train drew to a halt. He rose and picked up his bag,.

'Where will you go now?'

'Home. If you can call it that. You won't hear from me again.'

'Why not? I'd like to.'

'Now you know the truth, it's best forgotten. And so am I.' He held out his hand. My own felt lost when clasped in his large palm. He shook it once, then nodded and turned to climb aboard the train. I stepped forward and held the door open behind him.

'There's so much more I'd like to ask you.'

'And there's more I'd like to tell you,' he replied, looking back, 'but I've said enough. You have a husband and two children waiting at home for you. Their happiness is more important than my tired recollections of sadder times.'

'I wish you could meet them.'

'It's better that I shouldn't. If I were you, I wouldn't burden them with my story. Goodbye, Leonora. Go home. Be happy. Forget me.'

359

'How can I?'

'You will.'

I released the door and he slammed it shut. A whistle sounded behind me. I raised my hand and he touched his hat. Then the train began to move. He didn't lean out of the window, so the last I saw of him was a thin, refracted shape obscured by sunlight on dirty glass and the lurching, narrowing angle of the train. I followed it as far as the end of the platform, watched it fade rapidly from view, recalled that other train – that other parting – more than thirty years before, and when the dwindling shape had become a smoking speck and finally vanished, I realized how, for all he had confided in me, he had, at the last, still succeeded in eluding me.

What had he done, where and who had he been since walking away from my father that April morning in 1917? Why had he waited till now to see me? Was it that he could not do so till Olivia was dead? If so, was the reason connected with her decision to take me away from Grace Fotheringham? What had she hoped to gain by it? If John Willis knew the answers, it was too late to glean them from him.

I remember speaking to the man on the ticket barrier as I left, asking him what train the Witham service connected with.

'Anything on the main line, missus. One way as far as Penzance. The other to London and beyond.'

'The man I came on with earlier: you clipped his return ticket. Did you happen to notice where he was going?'

But he couldn't remember Willis, far less his destination. 'Don't *you* know?' he said. And, of course, I didn't.

As I walked slowly home, I realized how absurd it

would sound if I related Willis's story to Tony, then admitted that I'd not only kept his first visit secret but also had no way of contacting him again: no proof, if it came to it, that he was not a figment of my imagination.

When I turned into Ash Lane, I suddenly thought how acute Willis's advice had been. In a sense, I did just want to go home and forget him. Had he come to me ten years before, it would have been different, but the truth he'd brought now seemed somehow redundant in my ordered, settled life, far as it was from Meongate and all that had happened there. If I told Tony that I wasn't illegitimate after all, he might try to re-open the whole question of my claim on Olivia's estate, whereas I still wanted nothing of Meongate, no inheritance, however meagre, to suggest that I was beholden to the woman who'd tried to take my father from me. It was enough for me to know now that I truly was Captain Hallows' daughter. Yet I had no way of proving it. Indeed, to convince others, I would have had to expose him as a deserter. That was a secret I was happy, even proud, to keep.

So it was simpler to tell Tony nothing, safer to trust no one but myself with my new-found knowledge. Eight years of marriage had not entirely dispelled the secrecy of my youth. When I did act, it was cautiously.

The following weekend, I told Tony I was thinking of spending a day in London; shopping trips to town were a periodic treat in which he was happy to indulge me. Early on Wednesday morning, the tenth of June, I set off.

But I didn't go to London. I got off the train at Westbury and boarded one for Portsmouth. There I took the ferry to the Isle of Wight and another train, across the island, to Ventnor, retracing Franklin's journey of thirty-seven years before.

At Bonchurch, I found what I was looking for: a small, plain, white gravestone simply inscribed. LEONORA MAY HALLOWS, 1891–1917. The question Olivia had forbidden me to ask was answered at last. I filled the vase with water and left the flowers that I'd brought.

I sat in the churchyard for nearly an hour, wondering whether, one day, I would take you to see your grandmother's grave. Yet how could I? To reveal one part of Willis's story was to reveal all. And I already knew I wasn't equal to that. So I mourned my mother alone. I suppose, in my heart, I also wanted, now that I had something of her at last, to keep it to myself, to preserve her memory as my personal secret. I placed a standing order with a florist in Ventnor to replenish the vase regularly and have renewed it annually ever since. If we went to Bonchurch now, we would find fresh flowers on her grave. And we will go there – for now we can.

I left the churchyard reluctantly, knowing I had other business in Bonchurch.

Sea Thrift was much as it had been described to me. I entered nervously, wondering if, by any chance, Grace Fotheringham still lived there, if this was the moment when I would see again my pretty lady of long ago.

But it was not to be. A querulous, liver-spotted little man answered the door. He assured me that the name Fotheringham meant nothing to him. My enquiry seemed to irritate him.

'She lived here during the First World War,' I said.

'I can't help you. My wife and I bought this house seven years ago – from a Mr Buller.'

'She was a schoolteacher.'

'Mr Buller was a dentist.'

'At East Dene College.'

'Never heard of it.'

I asked at the post office. There too the name Fotheringham rang no bells. But when I mentioned the college, it was a different matter.

'Closed in '39,' the man behind the counter said, scooping ice cream from a pail for the cornet I'd felt obliged to order.

'Then nobody would remember somebody who taught there?'

'You could try Miss Gill. She was on the staff. Still lives in the village.'

He gave me the address: a crooked-roofed cottage perched on the wooded slope above the church. Miss Gill, a stout, panting, bustling lady, received me in her musty conservatory, where she was dispensing seed to a caged colony of song-birds.

'East Dene? Yes, I taught there for more than thirty years.' She peered at me round the end of a cage. 'Are you an old girl? What did you say your name was?'

'Galloway. And no, I never went there. I'm trying to trace somebody who taught there. A Miss Fotheringham – during the First World War.'

'Fotheringham?' She rattled the bars of a cage. 'Don't squabble! There's plenty for everyone. Fotheringham, you say? Ah yes – Grace Fotheringham.'

'That's her.'

'Left under a cloud, as I remember.' She clicked her tongue at the birds. 'Simply failed to turn up at the start of the autumn term: 1920 it would have been.'

'Do you know why she left?'

'Absolutely no idea. I had better things to do with my time than enquire into such matters. But she was clearly . . . well, not sound.'

'In what way?'

'She fostered an orphaned baby. Can you imagine? A woman in her position. Extraordinary. Quite extraordinary.'

'Any idea where she went?'

'None whatever. I think we were all glad to see the back of her.'

There was no more to be learned in Bonchurch. I returned to Portsmouth and asked a taxi driver to take me to the Mermaid Inn, Nile Street.

'There's no Mermaid in Nile Street.'

'There must be.'

'Not as I've 'eard of.' He leant out and shouted to the driver next to him on the rank. ''Ere, Reg; ever 'ear of a Mermaid Inn in Nile Street?'

'Yeh. Bombed out in the war. Never rebuilt.'

So I had him take me to Brickwood's Brewery instead, where I was referred to a Mr Draycott as having the most reliable memory for lapsed tenancies. I found him stooped over a desk in a busy office above the yard.

'The Mermaid? Yes, your information is correct. Destroyed in the Blitz: April 1941. We'd probably have closed it after the war anyway. Trade was contracting in—'

'It's the tenant I was interested in.'

He paused for a moment, then remembered. 'Nora Hobson. She ran the place with her brother. Fellow named Fletcher. Both killed in the bombing raid.'

Another dead end. I went to the library and looked up the same back copies of the local newspaper that Franklin had. It was all there, in verification of his account. I even found a report of the inquests into Mompesson and Cheriton. That too bore him out. But documents, it seemed, were now the only witnesses. The actors in the drama were beyond my reach.

My next step was disguised as a shopping trip to Bristol. In reality, I drove to Winchester and located the auctioneer who'd handled the sale at Meongate. However loathsome they were, Olivia's two paintings were embedded in the tragedy that had overtaken my parents: I'd begun to regret my rejection of them. And the book Olivia had taken from me, the book with which I'd fought off Sidney Payne: Willis's account had made me want to read it for myself, bloodstained or not. I'd almost begun to hope that Olivia hadn't destroyed it after all.

The auctioneer remembered the sale well; it was relatively recent.

'I'm trying to trace some of the items you sold, Mr Woodward,' I explained. 'Some paintings by an artist named Bartholomew and a book: a church committee report on poverty in Portsea at the turn of the century.'

'As far as the paintings go, I think I know the ones you mean.' He smiled. 'A pair of rather obsessive medievalist pieces.'

'That's them.'

'Let's see.' He thumbed through a ledger. 'Yes, here they are. Two oils, by P. Bartholomew. They went for twelve guineas. Not bad, all things considered.'

'Who bought them?'

He shrugged. 'A member of the public. Paid cash. He wasn't a dealer, that I do remember.'

'And the book?'

'Except for a couple of Victorian atlases and some Trollope first editions, we sold the contents of the library as a job lot to a local bookseller – Blackmore's in Jewry Street.'

Mr Blackmore was as helpful as I could ask. 'They were no great bargain, Mrs Galloway. I haven't sold many of them. I don't remember the book you describe at all. But you're welcome to have a look. They're rather scattered about the shelves now, I'm afraid.' I looked, but in vain.

There seemed, as I walked away from the shop, one more avenue worth exploring. At police headquarters, the officer behind the enquiries desk volunteered what information he could – but that wasn't much.

'The name Shapland means nothing to me, madam, though that's not surprising. If he retired during the First World War, he's probably dead by now, so even the pensions branch couldn't help you. Where did you say he was stationed?'

'I don't know for sure. Portsmouth seems likely.'

He pondered for a moment. Then: 'You could try George Pope. He's been desk sergeant at Pompey since Adam was a lad. If Shapland was stationed there, George would remember him.'

It hardly seemed worth the effort, but I was determined to trace every loose end that I could. A fortnight later, Tony went away for a few days to Manchester on business. I took the opportunity to drive down to Portsmouth. I'd telephoned ahead and established that Sergeant Pope would be on duty at the police station and he, it seemed, was expecting me.

'Are you the lady who phoned earlier?' He filled his large uniform with pride and looked at me with piercing eyes set in the large, sad face of a man who'd contemplated a lifetime of crime.

'I am, yes. I was very much hoping to have a word with you.'

'It must be my lucky day.' He smiled with sudden, endearing coyness. 'What can I do for you?'

'I'm trying to trace an Inspector Shapland. I think he

was stationed here and I was told you might remember him.'

He frowned. 'Do you mean Arnie Shapland?'

'I don't know his first name. He retired before the First World War – and was recalled during it.'

The great grey head nodded in slow remembrance. 'You *do* mean Arnie Shapland. He was an inspector here when I joined the Force. Prickly old . . .' His concentration returned to the present. 'But that was forty-two years ago. You're right: he retired just before the Great War. Why should a young lady like you be interested in old Arnie? He must be dead and gone these twenty years or more.'

'He investigated a case involving my family. It was never cleared up.'

'What case?'

'A murder. At Meongate, near Droxford, in 1916.'

'The Meongate murder?' he chuckled. 'Fancy you dredging that up. Yes, it was one of Arnie's. His very last case. He was put out to grass again straight afterwards.'

'He didn't stay on until the end of the war, then?'

'No. The case turned sour on him. The aristocracy were mixed up in it.' He caught himself up. 'Your family, did you say?'

'Yes, but do go on. You won't offend me, I assure you.'

'It's just that he claimed to have solved the case. *Insisted*, I should say. Went on insisting, long after he was told to drop it. Then he was taken off the strength, suddenly, as if . . .'

'As if somebody wanted to shut him up?'

Pope smiled again. 'As if his conclusions weren't too popular. Let's say that.'

'And what were his conclusions?'

'I was a raw young copper, Mrs Galloway. Arnie

Shapland wasn't about to confide in me – or anyone else.'

'His family, perhaps?'

He shook his head. 'I wouldn't have thought so. He was a bachelor. Lived over his sister's grocery shop in Goldsmith Avenue. Her son runs the place now.'

I shared Pope's scepticism, but it was no great hardship to drive across the city to M. & F. Lupson (Groceries & Provisions) and try my luck.

It was a dowdy, dun-painted corner shop at the end of a terraced street. From the other side of Goldsmith Avenue came the dull, heavy clanking of a railway goods yard. Otherwise, the populous neighbourhood was strangely still and silent, drugged by the sultry afternoon. Inside the shop, torpor and gloom prevailed. A thin, nervous-looking man was weighing and packing tea: its acrid scent hung in the air.

'Mr Lupson?'

'Er . . . Yes.' He turned, sank the scoop in the sackful of tea, wiped his hands aimlessly on his apron and looked wanly towards me. 'Can I help you?'

'I believe you're the nephew of Arnold Shapland, the police inspector.'

He frowned. 'Well . . . Yes . . .'

'He investigated the Meongate murder in 1916. Does that mean anything to you?'

'Meongate?' His words came slowly, in time with his thoughts. 'Meongate, you say?'

'That's right. I know it's a long time ago, but it's a tragedy that still hands over my family. I gather your uncle thought he'd solved the case and was then taken off it. I wondered if he might ever have . . . said something . . .'

Lupson's glasses had slid most of the way down his

368

nose. Now he pushed them back up, focusing his eyes with sudden, gleaming animation. 'The Meongate murder. You know about it?'

'My family lived at Meongate.'

'Well, well, well. So Uncle Arnie was right after all. It's just a pity you left it twenty-five years too late.'

'What do you mean?'

A smile had broken out on his drawn, pinched face – a lop-sided smile of strange, unfamiliar pleasure. 'He said we hadn't heard the last of it. He said he'd be proved right in the end. Well, well, well. Who'd have . . .' Suddenly, the smile dropped from his face and his mouth clamped shut. A moment later, I saw why. A hard-jawed woman with scraped-back hair had entered the shop from the rear. I had the immediate impression that she modified what she was about to say when she saw me. Even so, there was no gentleness in her tone.

'Maurice! When you've served the lady, I want these biscuit tins moved.' She went out again at once.

Lupson leant across the counter towards me. 'I can't talk now,' he whispered.

I found myself whispering as well. 'I wouldn't keep you long.'

'That's not the point. I'd like to discuss it, really.' He thought for a moment. 'I'll be doing my rounds in the van later. We could meet then, if you like.'

'I'd like that very much.'

'This end of South Parade Pier. Half-past four.'

I nodded in agreement. He swayed back into an upright position and, feeling foolish, I ordered a twist of tea.

Lupson was precisely on time. At 4.30, I was standing near the entrance to the pier, looking down over a low wall at the beach and the few bathers braving a keen

369

breeze, when his bull-nosed, rusting van pulled up beside me and he climbed out, sucking nervously on a cigarette.

'It's kind of you to have come,' I said, in an effort to put him at his ease.

He shrugged his shoulders awkwardly. 'Shall we walk a way?'

We moved slowly in the direction of Southsea Common. As we went, I told him what little I wanted him to know of my connection with the Meongate murder. I hoped it would draw him out and I was not disappointed.

'Mrs Lupson hated Uncle Arnie. That's why I couldn't talk earlier. When we first married, we lived over the shop with my mother and him. It was a tight squeeze. They didn't get on. Now, my uncle and me – that was different. I was closer to him than to my own dad. When I was a lad, he told me all about the Meongate murder. Other cases, too – but that one most of all. He'd always come back to it, like a dog to his bone. He'd take me for walks to Milton Park – or down to his allotment – and go through it, time and again.'

'Why did you say I'd left it twenty-five years too late?'

'Because that's how long he's been dead. He always reckoned we hadn't heard the last of it, you see. He always maintained that, one day, it would crop up again and he'd be proved right – right about who the murderer was. They didn't want to know – his superiors, I mean. They wanted it hushed up. But my uncle wouldn't stand for that – so they sacked him.'

'I understood he'd retired.'

'That's not the way he looked at it. He brooded on it endlessly, cooped up in his little attic room; ran through it, over and over, for my benefit.'

'What was his theory, Mr Lupson? I'd be fascinated to know.'

'You can read it in his own words. He sent a letter of protest to the Chief Constable about the case being closed. Typed it out laboriously on the old sit-up-and-beg machine he kept in his room. It sets all out in detail. I've brought the carbon copy he took. I thought you might like to see it.'

It was more than I could have hoped for. When we'd retraced our steps to the van, Lupson pulled an old attaché case from beneath the driver's seat, lifted out a bundle of papers, detached a crinkled clip of flimsy sheets and handed them over solemnly. Then he leant against the bonnet, smoking another cigarette and taking the air, while I read his uncle's letter.

It took the form of a memorandum, with neither address nor salutation.

CONFIDENTIAL
To: The Chief Constable
From: A. W. Shapland, Det. Insp.
Date: 13th November 1916
Subject: The Meongate Murder Inquiry

I realize you will not welcome another communication from me on the above subject, but I feel obliged to state my position clearly, since the plain implication of the Watch Committee report on this case is that its investigation was mishandled. That, I take it, is why my recall from retirement has been so abruptly terminated, although no formal explanation has so far been given to me.

If this case is to be considered closed, it must be on the basis that Lieutenant Cheriton murdered Mompesson before taking his own life. The only motive put forward to explain this is Lord Powerstock's claim that Cheriton was victimized by Mompesson on account of his dubious war record. It seems to me that there are three fundamental objections to this explanation.

1. Why should the gun used to kill Mompesson not subsequently have been found amongst Cheriton's possessions?

2. If Cheriton suffered from neurasthenia – as stated at the inquest – how did he manage to plan and execute such a cool and calculated murder?

3. If Cheriton really did kill Mompesson in order to refute his allegations of cowardice, why did he not make this clear in a note to be found on his body, when, by leaving no note, he only encouraged the assumption that he could not face returning to France?

I think it highly likely that, in fact, Cheriton did leave a note, that it was removed from his body and destroyed and that this was done because the note identified the real murderer. The only person in a position to remove such a note was Lieutenant Franklin and I believe he did so because he was the person named in it. To substantiate this, I bring to your attention the following.

1. Amongst Mompesson's possessions, I found a paper recording a date (June 13th) and an address in a slum district of Portsea. The address was later shown to be an unoccupied set of rooms above a woodyard. Mompesson had no known connection with Portsmouth, but you may recall that the first Lady Powerstock was implicated in the Mermaid Inn sedition case of 1904, centred on Portsea. She was known to have formed an association with one of the defendants, a radical agitator named Daniel Fletcher.

2. When questioned, Franklin claimed to have left the White Horse Inn *alone* at about 10 p.m. on Friday, 22nd September, i.e., about an hour before Mompesson was murdered. Major Thorley, on the other hand, stated that he saw Franklin leaving *in the company of another man* (whom he did not recognize).

3. Entering Meongate in the early evening of Sunday, 24th September, I surprised Franklin and Mrs Hallows reading and discussing the First Lady Powerstock's published account of her charitable work in Portsea.

4. Questioning Mr Gladwin, father of the first Lady Powerstock, that same evening, I asked him if the late Captain Hallows was really the son of Daniel Fletcher rather than Lord Powerstock and what event of significance had occurred at Meongate in the middle of June this year. He became unreasonably agitated and refused to answer any questions.

5. Mrs Hallows left Meongate early on Monday, 25th September and has not returned there since. I know she purchased a single ticket to Portsmouth at Droxford railway station that morning and I believe she is now resident on the Isle of Wight at an address known to Lord and Lady Powerstock. I understand they have given you an explanation of her departure from Meongate, but that explanation has not been passed on to me.

6. When I disclosed my knowledge of the Portsea address to Franklin on the morning of Tuesday, 26th September, he immediately left Droxford. He was followed first to the aforesaid Portsea address and thence to the Mermaid Inn, where he stayed overnight. The following morning, Wednesday, 27th September, he eluded our officer whilst boarding the Isle of Wight ferry. He returned to Droxford that evening.

I suggest the only conclusion that can be reconciled with the foregoing is as follows.

Captain Hallows did not die in France in April, as reported, but deserted, returned to this country and went into hiding with the aid and connivance of his wife. Daniel Fletcher, his natural father, sheltered him at the address in Portsea from 13th June onwards. At some point, Franklin was also let into the secret. I am unable to say how Mompesson discovered the deception, but, upon doing so, he attempted to use the information to blackmail one of all of the parties concerned. Franklin and Hallows met outside the White Horse Inn on the evening of 22nd September and agreed to silence Mompesson. One or both of them then entered Meongate and murdered him. They were seen leaving his room by Cheriton, for whose nerves this was the last blow. Mrs Hallows subsequently joined her husband in Portsea and they slipped away to the Isle of Wight. Alarmed that I knew of the original hiding place, Franklin followed in order to warn them. Having satisfied himself as to their safety, he returned to brazen out the inquest.

I very much regret having to end my career with an unsolved case, especially since I am certain it could have been solved had I been given the support I was entitled to expect. I deny that my questioning of Lord and Lady Powerstock – or any other witness – amounted to harassment and I wish it to be recorded that the order forbidding me to pursue my enquiries on the Isle of Wight fatally handicapped my investigations.

I urge you to re-open this case. In view of the evidence placed before you in this memorandum, I believe you have no alternative but to do so. I await your decision.

'He never received a reply, Mrs Galloway. It was the final insult. He served them faithfully for more than forty years – and that was his reward.'

Yes. He had done well. He had read the clues and reasoned his way to a solution. He was so nearly right. Of course Lord Powerstock would have had friends on the appropriate committees to say: 'Enough is enough.' Naturally, Olivia would have known which ears to whisper in: 'My stepdaughter is pregnant and has left our house in disgrace. Call this man off.' Who would believe Shapland's crazed theory of dead men walking and old allegiances come to the fore? Nobody. His only answer would be the blank wall of official silence.

'He always said we hadn't heard the last of it. He told me, time without number, that, one day, he'd be proved correct. Is that why you've come now, because, after all, he's been shown to be right?'

Lupson's face, lit by the sun where it slanted through the windscreen of his van, was strained by the strength of his faith in a childhood idol. I could read in it all the clinging bitterness of a dead policeman's exile from the one, last case he could never abandon. How could I tell his lone, gauche relative that, in the end, it had been for nothing?

'Yes, Mr Lupson. That's why I came to see you. I know the whole story now. Your uncle was right all along.'

They were the words Lupson wanted to hear. For myself, Shapland's letter of protest served only to remove the last shreds of doubt about Willis's story. It was true, in every detail. He and Shapland had struggled through the same maze and had emerged as ignorant as each other of what really took place at Meongate the night Mompesson died.

If I was to learn any more, I knew it would mean

talking, even pleading, with a man whom I'd hoped never to see again: Mayhew. If anybody could tell me why Olivia had acted as she had, how I'd come to be her ward rather than Grace Fotheringham's, then it was Mayhew. Next day, I rang his old offices. After some prevarication, they gave me his private address: a bungalow in the New Forest. I drove down there the same afternoon.

Mayhew's retirement home was near Cadnam, on the eastern fringe of the forest. I don't know what I'd expected, but it certainly wasn't a newly built, terracotta-roofed residence at the end of a recently concreted drive, with a screen of poplar trees behind the house and horses grazing in the field beyond. This wasn't at all the venue I associated with a grey-suited, grey-faced solicitor. Nor had I expected the door to be answered by a Mrs Mayhew, who looked twenty years her husband's junior and said she'd thought I was the man who came to clean the swimming pool. She directed me to the rear garden, where 'Larry' was 'dead-heading some roses.'

He seemed surprised to see me as I was to find him, dungareed and flat-capped, clipping at his hybrid tea bushes with a panting basset hound in attendance.

'Mrs Galloway,' he said. 'The very last person . . .'

'I'm sorry to call unannounced,' I said. 'I wonder if I might have a word with you.'

'Concerning Lady Powerstock's will?'

'Not exactly.'

'You could have written. I still visit the office once a week.'

'Could we talk now?'

'Very well.'

He led me to a garden table near the swimming pool

and we sat opposite each other in camp chairs. There was no offer of tea, no suggestion that my visit was anything other than an unwelcome invasion of his privacy. Accordingly, I dispensed with all preliminaries.

'What can you tell me about Grace Fotheringham?'

His face betrayed no reaction to the question. 'What do you wish to know?'

'The circumstances surrounding her surrender of me to my grandparents.'

'I'm not sure I can help you.'

'You corresponded with Miss Fotheringham at the time of my birth, giving her to understand that my grandfather wanted nothing to do with me. Is that not so?'

'I believe you're correct.'

'Did you correspond with her again?'

'Once, as I recall.'

'For what reason?'

'It was early in 1920. Lady Powerstock indicated that she wished to retrieve you from Miss Fotheringham's keeping.'

'Why?'

'The reason formed no part of my instructions. I wrote to Miss Fotheringham seeking her compliance. At first, she refused.'

'Only at first?'

'Since she was not your legal guardian, she could have been obliged to comply, but proceedings to that end did not prove necessary.'

'Why not?'

'I don't know. Lady Powerstock handled the matter personally. At all events, Miss Fotheringham relented and you were installed at Meongate.'

'What became of Miss Fotheringham?'

'Once again, I don't know.'

'She left the school where she was working, abruptly, in the summer of 1920. Do you know why?'

'No.'

'I'm not sure I believe you, Mr Mayhew.'

Even this insult failed to move him. 'That, of course, is your privilege.'

'I think you know a great deal more about my family's affairs than you've ever disclosed.'

'A family solicitor, Mrs Galloway, is not normally noted for his indiscretion. Lord and Lady Powerstock used my services for many years. I always respected the confidence they vested in me.'

'And now they're both dead?'

'As Lady Powerstock's executor, I still recognize an obligation to her.'

'But not to her granddaughter?'

'Not at any rate to you, Mrs Galloway.'

The subtle distinction was transparently unpleasant. It signalled that I would gain nothing by pressing the point. I rose hurriedly from the chair. 'Goodbye, Mr Mayhew.'

'Mrs Galloway . . .' He looked at me inquisitively for a moment. 'May I ask how you heard of Miss Fotheringham?'

'No,' I replied, smiling to spite him. 'You may not.'

I returned to Wells that day realizing that I had explored and exhausted every avenue – and learned nothing beyond what Willis had already told me. There seemed no choice but to abandon my search.

With a conscious sense of finality, I wrote to the Imperial War Graves Commission, seeking information about the man who'd died in Franklin's name. Their reply confirmed what I knew.

'First Lieutenant Thomas Blaine Franklin, Hampshire Light Infantry, died on 16th August 1917, aged 25, whilst attached to the Northumbrian Regiment. After the war, the Army Graves Service were unable to locate his grave and he is therefore commemorated by name on the Memorial to the Missing at the Tyne Cot Military Cemetery, Belgium.'

For all that I did not doubt Willis's word, it was hard to accept the thought that this, a stranger's name, was truly the record of my father's death and that Franklin wasn't really dead at all. How could I explain it to anyone when, sometimes, I scarcely believed it myself?

I wondered often if, one day, Willis would return, knock at the door one Sunday afternoon and walk back into my life. But he had said that he would not and time proved him as good as his word. I had no way of finding him. He had vanished. Sometimes, increasingly as the years passed, I wondered if he'd really come at all, if I hadn't just imagined his visit. There was no proof, after all, nothing tangible by which to remember him. That thought alone deterred me from confiding in Tony – or you, as you grew older. I told myself there was no point endlessly rehearsing the past, that to have learned the truth about my parents was enough. Willis was proved right. In the end, I did forget him.

TWO

By the time I was fifty, Ronald was at university and you were away at boarding school. Tony was working harder than ever because of Jimmy Dare's illness and seemed to spend less and less time at home. So, after twenty hectic years, I found my life slipping into tedium and solitude. Accordingly, when the past next intruded on my settled world, I no longer saw it as a threat to comfort and security, rather as a challenge to be welcomed.

In the middle of January 1968, I received a letter from a firm of Cornish solicitors, Trevannon & Roach, of Fore Street, Fowey. I'd never heard of them, but they, it seemed, had heard of me. I read the letter aloud to Tony over breakfast.

'Dear Mrs Galloway, We are acting as executors for the estate of the late Mr John Willis of 13 Bull Hill, Fowey, who died on 7th January and bequeathed to you, under the terms of his will, the house which he owned and occupied, along with its contents. It would be much appreciated if you could contact Mr Gerald Trevannon in order to make arrangements to take possession of the property.'

I'd instantly regretted reading the letter out. It was as shocking to me as it would be inexplicable to Tony. Why had Willis left me his house? Surely our one meeting fifteen years before didn't warrant such a gesture. Why deliberately hide himself from me, then send this eerie posthumous message? Was Fowey where he'd been heading when he'd boarded that train and left me without a clue to his destination – until now?

'Who's John Willis?' said Tony, his face creased by a puzzled frown.

His words broke into my thoughts. What was I to say? That he was a man I'd met once but never mentioned to my husband? That he was a friend of the father I'd never known? If I'd had time to formulate a response, I might have told him the truth then – complex and incredible as it was. Instead, I stumbled into a lie.

'I don't know. The name means nothing to me.'

'But he's left you his house!'

'I can't help that. It's as much of a mystery to me as it is to you.'

'Come on, darling. People just don't leave their houses to complete strangers.'

'Well, somebody seems to have done so in this case.'

It was clear Tony didn't believe me, yet it would have been unlike him to say so openly. Instead, he would wait patiently, trusting that eventually I would tell him the truth. I could read as much in the cautious, practised way he erased doubt and misgiving from the expression on his face.

'What will you do, then?' he said eventually, in neutral tones.

'Contact Mr Trevannon, I suppose.'

'Does he say how much the house is worth?'

'No.'

My reply gave him a safe topic on which to exercise his mind. 'Fowey's something of a holiday resort. The right sort of place might be worth a bit.'

'Yes. It might.'

'I suppose you'll want to go down there.'

'I shouldn't think I'll have much choice.'

'You know I can't get away. Not as things stand at present.'

'It's all right. I'll go alone.'

Alone was, after all, how I wanted to go. If Tony hadn't been so preoccupied, I suppose he might have insisted on accompanying me, but I think we were both secretly glad that he didn't, both content, in fact, to skirt round the truth for a little longer. I was not yet ready to share the urge I felt to learn what I could of the life and death of John Willis.

I drove down to Fowey the following Monday. It was a cold, wet, grey day in late January: raw and chill, with all Cornwall's charm squeezed out of it by the grip of winter. It was dark by the time I arrived. I booked into the Fowey Hotel – rambling, empty and buffeted by gales – and began to regret the impulsive journey. I'd been given a room with a view of the estuary, but, that night, all I could see from the window was a sprinkling of pale lights smeared by the trickling rain.

The prospect had changed by morning. The sky was clear, the frost stark on the lawns beneath my window, the sunlight winking and dazzling on the water. The town lay below me, a tumble of narrow streets and huddled roofs, smoke curling from cowled chimneys. Out in the estuary, bare masts stood like winter saplings above the cluster of anchored vessels. The *put-pat* of a slow-moving ferry boat reached me, amplified in the still air. To the south lay the broad, flat ocean, to the north the curving, enclosing slopes of a wooded valley. This was where John Willis had made his home.

My appointment with Mr Trevannon was for ten o'clock. He greeted me in his first-floor office above the busy main street of the town and bustled about, arranging coffee and a copy of the will. He was younger than I'd expected, tousled and ill-prepared, somehow reassuringly inefficient.

'As you see,' he said, stooping over a small electric fire to activate another bar, 'it's a straightforward document.'

'I see he stipulated cremation.'

'Yes.' He jarred a light-fitting with his head as he rose from the fire: the low-ceilinged office seemed altogether too small for such a tall and uncoordinated man. 'I'm sorry I didn't contact you beforehand. Would you have wanted to attend? He subsided into the chair behind his desk with a sigh.

'Possibly. But it doesn't matter. And a bequest of a thousand pounds to the Earl Haig Appeal Fund.'

'Mmm. Was he . . . an old soldier?'

'As I explained to you on the telephone, Mr Trevannon, I never knew Mr Willis. This inheritance has come as something of a shock to me.'

'Ah, yes. Of course. How odd.'

'I was hoping he might have explained himself to you.'

'Well, no. Actually, if you look, you'll see he made the will in 1954. The Trevannon who witnessed it was my father. I don't recall ever meeting Mr Willis. I knew him by sight, of course. Something of a local character.'

'Was he? Why?'

'Oh, I don't know. Not very sociable, let's say. But then, on the other hand . . .'

'It doesn't specify a house here. It merely refers to my receiving the residue of the estate.'

'After the bequest to the Haig Fund and the undertaker's bill, the house is really all that's left. Mr Willis wasn't a wealthy man. Although the house must have . . .'

'When did he buy it?'

'The deeds are still with the bank. But, from memory . . .'

A secretary minced in with coffee and biscuits. She leant across the desk for a confidential word with Trevannon. 'Mr Cobb's downstairs,' she whispered.'

'Oh God.' He grimaced. 'Well, tell him I won't be long.' She withdrew. 'Now, where was I? The house . . . when did he buy it? Early fifties, I think. It's probably appreciated a good deal since then.'

'So . . . may I see it?'

'Of course.' He raised his cup to drink.

'Do you have the keys?'

'Ah. Bit of a problem there.' He put the cup down again, as if to emphasize his difficulty. 'Actually, no. Ordinarily, I would have. But, in this case . . . To put it bluntly, Mrs Galloway, you have sitting tenants.'

'Squatters?'

'Oh no. They were there with Mr Willis's blessing . . . as far as I know. Lodgers, you might say.'

'So they have the keys?'

He smiled nervously. 'Well, naturally. I've explained the position to them, of course. They know you're coming.'

'In that case, perhaps I oughtn't to keep them waiting.'

'Go straight round, you mean? Good idea.' He raised his cup again, then changed his mind: it returned, still full, to its saucer. 'Perhaps I should . . . ah . . . tell you something about them. They're not . . . the sort of lodgers you or I might take in.'

'I'm sure they won't bite.'

'No . . . No, of course not.' Some coffee was finally consumed. 'You'll want some directions. Bull Hill's just round the corner. Number thirteen's at the far end.'

Bull Hill, an alley reached by a flight of steps behind the Lugger Inn, threaded between the backs of the house-tops in Fore Street on one side and a tall stone wall on the other. The estuary was visible beyond the jumble of roofs, but Bull Hill itself held a sheltered, hidden warmth, divorced from the bustle of the town.

Some way along, the wall to my left merged with the frontages of houses built on the slope above the alley and there, between two austere and shuttered properties, I found my strange inheritance.

Number thirteen was a narrow, three-storeyed build-ing looming above a low, crumbling wall and a neglected garden, pink-washed and slate-roofed, with paint peeling on the windows. The porched entrance was to one side, reached by a steep flight of shallow-treaded steps. At the top of them out of the sun, it was suddenly cold: a bitter, chill breath of winter. On the door I noticed a sheet of paper, folded in two and attached by a drawing pin. I rang the bell and then, hearing no sound, tried the knocker. There was no answer. Feeling only a little sheepish, I removed the sheet of paper and unfolded it. Three words scrawled on it in biro: *King of Prussia*. Then I tried the door handle. It wasn't locked.

A strange mixture of odours met me: dampness, furniture polish, stale food, cats and something else, sickly sweet, like incense. There were soiled dishes piled in the kitchen sink and cat food in a bowl beneath the draining board. The kitchen was to the rear of the house, looking out on to a patch of shade-blighted garden where two sheets hung despondently on a motionless line. The large front room commanded a fine view of the town and the estuary. The warmth of a paraffin stove still hung in the air, its steam heavy-beaded on the windows. There was a frayed leather sofa, a dark-wooded dining table much scratched and stained, and bookcases beneath the windows, their contents jammed and jumbled.

I knelt by one of the bookcases and ran my eye along the shelves. It was just possible ... but no. I didn't recognize any of them. Thrillers by Hammett and Chandler, some Zane Grey westerns, most of Scott Fitzgerald, poetry by Sylvia Plath, plays by Wesker: not at all what I'd have expected.

'Hello?' A voice came from behind me. I turned round to find myself looking at a slim, rather blank-faced girl in her early twenties. She had long blonde hair with brunette showing at the roots and wore an over-sized caftan coat over a cheesecloth shirt and tight, faded blue jeans. 'You must be Mrs Galloway.' There was a lilt of Cornishness behind the practised drawl.

'Yes, that's right. I'm sorry to have barged in. The door wasn't locked.'

'It never is. I'm Zoë Tefler. I live here.'

'I thought you must.' I held out my hand: she shook it awkwardly, as if the gesture was an unfamiliar one.

'We were wondering when you'd arrive. I'm sorry it's such a mess.'

'There was a rather odd note pinned to the door.'

She shrugged a knitted bag off her shoulder into an

armchair and laid her hands on the still warm stove. 'The King of Prussia's a pub. It means Lee's gone down there. You must have just missed him.'

'Pity.'

She laughed, then squinted back at me as if in need of spectacles. 'You're not really what we expected.'

'No?'

'Johnno never mentioned you.'

I decided to test her knowledge. 'He never mentioned you either.'

'He wouldn't, would he?'

'Why not?'

She walked to the window and lit a cigarette. I declined the offer of one. 'What will you want to do with this place?'

'I was hoping we could discuss that. Perhaps when . . . Lee gets back.'

She laughed, as she had before. As she drew on the cigarette and gazed out of the window, I noticed for the first time that she was really quite beautiful: long neck, high cheeks, large, almost luminous eyes, all carried with a casual air of waif-like awareness.

'Would that be possible? There's no hurry. I'm staying at the Fowey Hotel overnight.'

She frowned, then looked at me with sudden concentration. 'Mrs Galloway' – another drag on the cigarette – 'did you . . . mean something to Johnno?'

I was determined to give nothing away. 'I must have.'

'When did you know him?'

'I last saw him fifteen years ago.'

She nodded pensively. 'Why don't you come to dinner tonight? You could meet Lee then.'

I was taken aback by the abruptness of the invitation. 'Well . . . all right. Thank you. I'd love to.' Suddenly the abnormality of it all struck me. Zoë Telfer wasn't at all the sort of person I'd have accepted – or expected – a dinner invitation from.

'Do you want to . . . see round the place?'

'It's kind of you, but I shan't intrude. Perhaps . . . later.'

'OK then. Come round about seven.'

'Until seven then.' I turned to go.

'Mrs Galloway . . .' I stopped and looked back at her. She took a lengthy draw on the cigarette, then stubbed it out prematurely in an ashtray on top of the bookcase. 'I miss him, you know. It's funny really. I was hoping you'd be somebody I could talk to about him.' She looked at me with her frank, saucer-like eyes.

'To be honest, I didn't know him that well.'

'Nobody seemed to. And now . . . it's too late. It was so . . . unexpected.'

'A heart attack, Mr Trevannon said.'

'Yeh. Poor old Johnno.'

'How did it happen?'

'He was always up early. That Sunday, he hadn't stirred by midday, so I took a cup of tea in to him. At first, I thought he was still asleep. It must have been a very peaceful way to go. The doctor said he wouldn't have known anything about it. Like a clock winding down, I suppose. One day, it just stops.'

'I'm glad he wasn't in any pain.'

'Yeh, so am I. He was very good to us. Taking us in and all that.'

'How long have you lived here?'

'A little over a year. We moved in just before Christmas '66. Before that, he lived alone.'

'You'd not known him long then?'

'No, not long. Not really . . .' Her eyes seemed to drift out of focus, as if she was looking past me at something

388

that wasn't there. When I left, I'm not even sure she noticed.

I made my way to the other end of Bull Hill, where it rejoined Fore Street, then headed back towards Trevannon's office. The narrow thoroughfare was crowded with shoppers and delivery vans. Stepping into the doorway of a bakery to avoid a pair of old women with bags on wheels, I found myself standing next to a tall man in a duffel coat, holding the steaming remains of a pasty before him, swathed in greaseproof paper. It was Mr Trevannon.

'Hello,' he said, gulping down a mouthful. 'Have you been up to the house?'

'Yes. I met Miss Telfer.'

'But not her boyfriend?'

'You mean Lee? No, he wasn't in.'

'Just as well. Bit of a weirdo, actually. American. A draft dodger, I think. Funny choice for a lodger. Funny all round, really.'

'In what way?'

'See that over there?' He pointed to the shop opposite some sort of boutique-cum-pottery, with a metallic, copper-coloured awning. The midday sun, slanting between the houses, hit it with a dazzling glare. 'Mr Cobb's wife is disabled, you see. They lived above this bakery. He claims she can't sit by the window as she used to, and watch the world go by, because of that awning. Unless it's cloudy, of course.'

'I see his point.'

'So do I. But is it a public nuisance? That's what he wants me to prove, which is tricky, decidedly tricky. Some people would say Lee Cormack was a public nuisance. Evidently your Mr Willis didn't agree.'

389

'Evidently not.'

'As I say, it's funny. He didn't seem to have any friends. Lived alone till he took those two in. And left you with a bit of a problem. You'll want to evict them, of course.' He peered at the last fragment of pasty, then screwed it up in the paper.

'Evict his only friends, you mean?'

'You could look at it like that.' He glanced up and down the street, apparently in search of a refuse bin. 'Not his only friends, though. There was Eric Dunrich. You'd often see them together.'

'Could I contact Mr Dunrich?'

'Why not? He lives over the estuary in Polruan. Seaspray Cottage in West Street. Just round the corner from the ferry. Anybody will direct you. But I ought to warn you: he's a bit odd. Proves my point, really.'

Still uncertain what Mr Trevannon's point was, I crossed the estuary on the tiny, struggling ferry-boat early that afternoon. The air remained clear and bright, a cold sun lighting the whitewashed housefronts of Fowey as they fell away behind us.

I walked alone up the slipway on the Polruan side, while three housewives, laden with shopping bags, bustled past me to reach the ferry. On the jetty, one brave amateur artist sat muffled in the lee of a low building, dabbing at his canvas with a brush held in one mittened hand. I asked him for directions to Seaspray Cottage.

'Just around the corner. But I fear you will find nobody in.'

'How do you know?'

'Because I am the sole occupant.'

'Eric Dunrich?'

'Yes.' He shot me a buck-toothed grin from inside his scarlet balaclava. At once, I took more note of him. A dumpy figure, wrapped in sweaters, perched obstinately on his camp chair. His painting, propped on an easel before him, had an air of stubborn inelegance.

'Perhaps you'll have heard of me, Mr Dunrich. I'm Leonora Galloway.'

'Mrs Galloway!' In one maladroit movement, he jumped up from the chair, nearly capsizing his easel in the process, and swept off his balaclava, leaving a crop of grey hair spiked out at alarming angles. 'Delighted to make your acquaintance.' He seized my right hand but, instead of shaking it, held it flat and bowed stiffly.

I laughed nervously. 'I gather you knew Mr John Willis.'

'Yes, indeed.' He grinned. 'And you, I gather, are his beneficiary. Will you do me the honour of stepping back to my humble abode for tea? We might there discuss our mutual, much-mourned friend.'

I didn't know whether to take him seriously, but accepted the invitation none the less. He left his chair, easel and canvas where they were and took only his paints and brushes, bundled in a duffel bag, as he led the way up a narrow street between silent cottages that seemed to echo and amplify his high-pitched, piping voice.

'John never spoke of you, Mrs Galloway, but it is evident that you stood highly in his esteem. I am therefore honoured that you should seek me out.'

We turned in at the green-painted door of his tiny home, a spotlessly clean, strangely warm haven of potted plants and ceiling-high bookcases. He left me alone whilst he made the tea, but his voice carried clearly from the kitchen.

'I have no view of the sea from here, you understand, so, if I am to capture it on canvas, I must brave the winter chill.'

'Do you paint a lot, Mr Dunrich?'

'Ceaselessly, Mrs Galloway, ceaselessly.'

'Yet none of your work is displayed here.'

A serving hatch was flung open to admit his head and shoulders. 'That is because my paintings are consistently dreadful. My ceaseless striving is to produce one that I actually like.' Steam began to rise from a kettle behind him. The head and shoulders withdrew.

'That's a remarkably conscientious attitude.'

'To thine own self be true. Is that not essential? John reminded me of it, often enough.' He appeared suddenly at the door, teapot and cups rattling on a tray. 'He had the advantage of me, of course, being a gifted painter himself. Yet still he hid his works from view.' He deposited the tray on a low table and gestured me to an armchair.

'He painted as well?'

'Why yes. It was a shared interest, but not a shared ability. The talent was all his.'

'Had you known him long?'

He applied one index finger to his forehead. 'Sunday the eighteenth of November 1962. A little over five years.'

'You can be that precise?'

'Precision, Mrs Galloway, is a function of significance. Milk or lemon?'

'Milk, please.' He began to pour. 'I've visited the house.'

'A charming property, is it not?' He craned forward with my tea.

'Yes. Perhaps you can explain what nobody else seems able to. Why did he leave it to me?'

Dunrich held his cup motionless, halfway between saucer and mouth. 'Explanation relies upon understanding. Alas, I have insufficient. John was a good and loyal friend to me. To have asked for more would have been to trespass upon his privacy.'

'If I were you, I think I might feel hurt that he left everything to a stranger and nothing to his friends here.'

'Oh, but he did. He left his memory.'

'Wouldn't you have liked some memento?'

'You place me in a difficult position, Mrs Galloway. The fact is that John promised me just that. He sat there – in the very chair you occupy – the afternoon before he died. Epiphany, it was. He said that when he was no longer here . . .'

'He said that the afternoon before he died? He spoke about being no longer here?'

'An eerie coincidence, you mean? Neither, I would suggest. John was something of a seer. Or so I felt. But yes. Those were the terms in which he spoke – a matter of hours before he died.'

'If it lies in my power, Mr Dunrich, you'd be welcome . . .'

He held up his hand. 'Too late, dear lady. Alas, too late. What he intended, and I desired, has been mislaid.'

'What do you mean?'

'I gathered from Miss Telfer that the painting he promised me was not amongst his possessions. Sold, we must suppose. But, if so, why did he mention it? He was not given to cruelty, nor much to jokes at all.'

'There must be some mistake, then. I'll see what I can find out.'

'Pray cause no difficulty on my account. If John considered the two young people worthy of spare beneath his roof, I will not fall to quibbling about the consequences.'

'Why did he take them in, do you know?'

'They were homeless. Also there was, shall we say, an artistic purpose. Miss Telfer enabled him to complete a series of paintings. I had thought the process would bring him the contentment he once helped me to find, but the reverse appeared to be the case. When I saw him last, he was a troubled man. Would that I had done more to assist him.' Dunrich had grown suddenly gloomy, all the effervescence gone from him. He returned his cup to its saucer with a dull clatter.

'There's nothing anyone could have done about a heart attack.'

'No. Of course not.' He seemed to revive a little. 'More tea?'

Later, I walked back with him to the harbour. The ferry was waiting at the bottom of the slipway. I thanked him for his hospitality and began to descend.

'Call again any time, dear lady. I never stray far.'

'I forgot to ask, Mr Dunrich. What happened on the eighteenth of November 1962 that enables you to recollect the date so clearly?'

'Did I not say? That was the day I was to have thrown myself from St Saviour's Point. It's a sheer drop, you know.' He grinned. 'John dissuaded me.' I stared up at him in amazement. 'Do not dally, Mrs Galloway. The ferry is ready to depart.'

That night was still and frosty. The church clock was striking seven with leaden clarity as I climbed the steps to Bull Hill: the alley was deserted, inky black and silent.

Zoë welcomed me nervously. She was wearing a

blouse and long skirt: I think it was her attempt to look smart. She showed me into the front room, where the paraffin stove had induced a humid warmth overlaid with the scent of smouldering joss sticks. The mournful voice of Bob Dylan was droning from a record player.

A figure rose from the sofa, where he'd been slumped out of sight. Tall, thin and sinewy in jeans and a black shirt, a mop of dark, curly hair reaching to his shoulders, several days' growth of beard. He didn't smile or extend a hand in greeting.

'Hi,' he said levelly. 'I'm Lee. You must be our new landlady.'

'In a sense. I'm Leonora Galloway. Inheriting this property came as something of a surprise to me.' I heard my own voice bounce back to me off his hollow-eyed stare. A middle-aged Englishwoman with an unfashionable accent: what must he have thought?

'Dylan your bag?'

I smiled. 'Hardly.'

'Reckon not. Make you uncomfortable, eh? The thought that the times may really be a-changing?'

Zoë came in behind me. 'Turn that down, Lee, will you?' He shrugged his narrow shoulders and slouched across to reduce the volume. 'Would you like something to drink, Mrs Galloway?'

'Thank you. A sherry, perhaps.'

Lee sniggered. 'No sherry, ma'am. How 'bout a beer?'

In the end, I had nothing. Lee took swigs from a can and smoked roll-up cigarettes, sitting on the carpet by the stove, as if he craved its warmth. I sat on the sofa and tried to make conversation while Zoë busied herself in the kitchen.

'Which state are you from, Lee?'

'New Jersey.'

'And what brought you to Cornwall?'

'Vietnam. You ain't looking at a patriot. I'm here because we're there. Shocked?'

'No.'

'Yes you are. 'Course you are.'

'Was Willis?'

He snorted. 'How should I know? He didn't exactly volunteer his feelings – on anything.'

'He gave you a home.'

'He gave Zo a home. He gave me . . . house room.'

Zoë had made some kind of flan. That, and a bowl of baked potatoes, constituted the meal, taken round the table in a corner of the room, lit by a fat red candle that cast its flickering glow on Lee's drawn features and made him look gaunter than ever. On Zoë the effect was different. Her eyes, lambent and enlarged, regarded us both as from a distant plateau. Around us, Dylan's voice wailed on.

'Had he never told you of his intention to leave the house to me?'

'No,' said Zoë softly. 'He never so much as mentioned your name.'

'I can't understand it. He made his will fourteen years ago. Perhaps he forgot its provisions.'

'That man,' Lee put in with a slur, 'never forgot a damn thing.'

'I went to see Mr Dunrich this afternoon. He told me that Willis painted a good deal.'

'Yes,' said Zoë. 'He did.'

'He told me there was one particular painting, half-promised to him, that somehow went missing.'

'You talk to that creep,' Lee said, 'and you'll hear all kind o' things.'

'You don't like him?'

Lee scowled, but it was Zoë who answered. 'Johnno liked him. but sometimes he's rather . . . confused.'

'Are there no paintings, then?'

'Yes. There are paintings. Johnno used the top floor as a kind of gallery. It was his . . . particular place.'

'Could I see them?'

Lee began to frame an objection, but Zoë cut him short. 'Of course. Everything here is yours now. I'll take you up after dinner.'

'That's right, ma'am,' Lee said. 'Everything here is yours. We come with the property, body and soul.' He smiled defiantly.

Later, when Zoë showed me upstairs, Lee stayed behind, reclining by the stove, drinking and smoking, singing along with the music under his breath.

The narrow, enclosed stairs led to two bedrooms and a bathroom on the first floor: I glimpsed a mattress and disordered blankets behind a bead curtain. Another flight led to a single room at the top of the house. Bare boards, with low windows set in the eaves, in one corner a strip of carpet and a narrow bed, elsewhere a jumble of easels, chairs and cupboards. I glanced around at the stray tea chests and irregular stacks of canvases, all with their faces turned to the wall.

Then I saw it. A shape by one of the windows, concealed by a sheet, too small to be an easel, somehow familiar. I stepped across and pulled off the sheet. It was the telescope from Meongate. I had no proof it was the same one, no way of being sure, other than the certainty I felt when I looked at its polished brass tube, the surface minutely pitted with scratches, or the splayed wooden pedestal, spotted with paint.

'What's the matter?' said Zoë from behind me.

'I recognize the telescope. Was Willis an astronomer?'

She stood beside me in the black, uncurtained window, the light from a bare bulb falling coldly between us. 'He was many things. So many things.'

'And the paintings?'

'They're here.' She pointed to the stacks.

I went across and turned the canvases around, one by one. Local scenes: seascapes, river views, clifftops, crumbling castles, redundant tin mines. As Dunrich had said, there was skill in them. But, for all that, the subject matter was unremarkable.

'Eric came here a few days after Johnno died and sorted through them.'

I pushed the canvases back against the wall and rose to her eye level. 'Mr Dunrich suggested that Willis took you in because he needed your help – yours, not Lee's – to finish a series of paintings. Is that true?'

'We had a caravan out at Lankelly. It was meant to be just a summer let. We couldn't have stuck it through the winter. We'd met Johnno in the King of Prussia several times. When he asked us if we'd like to share this house, we were in no position to refuse. And I didn't want to. He didn't charge us any rent. He only asked me to . . . dye my hair. And let him look at me.'

'Why did he want you to dye it?'

'There was some resemblance he wanted, that he needed to capture in his paintings.'

'You were his model?'

'Yes.'

'But the only paintings here are landscapes. Where are the others, Zoë? Where have they gone?'

'Say nothing, Zo!' It was Lee's voice, raised and peremptory. I turned to see him walking slowly up the stairs, a sullen look of anger on his face. 'Any questions, ma'am, you direct 'em to me. But I have to tell you: you won't get any answers.' He moved across to join us. 'This is your house now, right enough, so if you want to give us notice to quit . . .'

'I never . . .'

'If you want to, that's fine. That's your privilege. But as far as what went on here before you showed up, then I advise you to keep off. If there are any pictures missing, it's because the old man sold 'em before he died.'

'But he promised Mr Dunrich . . .'

'You heard what I said. That's my last word.'

I too had grown angry. 'Then here's mine. I hadn't made up my mind to ask you to leave. I wasn't sure I had a right to. But now I am sure. You'll hear from me through Mr Trevannon. I dare say he'll know what notice is reasonable. Good night to you both.'

I left them there and only silence followed me down the stairs.

The anger had gone by morning, but the resolution remained: I would be rid of them and shortly rid of the house. If Willis had left it to me because of a debt he felt he owed my father, then he could hardly object to what I chose to do with it. Niggling, undefined suspicions remained. He could only have obtained the telescope by buying it at the Meongate auction. Why hadn't he told me of it when he'd visited me in Wells? What else had he bought there?

It was useless. I couldn't interrogate a dead man. I returned from a walk to Readymoney Cove more sure than ever of what I would do.

At the hotel, the receptionist told me I had a visitor waiting in the lounge. It was Zoë. She was sitting by one of the picture windows that looked out over the estuary. She seemed out of place among the deep leather sofas and stately rubber plants, a vulnerable Cornish girl ill at ease in plush surroundings.

'Hello,' I said. 'I wasn't expecting to see you here.'

She looked up at me with pleading, innocent eyes. 'I wanted to apologize for what happened last night.'

I sat down beside her. 'It wasn't your fault.'

'It was, partly.'

'Would you like me to order some coffee?'

'No. No thanks. Not for me.'

'It's kind of you to have called. But I don't think you'll change my mind. Lee . . .'

'I've come to tell you the truth.' She lowered her voice. 'We sold the other paintings. The day after Johnno died, Lee took them to a guy he knows in Plymouth. To be honest, we needed the money. But we didn't know Johnno had left the place to anybody then, so it didn't really seem like stealing.'

'I can understand that. But why didn't you sell all of them?'

'The rest weren't worth anything. You see, the ones we sold weren't by Johnno, except for the last one. He'd painted that in the style of the others – somebody else's style.'

'What do you mean – a forgery?'

'Not exactly. I don't think he meant to pass it off as the other artist's work. He just . . .'

'Who was the other artist?'

'I'd never heard of him. But Baz – that's Lee's friend in Plymouth – reckoned they were worth a bit. He said they were by somebody called Bartholomew.'

So. He had bought more than just the telescope. 'How many pictures were there?'

'Three in all. Two genuine and the one that Johnno did. It wasn't like his other work. It was kind of . . .

weird. It's the one he wanted me to model for. He had me dye my hair and wear an old-fashioned dress. Sort of Edwardian, I suppose.'

'Was it you he was painting, Zoë? Or somebody you resembled?'

'I reckon you must know who it was. When I said he never mentioned your name, I wasn't telling the truth – not exactly. I remember, when he'd finished the picture, he stood back and looked at it and said something. Just a whisper really. I don't think he realized I could hear him.'

'What did he say?'

'He just said your name. "Leonora." That's all. But it isn't you he meant, is it?'

'No. It isn't me.'

I drove to Plymouth that afternoon. Zoë had given me the address: Barbican Fine Arts, Southside Street. It was in a cramped arcade near the fish quay, a ground-level display inspired by Dali and Bosch luring the unwary to a cavernous, first-floor studio hung with trawling nets and skull-like seashells. Luridly coloured beams supported a bewildering array of the old and the new: eighteenth-century spaniels in torment alongside modern-day images of Daliesque surrealism, with Wagner playing ominously in the background. I felt and must have looked absurdly out of place.

'Can I help you?' The assistant was female, emaciated and mini-skirted, shivering in the sail-loft chill and sniffing as she spoke.

'I'm looking for Mr Basil Gates,' I said.

'You a friend of his'

'I'm a friend of Lee Cormack – you might say. Is Mr Gates in?'

'I'll go and see.'

She left me gazing at a vast and lividly wrought representation of some vaguely East European village. In every hut and hovel, a bestial act was in progress, visible through open doors or windows: a kind of advent calendar of sundry perversions. It was skilfully done and that only made it worse.

'One of mine.' The voice came from behind me, deep and mellow with a sickly sweetness. 'Do you like it?'

I turned round. My questioner was tall, willow-thin and nordic blond, clad in jeans and a smock, beads hung about his neck. His bright little eyes glinted at me from behind circular, slender-framed glasses, a pointed Cavalier-style beard adding a narcissistic note to the bohemian air. 'I think it's very well painted,' I said.

He smiled, displaying a row of jagged yellow teeth. 'You don't like it. I'm glad. You're not meant to.'

'You're Mr Gates?'

'The very same.'

'I believe you're a friend of Lee Cormack.'

'I know him, yeh. What's it to you?'

'I'll come straight to the point. Lee sold you three paintings by the late-Victorian artist Philip Bartholomew earlier this month.'

'He could have.'

'They weren't his to sell. They belong to me.'

'I wouldn't know about that.'

'I don't want to cause you any trouble. I accept my neglect was partly responsible. I'm simply trying to recover them. Do you still have them?'

He smiled again. 'Bartholomew's not strictly my style. You can see I wouldn't have wanted to hang on to them.'

'So what did you do with them?'

'I have contacts. Some are into that kind of thing. I'd have disposed of them that way.'

'I'm anxious to get them back. Would you be willing to give me the name of your contact?'

Once more the twisted grin. 'You have to consider my expenses.'

'How much do you want?'

'Look on it as a contribution to the struggle for artistic integrity.'

'How much?'

'That's up to you.'

I opened my purse. He reached forward, with slender, questing fingers, and drew out a five-pound note. 'I took them to London. Knew a feller mounting an exhibition of that kind of stuff.'

'His name?'

'Toby Raiment. He runs a shop in Camden Passage, Islington. Don't say I sent you.'

I phoned directory enquiries from the nearest call box and they gave me Raiment's number. But the man who answered was only 'minding the shop'. He suggested I ring again in the morning.

I did so from my room at the Fowey Hotel. Mr Raiment had one of those opulent voices which sound as if their possessor is permanently engaged in chewing toffee.

'Bartholomews? Yes. I had three in my major retrospective on neglected late-Victorian artists. It runs until the end of February.'

'You say you *had* three – not *have*?'

'Sold one. They're greatly in demand, you know.'

'Could I possibly come and see the other two?'

'Of course. Do you wish me to put them aside for you?'

'Yes. Yes please. Would Saturday morning be convenient?'

He took my name and we agreed a time.

I climbed Bull Hill later that morning, conscious that it might be for the last time. The alley was silent but for my own footsteps and the distant bark of a dog. The door of number thirteen was ajar, so I knocked and went in.

'Hello?'

Zoë's voice came to me from the front room. 'In here.'

She was sitting on the sofa, reading, with her legs curled beneath her and the cat dozing against her feet. A Simon and Garfunkel record was playing softly in the background. She looked up as I entered and I saw at once that her right eye had been blackened.

'Zoë! What happened?'

'Lee found out I'd been to see you – and why. That is, I told him why.'

I sat down on the sofa beside her. 'You poor thing. Is there anything I can do?'

'Don't worry. It won't happen again. Lee's gone, you see.'

'Gone?'

'To London, I think. He has friends at the LSE. It's been coming for a long time – since before Johnno died. And now – well, he didn't want to answer any awkward questions about the paintings, I suppose. He can't risk being sent back to the States as things stand at present.'

'I'm sorry it's come to this. I really am.'

'Don't be. I reckon it's for the best.'

'Will you stay here on your own? You can, you know. I never . . .'

'No. I wouldn't want to do that. Now Johnno's gone. I don't really want to stay. My sister and her husband run a restaurant in Truro. They've often asked me to go and help. Now's the time to take them up on it.' She smiled, proudly, through the bruise; seemed, for a moment, very like my own or any mother's daughter. She held up the book she'd been reading. 'Do you know the poems of Stevie Smith?'

'I don't think so.'

'I'll read you one. It's called "Not Waving but Drowning". It always reminds me of Johnno.

> "Nobody heard him, the dead man,
> But still he lay moaning;
> I was much further out than you thought
> And not waving but drowning . . ."'

The images of the poem stayed with me as, later, I walked away down Bull Hill, images of drowning mistaken and strangely familiar, images that hovered at the edge of the mind like an often used name which, suddenly and infuriatingly, one cannot recall.

> 'I was much too far out all my life
> 'And not waving but drowning.'

After she left Fowey, Zoë sent me postcards at sporadic intervals over the next year or so. The last one said simply, 'I've been happy for quite a while now,' and was post-marked Dublin. When I think of her, it's not as Zoë Telfer, making her way in the world; rather, as she was that last day, reading poetry to me with a bruised face, the play of weak sunlight on her hair giving notice that soon, all too soon, the blonde dye would be gone and, with it, an illusion, gone, like another illusion, at another time, for ever.

I was home again that evening. Tony seemed relieved to hear that Zoë would go without protest and volunteered to take charge of the house sale. As for my 'shopping trip' to London on Saturday, he appeared blithely unsuspecting.

You probably don't know Camden Passage and I've never been there since. It seemed, on a day of leaden skies and steady rain, merely one turning among many off the grey, congested streets leading north-east out of central London. The taxi-driver dropped me at the corner. Raiment's Gallery was flanked by an antique shop and an Italian restaurant. I went straight in, setting a bell above the door jangling frantically.

Display cases in the centre of the shop held tinted country maps, illustrations from *Punch* and a miscellany of period prints. The walls were hung with Raiment's 'major retrospective', comprising a mediocre array of family portraits, London sunsets and alfresco tea parties, interspersed with stags' heads and stuffed badgers. As I surveyed them with growing distaste, a strip curtain at the back of the shop parted and I was joined by the proprietor: tall, fleshy, with a mane of ginger hair and a crested blazer. Signet rings, brass buttons and cufflinks glittered in the gloom. I introduced myself.

'Of course. The Bartholomew lady. Come with me.' He led the way through the strip curtain and down a short flight of steps to a longer, lower room, where prints were piled in disorderly profusion amongst empty frames and stretched canvases. He turned to the right-hand wall with a gesture of triumph.

They were the two paintings I'd rejected when offered

them before the auction at Meongate, the same two unsavoury reminders of the artistic imagination of Philip Bartholomew. I might have guessed, but had dreaded to guess, that these were the two unsold.

'I'm very sorry,' I said. 'It's the third one I was interested in.'

'You're intimately familiar with the works, then.' Mr Raiment sounded annoyed.

'As a matter of fact, I am. You bought all three from Basil Gates, the Plymouth dealer.'

'I really don't see . . .'

'The point is that the third work was on the same theme, but somehow distinctive. Wasn't it?'

'Possibly.'

'Would you feel able to tell me who bought it?' He smiled and was about to refuse, so I cut him short. 'Mr Raiment, I do appreciate that I've inconvenienced you. That was not my intention. If I could, in some way, defray the costs . . .'

'I took them out of the sale. You may have cost me a customer.'

'I doubt it, don't you?'

For whatever reason, his mood softened. 'It's unlikely, I grant you. The third one was better than I'd have expected of Bartholomew.'

'You're sure it was authentic?'

He gestured to the walls. 'My gallery, madam, is a shrine to authenticity. I have nothing to hide. Not even' – he sighed - 'the name and address of a customer.' He moved to a filing cabinet in the corner and pulled open a drawer. 'The purchaser of the Bartholomew had the painting delivered. Copies of the invoice and delivery note should be here . . . Ah yes. Indeed they are.'

By now, I was standing next to him. Over his

shoulder, on the flimsy sheets of paper, I saw a name I knew.

Miss G. M. Fotheringham, 121 Catesby House, Dolphin Square, Pimlico, London SW1.

I walked along the Embankment early that afternoon, the rain having given way to flecked skies and a bitter wind. Battersea Power Station loomed reassuringly on the other side of the Thames whilst, behind me, beyond railings, above tended gardens, an ordinary, prosaic block of windows held the answer I'd sought so long to the questioning blanks of my childhood. Why did I wait? Why did I hesitate? Mostly, we don't know when life is about to present its greatest challenges. But this was different. This couldn't be disguised as a social call on a Saturday afternoon. What I was about to learn could never again be forgotten.

A porter showed me the way through the well-appointed warren of apartment blocks. Windowless, carpeted corridors between stern, spy-holed doorways. Somewhere, the faint hum of a heating system. Through one door, the plangent notes of a piano: somebody was playing Chopin.

The porter left me by the door of number 121 and walked slowly away. I waited until he was out of sight, then rang the bell and waited again, wondering if I was being observed through the spy-hole.

The door opened. The woman who stood there was slightly taller than me, had once, perhaps, been athletic and still carried herself erect, was obviously old but not unfashionably dressed, her grey hair simply but elegantly styled, her face lined but far from drawn.

'Miss Fotheringham?'

'Yes.' She conveyed as she looked at me none of the meekness or vulnerability often associated with old age. Whether from the inclination of her character or the necessities of an independent life, she seemed to have drawn a robust and quiet dignity which was at once disconcerting and yet intriguing.

'I'm . . . Well, you don't know me. But, in a sense, you do. My name . . .'

'Don't say it. I know who you are.' She smiled as she spoke, deepening the dimple in her cheeks and melting at once the challenging directness of her gaze. 'Had your mother lived, she would have come to resemble you. Hello, Leonora. I've waited a long time to meet you again.'

We did not kiss, or close the gap of nearly fifty years with anything more than a stilted handshake. That was how, at last, I found my pretty lady.

We sat in her lounge overlooking the Embankment and took tea with every semblance of normality. I looked around but hardly noticed my surroundings, may have declined a slice of cake and certainly did not taste any of the tea that I drank.

'How did you find me?'

I described the trail that had led me to her and she listened attentively, in the way the schoolmistress she'd once been might have listened to a pupil's exposition.

'I was surprised when I saw Bartholomew's work advertised for sale,' she said when I'd finished. 'Your mother had often referred to him, so I went along to take a look. Since buying one of the pictures, I've half-expected something like this to happen.'

'You expected it to lead me to you?'

'Nothing as definite as that. But I sensed buying it wouldn't be the end of the matter. I sensed it would put me back in touch, however indirectly, with all those people and places I thought I'd left behind.'

'So why did you buy it?'

'Because I knew it couldn't be genuine. Because it depicted my friend, your mother – and Bartholomew could never have met her.'

Before seeking answers to all my other questions, I had to satisfy a more urgent longing. 'May I see the painting?' I asked, as calmly as I could manage.

'Of course.'

She led me down the short hallway to the bedroom, pushed the door open and stood back to let me pass.

The painting was hanging on the opposite wall, where daylight from the window clarified its every detail. The gilt frame and sombre colouring were reminiscent of Bartholomew's pictures as they'd hung at Meongate and the scene – a castle bedchamber – seemed, at first sight, identical. Yet there was something different, something strange deceptive, in the similarity of style and subject. I stepped closer.

Then I saw the third Bartholomew for what it really was. It's hard to recall now what I noticed first, hard to be certain how quickly I perceived all of its poignant associations. They declared themselves selectively, as if content in the knowledge that to all save a few they were merely an amalgam of imitated impasto. Yet towards the few, of whom I was one, meaning crept from beneath the layers of paint.

It was not a castle bedchamber. The grey-hued walls which had suggested as much were papered, the floor-length curtains woven of some fine and modern fabric. Nor was the point of view the same. In the foreground were two figures cast in shadow, silhouetted against the only source of light in the room. So indistinct were they that only implications of shape and position identified them as the man and the woman from Bartholomew's paintings, the woman reclining on the bed, propped on one hip, her back to the light, the angle of a raised elbow suggesting that she had thrown her head back against her hand, as if to look, or laugh, at the man now stooped above her. He appeared to be in the act of quitting the bed, the spread of his arms and the angle of his back hinting at haste and dismay, perhaps even the panic of one discovered. Certainly his head was turned anxiously towards the light, as if its source embodied his worst fears.

As well it might. The door of the room stood open, revealing, on the threshold, a woman holding aloft a silver candelabrum, whose three flickering flames shone on her face and clothing. The play of candlelight on this central figure was the most strikingly artistic feature of the painting. It caught the dark blue folds of her gown, the blonde, unbraided lustre of her hair, the pale, open features of her face. It sparkled in the pained, enlarged circles of her eyes and glistened in the slender band of gold on one finger and her left hand where it grasped the stem of the candelabrum. It revealed enough to suggest that the woman was pregnant. It declared too much, and that too well, to doubt who the woman was.

'Is this,' I said at last, 'a true likeness of my mother?'

'Uncannily so,' Grace replied from just behind me. 'When I saw it, I felt it could only have been painted by somebody who knew her well, who had, perhaps, loved her. I thought at once of your father.'

Of course. The deception was clear. Willis had completed Bartholomew's series in his own way, making amends for what he'd once suspected my mother

411

capable of by reviving his fear of being capable of it himself. Yet to Grace Fotheringham, who did not know all that I knew, Franklin was long dead and only my father could have seemed responsible for the portrait of her friend.

'I have no way of knowing when he might have painted this,' Grace said, 'although it doesn't look very old.'

'It was painted last year,' I murmured.

'Last year? Then he's still . . .'

'Alive? No. My father died many years ago. There is a great deal I have to tell you.'

We returned to the lounge and there I recounted the story Willis had told me fifteen years before. Grace listened in virtual silence, with concentration and a measure of scrutiny. She remained distant but vigilant, as if comparing what I said with what she knew, as if verifying my every word by reference to her own knowledge. When I'd finished, it was growing dark outside.

In the silence that followed, Grace moved around the room, switching on sidelights. She turned up the fire and drew the curtains. Then, quite deliberately, she walked over to me and kissed me on the forehead and smiled for the first time. The warmth of her spirit emerged, as if a door had been opened, leading from a wintry house into a scented spring garden.

'Bless you, Leonora,' she said suddenly. 'Bless you for finding me.'

'Since Willis – or should I call him Franklin? – came to me, you're the very first person I've met who could corroborate his story.'

'We first met in just the way he told you.'

'And you last met?'

'Again, just as he told you. Leonora convinced herself

– and me – that John had taken his own life. Accordingly, the only visitor I expected after her death was Franklin. At first, I couldn't understand why he left Sea Thrift so abruptly, but, when he didn't return, I began to think about what he'd said – and realized that he didn't think John was dead after all. I went to the churchyard – but there was no sign of anybody. I told myself that he must have realized he was wrong, that if John were alive, he wouldn't have abandoned his daughter. Suicide seemed the only possible answer, the only honourable alternative to coming forward and being tried as a deserter. When I read of Franklin's death a few months later, I had no idea that I was actually reading of just such an honourable alternative.'

'Yet you thought my father was alive when you saw the third Bartholomew.'

'It seemed the only possible explanation. In a sense, that's why I bought it – to hide the evidence, if you like. I'm glad it also served . . . to reunite us.'

'Did it have to wait for me to seek you out?'

I'd tried to erase all hint of condemnation from my voice, yet Grace leant forward in her chair and frowned when she replied, as if some implication had reached her none the less. 'You must understand, Leonora, that I thought you knew nothing of me. And so you would, if Willis hadn't . . .'

'No,' I said, 'I've been looking for you far longer than that. In fact, for as long as I can remember.'

She looked at me incredulously. 'How can you have been?'

I told her then of my earliest memory, of the strange parting at Droxford station dimly recalled.

When I'd finished, she said: 'So you remembered. We didn't think you would.'

'We?'

'Charter and I. You were barely three.' Suddenly, she began to cry. When she pulled a white handkerchief from the sleeve of her cardigan, I thought instinctively of the last time I'd seen her cry and realized what I should have done when she'd first opened the door to me. I sat beside her on the sofa and hugged her and she dried her tears. 'Forgive me,' she said. 'It's just that I thought you would forget, that I thought you would be happier if you forgot.'

'Hardly. Meongate was not a happy place.'

'No. I feared it wouldn't be.'

'Then why did you let me go back there? I've spoken to Olivia's lawyer. He says you could have been forced to – but that it never proved necessary.'

'I was forced – but not by the law. Olivia persuaded the Headmistress of East Dene to dismiss me. How she achieved it I never knew. In those days, one had few sanctions against dismissal. I had simply to pack my bags and go. Sea Thrift was owned by the school, so I found myself homeless as well as unemployed. In the circumstances . . .'

'You had no choice but to hand me over.'

'That is how I excused my abandonment of you, yes. But there is always a choice. I'm sorry I failed you.'

'You didn't. If Olivia was determined to get me back, you couldn't have stopped her. What I don't understand is why she wanted to.'

'I don't understand that either. I only met her once and she was in no mood to explain her reasons. She seemed to me a woman used to indulging her whims – and her vices. Leonora told me nothing good of her. And my one attempt to defy her ended in total failure.'

'What did you do after leaving Bonchurch?'

'What I'd have done I can't imagine – if Charter hadn't come to my rescue. Dear old Charter, the only one from Meongate who attended Leonora's funeral. He came to see me just before I was due to quit Sea Thrift and loaned me money with which to set up a private school in Yorkshire. Thanks to him, I pulled through. Thanks to him, I had that last sight of you at Droxford.'

'I was told he moved to Yorkshire himself.'

'Yes. He'd opposed Olivia too openly to remain at Meongate. I imagine helping me was the last straw. He bought a little cottage at Robin Hood's Bay, near Whitby, his home town. I visited him there often. He died in 1924, before I'd even begun to repay his loan. But he wouldn't have minded. He was a dear and lovely man. I miss him still.

'I retired from schoolteaching ten years ago and moved into this little flat. I lead a quiet life – but not an unhappy one. Until I saw Mr Raiment's advertisement two weeks ago and visited his gallery, I never expected to have any further contact with your family. But, then, I never expected to find the third Bartholomew.'

We went and looked at it again. Artificial light seemed only to add to its mysteries, deepening its shadows and enhancing the candlelit figure of my mother. I remembered what Willis had said within Zoë's hearing when he'd finished it only a few months before: he had brought back Leonora. But back to what? To repel the darkness threatening to engulf him? To discover the guilt he felt? If Olivia was the woman on the bed, as in the other two paintings, who was the man? Bartholomew? Mompesson? Or Willis himself? There was no answer in the placid, solemn beauty of my mother's face.

When I got off the train that evening at Bath Spa, I

was tired but elated. Whatever old sadnesses Willis's painting had revived, it had brought me happiness in the present: the rediscovery of the pretty lady of my childhood. Grace had agreed to visit me in Wells soon and I was busily considering how much – or how little – to tell Tony about her. As a consequence, he was the last person I expected to see waiting for me at the station. Yet there he was, kissing me dutifully and ushering me towards the car.

'How did you know which train I'd be on?' I said.

'I didn't. I've been here since six.'

'There was no need.'

He started the car. 'Oh, but there was. I know you think I'm a blind and insensitive clod – and at times I can be – but you're mistaken if you think I've been unaware of all that's happened this week.'

'What do you mean?'

'A mysterious benefactor. Sitting tenants. A flying visit to London. Why don't you tell me what it's all about? And don't say you'd never met Mr Willis before.'

Tony's timing was, as ever, impeccable. It was one of his greatest gifts. I suppose it also embodied his Englishness – his rather old-fashioned, buttoned-up, ironical manner that could master the strongest emotions. He'd known better than to demand an explanation when all I'd offered was a transparent pretence that Willis was a stranger. He'd bided his time when I'd returned from Fowey clearly still distracted. Now he'd somehow divined that his time had come.

We stopped for dinner at a country hotel south of Bath and, in the end, spent the night there. I recounted Willis's story and explained as best I could why till then I'd kept it from him. I described my experiences in Fowey and enlarged on what Grace Fotheringham had said to me. And later, safe in his arms in the small hours between midnight and dawn, I told him what I should have when he first asked me to marry him twenty-three years before.

'Now you see,' I murmured at the end of all my confessions, 'why perhaps you should have heeded the village gossip.'

'Stuff and nonsense,' he replied, kissing me. 'I always knew you had secrets. They made you different from the rest. They made me love you.'

'Would you have married me if you'd known I was a deserter's daughter?'

'You know I would.'

'And if you'd known I was responsible for Payne's death?'

'That too. If you *were* responsible.'

'Why do you say *if*?'

'Ask yourself why Olivia didn't accuse you of it when I told her I intended to marry you. You can't believe she held her tongue out of affection for you.'

'I've never understood why she said nothing. But I've always been grateful.'

'Then don't be.'

'Why not? She didn't say anything, did she?'

'No. Not then.'

'What do you mean – "not then"?'

'I mean she told me later.'

I sat upright in the bed and stared at him. 'You knew?'

He smiled disarmingly. 'What there was to know, yes.'

'When?'

'Early in '53, when we heard she was dying. I went down there alone, remember? Well, that's when Olivia chose to tell me.'

'You said nothing about it.'

'Perhaps now you'll understand it made no difference. I knew you'd tell me yourself in the end. I was happy to wait. Besides, I realized that if Olivia had chosen to hold the accusation back until then, confronting you with it would only serve her ends. Now you have told me, I see that I was right.'

For fifteen years, I realized, I'd manufactured reasons not to tell my husband something he already knew. I'd left him to pit his love for me against the worst that Olivia could imply. I'd thought him obtuse and unobservant where he'd been patient and sensitive. I'd been a fool. 'What did she say?' I asked him at last. It was time, I knew, to hear the worst.

'When I arrived, Nurse Buss told me Olivia had been unusually alert all day and was eager to see me. I went up to her room alone. She had her bed by the window, where she could look at that picture of her first husband's, surrounded by shawls and potions and scraps of food. The place gave me the creeps.

'For a moment, when I went in and saw her lying there, so wizened and still, I thought she was dead. Then she opened her eyes and looked at me. Burning, bitter eyes. She told me to sit down and pour her some whisky. I obeyed. Even at death's door, she retained her power to command. Then she began talking, between sips of whisky, urgently and fluently – at least at first. As Nurse Buss had said, she was alert – unnaturally so. The reason was the need she felt to talk. I'd been brought there for only one reason – to hear what she had to say.'

THREE

This has been the worst year of my life. Entombed in an empty house with only that harridan of a nurse for company. The windows rattle at night and the rain rushes like needles against the glass. Here I lie now, sick, dying, old, worn to a husk: there is nothing here for you to envy or admire. Or so you think.

How is Leonora? How is the knight on his white charger who carried her off into a happy ever after? You sit before me and smile politely and ask how I feel, but you don't want to know. You really want to know when I'm going to die. That's it, isn't it? When is this frayed old remnant of a woman going to oblige you by vacating her fraud of a life?

If I had the energy, I'd laugh in your face. There was a time when I could have wrapped you round my little finger, a time when you would have been my plaything. Yes. Smile as much as you like. You would have been. I can see your mouth quiver with distaste. You find the thought disgusting. But you wouldn't have then. None of the others did.

All men and most women are fools. My mother was

a fool, who gave herself to an Italian dancing instructor and got me for her pains. I, on the other hand, learned from other people's mistakes. I didn't model nude for so-called artists because the money was good. Oh no. There was more to it than that. I was cleverer than the whole pack of them, but they wouldn't have thanked me for letting them know it. What they wanted of me was the hire of my body. I was superb. Still am in foolish Philip's painting. He only realized I'd ensnared him when it was too late. I let him have his fill of me – visually. He could ask me to sit or bend or lie before him and I would. I would pose for him in any position – and some were not for painting. And he would stand beneath the dais, pretending to study proportion, six inches from my breasts, and would see my eyes move to the bulge in his trousers. But he could not touch me.

Disgusted? I said you would be. I see you look away, but I see also the thin film of sweat on your stiff upper lip. Go on, look at the painting, I was magnificent – wasn't I?

He married me because he had to touch me. And once he'd married me, he couldn't bear to. I made sure of that. I betrayed him, with other artists of course, but most splendidly – most obscenely – with his own sister. That destroyed him, and it was meant to. It's her I'm looking at in his painting. At least, I believe that's what he intended. For all our sakes, it's as well he didn't finish the series. I should think he was drunk when he went over the side of the ferry. It would have been unlike him not to be. I was waiting for him in our cabin. Perhaps he couldn't face me. I didn't raise the alarm till morning. Something that may once have been him was washed up on the coast of Normandy three weeks later.

I believe his sister identified him. She was suitably distraught.

The desirable young widow of a notable artist: it wasn't a bad transformation. And my reputation wore so much better than Philip's. Lizzie Kilsyth introduced me to Edward at one of her soirées. He was in a morbid swoon of bereavement at the time, but was still able to recognize my beauty as a desirable acquisition. He looked on me as he would a Wedgwood vase: elegant, expensive and a sound investment. Water ran through his veins: passion was to him a foreign country. I didn't mind that. He made me Lady Powerstock and left me free to find pleasure where I would.

What was it that drew me to my own stepson? There were obvious factors: his youth, his good looks, the time that hung so heavily here during the early years. Above all, of course, because it was forbidden. He saw me looking at him: I let him. I hinted – only hinted, with an oblique word here or there, angled like a glass to reflect the sun – that the woman in the painting was indeed me and could, in certain circumstances be his.

I'm talking about Leonora's father. Dead old men were once young and handsome, virile and vulnerable. Did I say dead? Let's pretend he's dead – for a little longer. He wasn't dead then, not to my suggestions. That's all that really matters. He spied on me from the observatory, if you can call it spying. I took care to undress in the window, where I could be seen through the telescope, to undress slowly, to pose, if you like, thinking of the agonies of mind and body he would be going through, watching me.

Then Miss Leonora Powell walked demurely into his life – and he was lost to me. He'd been tempted: we both knew it. Later, when I told his wife of it, she refused to believe me. I think truly she couldn't imagine it. But I don't think John ever forgot. When he went away to the war, I came to hate Leonora for her purity and her loyalty. I tested both qualities – and found them nauseatingly impregnable.

I've never loved anyone in my life except myself. You ought to know that. It's true of more people than would care to admit it. Those who do admit it earn my respect. That, I suppose is what marked Ralph Mompesson out from the rest. That and the fact he was twice the man the Honourable John Hallows could ever be. He didn't hide his desires. He was proud of them. We met him at a fund-raising event about the time Edward decided to parade his patriotic soul for inspection by taking in convalescent officers, one or two of whom I enjoyed. They were generally too conscience-stricken to enjoy me.

Avert your gaze if you like, Captain Galloway. You don't fool anyone. If you'd come here then, you'd have worshipped me too: I'd have made sure of that. Maybe you'd have fallen in love with me, like that young idiot Cheriton. He shot himself here, you know, blew his brains out with a pistol. And why? Because he was afraid of going back to the war? Oh no. That would have been too sensible. He shot himself because I told him Ralph had been my lover. Can you imagine? He even left a note, which, mercifully, nobody read. Sometimes the stupidity of your sex surprises even me.

But Ralph was different. I'll grant him that. A woman's man, you might say. The plan he evolved to acquire Meongate would have worked, though it would have benefited me more and him less than he supposed. But it had his swaggering, cocksure elegance: it would have worked. We knew John hadn't died in

France and that Leonora's pregnancy by him could be used to destroy both them and Edward. We would have been their joint beneficiaries, master and mistress of Meongate. Then I wouldn't be croaking out my last days over cheap whisky in a cold house. Pour me some more. And have some yourself. You look as if you need it.

Somebody murdered Ralph, somebody who knew what would happen if he wasn't stopped, somebody who outwitted him – and me. But only in a sense. Theirs was a truly pyrrhic victory. The police didn't know where to look, but I knew who the murderer was. There was only one man desperate enough to have done such a thing: the Honourable John Hallows. He knew my mind better than most. I'll admit it was clever of him. But foolish as well. By killing Ralph, he made sure he could never come back, made sure he would have to stay in hiding for the rest of his life.

When your battalion camped in the grounds in the spring of 1944, I had you marked from the first as Leonora's knight errant. I watched from an upper window when you met for the first time. And all those other times? Did you think I didn't know what was going on? All those letters via the post office? I knew. I knew everything. So I had plenty of opportunity to decide what to do when you finally deigned to tell me you wanted to marry her. I could have told you enough to frighten you off. Be in no doubt of that. Instead, I said nothing. I let you marry. I let you have children. Now I'll tell you what you've married. Now, at last, you can have my wedding present.

Leonora's mother went away and obligingly died giving birth. To the very end, she preserved her saintly air of self-sacrifice. Her friend, the schoolteacher, Miss Fotheringham, proposed to raise the child herself. I could have let her. But I didn't. At first, she resisted, so I was obliged to discredit her. Her headmistress was indecently eager to believe that I had letters suggesting Miss Fotheringham and the child's mother had formed an unnatural attachment. To avoid any breath of scandal, Miss Fotheringham was dismissed from her post and the child consigned to me.

You pretend indifference, but I can see you want to know. Why did I take her back? Why? Because the war was over and my murderous stepson could feel free to show himself at last. He would want his daughter to remind him of his wife. He was too insufferably decent to forget her. When he looked for her, he would have to come to me. And when he came I would show him no mercy.

Why didn't he come? He'd chosen to defy me, but I had the only thing left for him to cherish: Leonora. She suffered on his account. I don't deny that. But still he didn't show himself. It's too late now. An obscure suicide? Probably. And yet, and yet . . . Sometimes, I dream he's up there in the observatory still, looking at me, always looking. Is he out there somewhere, do you think? It doesn't matter. I've won anyway. He's won nothing. Nothing, do you hear.

After Edward's death, I learned from his accountant that he'd invested heavily in American stocks during the war on Ralph's advice. Good advice when given. But since 1929 the shares had been worthless. I was suddenly obliged to marry for money. Sidney Payne, you understand, was a brutal necessity. Nothing else. When he went bankrupt, the necessity left our relationship, and of brutality I had no need. It was at my suggestion that he looked to Leonora for satisfaction.

You may have been told my third husband died from

a fall. It's true. He did. He was drunk and upset at the time, upset because I'd just discovered him in bed with Leonora. Ask her yourself. She'll say he attacked her, that she struck him with a heavy book in self-defence, that the blow may have caused the fall, that she said nothing for fear of being blamed for his death, that I have the blood-stained book to prove it. Well, I have the book. That much is true. You can see it if you wish. Not now. Later. If there was no resistance, of course, that would be quite another matter, wouldn't it? Tell me, is that the whisky or something else causing you to flush?

By the way, I've left the house to Walter Payne. He's told me all about his plans for it. Some nonsense about a country club. It sounds entertainingly awful. If you're thinking of contesting the will, I strongly advise you to think again. Mayhew can prove Leonora wasn't legitimate and that's what she believes anyway. You could tell her the truth, of course, if you think she'd welcome it. I leave that to you.

Why is it so dark? It can't be evening yet. Not yet. Call Buss. No. Better still, don't.

I consulted a clairvoyant once. She said he was still alive. What do they know? If he were, he'd have come looking, wouldn't he?

The comet was like a flaming dragon. Philip had once been to China, you know. Dragons dance in the streets there.

John talked about its course and what brought it back. I'd left a light in my window. I pointed down to it and said I hadn't realized he could see me from the observatory – if he cared to look. It wasn't cold. It was a balmy night. But he was trembling.

They watched me often. It was my power over them. Strong young men with artistic fingers. Not like Ralph at

425

all. The first time he took me, it was no better than rape. That's what made it so . . . delicious.

Philip left the painting to haunt me. But I laid his ghost – many times.

Why didn't he come? Last summer, once . . . I almost thought . . . He's won nothing. Nothing, you hear?

I read that Franklin died at Passchendaele. As good as putting a gun to his head. The fool.

He outwitted Ralph, not me. But how? How could Ralph let it happen? Miriam's book is in the drawer. That's her secret. That's your answer.

FOUR

'After it was over, I sent Buss to phone the doctor. She'd closed Olivia's eyes, but still, through the blank lids, I felt her watching me. The book was where she'd said, in the drawer of her bedside cabinet. There was no bloodstain. I suppose I'd known there wouldn't be.'

Then, for the first time, I understood Olivia. Perhaps, if the word meant anything to her, she had loved Ralph Mompesson. In everything else – at least until her powers began to wane – she had her way. But Mompesson's murder wrecked her ambitions for what they might have achieved together and for that she held my father responsible. It was to serve her desire for revenge that I'd been taken to Meongate. I knew now why her hopes of luring my father from hiding were doomed from the first. I knew now why I'd borne the brunt of her frustrated need to be avenged upon him. I knew at last what had cursed my childhood.

'She was an irredeemably evil and cunning woman,' said Tony. 'Even at the end, she was more concerned with trying to make me believe you'd responded to

Payne's advances than with making her peace with the world she was about to leave.'

'I never saw the bloodstain, Tony. She told me there was one and I believed her. Now, when I think about it, I don't suppose I had the strength to draw blood. If you'd asked me as she suggested . . .'

'Your answer would have seemed to incriminate you. That, of course, was what she hoped would happen. But she'd revealed too much hatred for me to believe anything, she said. That's why I said nothing to you. It was the only way to defy her.'

'What did you do with the book?'

'It's in the loft at home, tucked away in the suitcase where I keep my old uniform. I could have destroyed it, I suppose, but that too would have seemed a victory for her. So I kept it, safely hidden, against the day when you might want to tell me all that you've told me now.'

Irony upon ironies. The book I'd feared Mayhew meant when he'd spoken of Olivia's bequest to me, the book I'd hunted for in Winchester: all the time it had lain hidden in my own home. Tony had known its secret better than me. I should have guessed it had played no part in Payne's death, that Olivia merely claimed it had, the better to suborn me. And so I would have guessed, but for the extent of her domination over me. She had set out to crush me and had nearly succeeded, but Tony had been better than I deserved. His long and faithful silence had sealed her defeat.

As I pondered what he'd revealed, I began to appreciate the cool-nerved subtlety of my patient, unassuming husband. 'Tony Galloway,' I said. 'All these years you've known exactly what's been going on in my head – yet said nothing.'

'I told you: I was waiting for you to speak.'

'You knew Olivia had disinherited me. That shocked outrage on my account was mere play-acting. And you knew I wouldn't contest the will.'

'True,' he said with a smile.

'What did you think when you heard about the house in Fowey?'

'That Willis was your father. It seemed to make sense in view of Olivia's insistence that he hadn't died in the war.'

'But still you said nothing?'

'I didn't force the issue because I hoped that after you'd been down there you might feel able to tell me the truth of your own accord. And so you have, though the truth turns out to be somewhat different from what Olivia led me to expect. In a sense, that makes it all the better.'

The following morning, after breakfast, we walked round the hotel garden in the clear, cold air of a new day, luxuriating in the intimacy our revelations had revived.

'When I walked round Meongate that first morning, in 1944,' Tony said, 'I sensed that fate, rather than a whim of military logistics, had brought me there. When I saw you in the orchard, the girl they'd whispered about in the village, I sensed it again: that you were my future. Perhaps that's why, later, not telling you how much I knew seemed the only right thing to do.'

'And now, Tony? What's the right thing to do now? What do we tell our children?'

'That's for you to say, Leonora. It always has been.'

Once again, I decided you should not be told. I justified my reluctance to speak by reasoning that you hadn't known the people involved and would have no use for the tangled tale of a dead generation, that you were too young, too self-centred, too obsessed with the present. But none of that was the real reason. The truth was that sharing my past with Tony had bound us together. By sharing it with others, I feared our new-found rapport would once more fade.

That's why Grace Fotheringham was introduced to you as nothing more than a former teacher of whom I was fond. That's why I normally arranged for her to visit me when I knew you wouldn't be at home.

The first such visit took place just before Easter 1968, a few weeks after I'd sought her out in London. I'd already written to her with the sordid truth about how Olivia had ousted her from East Dene: she'd taken the news philosophically. Now, when I recounted all that Tony had told me, she still seemed unmoved by Olivia's malice, still strangely sympathetic towards the woman who'd tried to ruin her. The reason, I soon discovered, was that, unknown to me, she had the advantage of her in one vital, triumphant respect.

'Poor woman,' I remember her saying, shaking her head and gazing out of the window at the daffodils waving their heads in the garden. 'Poor foolish woman.'

'Grace!' I exclaimed. 'How can you be so charitable?'

'Because she did it all for revenge, and revenge is the hardest taskmaster. I always pity those who allow themselves to be controlled by it. It sounds to me as if it consumed her in the end.'

I experienced then, as we sat over our tea cups in the conservatory, the sensation that Grace Fotheringham alone of Olivia's victims had escaped her unscathed and spoke of her now with the compassion of one who was always her superior. It could have been, I knew, the schoolmistressly manner of a natural benevolence. But I sensed it was something more.

430

'There is an irony, isn't there,' she continued, 'in the thought of her waiting all those years for your father to reappear, when we now know she was waiting in vain?'

'Do you think she may have been right on one score at least?' I said. 'That my father killed Ralph Mompesson? I know he denied it to Franklin, but mightn't he have been trying to spare his friend's feelings?'

Grace looked at me intently. 'That's what you want to believe, isn't it? It's what your mother believed, after all, and it's what I believed too – at one time.'

'Until I told you Willis's story?'

'No.' She looked away for a moment. 'No, Leonora. I've known for a long time who really killed Ralph Mompesson. You see, Olivia tried to ruin me, it's true, as her lover tried to ruin your family, but there was one man who was too clever for both of them, one man who came to my rescue just as he came to your mother's. That man was Charter Gladwin.'

'Charter?'

'Yes. As I told you, he gave me the capital to establish Marston College and I used to visit him every other Sunday, in his cottage near Robin Hood's Bay. It was set among fields near the top of the cliffs, terribly exposed in winter. You could always hear the sea, and the gulls, and the wind rushing in the chimney, whatever the season, but inside it was cosy and welcoming, full of Charter's mementoes of a long life. I looked forward to my visits to him as a fortnightly refuge from the cares of the world. I can still remember the smell of the logs burning on the fire there and the tang of the mackerel he'd grill in front of it.

'One Sunday, after I'd agreed to join him in a glass of rum, we talked about your mother. She was a favourite topic of ours: a friend to both of us. At some point, I said much what you've said now. As one who'd lived at Meongate at the time, did Charter think Leonora was right to believe that John killed Mompesson?

' "Oh no," he replied. "John didn't kill him." '

' "How can you be so sure?" I asked.

' "That's very easy, my dear," he said. "I can be sure because I killed him myself." He smiled. "Yes. You may as well know. I shot Ralph Mompesson for his pains."

'I was as you may imagine, taken aback. Murder was the very last act I would have associated with dear old Charter. But, in his account of it, the concept changed in my mind. When Charter described how he'd come to kill Mompesson, it sounded the most natural thing in all the world.'

FIVE

I first met Ralph Eugene Mompesson in the summer of 1915, when Olivia began entertaining him at Meongate. I choose my words carefully, because I'm damn sure he'd been bedding her in London for months past. Not that I cared. If Edward hadn't the sense to see the woman couldn't stand comparison with my Miriam, that was his look-out. Live and let live, after all. I couldn't claim a morally blameless youth, so I didn't propose to start casting stones in my dotage.

Until the news came of John's death in France at the end of April 1916, I didn't think of Mompesson as anything more than the man Olivia kept to satisfy her in ways her husband never could. As such, he was somebody I could quite happily ignore. All that changed when I realized he had his sights set on Leonora. I watched him, watching her, as she played the piano of an evening, and I didn't like what I read in his eyes. I'd seen him walking the lawns, smoking his foul cheroots and looking at the house as if he was certain he would one day own it, and I knew that, sooner or later, he'd have to be faced.

My one advantage over him was my age. It made him discount me as a threat. Perhaps he should have been more curious about my past. Then he'd have known I was no stranger to his homeland. In 1863, I'd run the Unionist blockade of the Southern States. The risks were considerable, but the profit in Liverpool on a cargo of cotton made them worth taking. The exploit made me several enemies – and one firm friend: Wesley Maitland, then a struggling Georgia landowner, later an eminent senator. I wrote to my old friend in his retirement, asking him to dig up what he could about Mompesson – his past and his present. I wanted to know why he'd come to England and what he'd left behind. Before I moved against him, you see, I wanted to be sure of my ground.

Because of the war, communications with the States in 1916 were subject to all manner of delays. I knew I might have to wait many weeks for a reply, maybe months. Meanwhile, it was imperative that Mompesson should have no cause to suspect I was enquiring into his background. Accordingly, I cultivated my reputation as a harmless old idiot and bided my time, with what patience I could muster.

Old men don't sleep well, especially when they have something on their mind. I was awake before dawn most mornings and that's how, on Sunday, 11th June, I came to know that my grandson wasn't dead after all. I heard a door close down the passage: it sounded as if it was Leonora's. But the footsteps that came from that direction and passed my own door weren't hers. They were too confoundedly masculine. If I'd thought about it longer, I'd have dismissed the idea that it might be Mompesson as nonsense – and unworthy nonsense at that – but I didn't have time to think. I moved to the door and eased it open, just in time to see a male figure turning the corner in the passage, as if heading towards the back stairs. It wasn't Mompesson. It was my grandson John, come back from the dead. I nearly cried out to him, but the words died in my throat. Then he was gone.

Unable quite to believe the evidence of my own eyes, I fetched the key and went up to the observatory. It commanded a view of the whole house and grounds and I knew that, if John really was there, I could be certain from that vantage point of seeing him go. The sun was only just getting up, but it was light enough to show a lone figure, stealing away across the park. There was no mistake. It was John. He looked back once, then vanished into the trees.

Out of the corner of my eye, I saw a drift of smoke from the window of one of the guest rooms below me. The rising sun was shining on the raised pane and there I saw, standing behind it, clad in a dressing gown and smoking a cheroot, none other than Mompesson, smiling to himself and staring fixedly towards the spot where John had just slipped from view. So Mompesson knew as well – and the knowledge gave him the hold over Leonora that he might have prayed for. By succumbing to the temptation to visit her, John had handed his enemy the weapon he needed.

At first, I expected Mompesson to denounce John as a deserter. God knows, there was nothing I could do to stop him if he chose to – nothing, that is, short of the one step I hadn't yet realized I would have to take. But nothing happened. It was as if I'd dreamt it all. Leonora gave no signs that she was not a widow. Mompesson refrained from showing his hand. I concluded he wanted more proof before taking action. So long as he lacked it, we were safe.

In early September, Franklin came to stay at the house. As a friend of John's, he was, unwittingly, as much of an enemy as an ally. Out of sheer confounded loyalty – and, I suspect, a growing affection for Leonora – he threatened to stumble on the truth. I wish I could have been more open with him, but I knew I must not be. For Leonora's sake and for John's, I had to keep my own counsel.

On the morning of Friday, 22nd September, I heard from Maitland at last. His letter had taken six weeks to reach me. What it told me was worse than I'd expected.

'I hope this information will be valuable to you,' he wrote. 'Getting it cost me near as much as selling you that cotton in '63. Ralph Mompesson, as far as I can judge, is the sort of man who'd have taken your money, then shot you in the back and sold the merchandise all over again.

'What he's told you about himself is true as far as it goes. His family owned a lot of land in Louisiana before the Civil War. But his father went to the bad and sold it all for a pittance to a carpet-bagger. Young Ralph, it seems, was neither hero nor fool. He served briefly in the army during the war with Spain, then went north. I gather he made a pile in the Northern Pacific Panic of '01. After that, he never looked back. He was mixed up in every railroad swindle going – of which there were plenty, believe me. But he'd served with Roosevelt in Cuba and, while Teddy was President, he was fire-proof. When Roosevelt retired in '08, it was bad news for our friend. Federal agents began to enquire into his dealings and I've no doubt they'd have called time on him in the end.

'In fact, though, it was the suicide of a Massachusetts heiress in the summer of 1913 that brought the roof down on him. They were engaged at the time and, through her, Mompesson stood to get his hands on the Reveson banking fortune. It must have been a blow when she took her life. She left a note saying some damned unsavoury things about him. Nothing actionable in law, but worse, in a sense. Brutality, perversion, sadism – that kind of thing. Old man Reveson didn't want it brought into the open, but he did want rid of Mompesson, so he paid his passage to Europe and had done with him. Maybe Mompesson reckoned it was time to quit. From what you say, he's started all over again.'

I sat down to breakfast that morning, my old head whirling with all that Maitland had told me. A villain, a fraudster – and something worse. Mompesson had to be stopped. That much was certain. But how?

Amidst all my ponderings, Franklin joined me at the table, cast down for reasons of his own. He reminded me that Mompesson was to join us that evening for the weekend, though, God knows, I needed no reminding. Then he delivered a shattering blow.

'I have it from his own lips,' he said, 'that he hopes to marry Leonora.'

I laughed it off as best I could, but that's when I truly had the measure of Mompesson's capacity for evil. To protect John, Leonora would have to submit to a bigamous marriage. Mompesson could expose the crime whenever he chose, posing as its innocent victim; yet, in the meantime, could demand his marital due. I wondered if Olivia knew of his plans and approved, but it didn't really matter what she thought. Only Mompesson's intentions counted for anything.

That afternoon, pacing the grounds, I rehearsed my options. They were pitifully few. I clung to the hope that

Franklin might be mistaken. But it was a faint hope.

Then I saw Leonora walking up the drive towards me. She looked strained and upset. Wherever she'd been, it had done her no good. Even to my old eyes, it was obvious she'd been crying.

'Hello, Charter,' she said. 'What, no smile? Are even you depressed?'

I put my arm round her and led her towards the house. 'Only at the thought of you being unhappy.'

'It's not so bad,' she replied, smiling bravely.

'If you're in any kind of trouble . . .'

'No. There's no trouble – nothing for you to worry about.'

'I worry about Mompesson. I think he might have his eye on you.'

'What nonsense!'

'If you say so. Can I take it, then, that if he had the nerve to ask you to marry him, you'd reject him out of hand?'

She stopped and looked at me intently. 'What makes you ask such a question?'

'Just idle curiosity, my dear.'

'What would you think if I accepted such a proposal?'

'I would think you had your reasons.'

She squeezed my hand. 'It's good of you to say so.' Then she trembled. 'I must go in. It's becoming cold out here.' She stepped free of my arm and moved on towards the house. I watched her go, certain at last what I should do. She'd not answered my question, but I had my answer all the same.

I spent the hour before dinner in my room. From the old trunk where I kept it, I took the derringer I'd bought in Savannah in '63, when I'd thought I might need it. Now the need had arisen. I cleaned and oiled it, checked the action, loaded it and put it away again. Then I went down to dinner, smiled benignly at Mompesson over the table and weighed my chances of surprising him.

He was the last to go up afterwards, leaving me asleep by the fire – as he supposed. After a few minutes, I followed him upstairs. I fetched the gun, slipped it into my pocket, then made my way to his room. I knew neither Thorley nor Franklin was back yet, so only Cheriton's room, among those nearby, was occupied.

I went in without knocking. Mompesson was on the other side of the room, by the dressing table, taking off his cufflinks, his back towards me. Without turning round, he said: 'You're early. You wouldn't want to be thought over-eager, your Ladyship – would you?' Then he turned and saw it was me. 'What in hell do you want?'

I told him. 'I want you out of this house – and out of my family – for good. And I want you out . . . tonight.'

He laughed – as I knew he would. 'Go back to the fireside, old man, before they put you away in a home for the senile.' He turned away again.

There was a discarded towel lying on the chest of drawers beside me. I lifted it up and draped it over my hand as I drew the derringer from my pocket and moved towards him. I knew I had to use the gun at close range, which was just as well: my eyesight wouldn't have been up to it otherwise. Yet I knew also that I'd regret it if I gave him a chance to overpower me.

'Still here?' he said, noticing me out of the corner of his eye.

'The problem is: you're still here. I know what you've done since coming to this house and I mean to put a stop to it.'

'The hell you do,' he began. That's when I shot him, while he was still turning to look at me. It was a clean shot. He died instantly, with a fixed look of surprise on his face. He was a clever man, whose one mistake was to think he could treat me like a fool. But playing the fool and being a fool are two very different things. I don't think he ever understood that.

When I left the room, the house seemed quiet. Nobody had stirred. Or so I thought. Then, as I crept along the passage, I saw him. Cheriton, deathly pale, standing in the doorway of his room, wide-eyed and shivering. He looked at me as if he couldn't believe what he saw. Whether he noticed the bloodstained towel, bundled, and slightly singed, in my hand, I don't know.

'I . . . I thought I heard . . . something,' he stammered. 'Like a . . . a shot.'

'I heard nothing,' I replied. 'Perhaps you dreamt it.'

'Perhaps. I dream a lot . . . these days.'

'Go back to bed, young fellow. That's my advice.'

And off he went, meekly, without further ado, closing his door gently behind him. I went back to my room, cleaned the gun, hid it beneath the floorboards and burned the towel on the fire. I'd just climbed into bed when Fergus came knocking on my door to raise the alarm. Olivia had found Mompesson – as I'd expected she would. Her claim to have heard the shot was a lie, designed to explain why she'd gone to the room. As for Sally, I don't blame her for backing up her mistress. She had her livelihood to consider, after all.

I said nothing to Cheriton the next day. I hoped he would believe meeting me was a dream, if he remembered it at all. Now I think he probably did believe he dreamt it, as he may have thought he dreamt many things in that house. I must take my share of the blame for his suicide. We all failed him. It was a bad business.

So bad I even considered confessing to the police, would you believe? The man they put on the case – a fellow named Shapland – came to question me two days afterwards. Cheriton's death had knocked all the stuffing out of me. I didn't want him to be blamed for killing Mompesson as well as himself, the conclusion which Edward and Olivia were both eager to draw, so I proposed to lay all the facts before Shapland and make a clean breast of it.

It never came to that, entirely because of the fellow's brass-necked insolence. I don't know what fanciful theory he was cooking up, but he dragged in Miriam's death and the old story that she had some connection with an industrial agitator named Fletcher. He had the confounded cheek to ask me if I thought Fletcher might have been John's father, rather than Lord Powerstock.

My immediate reaction was to throw the blighter out, but then he asked another question: what significant event had occurred at Meongate in the middle of June? My blood ran cold. He could mean only one thing by it. He knew, or suspected, that John wasn't dead. Suddenly, Inspector Shapland became a dangerous man. Confession was out of the question if it might lead him to the truth. I told him it was past my bedtime and showed him the door.

I was mightily relieved when the inquest failed to name Cheriton as the murderer. It eased my conscience more than a little. By then, there was nothing to be done but hold my tongue and trust that matters might turn out happily. Alas, they didn't. Leonora died, Franklin was killed and John stayed in hiding. I've often wondered since where he might be, but now I don't suppose I'll ever find out. There's nothing more I can do to help him. I'm glad, at least, that I was able to help you.

If I had my time over again, I still wouldn't hesitate to kill Mompesson. You were Leonora's friend, so you'll understand: I did it for her. She needed a helping hand – I gave her mine. When you're my age, the risk of being hanged doesn't weigh too heavy. And I knew there was only one way to deal with Mompesson. I'd met his type before, you see. He reminded me of a Russian nobleman I ran into in St Petersburg in the winter of '61. I ended up killing him too. Did I ever tell you about that?

SIX

'Even had I not been indebted to Charter in so many ways, I would have kept his secret. When he died the following year, I found the derringer among his possessions and disposed of it, over the cliff, before it could arouse anybody's curiosity. I admired him for what he'd done to help Leonora. I thought often of all the younger, better-qualified men at Meongate who might have gone to her rescue and reflected that only old Charter had had the nerve, and the sense to do what needed to be done. You should remember, if you ever think your father failed you, that your great-grandfather avowedly did not.'

That, then, was Charter's victory over Olivia. She'd wasted her life – and a portion of mine – seeking the man she thought had killed her lover: a foolish fate indeed for one so proudly impervious to feeling. Hatred had snared her where love never could. Yet it had also deceived her. In all her serpentine imaginings, she had never so much as glimpsed the truth. The rumble-voiced man with the white whiskers, who'd held me in his arms at Droxford station all those years before, had escaped her, to laugh away his days in his cottage by the sea. The fat old man they'd thought a fool had been too clever for all of them.

'I'm sorry if I've shattered an illusion,' said Grace. 'Did you want so badly to believe that your father killed Ralph Mompesson?'

'I suppose I did,' I replied. 'It seemed to make up for . . . everything else.'

'You blame him for deserting you?'

'A part of me did, when Willis first told me that he hadn't died as I thought. But not now. Now I don't blame anyone. It is enough . . . to know the truth.'

As if to prove that the truth couldn't hurt me any more, I persuaded Tony to drive all three of us down to Meongate the following day. It was a dare, if you like, a conscious act to exorcize all that the place had meant to me – and it seemed to work. It was the same time of year as when Tony and I had first met, and Grace had not been there since my parents' wedding, so, for all of us, its associations were never worse than mixed.

Droxford had changed less than I'd expected. We stopped at the White Horse, then drove round to the disused railway station and on, down the lanes, to Meongate.

The Forest of Bere Country Club had once been my home, of course, but as we sat in the bar, formerly the morning room, looking out at the neat little putting green and the golf course beyond, I could not rid myself of the sensation that Meongate had gone, vanished to the last brick from beneath my feet, faded beyond the last haunting from my mind. They played bridge now in the bedroom where Mompesson had been shot, held committee meetings in the library where

Bartholomew's first painting had hung, drove tee shots over the remnant of orchard where I'd come upon Tony one distant spring morning. I was glad to have gone there again, glad to have found it cleansed of all my memories.

When the waiter came with our sandwiches, Tony asked him whether Walter Payne still owned the club.

'Yes, sir, though we hardly see him here. Lives in the Channel Islands now. Tax reasons, I believe.'

'Of course,' said Tony, with a rueful glance in my direction.

'Still president of the club, though. Are you acquainted with him?'

'My wife knew him' – he gestured towards me – 'a long time ago.'

'When this was still a private house,' I added.

'You'll have noticed lots of changes, then, I should think.'

'Only for the better.'

'Tell me,' the waiter said, stooping over the low table conspiratorially, 'do you remember the murder here? They say a wealthy American was done in.'

'I believe so,' I said levelly. 'But that was before I was born.'

'Unsolved, I gather.' He winked. 'They're the best kind.'

'As you say,' I replied, glancing at Grace. 'The very best kind.'

EPILOGUE

Another day, another place. And yet the same, in memory and meaning. Dead flat, heat-stunned, a green warming pan beneath a dome of flawless blue. This is the Belgian hinterland on a warm, still afternoon of early October, blanketed with such motionless peace as only centuries of war can bring. This is a narrow turning off the Zonnebeke to Passendale road, flanked by fields of head-high, static maize or sleeky coated, cud-chewing cattle recumbent in their pastures. This is the end of Leonora's story – and yet the beginning. This is where she has taken her daughter, at the close of all her confessions, to open one last portal on her father's soul.

This very morning, Leonora and Penelope Galloway arrived at Lille by train from Paris. There they hired a car, crossed the Belgian border and drove north, by roads dotted with the white oases of thickly planted war graves, to Ieper, a new name for the old, shell-scarred city of Ypres. Skirting the city walls as far as the Menin Gate, they had no time to inspect this other vast placard to the missing dead but drove on, north-east through Zonnebeke towards Passendale. Of the mud and mayhem synonymous with the discarded name of Passchendaele they saw no trace, perceived no sign, heard no whisper in the bright, clear air.

Now they have arrived. A bend in the lane, then a long flint wall on their right and a delta of white-faced gravestones declaring itself on the gently sloping ground beyond. Sooner, vaster, brighter than expected, their destination prepares itself to meet them.

Penelope pulls the car off the road and listens to the silence that follows and surrounds them as the engine dies. They climb out into the windless hush of the empty countryside and look across the road towards the farm fields of peacetime Flanders. A distant barn ripples in the heat haze and a cow by the nearest gate eyes them with long-lashed serenity. Behind them, the gravestones of Tyne Cot Military Cemetery await in immaculate, incongruous order.

The two women stand for a moment in the flintstone lych-gate and gaze up the central avenue between the graves towards the Great Cross of Sacrifice where it gleams atop its pyramid of white stone. Then, without a word, Leonora turns and opens the small metal door set in the right-hand gate pillar. Within are lodged the bound registers of the cemetery, twins to those she consulted at Thiepval. Finding the one she wants, she begins to turn its crinkled pages.

Penelope does not wait for her mother to find the entry she seeks. It is enough for her to know that here, under another man's name, her grandfather is commemorated more fittingly than that other mistaken record of his death. She enters the cemetery alone and begins to walk up the long aisle between the graves, the grass beneath her feet green and damp from recent watering. Here, she has read, are buried 11,908 men who died in the Ypres Salient between August 1917 and November 1918. Here it is the sheer quantity of their headstones, pure white, lovingly tended, shrub-fringed and rose-adorned, that shocks as much as the altimetric lists of the missing at Thiepval.

At the top of the avenue, she pauses beneath the soaring Cross of Sacrifice and looks back towards her mother, who is progressing slowly in the same direction. At first amazed, and later awed, by Leonora's account, Penelope has begun, since leaving Paris, to resent her long exclusion from their family's tragic history. She would have paid more attention to Grace Fotheringham if only she had known who she really was. She would have visited Meongate and Bonchurch. She would have come here sooner. She knows it is pointless to complain, yet still it seems unjust that she should have had to wait so long.

Leonora smiled breathlessly towards her daughter as she approaches. 'I found the entry,' she says. 'The register shows he was killed on 16th August 1917, during the advance on Langemark.'

'Is he buried here?'

'He may be. Many of the graves are unidentified. But it's more likely he lies somewhere on the battlefield, like so many others.'

Tyne Cot is itself the shape of a giant headstone, the graves in front of the Great Cross arrayed in serried rectangles, those behind fanned out on a terrace beneath the enclosing curve of the flint-walled Memorial to the Missing. Here, on stone panels, the names of 34,888 men who have no known grave are recorded. And here, amongst the division of the Northumbrian regiment to which he was attached, the two women find the name they seek: Lieutenant T. B.

Franklin. Though that, of course, is not the name Penelope seems to see, written between the letters on the stone. Unable to disguise her thoughts any longer, she looks at her mother and says:

'Why didn't you tell me sooner?'

Leonora returns her gaze with soulful intensity. 'I've given you all the reasons, Penny. The good and the bad. The vaguely noble and the frankly selfish.'

'Somehow, Mother, none of them quite measures up.'

'I was afraid you'd say that.'

'Why?'

'Because I've felt it myself often enough. Something always held me back, something beyond inbred caution and the wish to cherish it all as a secret between your father and me. I could never quite understand the instinct, but I always obeyed it.'

'So why break your silence now?'

'Because now I know what it was that I sensed. That's why we've come here. That's the last strand in my story.'

The two women cross to a nearby bench and sit, gazing out across the dazzling expanse of gravestones towards the distant, invisible sea. Leonora's story has already brought them immeasurably further than the 116 kilometres from Thiepval to Tyne Cot. Yet still, as Penelope is about to learn, it has one more step to take.

Grace spent her final years where she would least have wanted to: a nursing home. Fortunately, she was largely oblivious to the fact. I should have visited her more often, but she'd retreated increasingly into her past, sometimes not recognizing me, sometimes taking me for my mother. In the end, I found excuses not to go and understood at last what she'd once told me: that few were lucky enough to enjoy old age with the style and splendour of a Charter Gladwin.

Then, in contrast to Grace's slow and sad decline, Tony died with devastating suddenness. That put my old friend out of my thoughts completely. When I heard of her death in the summer, I felt firstly relieved and secondly horribly guilty at the thought of my long-standing neglect of her.

What never crossed my mind was that Grace might have mentioned me in her will. All her capital had gone in nursing fees, but her possessions had been put into store when she'd left Dolphin Square. From amongst them she'd reserved for me Willis's painting, the third Bartholomew, which had served to reunite us nearly twenty years ago.

To be honest, I hardly registered the fact until the very day the delivery van arrived. The driver and his mate carried their cargo into the hall, stood it against the wall, handed me a bill and left. Then I knelt before it and slowly stripped away the cardboard wrapping.

And there, as I'd know it would be, was my mother's face, shining more brightly than ever it seemed, in the pool of candlelight, amidst the shadows and suspicion, amongst the dim figures and dark purposes of that crepuscular scene. It was not simply a daughter's adoration that made it easy to understand why she should have been loved. Serene and self-possessed, she entered Willis's extrapolation of Bartholomew's theme as one elevated beyond its reach. Perhaps that, after all, was Willis's intention, to reflect in her beauty all the folly of those who had succumbed to Olivia's snares.

Kneeling there, in the hallway, I suddenly realized what I should do with Willis's painting. It would only have depressed me, as I felt at the time, to have it about the house and Willis himself had promised it to Eric Dunrich. Therefore, I resolved, to Eric Dunrich it should be entrusted.

From a regular exchange of Christmas cards, I knew that Dunrich was still ensconced at Seaspray Cottage, Polruan, with his horde of cheerfully inferior paintings. Accordingly, I wrote him a letter, suggesting a date for a visit, and received a reply by return, crayoned in a sprawling hand on the back of a postcard. 'The artist will abandon his fruitless toil in honour of the occasion. Delighted and flattered. E. D.'

Three weeks ago today, I set off at dawn, with my gift loaded in the back of the car. Early mist cleared to a mid-morning of startling, cloudless brilliance. It was one of those rare, peerless days which only spring or autumn in all their fickleness can breed, when the elements conspire to invest the English countryside with a casual, luminous beauty. That, or the undertow of my persistent grief, might explain the omens of significance I seemed to detect in the every mile covered towards Cornwall and a batty old artist in his cottage by the sea. Whatever their origin, after I'd taken to the minor roads that amble south from Liskeard and began to glimpse the sea, winking and glinting at me through the folds and creases of jumbled farmland, those omens began to close in upon me.

True to his word, Dunrich wasn't painting on the harbour wall at Polruan, despite the favourable conditions. Instead, when I walked round to Seaspray Cottage, there he was at the window, bobbing up from a chair and waving when he saw me. The door was flung open and he greeted me with his remembered toothy grin.

'Fair day attendeth fair lady,' he declaimed. 'It is, of course, the keenest pleasure to see you once again.' He took my hand and bowed awkwardly. I mentally diagnosed rheumatism from too many days sitting in the wind and noted that his grey, spiky hair had turned white and his face looked thinner but that he was otherwise a puckish and sprightly as I recalled.

'I have a present for you, Mr Dunrich.'

'For me?' His eyes lit up with childish glee.

'But you'll need to help me unload it. My car's just down the road.'

So it was that Dunrich himself carried the third Bartholomew into his house and unwrapped it on the table in his tiny lounge. If he'd already guessed what it was, his expression of surprise did not betray the fact.

'John's last picture,' he cooed, stooping low over the canvas. 'Lost, as I thought, for ever. But now, *mirabile dictu*, come once more to delight me.'

Over lunch, I explained to him how it had come into my possession, though of all that it might symbolize I said nothing. Not that he pressed me on the point: despite the sharpness of his wits, he was a strangely incurious man. For Eric Dunrich it was seemingly enough to gaze at a painting he'd once been promised. Perhaps, I thought, it was his simplicity that had endeared him to Willis, his ability never to enquire where enquiry was unwelcome.

After lunch, he suggested a stroll and led me up the lane to the headland above the estuary, where an un-attended coastguard look-out and the crumbling wall of an old fortification clung to a rocky prominence at the top of sheer cliffs. The sea washed the flat rocks below in foaming sweeps but presented, further out, as calm and placid a face as the day itself. A single figure in the

452

stern of a fishing smack bound for Polruan raised his hand in greeting when I waved. The sun sparkled benignly on the boat's wake. Gulls swooped and soared. All was warm, breeze-fanned contentment.

Dunrich settled himself on a rough bench formed by a single plank secured between two buttresses of the ruined wall that adjoined the outcrop of rock. I sat beside him, closed my eyes and let the warmth of the sun seep through my skin.

'It's a lovely spot,' I said. 'Do you come here often?'

'I hoped you would enjoy the view, dear lady,' he replied. 'But no, I seldom venture here. It is, for me, a place laden with memories.' I opened my eyes and saw that he was smiling. 'This is where I first met John Willis. The return of his painting reminds me of all that he did for me. Not that I am ever likely to forget. He saved my live on this spot, twenty-four years ago.'

He sighed and looked out to sea, as if he intended to say no more. But, this time, there was no ferry boat to bear me away. 'What happened?' I said quietly.

I knew he would tell me. He'd taken me there because both of us needed to hear his story and only in that place could it be told. Only there, in that moment, could understanding be mine, as only now can it be yours.

John could not teach me to paint as well as he did. That, I fear, is not a transferable gift. But one art he did succeed in teaching me: that of living with one's own imperfections. Had I possessed it when younger, life might not have proved so fraught, but, by the same token, I would never have met him – or you. So, be assured, I am not about to bemoan my lot.

I believe I convinced even myself that I had a

vocation for the priesthood. When I discovered that it was really only a sensual addiction to the forms and rituals of worship, I should have abandoned the cloth at once. Instead, I allowed myself to be snared by my own faith. Why surrender something which I could so easily simulate? The answer I fear, lies nearer the heart of my addiction.

Let brevity be the soul of candour. I was choirmaster at a cathedral school, arrested one day on a charge of having committed an act of gross indecency with a boy chorister. Arrested and subsequently convicted. It scarcely matters that I was falsely accused, since I was, undeniably, tempted. So, though not strictly guilty, nor was I strictly innocent. Two years' imprisonment may have been a harsh punishment, but I cannot claim that it was entirely unjust.

What I failed to appreciate was that my punishment did not end with my release: it merely entered a more subtle phase. I came to Polruan because it was far from home and because I had once spent a happy holiday here as a child. It seemed an ideal refuge. But scandal's winged chariot swiftly overhauled me. I became a marked man, reviled by one and all. Even when neighbours were not whispering about me, or warning their children against me, I imagined that they were.

On Sunday, 18th November 1962, I resolved to make a dramatic exit from this vale of tears. It was a day of wind and rain. When I stood here, late that afternoon, on the very edge of the cliff, the gale tearing at my clothes and the spray stinging my face from the crashing surf below. I knew that I had only to take one step, one small step, and the rocks and surging waves would take me in their arms and bear me away. The coastguard look-out was unmanned. The light was failing. Nobody would be out walking in such weather. Nobody would see me – or care if they did. that day, I yielded to temptation. I stepped from the brink.

John was sitting where we are sitting now. I had failed to notice him in the rain and gathering darkness. He had watched in silence as I stood on the edge of the cliff and summoned my courage to leap. He must have wondered what my intentions were, must have assumed – until the very last moment – that they could not be what they seemed.

As I made to jump, he seized me round the waist. We fell sideways, away from the sheer drop, on to shelving ground where there were boulders and bracken to cling to. Even so, I nearly took him with me. But his strength was that of ten men. He hauled me back up to this platform, where we crouched, panting for breath, and the rain fell in torrents. My clothes were ripped, my hands bleeding from the sharp rock, my face washed in rain and sweat. I began to weep. He dragged me to this bench and made me take some whisky from his hip flask, let me gather my wits and catch my breath.

I looked at him: an older man than me, no less shabby or desperate, to judge by appearances but with a glint in the eye some would call crazy, others a passion for life. His very spirit shamed me.

'You're Eric Dunrich, aren't you?' he said.

'Yes.'

'I've heard people gossiping about you. I expect you can guess what they say. Is that what brought you here?'

'Yes. Death seemed to offer some kind of solution.'

'It never does that, my friend. Death is only ever a defeat. Why defeat yourself?'

'I already have done. Didn't you listen to what they said?'

'I could hardly not. But do you seriously suppose there's a man in this village – me included – who hasn't at least one secret to hide that's every bit as shameful as anything you're supposed to have done? What you fear isn't the truth about yourself, but the prejudices of others. They're worthless, believe me. Accept an offer of friendship. Begin again.'

I said nothing. I was too shocked at my own susceptibility to what he had said. What was my iron resolve worth if it could be so easily undermined by a stranger? It was laughable.

After a moment, he spoke again, more earnestly than before. 'If you want to go through with it, I won't intervene a second time. But if you decide not to, you'll be doing me a favour as well as yourself.'

What I said next was out of embarrassment at my own weakness as much as resentment that my grand gesture had been frustrated. 'Why should you care?'

'Because this has happened to me before,' he replied. 'I once offered a friend a way out of certain death – and he refused. By stopping you just now, I was giving both of us a second chance.'

I stared at him incredulously. 'You make a habit of this?'

'Far from it,' he replied. 'The man I refer to had suffered much on my account. I offered him the only thing I had: my life in exchange for his. I offered to die in his place. But he refused. I've never stopped wondering what would have happened if he'd accepted, never stopped imagining how it would have been. But he didn't accept. He turned his back and walked away to his death. It stayed what it always was. A dream. An illusion. A lie I told to others and to myself. For my sake as well as yours, don't turn me down a second time.'

As you see, he was successful in his plea. We heard each other's confession, Mrs Galloway, then and later. The unfrocked priest and the unshriven sinner: a pretty combination, do you not think?

Judge not, that ye be not judged? Let him who is without sin, et cetera? None of that suffices, I suspect. Then what? He would have died for his friend, but his friend was too great a friend to let him. I know that he came to you with a lie, another man's story, a tragedy marginally different from his own, yet I beg you not to think harshly of him. His errors were borne, not of cowardice, but of love. He wished only to give you the memory of a father to be proud of. It is not an unworthy wish. All that he told you was true, save in that one particular. All that he learned from exile was barren, save in that one pretence.

He painted the third Bartholomew in order that he might face squarely all that was worst in himself and best in the woman he loved. Yet what he achieved transcended his purpose. It is why I so dearly wanted the picture and why, now that you have given it to me, I have broken my pact of secrecy with a long-dead friend.

Driving home from Polruan that evening, I pulled off the road halfway across Dartmoor and got out to watch the sunset: a fading slash of red on the horizon far to the west, somewhere beyond Cornwall. A breeze was getting up on the moor, tugging at the gorse and bracken and draining the warmth from the day. But I was in no hurry to return to the car. My mind was still on Eric Dunrich's parting words as I'd left Seaspray Cottage an hour or so before.

We'd hung the third Bartholomew in a place of pride, on the chimneybreast in the tiny, congested sitting room. I took a final, wistful look at it, then turned away and walked out to the front door, where Dunrich was waiting for me. He was smiling broadly, with something akin to exultation suffusing his features.

'You've seen it too now, haven't you?' he said. 'You've seen it in her face. She's forgiven him, Mrs Galloway. I am glad of it. Not merely because he was my friend, but because he was the finest man I ever knew.'

Tyne Cot is still and silent in the hottest hour of the day, its gravestones massed in obedience to the purposes of the dead and the pretences of the living. In all its vast immobility of names, nothing moves save two figures progressing slowly down the sloping avenue towards the lych-gate and the Passendale road beyond.

Leonora Galloway has completed her story. She has made her peace with the past and paid her debts to the present. She walks erectly, almost proudly, as they leave the cemetery and move towards the car. By contrast, her daughter Penelope seems hunched, bowed and thoughtful in the face of too much knowledge. She unlocks the car, climbs into the driving seat, leans across to open the passenger door for her mother and starts the engine.

Before climbing into the car herself, Leonora takes a last look back at the cemetery beyond its perimeter wall. On the Memorial at its summit, she knows that the sun still etches in shade the name of one of the missing, whilst far to the south, at Thiepval, another name commands in place on a lofty pillar. Two names for the same lie – if a lie forgiven should be called a lie. This, then, is whence her search ends. And where did it begin? She remembers it well, to this day: Droxford railway station, all those years before. But now, for the first time, another fragment of that memory crystallizes in her mind.

A woodland path, a shady summertime route back to Meongate. Charter carried her on his shoulders. She pulled at the straw of his hat. The sun-patched grass between the stretching boughs was as green as the trimmed blades at Tyne Cot, the shadows of the arching branches as deep as those beneath the pillars at Thiepval. He made her laugh. She cannot remember how, but he made her happy, for that brief space, after the sadness of parting. At the edge of the wood, by the stile that led into the grounds of Meongate, he lifted her down, sat her on the rail and leant beside her, recovering his breath and mopping his brow. He must have said something to amuse her, though all she can remember is laughter – his and hers.

Leonora climbs into the car and closes the door. She has a train to catch, a home to return to, a present to re-join – and a long forgotten promise to keep.

'How does it make you feel, Mother?' says Penelope as she pulls away. 'The knowledge that, in the end, he deceived you?'

Leonora's attention is elsewhere. When she replies, it is in response not to her daughter's words, but to her great-grandfather's. 'I will.'

'Will what?'

'Be happy.'

> *Then, scanning all the o'ercrowded mass, should you*
> *Perceive one face that you loved heretofore,*
> *It is a spook. None wears the face you knew.*
> *Great death has made all his for evermore.*

LONG TIME COMING

Robert Goddard

For thirty-six years, they thought he was dead...They were wrong...

Eldritch Swan is a dead man. Or at least that is what his nephew Stephen has always been told. Until one day Swan walks back into his life after thirty-six years in an Irish prison. He won't say why he was locked up - only that he is innocent of any crime.

His return should interest no one. But the visit of a solicitor with a strange request will take Swan and his sceptical nephew to London, where an exhibition of Picasso paintings is the starting point on a journey that will take them back to when the pictures were last seen - on the eve of the Second World War.

Untangling the web of murky secrets, family ties and old betrayals that surrounds their mysterious reappearance will prove to be a dangerous pursuit for the two men. Because watching their every step is a sinister enemy who will do whatever it takes to stop the truth emerging...

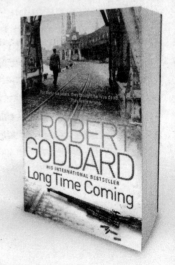

'The master of the clever twist'
SUNDAY TELEGRAPH

FOUND WANTING

Robert Goddard

The past will never let you go…

'The car jolts to a halt at the pavement's edge, the driver waving through the windscreen to attract Richard's attention. He starts with astonishment. The driver is Gemma, his ex-wife.

He has not seen or spoken to her for several years. They have, she memorably assured him, nothing to say to each other. But something has changed her mind – something urgent…'

Immediately Richard is catapulted into a breathless race against time that takes him from London, across northern Europe and into the heart of a mystery that reaches back into history – the fate of Anastasia, the last of the Romanovs. From that moment, Richard's life will be changed for ever in ways he could never have imagined…

'Everybody involved is double, triple and quadruple crossing everybody else…Goddard writes and plots with accurate precision; you feel he knows every setting and was witness to every scene'
LITERARY REVIEW

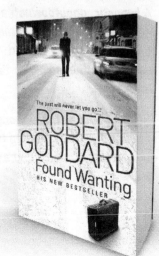

CAUGHT IN THE LIGHT

Robert Goddard

On assignment in Vienna, photographer Ian Jarrett falls passionately in love with the mysterious and beautiful Marian. Back in the UK, Ian resolves to leave his wife for her – only to find Marian has disappeared, and the photographs of their brief time together have been savagely destroyed.

Searching desperately for her, Ian comes across a quiet Dorset churchyard. Here he meets a psychotherapist, who is looking for a missing client of hers: a woman who claims she is the reincarnation of Marian Esguard, who may have invented photography ten years before Fox Talbot.

But why is Marian Esguard unknown to history? And who and where is the woman Ian Jarrett has sacrificed everything for?

'A hypnotic, unputdownable thriller...
one can only gasp with admiration
at Goddard's ability to hold
readers spellbound'
DAILY MAIL

'His best book yet, a sinuous structure
of twists and traps leading to an
unexpectedly sinister climax'
THE TELEGRAPH

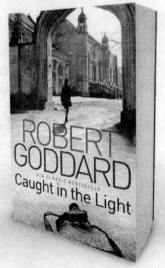